Praise for Nermin Bez

"The author weaves a tale of embroidered delight propelled by a rich pageant of colour and character. Whilst retaining a detailed and honest record of history, she unravels a love story that astounds as well as captivates with equal measure. Her in-depth research has, combined with a mastered use of language, engineered a narrative worthy of considerable praise."

—H. Pilkington, *independent editor*

"A brave undertaking most cannot dare. Written in the style of Tolstoy, Balsac, and Zola, in the expression of the nineteenth century. Narrates the era very well with the structure of a good novel. This is what I call a classical novel."

—Attila Ilhan, *poet, author*

"Extraordinary! It is so full of emotion that I read with tears in my eyes."

—Dr. Nihan Atay

"A dramatic documentary! A breathing novel. From the Czarist Russia to the imperial Istanbul of 1920s, [all the historical details] have been embroidered with the meticulous detail of an academician."

—Jack Deleon, *researcher, author, columnist*

"A book you can't put down. A book different from others in its classical writing style as well as its ability to marry romance and historical detail. The author's meticulous research gives this novel a documentary value."

—STEPS, *a publication of Bosphorus University*

"[With this book] Nermin Bezmen has landed in the literary world like a comet from outer space!"

—Hami Alkaner, *journalist*

"[This novel] has the magnificence of the classical ages."

—Ayhan Hunalp, *journalist, literary critic*

"Nermin Bezmen narrates the universal sorrow of all humans suffering from a diaspora."

—*Yasar Aksoy, journalist, author*

"I was born in Russia and completed my education in Saint Petersburg. I felt like I was reading an original Russian book by a twentieth-century Russian author. From its streets to its people, only a Russian can describe Russia as you have. Congratulations!"

—*Elvira Kazas, Crimean historian*

"This book is very valuable to our library because, unfortunately, we have not a single book on our shelves about the years before 1944."

—*Tatyana Sheksheyeva, head librarian of the Library of Alushta, Crimea*

"This is the single most important source book in our library that writes of our people and our history with such meticulous detail. Thank you, Ms. Nermin!"

—*Firuze Mehmedova, assistant to the head librarian of the Library of Alushta, Crimea*

"This novel and the photographs within are a gift to us. Your past is our past, and we just started finding out about it."

—*Yura Kochigarov, director of Alushta Museum, Crimea*

"I found this book, which is based on true life experience, to be absorbing and compelling. Readers will find the story at once heartrending and inspiring and will envy the author that her family history yielded a story of so much romance and passion. The author has truly made her characters come to life, and the story is enhanced by the author's account of searching for and encountering them. The story takes place in a wealth of contrasting settings, which are described vividly and will thrill the reader..."

—*A. Austin, literary fiction critic*

KURTSEYT & SHURA

KURTSEYT SHURA &

NERMIN BEZMEN

Translation from Turkish by
Feyza Howell

Kurt Seyt & Shura

Printed by CreateSpace, an Amazon.com company

Original Title: *Kurt Seyt & Shura*
Copyright © 1992 Nermin Bezmen
English Translation Copyright © 2017 Feyza Howell

Originally published in Turkish in 1992 by
PMR Dijital Tasarım, Bilişim, Yayıncılık, Tanıtım ve Pazarlama Ltd. Şti.

Cover Design: Pamir Cazim Bezmen
Cover Image: Ay Yapim
Author's Portrait: Pamira Bezmen Photography

English paperback printed in the United States December 2017

ISBN-13: 9781977698315
ISBN-10: 197769831X
Library of Congress Control Number: 2017919006
CreateSpace Independent Publishing Platform
North Charleston, South Carolina

About *Kurt Seyt & Shura*

A N INSTANT BEST seller since its debut in 1992, Nermin Bezmen's *Kurt Seyt & Shura* is a classic of contemporary Turkish literature, a sweeping romantic drama set around the time as the splendor of imperial Russia is obliterated in the wake of the Great War. Bezmen tells the story of two star-crossed lovers fleeing the wave of devastation wreaked by the Bolshevik Revolution—and does so with great sensitivity: one half of this couple was her grandfather.

Translated into twelve languages, *Kurt Seyt & Shura* inspired a sumptuous TV series that continues to enchant millions of viewers across the world. With the publication of this novel in the United States, fans there will now be able to read the true story of this great love affair, which triumphed over so much adversity yet failed to overcome human fallibility.

Kurt Seyt, the son of a wealthy Crimean nobleman, is a dashing first lieutenant in the Imperial Life Guard. Injured on the Carpathian front and later sought by the Bolsheviks, he makes a daring escape across the Black Sea. Too proud to accept payment for the boatful of arms he hands over to the Nationalists, he faces years of struggle to make a new life in the Turkish Republic rising from the embers of the dying Ottoman Empire. All he has is his dignity and love.

Shura, an innocent sixteen-year-old beauty enchanted by Tchaikovsky's music and Moscow's glittering lights, falls in love with Seyt. A potential victim of the Bolsheviks due to her family's wealth and social standing, she is determined to follow her heart and accompanies Seyt on his perilous flight over the Black Sea.

Their love is the only solace to their crushing homesickness for a land and family they will never see again, two lovers among hundreds of thousands of White Russian émigrés trying to eke out a living in occupied Istanbul.

Nermin Bezmen

Nermin Bezmen is an accomplished artist, art teacher, yoga instructor, and broadcaster whose meticulous research into family history led to the publication of *Kurt Seyt & Shura* in 1992. This fictionalized account of her grandfather's life became an instant best seller and is now considered a masterpiece of contemporary Turkish literature; in fact, it has reached textbook status in several secondary schools and universities.

Exquisite detail distinguishes her writing as she proves that truth is indeed stranger than fiction and that our ancestors call out to us from the pages of history. Her powerful character analysis and storytelling skills invite readers to explore their own dreams, sorrows, anxieties, and even fleeting fancies.

Bezmen has published seventeen novels, two of which are biographical and one of which is a fantasy. In addition, she has a children's novel, a collection of short stories, and a book of poems to her credit. She has two children and three grandchildren and lives with her husband, actor Tolga Savacı, in New Jersey and Istanbul.

Feyza Howell

Born in Izmir, Howell graduated from Robert College in Istanbul with a UK honors degree in graphic design. She holds an impressive backlist and is experienced in various aspects of international business, including design, advertising, TV production, marketing, product management, and business development. Throughout this period she has always drawn, written, and translated. Her interests include tennis, yoga, and dance.

Howell is married, has a son, and lives in Berkshire

My dear readers,

This is a true story.

It is a journey full of adventures. I immersed myself in thorough research in order to uncover the truth of the past, while filling in some of the details with my own imagination, where it would have been otherwise impossible to know intimate scenes between my characters.

I felt equally happy and sad as I concluded the final sentence of the fictionalized account of my grandfather's life. Little did I know at the time that *Kurt Seyt & Shura* would lead to four sequels!

I came to know my characters so well while breathing life into them through my words that parting from them became truly heartwrenching. As I returned to my own life, I knew I would always miss them and find inspiration in their loves, sorrows, and yearning. I would like to pay tribute to the heroes and heroines of my novel, above all for their indomitability of spirit.

May they all rest in peace.

I hope that you will find inspiration and deep love in this story as much as I did. May we all unite in the universal and eternal spirit of human love...

Nermin Bezmen

My beloved grandfather,

I dedicate my book to you.
Now I understand you better and miss you more than ever.

Nermin

Ode to Shura

A vision in a troika gliding
over the snow,
Blond hair glittering
Under a snowflake halo—
Bells tolling in a distant steeple
Invoke a saint's grace;
Chanting priests lead a choir.
Grandfather's little angel,
The first time I ever saw your face
And your eyes of sapphire.

The wind whistling,
The snow pounded into powder
By three horses trotting
Before breaking into a canter—
If only I could watch you,
Unforgettably lovely—
In his heart and on his lips your name,
As Grandfather watched you,
Seeking solace in memory,
His eternal flame.

Lost in an ancient Russian song,
A shot or two of something,
Memories flying along

That troika Grandfather was chasing—
Vodka glass in hand
Unshed tears glistening
For his lost Crimea and Russia—
Forsaken homeland,
But mostly yearning
For you, and you alone, Shura

Translator's Notes

Pronunciation of *Kurt Seyt & Shura*:

Kurt: This is Seyt's nickname, which means *wolf* in Turkish. It is pronounced with a flat *u*, as in *book*.

Seyt: This is the standard Russian pronunciation of Seyit (read as *say-it*, with the stress on the second syllable), our hero's given name. Both versions are used in the book.

Shura: Read as *shoo-ra*, this short form of Alexandra is an endearing nickname used by loved ones. Another variation used in the book is *Shurochka*.

Proper nouns in Russian have been transliterated in accordance with the latest convention, and modern Turkish spelling has been used for those in Crimean Tatar and Turkish, which are close enough for native speakers to understand one another with relative ease.

Turkish spelling is phonetic:
a = shorter than the English *a* in *father*
c = *j* in *jack*
ç = *ch* in *chat*
e = *e* in *bed* (never as in *me*)
    but *en* = *an* as in *ban*
ğ = "soft g" is silent; it merely lengthens the vowel preceding it
ı = *schwa*; the second syllable in *higher*

i = *i* in *bin*; never as in *eye*

j = French *j* in *jour*

r = *r* in *read*; at end of syllables closest to the Welsh, as in *mawr*

ö = *i* in *bird* or *u* in *burgundyü* = the closest English sound is as in *beautiful* or *fuel*

s = *s* in *sing*

ş = *sh* in *ship*

y = English *y* in *yellow*

On Turkish names:

Given names usually are accented on the final syllable, so *se-YİT*, *za-hi-DE*, and so on.

Honorifics follow the first name: *bey* (sir), *hanım* (lady), *efendi* (squire, often used to address someone of a lower social rank), *abi* (big brother), *abla* (big sister), and *hacı* (someone who has performed the pilgrimage).

On Russian names:

Customarily used as middle names in Russia, patronymics are formed by adding to the father's first name (*–ovich* or *–evich* for males and *–ovna* or *–evna* for females). Surnames take similar gender-specific endings: Verjensky—Verjenskaya and Moiseyev—Moiseyeva, for instance.

Close friends and family almost always use a contraction of the first name.

Acknowledgments

M Y DEAR GRANDMOTHER, Seyit's Murka, for relating your memories, which were as fresh as though the events had just taken place, and for sharing courageously so much that you might have preferred to forget;

My dear mother, Leman "Lemanuçka" Ulus, for the clues provided by your memories;

My dear paternal aunt, Saniha Görgülü, for relating events that merited a book in their own right, a brief instance of which I used in this novel;

Dear Jak Deleon for helping me discover the trail of my real heroine, Shura, and for your untiring researcher's spirit;

And dear Zeynep Deleon for sharing my passion during my research—I thank you all.

Dear Baroness Valentine "Tinochka" Clodt von Jürgensburg provided memories and photographs that shed light on Shura's early years and spurred me on with renewed enthusiasm. I wish I had met her earlier. In her final few months, we grew close enough to fit ninety years into our friendship. Our conversations brought back to life the years and loved ones she had been holding in her heart and mind—all the people and events she still longed for. She was so looking forward to Shura's novel! She wanted to learn about many lost years in her sister's life, and I was devastated when our baroness left us in the spring of 1992, as the novel was about to go to print. Wasn't it one of those unfathomable miracles of fate that brought us together—so late in the day, so close to her death—and helped us both fit the pieces of a puzzle together? I will miss you very much, Baroness.

Dear Theodor "Todori" Negroponti, Valentine's best friend and beloved companion of forty-seven years: I will never forget the nostalgic moments you shared with us.

Dear friends Mine Koyuncuoğlu, Lola Arel, Leonid Senkopopowski, and lawyer Vassaf Arım: thank you for the helpful advice in your specific fields.

My gratitude to the great writer Attila Ilhan for sparing the time to read my novel and for encouraging me on this journey across the vast ocean of literature, which I'd set my heart on.

Dear friend Vladimir Alexandrov, thank you very much for the support, encouragement, and information you have given.

My precious daughter, Pamira, and son, Pamir Cazım: your understanding maturity—even when I was exhausted and tense—proved once again how lucky I am to be blessed with such perfect children. My dearest son deserves extra praise for designing such wonderful covers and humoring me by refreshing the cover design from time to time. My dearest daughter guided me into the process of self-publishing and supported me in my dream to reach the American reader.

My dearest late husband, Pamir: I would never have been able to pursue my dreams with such determination without your trust, belief, and great support. I am truly grateful to you.

My dear, devoted fans across the world, who embraced *Kurt Seyt & Shura* from the very first day by letter, telephone, fax, e-mail, and social media and unwaveringly immersed themselves in the world of souls I had created, thereby becoming a part of my novel's family: I offer you my heartfelt thanks.

I owe thanks to the lavish TV production of *Kurt Seyt & Shura*, whose gripping account of this romantic saga in a tumultuous time enlarged the family of fans.

And last but not least, my translator and friend Feyza Howell: for your meticulous attention to detail, enthusiasm, and superbly flowing translation into English.

And my CreateSpace team, especially my editors, thank you all!

Contents

A Night in
Petrograd, 1916

S NOW FELL IN fat, lazy flakes, an immaculate white blanket settling over the sleeping city. The carriage turning left at Alexander Nevsky Square laboriously carved a wide arc through the snow that had piled up all night, rounded a corner, and drew up to the pavement outside a three-story house.

A few snowflakes fluttered at the windowsills, stuck to the panes and frozen solid. The coachman gazed upward as instructed; a net curtain parted, and a shaft of light beamed out. A male figure wiped the glass, waved, and withdrew.

***

The young man consulted the pocket watch he'd left by the lamp on the bedside table: it was coming up to four; he still had plenty of time. Carefully, so as to avoid rousing the sleeping woman, he lifted the duvet and got back into bed. He reclined against the pillow, still holding his watch. Then, a little more determined, he flung aside the covers and got up. He drew the curtain back a little more and looked out. The moon illuminated the whiteness starting directly outside the windowpanes, sweeping unbroken over the garden, the railing, and the broad expanse of road. A world in white. Everything sparkled when the moon shone between the scudding clouds, and the world looked more splendid under this white coat.

Heavy curtains kept the world outside the windows, where it belonged. In the semidarkness, the room spoke in scents: perfume revealed a woman's presence, and vodka testified to earlier indulgences, both mingling with the lavender emanating from the bed linens.

He turned toward the bed for a look. Amplified by the snow, the moonlight cast a bright-white light on the sleeping woman's bare back. He recalled what the darkness sought to conceal: the deep auburn of her hair, now cascading over the pillow in waves; the groove of her spine dipping delightfully from the nape all the way to her waist and vanishing under the covers; and the right shoulder glowing in the playful light, a flawless expanse of alabaster.

Seemingly oblivious to the cold, he leaned his bare back against the window; then, grinning at the memory, he moved to the round table by the fireplace. The fruit platter, carafe, and glasses still stood where they had been left: half eaten and half drunk from. She was an impatient one, that Katya. Or was it Lydia? Whatever. The auburn beauty had excelled at entertaining him that night.

He picked up one of the half-full crystal glasses, downed it in one go, and shook his head as the alcohol stung his throat. He lit the pink opaline lamp in front of the mirror, and the soft light of gas spread into the room. Digging into the jumble of garments on the sofa, he gathered his own clothing and collected his underwear. He was moving toward the bathroom when the woman spoke sleepily.

"Why so early, darling?"

He strode toward her, still carrying his clothes. She stirred, rounded shoulders and full breasts braving the cold, her face now more distinct. Sweeping her hair up with one arm, she reached out with the other. He stared with barely disguised lust; the charming armpit thus exposed looked as arousing as the ample breasts bathed in the pink light. The sleepy gaze was not necessarily reserved for this time of night: she had proven her expertise in seduction with those large dark eyes framed by long eyelashes, eyes that spoke of the bedroom, of the pleasures of the flesh. Full lips pouting in anticipation, she waited, eyes shut, arm still outstretched. Smiling at her unrestrained behaviour ravenous appetite, he sat down on the edge of the bed. Her provocative scent mingled with the bedclothes, fragrant from passionate hours. He yielded to the invitation of the arms wrapped around his neck. Languid eyes smoldered into his as she tugged away the bedclothes separating them to free her warm, buxom figure and snuggle up to him. She stroked his back and the muscles in his arms, pressed his head against her breasts, and presented her nipples to his lips. Effectively captured by her skillful limbs—surprising on such a petite woman—he enjoyed a lingering kiss before drawing back.

"It's time I got ready. You might like to get up too; I'll have you dropped off."

She pouted with a half shrug. "Couldn't we stay just a little longer?"

"I need to set off."

"Where to?"

"Moscow."

"When will you be back? Will you call upon me again?" She stirred as if to get up during this barrage, hoping to tempt him to change his mind.

All she got in response, however, was a jaunty smile and a pinch on the cheek before he walked toward the bathroom. He mused as he washed; he couldn't remember her name—just another one-night stand. Someone he had met at a wild party where the drink had flowed like water...and they had left together. She was no petty commoner, if the splendor of her dress and jewelry was anything to go by. In all likelihood, she'd arrived on someone else's arm—probably the man who'd paid for that splendor.

As he shaved, his thoughts strayed to the journey ahead. Best to get a move on, given he had arranged to meet the others at the station in an hour.

By the time he'd returned to the bedroom with a towel wrapped around his waist, she was already dressed. He patted his cheeks and neck with lotion from a bottle on the console. "Wouldn't you like to take a bath?"

"I never take a bath on my own," came the flirtatious reply.

An irrepressible grin lit up his face as he combed his hair, thinking, *Her husband—or lover, whoever it was—certainly has his work cut out.* He dressed, ignoring his audience, who sat on the edge of the bed to admire the view.

Muscular and fit, the young man in his early twenties carried himself with an aristocratic posture and demeanor. His moustache and floppy fringe were chestnut. A cleft chin seemed to complete his striking looks: flashing dark-blue eyes, a straight nose, and a perpetually sardonic mouth.

The redhead patted her curls back into place and sighed. Her questions were destined to remain unasked as the young man, now in full uniform and boots, strode between wardrobe and dresser, clearly lost in his own thoughts. He picked up several items from drawers, and some books went into a suitcase. She watched, astonished that he appeared to have forgotten the many wonderful hours they had shared in bed. Her wiles had failed to hook him. She leaned back with another sigh.

Taking a ring from a box by the mirror, he placed it on his finger and then put a watch in his pocket. She remembered openly admiring them last night— she adored jewelry after all, and he'd said the sapphire-and-diamond ring was a family heirloom. The enameled gold watch adorned with rubies was a gift from Tsar Nicholas II, he'd told her.

Soon they were ready to leave. A muffled clatter rose from the street. The second carriage had arrived. He picked up his coat and hat. "All right, let's go," he said. "I'll have you taken home."

He extinguished the lamp and walked to the door. She followed, surprised and not a little disconcerted at the absence of one last kiss or a plea for another meeting, as if there had been nothing between them.

The coachmen leaped down and ran over the snow. The young man turned to his guest, took her hand, and said, "Aktem will drop you off. Fare thee well, my lovely." Her name wasn't even on the tip of his tongue.

"Will we meet again?" she tried one last time.

"Why not?"

Happier now, she presented her cheek for a kiss, unbothered by the coachmen's presence. Finally, gathering her courage, and with a bashful smile, she asked the one question that had plagued her all this time. "Tell me your name again?"

His merry laughter rang in the snowy street's early morning silence. So the night had not been *that* memorable for either of them! Except for the ending, that is. He bowed, as if they had just met, and enunciated deliberately: "First Lieutenant Seyit Memedovich Eminof."

***

As the two carriages drove away in opposite directions, the auburn beauty who had sweetened his night was already slipping from his mind.

Moscow, 1916

THE KREMLIN FORTRESS, a commanding structure with formidable brick walls, included fairy-tale palaces with soaring towers and churches, dominated the entire stretch of the Krasnaya Ploshchad.

That night, leisurely snowfall against the deep-blue sky intensified the illusion of fantasy, as did the golden light that spilled from the windows of the Kremlin's palaces and grand entrances, bathing the flagstones. A troika crossed the Krasnaya Ploshchad, appropriately named Beautiful Square, toward Mokhovaya Road, the jingle of its bells a high note over the deeper thumping of the horses' hooves on the snow. The Kremlin clock rang eight times.

Snug in their fur hats and muffs, two young girls flanked their father in the troika, their arms through his, fascinated by these magical sounds and lights.

Alexandra, the younger girl, withdrew one hand from her muff to brush snowflakes off the golden bangs escaping from her hat and turned to smile at her watching father. Julian Verjensky responded with an equally affectionate smile. Happiness shone on his drained face as he stroked Alexandra's hand and then looked left at his elder daughter, Valentine. Dragging hers eyes away from the wondrous enchantment of the night, Alexandra observed him surreptitiously. He looked so tired, so exhausted, her poor papa. That was the reason they had come here from Kislovodsk in the first place. Upon the express recommendation of their family doctor, Julian Verjensky had agreed to undergo a checkup in a Moscow hospital and had brought his daughters along. He was due to be admitted for an operation the following day. Alexandra didn't necessarily understand all the details, but she knew her father's lungs were ailing. Fearful of terms such as *surgery* and *malady* and terrified of losing her papa, she fought hard to suppress tears as Julian continued to recount the Kremlin's history.

"According to some accounts, the original walls date back to 1367, to the reign of Demetrius Donskoi, and the clock in the bell tower was brought by a Serbian monk who came from Athos in 1404." He paused to turn to his younger daughter, who watched him with a sorrowful expression. "What is it, Shurochka?" he asked her. "Are those tears in your eyes?"

Embarrassed, Shura forced herself to brighten up in response to the familiar version of her name, and she feigned wiping something from her eyelids.

"I must've got a snowflake in my eye." She gave him a sweet smile.

"You're not cold, are you?" asked a concerned Verjensky.

"No, no, Papa. I'm fine—please believe me."

"Moscow's weather's not like ours in Kislovodsk, you know."

"It's lovely all the same."

Throwing her head back, Shura took a deep breath, inhaling the chilly evening air and the smell of snow. Julian beamed as he patted her hand.

Soon they were at the gate of the Borinsky mansion, where carriages queued to drop guests off at the broad marble staircase. Beautifully dressed ladies flicked snowflakes off their furs and muffs and, holding their full skirts up, ascended on the arms of their gallant escorts.

When their carriage passed through the grand gate, Shura felt a thrill. This was her first ever adult dinner dance! She was still two months shy of her sixteenth birthday. Their parents had taken Valentine, who was a year older, to several similar parties in Kislovodsk already. Handsome aristocrats and officers competed to ask young ladies to dance at such sophisticated soirees, Valentine had pronounced knowingly.

As she climbed the steps beside her father, Shura's heart was beating so fast that she feared it might just stop. She felt as if wonderful things were about to happen. She had no idea what the evening would bring, but something told her it would be magical.

They handed their cloaks and hats to the bowing servants and mounted a few more steps. The hallway and lobby rang with music from the hall. An usher waiting importantly at the door took a step into the hall, rapping his staff on the floor. He announced the arrivals: "Monsieur Julian Verjensky! Mademoiselle Valentine Julianovna Verjenskaya! Mademoiselle Alexandra Julianovna Verjenskaya!"

He stepped back as Verjensky started descending the crystal-banister staircase, flanked by his daughters. Several guests glanced up at the new arrivals before resuming their conversations. Their host, Andrei Borinsky, slipped away from the crowd and approached the steps, his genuine warmth indicating that these were special guests. Borinsky and Julian Verjensky were shareholders in the same oil company; they might meet seldom, yet they were close. After a friendly handshake with Julian, Borinsky turned to the girls.

"Oh, my word, Julian!" he exclaimed. "I can't believe these are your pretty little daughters! Well, still beautiful—if anything, they are even lovelier now but children no more. How time flies! Come; let me introduce you to my friends."

The young ladies followed their father and host as they mingled with the other guests. Valentine exuded confidence, whereas Shura was still fraught. Anxious and worried about revealing it, she looked down, lest she catch some stranger's eye. She whispered, "Tinochka, please don't leave me, all right?"

Valentine smiled back as she glided forward, holding the skirt of her dusky pink gown. "Don't worry...you wouldn't say that if you'd spotted your admirers!"

Shura stole a timid glance to her left, certain Valentine must be teasing—and her gaze met a pair of eyes watching her.

It felt as though an electrical current passed between her and the stranger. Blushing furiously, her heart racing, she dropped her eyes at once. Her father was talking to a baron he'd just been introduced to, and Valentine was chatting with a plain girl she'd met at a party in Kislovodsk—an acquaintance whose name Shura had been unable to catch.

She could feel the young man staring but didn't dare look in his direction. She squeezed the silk cordon of her bag, which matched her violet gown. Her waist-length blond hair had been piled on top of her head in curls, her first ever updo. Recalling how she'd secretly concurred with her father's and sister's earlier compliments, she realized all her confidence had vanished. Now all she felt was childish and callow among all these lovely, elegant ladies. How was she going to mingle with this crowd, and even dance with strange men, when she flinched at a single male glance from afar? Chances were none of these things would happen, she thought; instead, she would sit in a corner all night, a wallflower destined to watch others have fun.

Silently indicating Shura should accept the glass of wine held out by a servant, Verjensky resumed a heated debate with the host and two other men on the oil company shares, strikes, and other matters. Valentine and her friend, meanwhile, were still entertaining each other with the tales of that party. Shura took a tentative sip and then a bolder one. A little fortitude from the wine might help with the shyness after all.

Hoping to catch that unforgettable gaze again, she looked back at that spot, an act she regretted immediately; he wasn't there. She took another sip. She felt a little less tense now. She directed her attention to the orchestra playing a Tchaikovsky nocturne. All of a sudden, she sensed the same electric current as the same gaze locked onto her eyes.

Shura thought she must have drunk far too quickly. The music suddenly sounded distant. She failed to even make out a conversation right beside her. Her feet seemed to have lost touch with the ground, and she thought everyone could hear her heart pounding. This time she did not look away. He stood in a group of friends, also in uniform; he joined in the conversation from time to time but never took his eyes off the pretty girl in violet. When their gazes met, he smiled and bowed in a barely perceptible salute. Shura turned around with a bashful smile. She pretended to listen to Valentine and her friend, but her heart was fluttering like a bird. She downed her glass.

"Shurochka, if you keep drinking at this rate, you won't be able to stand up, never mind dance. The night's still young, you know!" Valentine cautioned.

Shura smiled back in reply, feeling her cheeks burn and eyes sparkle.

The polka beckoned couples onto the dance floor. It was just as Valentine had said: young men were inviting young ladies to dance one by one. Shura wanted the impossible: to leave the hall, vanish if she could. She was terrified it would be her turn next. Then she spotted the owner of the flashing blue eyes chatting with the host and another young man. A beaming Andrei Borinsky brought his entourage over to the girls. "Dear Valentine, dear Alexandra, allow me to introduce these two young men. My son, Petro Borinsky, and his good friend Seyt Memedovich Eminof—fresh young first lieutenants in the tsar's *Leib Guvardia*."

The young officers concluded the introduction ceremony with gallant bows. Imitating her big sister, Shura smiled with a faint nod.

When Petro invited Valentine to the dance floor, Shura floundered: it was clearly her turn next.

"Will you grant me this dance?"

He'd offered a barely heard invitation that she was too nervous, too powerless, to respond to. That earlier anticipation of something wonderful had been vindicated. She had never imagined that any man could have such an effect on her. His piercing stare made her feel naked. He looked so magnificent with his medals, ceremonial sword, and glossy knee-high boots that when he grasped the hand she had extended during the introduction and guided her to the dance floor, she was unable to refuse—or reply. Wordlessly, she abandoned herself to the arms of this total stranger, to his courteous yet firm hold. Her heartbeat in her ears, her cheeks pink, and her blue eyes sparkling in the excitement of the moment, she thought this was a lovely dream as she began spinning around the dance floor. She averted her eyes, however, from his probing gaze, which was as exciting as it was intimidating. She had no idea how to respond or what to say if he were to ask anything. Nor did she have any idea how long this sweet torment would last. It was as though he had taken hold of all her thoughts and actions.

The other couples changed partners several times, but Shura and Seyt did not. If she left now, she might never see him again, which was the last thing she wanted. As she danced around her kneeling partner, one hand in his and the other holding her skirt, their gazes met. She was intoxicated by the sardonic, teasing, proud, passionate, infatuated, and tender glints in his deep blue eyes. Her dainty hand in his strong, warm, and reassuring hold sent exhilarating shivers up to her wrist and from there to her entire body.

A merry polka played on as he slowly guided her out of the circle. Overwhelmed by a thrilling sense of adventure, and without speaking or asking, Shura submitted to his command and walked in his wake, her hand clutched in his. This stranger she had just met led her out of the hall, picked up her cloak, and draped it over her shoulders. They crossed a whole series of interlinked rooms and emerged onto a veranda at the rear of the mansion. Shura fleetingly wondered whether her sister or father might have noticed or whether they might worry. She could not believe all that had happened or her own audacity. Goodness knew what people would think. Her anxious eyes strayed to the door, but it was obvious they had not been followed: their only witness was the hazy light through the net curtain billowing in the wind. She held her breath, concerned he might misjudge her, think her accustomed to parties and flirting—not that she could disabuse him of the notion.

They had yet to exchange small talk. She shivered self-consciously in anticipation, too timid to raise her head for a look. Then she noticed his hand reaching out.

"Are you cold?"

His voice was low, tender, and warm, speaking as if he did not want to be heard. Tucking her into her cloak, he tugged the collar closed. Shura felt her heartbeat speed up at the touch of the hands on her neck and chin. At a loss for something to do with her hands, she brought them up to grab the collar, and their hands touched. A fever washed away the chill in the air. Her cheeks burned. She did not dare to raise her head and meet his eyes.

***

As Seyit gazed at the lovely, demure girl looking down, he felt an unfamiliar warmth inside. She was totally different from every one of his conquests so far. She had to be much younger than him, and even the cloak between them could not disguise the racing of her heart. She was a picture of angelic beauty with baby-blond locks falling over her temples and forehead; a pair of enormous, slanted blue eyes shaded by long dark-blond lashes; and a neat upturned nose. She was no little dalliance. Afraid of hurting this vision of innocent loveliness, he took a single step, fully intending to return her to the dance hall just as he had taken her out.

Then their eyes locked. Seyit was surprised at how this slip of a girl, and such an unassuming one too, had the power to shake him after all his conquests, after all those women he had bedded. It was the first time they had gazed at each other openly. He too felt the tremendous electricity between them. Shura's sparkling eyes, blushing cheeks, heaving bosom, and lips on the verge of bursting into speech seemed to promise unfamiliar delights and tender love. He felt enveloped by the warmth he had always longed for in his loneliest moments. A total stranger held such an overwhelming power over him!

He changed his mind. The last thing he wanted was to take her back now. Instead, he wanted to keep her to himself, here, far from everyone else, and get to know her. He might well be looking at his destiny, singled out for him and him alone.

Seyit touched her shoulder and drew closer gently, lest he frighten her off or hurt her.

In the enchantment of the night and her eyes locked on his, Shura could have been in a fairy-tale, snow-covered garden glittering in the moonlight, surrounded by music emanating from the house. Plucking up her courage, she lifted her gaze for a closer look at the face of the man who had led her away from the dance hall. They drew closer, the mist of their breaths mingling in the chill. It was too late to draw back, she knew, as she submitted her lips to his kisses. The snowflakes fluttering in front of the ornate gas lamps, the melancholy tunes of the balalaika and the piano—everything was part of a wonderful dream. Just when Shura felt on the verge of floating off, the kiss setting her lips on fire stopped. Her head tilted back, she was half fainting, half drunk, and breathless…She thought she heard snatches of something. Cupping her face in his hands, he was asking if she had any objections to staying out here for a while. Shura answered in a trance, barely able to hear her own voice. Perhaps she had not even spoken—she had no idea. She simply shook her head. She knew she should be inside; her sister and father would be looking for her, but she was imprisoned by the arms embracing her; the lips wandering on her face and neck; and the imperious, infatuated gaze. And she was a willing prisoner in the magic of the moonlight and music. She did not want to get away or socialize. She had no desire to go anywhere any longer. She could stay here for years. Closing her eyes, she waited, frightened of losing the magnificent spell enveloping her. But the risk of being caught in this remote corner with some stranger prompted her to protest softly, "I'd better go back. They'll get worried…"

Gripping her by the chin, Seyit gave her a lingering kiss and drew back. "Will I see you again?"

"Are you leaving?" Thinking he was about to go away, Shura flinched.

"No, no, I'm here tonight. I meant later, some other time. Where are you staying? Can we meet?"

She could not believe her ears. This stranger wanted to meet her. But how would they arrange it? "My father...my father's due to be admitted to the hospital tomorrow. I'm not sure. I don't think I could leave the hotel on my own."

"What about the weekend? Aren't you coming to the Borinskys' reception?"

Joy washed away despair. "The reception at the opera? Yes, oh yes, Uncle Andrei was talking to Papa about it—something about Valentine and me going. It all depends on Papa's health, but we might be able to come."

Seyit stroked her cheek with a smile. "Wonderful! So we shall see each other again. Now allow me to escort you back to the dance hall."

As if awakening from a dream, Shura pulled herself together and walked toward the door. It was best to stay as calm and composed as possible, lest she give herself away.

They were about to leave the dim, silent room, when, at his touch on her shoulder, she turned to face him. Repressing the urge to gather her in his arms once again, Seyit opened the door.

Soon they were back in the tipsy crowd. Shura's relief at not having been missed gave way to an inexplicable sense of perturbation, the disquieting possibility that she would fall head over heels in love with this young man, and she would lose him. She did dance with others and paired up with Seyit several times as they swapped partners in the polka; every time he drew near, her heart started pounding, and every time they drew apart, anticipation gave way to resentment and jealousy.

Like every dream, this too came to an end. It was past midnight when Julian Verjensky said they had to leave. Much as they would have loved to stay, the girls followed without protest, knowing their father must be exhausted and that a long and anxious day awaited them all. As they took leave of Borinsky, Shura's eyes wandered over the crowd in the hope of one last sight of that young man. He was nowhere to be seen. *Goodness knows which girl he's courting now!* she thought. She could have kicked herself for building her hopes up like a child and for making such a big thing of it all. She had behaved quite foolishly. She wasn't staying there—even if Papa insisted. All she wanted to do was return to their hotel room and cry in peace. Her eyes were welling up already. Fumbling to put her hand through the handle of her bag, she dropped her muff, gathered her skirts, and bent down—and she heard his voice. Yes, here he was again, his touch warmer than the fur. He murmured with a sweet smile, gazing deep into her eyes, "I shall be looking forward to Saturday night."

Mumbling something between thanks and a farewell, Shura skipped down the staircase behind her sister and father, her heart fluttering like a bird. Now she could weep tears of joy. So she hadn't been mistaken. So his attention was not a fleeting one. She would see him again.

"Lord! Please help me, Lord; please help me see him again!" she prayed. She suddenly remembered her father was due to undergo an operation the following day. She prayed to God and the Virgin Mary throughout the trip back to the hotel for her father's health and to meet the young man she had fallen for.

***

The waiting room of the Golitsyn Hospital looked not so much like a hall typical of such establishments as the lounge of an elegant home. Only the smell of disinfectant seeping in from the corridors betrayed the building's real purpose.

Valentine and Shura held hands for comfort as they waited for news from the operating room. It had been four hours since they had kissed their father, as he was stretchered away. With no word as yet, anxiety was gradually giving way to fear as the sisters prayed, afraid to make a single sound.

The door opened, and they leaped up: it was Andrei Borinsky. Eyes sparkling with unshed tears they rushed over in the hope of some news.

"Uncle Andrei! Is the operation over?"

"How is Papa? Please tell us!"

Borinsky put his arms around their shoulders. "Calm down, calm down. I'm sure everything's all right."

Valentine mumbled in a voice that suggested she was far from convinced. "But it's taking so long, Uncle Andrei! Are you certain Papa's all right?"

"I am, child; I am. According to the surgeon, everything's proceeding as anticipated. Don't forget your father's undergoing a major operation. It will take some time. But believe me, everything is fine. And I'll be waiting here with you; don't worry. They'll send word as soon as Julian's out. Now calm down. Come, sit down, and tell me a little bit about Kislovodsk. How's life over there? Is it as vibrant as in Moscow?"

As Valentine answered Borinsky's questions, Shura stared at the hospital garden. Wiping the windowpane clean of the fog from her breath, she rested her forehead against the glass and traced the fall of snowflakes outside with her right index finger. It all looked so calm, so silent. Her eyes filled up. She didn't even want to consider the possibility that her father might die. Clutching the cross that hung from the gold chain on her neck, she looked up to the skies, which were heavy with gray snow clouds. Her anxiety grew. All she wanted just now was for her father to get better. She felt ashamed of her prayers the previous night. If God were to hear her prayers, they should to be all for her father. Instead, she had also prayed all night to see a total stranger again. She would never forgive herself if something happened to her darling papa.

When the medical director finally entered the waiting room an hour later, he found all three waiting with bated breath. "Good news," he said. "It all went very well. Your surgeon will arrive presently to give you more information."

The sisters hugged joyfully and asked to see their father at once.

"Not just yet. He's in a deep sleep at the moment. I assure you, however, that he is much better. Frankly, the best thing you can do is go and rest a little yourselves. Come back in the morning for a brief visit."

He was adamant, and there was no point in insisting. Borinsky resolved to take the girls away. "Come along then; we'll go over to our place...and I'll have none of your excuses either. Surely you didn't think I'd leave the daughters of my dearest friend all on their own—and in a hotel room at that."

"But Uncle Andrei, everything we have is in the hotel!"

"That's no problem at all: We'll call in there first. You can collect your belongings, and we'll go directly to our place. We'll be back in the morning, at any rate. And we can inform your father then that you're staying with us. To be honest, I have no idea why we've not thought of it earlier."

Later that day, in their rooms in the Borinsky mansion, the girls could barely contain themselves as they waited for morning to come.

Sadly, that first visit would be an enormous disappointment. The patient was still in critical condition, and no one was allowed to enter his room.

All they could do was to wave from the door and try to hide their horror. He looked unrecognizable now that the full beard and moustache had been shaved off for the first time in years. His eyes looked smaller, and his cheeks were sunken in that haggard face; several tubes snaked out of the dressings covering his neck. The doctor at his bedside said something and held up the pillow and tubes so that Julian Verjensky could turn his head for a look at his daughters. His ashen, resigned face brightened up at once; gathering his strength, he beamed at them. Choking back tears, Valentine and Shura waved back, smiling. That tiny movement had been enough to tire him out, and Julian closed his eyes with a moan. As the doctor settled him back into the bed, he signaled for Borinsky and another doctor to lead the girls away.

Shura was crying as Valentine confronted the doctor. "What's wrong with Papa? I thought he was supposed to get better!"

"Your father is quite well, young lady. But it wasn't at all an easy operation that he's undergone—" the doctor reassured her in a confident voice.

Borinsky interrupted. "Best to tell them everything, Doctor—best thing to set their minds at ease."

Some of it sounded quite incomprehensible; among the profusion of medical terms, the one thing Shura could make out was that her father would be breathing through a tube in his throat from now on. Valentine might have understood more, but Shura didn't dare ask her. They returned home in silence. In an effort to lift their spirits, Borinsky clapped his hands with a jolly laugh. "Come on then; pull yourselves together! Your father's getting better. He'll be back on his feet and joining us in a few days. I'm sure he'd be heartbroken if he could see you two sulking. Come to your senses now. The last thing I want on Saturday night is two miserable girls moping beside me. All right?"

Shura's heart leaped at the mention of Saturday night. How could she have forgotten? She wasn't even sure they could go to the reception at the Bolshoi. How could they have fun while their father was in the hospital? Just as Valentine was about to protest, to say something to that effect, Borinsky raised a hand to indicate he would brook no excuses and shook his head.

"Tsk, tsk, tsk...I won't hear of it. There's nothing you can achieve by sitting here. Not to mention that your father actually wants you to go. And how can you cheer him up if you can't shake off your own gloom? Don't worry; I will take you to the hospital every day. You will see him every day. And you will be able to spend as much time with him as his doctor allows. But you will also enjoy your own lives; are we agreed?"

Borinsky's bright, cheerful, and hopeful voice was heartening; he was right, the girls thought, as they climbed the stairs to their rooms.

The next morning, Julian looked much better; his face had regained some of its color, and even his eyes were brighter. But he was not allowed visitors and couldn't speak yet, stated the doctor; what the patient needed now was time. And their cheerful support, thought the girls as they left the hospital in much better spirits than the previous day. They concurred with Uncle Andrei. Their father would be missing their mother too, and it was up to them to jolly him along until their return to Kislovodsk.

Saturday morning's visit was more heartening still; they were allowed into their father's room for the first time and exchanged a few words. Delighted that he was on the mend and would be discharged within the week, Valentine and Shura launched into feverish preparations for the evening with clear consciences.

Shura's stomach was gripped by cramps from noon onward. They were not symptoms of any ailment, feeling light headed as she did, her heart racing and her legs buckling under her. This was love. She had no desire to discuss anything with anyone; by focusing her thoughts on the mysterious stranger, she felt she might bring him closer. At times a thought flashed into her mind: it would be nothing short of a miracle to find him in that crowd, not to mention the possibility that he might be escorting someone else—a thought that sank her spirits. In two minds about the evening, therefore, she scrutinized her wardrobe over and over again, unable to decide what to wear. She might well have to consult Valentine. The violet gown flattered her the most, but she had worn it the other night. She picked up the yellow dress embroidered with white flowers on the collar, shoulders, and skirt. She put it on, moved to the mirror, and lifted her hair with both hands and piled it onto her head. Turning on the spot, she watched her reflection. Dissatisfied, she pouted, removed the dress, and flung it on the bed. That yellow competed with the blue of her eyes and her blond hair. She briefly considered the pink organza—her sister certainly would not wear pink tonight—and discarded the idea as soon as she held the dress up to her face: those iridescent pinks did nothing for her. She had to look different and much more beautiful than ever before tonight. She finally decided on the turquoise silk taffeta gown.

They still had four hours to go. Time seemed to be standing still. The arrangement was to meet in the large hall downstairs at eight and set off. At seven thirty, Valentine came over to find Shura pacing in her room, crushing a handkerchief.

"Shurochka, you look lovely! Just like a fairy-tale princess."

Shura returned the compliment, admiring her big sister, who wore a white gown adorned with silk ribbons. "You too, Tinochka! You look radiant, by God!"

Hugging and kissing joyfully, the girls occupied themselves with final touches to each other's hair and skirts, more excited than ever before. When the clock in the entrance hall finally rang eight, they knew it was time to go downstairs. With one last critical look in the mirror, they left.

They had barely taken a few steps down, Valentine leading the way, when they spotted the group waiting at the entrance to the hall. Shura gasped, her heart pounding. Pausing momentarily, she grasped the banister with her right hand. Her sweaty palm felt even more feverish at the contact with the cool crystal. Her left hand went up to her bosom, as if to still her racing heart. Andrei Borinsky was waiting with two men in uniform—none other than Petro Borinsky and Seyt Eminof, the young man Shura had been dying to see again. She thought she might compose herself if only she could slow her descent, but feeling the stares on her, she followed Valentine at the same unhurried pace.

Borinsky saw no reason to disguise his admiration. "My God! We are indeed fortunate tonight, aren't we?" He winked at the young men to indicate he really meant it was they who were fortunate. "Tonight we'll be escorting the most beautiful and graceful young ladies to the Bolshoi. I am delighted."

Approaching the stairs and taking the girls by the hand, he led them to the middle of the hall one after the other as the two young men bowed.

"It is time to leave. I'd have loved to offer you a glass of something if I weren't hosting this evening, but we must get there before anyone else."

Followed to the door by his smiling guests, he climbed into the first carriage and invited the girls inside as well; the officers boarded the second carriage.

As Valentine chattered with their host with her customary confident charm, soft brown hair framing her glowing face, Shura consciously avoided turning around for a look throughout the trip.

The snow that had fallen all day had settled into perfect silence. The wind had dropped. They drove along the glittering Mokhovaya and Herzen Roads until the carriages slowed down at Teatralny Square. The monumental theater rose before them in the white darkness, magnificent and twinkling with a myriad of lights.

"And this is our legendary Bolshoi," announced Borinsky.

"It's lovely! Just like a shrine!" exclaimed Shura, audibly letting out the breath she had been holding.

"Yes, dear child, just like a shrine," said her host with a burst of laughter.

The carriages drew up before the eight-column portico. Shura was getting ready to descend when she noticed the hand extended toward her. Gathering her skirts with her right hand, she laid her left in Seyit's palm.

She ascended the stairs alongside him, her hand in his warm, strong, yet gentle grasp, musing that this could be the continuation of the dream of the other night. Alert to his unwavering gaze, she didn't dare turn her head toward him; that surreptitious stare was still profoundly flattering though. She had to offer a sign of her interest. One look couldn't hurt, and they might never see each other again. Just as they were about to enter the hall, she gathered her courage, turned her head, and flashed him a look. The sparkle in his eyes was no different from hers. They might never see each other again, yet he had taken her captive, a lifelong captive, with a single look. Shura trembled. Something told her she was hopelessly and eternally in love...and would suffer greatly.

It was not long before Andrei Borinsky's guests filled the lobby. Every time Shura and Seyit caught occasional glimpses of each other, she stole another look and offered a furtive smile, and every time that happened, Seyit pondered ways of getting to know this timid beauty more intimately.

After a light service of caviar and French champagne, the guests filed into their seats. Shura and Valentine were in the box nearest the stage. The lights were about to be doused when Borinsky slipped in and sat down behind them.

"I hope you'll like your seats, and I hope you will forgive me, but I do have to visit my guests in the other boxes. Essential to avoid offending those not invited back to the house afterward, you know. But I will find you again before the end of the show. Please don't worry, and wait for me here, all right?"

His excuses thus made in the blink of an eye, he rose and vanished behind the heavy velvet curtain. The girls giggled. Shura surveyed the other boxes, where heavily made-up elegant ladies sat in their finery, priceless jewels adorning décolletages that exposed the slightest trembling of their breasts. They seemed to be competing with one another and the splendor of the Bolshoi itself. She looked nothing like them in her plain turquoise dress and wore only a gold cross on her neck. Her glance strayed to the chatty young lady in the next box, whose smoldering jet-black eyes—the same color as her hair—were employed to full advantage. She seemed to be talking with her entire body and not just her mouth as she wielded her eyes, lips, hands, and shoulders, fingertips lightly wandering on her throat. Her escort's rapt attention suggested that she was succeeding. Astounded at the movement of those breasts, Shura stole a glance at her own chest. No matter how deeply she might inhale, her own assets would never overflow in the same way. This lady must be breathing in some other manner.

Valentine interrupted her musings. "Shurochka, look who's over there!"

Shura's eyes followed the pointing finger, and she failed to spot any familiar face in the next box but one.

"Look—it's Lola Polianskaya, my friend from Kislovodsk. She was at Uncle Andrei's party the other night. She's here with her parents. And look, she's beckoning us. Come on; let's go."

Shura had no intention of spending the whole evening with a girl she didn't know. "We've got great seats, Valentine—and look, the curtain's about to rise. I don't want to go."

"Come on, Shura; come on, sweetie—it's only two boxes away. We'll get there in no time at all! Look, they're calling us!"

"You go. Anyway, Uncle Andrei would miss us when he comes back; it would be terribly rude. I'll stay."

Valentine hesitated, still on her feet. "But I can't leave you alone here!"

"Don't be silly, Tinochka; I'll be fine. You go. Go on; join your friend. Quick, it's about to start; you'll be stuck here otherwise."

Valentine had just vanished behind the curtains to the corridor when the orchestra struck up the *Swan Lake* overture. Placing her clasped hands on her lap, Shura surrendered to the magic of Tchaikovsky's music. The curtain rolled up inch by inch, teasing the audience with the magnificent scenery beyond. The castle formed the backdrop to Siegfried's birthday party. The happy young prince was greeting arrivals as two female dancers and a male executed a faultless *pas de trois*.

Shura abandoned her fluttering heart to the enchanting tale. Soon she was floating on Odette's wings and welling up at the Swan Queen's hopeless love. Uncontrollable tears that no one else could see, she hoped. Engrossed in the romance before her eyes, she was happy to be on her own—so much so that she never noticed the silent parting of the curtains. Startled by the soft touch on her hand, she turned to the silhouette sitting behind her in the dark. He tucked a handkerchief into her hands. Was she confusing the fairy tale on the stage with her own daydreams? It was hard to tell where fantasy ended and reality began.

But then...didn't life turn into a dream whenever she was with him? Every dream had an end, as ultimately this one must. Fine. Then she was going to enjoy it while it lasted. Her eyes on the stage, she dabbed at her eyes, hoping she wasn't the focus of attention. Her hands had been lying on the folds of her voluminous skirt, but now she surrendered her right hand into his. The warmth spreading into her whole body from the wrist felt as heady as it had been the other night.

On the stage, it was dawn, time for farewells: Odette parted from her prince, and the swans bade good-bye to the hunters. The happy time was over.

"Stop crying now; the curtain's about to fall."

She turned eyes sparkling with tears toward him as the curtain fell, but a smile played on her lips. Seyit's voice was nearly lost in the applause.

"My God! You're so innocent—and so beautiful!"

They weren't destined to stay alone for much longer though. Valentine, her friend Lola Polianskaya, and Petro Borinsky joined them soon after the curtain fell. Drinks circulated once again during the fifteen-minute intermission. She took the champagne Seyit pressed into her hand, holding his gaze for the first time instead of shying away. Quite the opposite—as the evening progressed, it occurred to her that she wanted to see more of him. They would have to part forever soon enough, anyway. This would undoubtedly be little more than a longing romance across a vast distance, since she was due to return home in a few weeks. As for this total stranger, he was obviously a guest in Moscow for no more than a few days. In a flash, she realized she would do anything to be with him, take anything that came along, no matter the consequences—an idea and a foolish audacity that surprised her briefly, but the voice of the heart stilled common sense. She was hopelessly in love, far more than the swan queen Odette.

Every seat in the box was filled for the second act now that Valentine, Petro, and Andrei Borinsky had all returned from their visits. It seemed Shura's chance for a tête-à-tête with Seyit had come to an end, at least for the night.

***

Twenty or so carriages waited to take the party, which now included several dancers, back to the Borinsky mansion for the second part of the evening's entertainment.

Seyit and Petro escorted Shura and Valentine to the exit. Shura was discomfited at Petro's furtive glances at her as he escorted Valentine. She hadn't taken to him much in the first place; his looks might turn many a young girl's head, but there was a suggestion of deceitfulness in his nose—just a little too short and too upturned for a male face—and squinting eyes. She couldn't quite explain why, but Shura felt uneasy in his presence.

The four young people entered the same carriage. The trip back took no longer than ten minutes, and most of the conversation flew between Valentine and Petro, while the other two just locked eyes. Shura no longer felt so timid. She was doing nothing wrong, was she?

By the time they arrived, drinks were already flowing in the music room. A lavish meal waited on a table in the dining room. The night could have been just starting, as music and laughter filled the house in no time at all. The Bolshoi ballet troupe stood to one side, clearly the focal point of the evening. Males young and old blatantly courted the beauties they had watched on stage earlier.

Shura watched, amazed, as the ballerinas teased them all with sultry laughter and graceful movements.

Then she spotted Seyit in the same group. It broke her heart. Now there was no point in staying. She considered sneaking out and going up to her room, but before she could, Seyit and another man approached, flanking a dancer. They looked like very close friends. Nailed to the spot, Shura waited until Seyit offered introductions that set her mind at ease.

"Dear Tatiana, allow me to introduce you to this lovely young lady: Alexandra Julianovna Verjenskaya." Turning to Shura, he introduced the others. "Tatiana Tchoupilkina, principal with the Bolshoi, and my dear friend, Lieutenant Celil Kamilof."

Shura looked them over during this brief ceremony. Tatiana had to be much older, even older than the two young men. She moved with an exquisite fluidity as though permanently on stage, and her large black eyes still wore the heavy stage makeup. Perhaps it was the cosmetics that made her look so much older. Her complexion was porcelain white and clear. *No other neck could be longer or more slender, more suited to represent a swan on the stage,* thought Shura. Tatiana had the flat chest of a little girl, yet the way she shaded those flashing black eyes with her long eyelashes was magnetic. A fetching smile gleamed on her lips.

Artistic her demeanor might be, but she wasn't in the least bit pretentious. She was also quite obviously with the other man. Shura breathed a sigh of relief and warmed to the dancer at once. Celil's love was apparent for the whole world to see, in the way his twinkling, slanted eyes gazed at Tatiana. He had a bright, distinctive face, quite handsome in his own way.

It didn't take long for Shura to relax in their company, enough to forget how much younger she was. When the officers went to top up their glasses, Tatiana laid a hand on Shura's. "Dear Alexandra Julianovna, I wish you could stay here for longer. We'd have such a great time."

Shura replied equally frankly. "I can imagine, Tatiana Tchoupilkina…"

"My close friends simply call me Tatya."

"Very well, Tatya."

"Sadly, Celil and Kurt Seyt are also due to leave Moscow soon."

"Do they come here often?"

"Not really. In fact, you never know when and where they will be next. On the whole, where Tsar Nicholas goes, there they go. Can't say they don't enjoy a colorful life!" A peal of laughter. "You know, dear Alexandra—"

"My close friends call me Shura."

Tatiana continued, still laughing, "Yes, dear Shura, you know, if I weren't a dancer, I'd have wished to be a man, and in their place!"

The idea that a famous beauty surrounded by male admirers should wish to be a man was inconceivable. Shura's quizzical look prompted Tatiana to let loose another of her celebrated peals of laughter. "If you had any idea just how colorful their lives are, I have no doubt you too would want to be in their place."

The girl couldn't help but smile as she shook her head. "I don't think I would ever want to be a man."

Tatiana pointed to Celil and Seyit, who were parting the crowd to return, carrying their glasses.

"Take a look at them, dear Shura: they're handsome, moneyed, in the tsar's court, and permanently surrounded by aristocratic beauties. Their escapades would make a book, young as they are now—trust me."

Shura was astounded at this calm and happy acceptance. "So you know of Celil's escapades, Tatya?"

"Of course I do. Don't be so surprised. I'd have to be a fool to think I was the only woman in the life of a handsome officer shuttling between Moscow, Livadia Palace, and Saint Petersburg." She flapped her hand. "Oh, I know it's now called Petrograd, but to me, it will always be Saint Petersburg! At any rate, all I care for is the time we have together. And also, I'm sure he loves me most, which is enough for me." She paused to take a look at the girl listening in amazement. "Good God! What am I saying? I've shocked you, haven't I, dear Shura? Totally forgot you're barely a child. How old *are* you, as a matter of interest?"

"I'll be sixteen in April."

"Oh my God! Still fifteen then? You do look older, I must confess. You won't be cross if I don't tell you how old I am, will you? I am much older, I assure you. And please forgive me; I hope I've not embarrassed you, prattling on like that. That would be the last thing I'd want—for you to misunderstand me. But believe me, if only I'd known you were just sixteen..."

Shura knew Tatiana meant well. Truth be told, she was flattered by the misjudgment that had led to the shared confidence. Despite the disparity in their ages and styles, Shura smiled, sensing they could become close friends. "Oh please, Tatya; I can't claim not to have been shocked, but believe me, I do enjoy your company."

When the men returned, Tatiana whispered into Seyit's ear as she picked up her glass. "Seyt Eminof, I've never seen you devote yourself exclusively to one lady all night. She's obviously got some sort of pull over you. Indulge me to warn you, however: She's far too young yet. She's not like anyone else you've had before. Don't you dare hurt her."

Seyit felt his insides warming as he looked at Shura chatting with Celil. "You seem to have taken a shine to her, Tatya."

"I have, indeed."

A grinning Seyit winked. "Who knows? I might too!"

Moving to Shura's side, he touched her lightly on the elbow. "Shall we take a walk in the garden—that is, if you won't get cold, Alexandra Julianovna?"

Not deceived by the formality, Shura shivered deliciously at the prospect of being alone with him in the half light of the garden. In order to spare her blushes before the other couple, she asked Tatiana, "Wouldn't you like to come along, Tatya?"

"You two enjoy yourselves; Celil and I have something to discuss. We'll still be here when you return," said Tatiana, beaming at Celil. She took his arm and led him away without waiting for a reply.

When they emerged onto the veranda in the rear, Shura was astonished to find herself speechless once again. They halted at the top of the steps leading down to the garden.

"Are you sure you won't get cold?"

Shura shook her head. She wasn't in the least bit cold, yet something inside shivered inexplicably. Moving closer, Seyit held her arm tenderly. "Don't tell me you're not cold; see how you tremble!"

"I am not, I assure you."

The stranger who felt like a lifelong companion held her by the elbow and guided her down the steps to the garden.

"Then you're probably homesick. Homesickness makes you feel this way." Shura looked at his face, where the melancholy in his voice echoed. "You feel cold when you feel alone—something I know all too well."

She relaxed as tender concern for her escort replaced timidity. "Is your home very far?" she asked softly.

Seyit smiled. "My home? Homes? Yes, they're all very far now."

They halted by the fountain momentarily to listen to the burbling of the water pouring from bowls held by four cupids, which stood back to back on the marble plinth in the center—a sound in harmony with the tunes rising from the house.

"It's all so lovely," said Shura, but before she could finish, his hand was in her palm. Their eyes met.

"You're even lovelier," he replied, planting a kiss in her palm.

Intoxicated by the warmth of his fiery lips but uncertain of the attitude she must adopt next, Shura closed her eyes briefly and found herself in his arms.

He just hugged her slender figure tight for a while without moving, lest he frighten her. Shura laid her head on his chest, her heart racing. She submitted to the powerful embrace of the man she had fallen in love with, a totally unfamiliar emotion that brooked no protest. She did not know him, but this had to be the man she wanted beside her for the rest of her life.

The snow fell in weary, lazy flakes.

"Let's go back in if you like."

Reluctant to leave, Shura looked up into his eyes. His eyes flashed in the darkness, and Seyit finally gave in to temptation; he could no longer content himself with merely staring at this wonderful beauty. He placed a lingering kiss on her forehead. Filling his lungs with the smell of her hair, he cupped her face in his hands. Then, still hugging her, he all but dragged her to the trees to the rear. He leaned against a tree and drew her close. Tilted her head up by the chin and leaned down toward her lips. The chilly moonlit night, the flickering lights of the gas lamps, the music, and the burbling of the fountain all seemed to be inviting them to love. Shura opened her eyes and gazed at his face, now certain this was the only man she would ever want for all her life. But how long could they stay together? They might meet once, perhaps twice at most, after which they would go their own ways. A profound sadness deflated her ardor. No, she did not wish to lose him.

"My little Alexandra! You're so lovely, so sweet!" repeated Seyit as he covered her cheeks and throat with kisses.

Aroused by the kisses and breath at the base of her ear, and despite a brief panic at this inexplicable pleasure, Shura raised her arms and wrapped them around Seyit's neck. As he held her captive in his arms, their lips met once again. Seyit experienced an unfamiliar rush of warmth at the unaffected, guileless, innocent, and inexperienced love on offer. This sweet young thing had submitted so readily; he wanted to take her away from here, to somewhere they could be alone together. But how long would the thrill last? How could this be a genuine relationship? They were embarking upon something they could never see through. He had to restrain himself.

"Alexandra." He buried his face in her hair.

"Yes?" asked Shura, virtually inaudibly.

Seyit couldn't believe his ears when his mouth uttered the total opposite of what he had planned to say. "I want to see you again, to be alone with you." An idea popped into his mind. "Tomorrow...how about I collect you tomorrow morning, and we can spend Sunday together?"

She replied without removing her arms. Her voice was still low and trembling. "We're going to visit my father in the hospital tomorrow morning. And afterward, I'm not sure...I don't know how to get permission to go out."

Seyit caressed her cheeks. "But would you like to be with me too?"

Too bashful for a straightforward reply, Shura just nodded.

"Are you sure you really want to? I want to hear you say it."

"Yes...yes, I do."

"Then leave it to me; I'll think of something. Perhaps I'll take you to the hospital. And then give you a tour of Moscow."

"But...Uncle Andrei?"

"Don't worry. Andrei Borinsky has known me since I was a child. I don't think he'll make an issue of it." He brushed at the snow sticking to her hair and forehead; it was falling much more heavily now. "Come on, let's go back in. I don't want you to get sick."

Shura couldn't even begin to guess how long they had stayed outdoors. She felt as if they had been together for many, many years, yet at the same time, she felt as if everything had begun and ended quite unexpectedly—as if she had been dispatched to a fantasy world and tugged back by a magic wand. Her real life waited just there, just beyond the stairs and the door. The idea of parting from Seyit was heartbreaking. They walked hand in hand for a little while, as slowly as they possibly could. Seyit pointed to the cupids as they passed the fountain.

"You know, I'd like to swap places with them. I'd like to freeze with you in my arms as I kiss you. Then you'd be in my arms, kissing me for all eternity."

Shura couldn't suppress a bashful smile at those words, no less thrilling than the warmth of his hands wrapped around hers. "Then you'd be cold under the snow for all eternity."

Seyit halted and grasped her shoulders; he was smiling. "My little darling! With you in my arms? No, oh no; I hardly think so."

The moment they stepped into the house, Shura realized just how cold she had gotten—not that she cared, floating in ecstatic anticipation as she was. Removing her cloak and brushing the snow from her skirts, she rejoined the party with the man she loved.

They found Tatiana and Celil again, and Seyit vanished briefly. Shura stole a look to follow him in the crowd but then turned her head back, lest she be found out by others. His return about fifteen minutes later flooded her veins with warmth. *This must be what they call love,* Shura thought.

"Marvelous arrangement for tomorrow," announced Seyit in high spirits, drawing intrigued stares from the group. "Dear Alexandra Julianovna, I have spoken with Andrei Borinsky and obtained his permission to take you out tomorrow. I will collect you after your hospital visit, and Celil, Tatya, and I will show you Moscow."

She couldn't believe her ears. It all sounded far too easy. But...

"But...Valentine? I can't leave her alone!"

"I believe she will be visiting another friend with the Borinskys tomorrow."

Tatiana's delighted laughter rang out. "Excellent! Excellent! We'll have a wonderful day, I'm sure."

From that moment on, Shura could think of nothing else. The rest of the night flew by as if in a dream. It was some early hour in the morning when the last of the guests departed—and that happened to be none other than Seyit. The two young people exchanged good-byes, gazing into each other's eyes.

On kissing her big sister good night, Shura briefly considered telling her what had happened but discarded the idea at once. Valentine might disapprove or even reprimand her. Worse still was the risk of jeopardizing the following day's arrangements. All she wanted to do was to get into bed as soon as possible and revel in her dreams. She relived the moments in the garden over and over again once she had turned out the light and snuggled under the duvet, and she re-called every single word they had exchanged, every kiss, every touch. When at last she fell asleep, Seyit's touch on her lips and embrace on her body felt no farther than her dreams.

It was nearly noon when the household finally rose the next day. After a lavish breakfast, Andrei Borinsky took the girls to the hospital. This was Julian Verjensky's best day since the operation. He was due to be discharged in a few days, and the girls had their longest visit yet, sitting on either side of his bed and chattering away happily about life at the Borinsky mansion as their father watched his beautiful daughters. He couldn't speak, but he was able to com-municate by blinking and nodding. After half an hour or so, the doctor led them out. It was time for the patient to rest.

Valentine had arranged to visit with a distant relation, accompanied by Andrei and Petro Borinsky, just as Seyit had said. All the same, Shura invited her sister to join her party, but Valentine much preferred a house visit to traipsing up and down Moscow's streets in the bitter cold for hours and hours.

Her stomach cramping, her head spinning as if drunk, Shura wore a navy-blue dress adorned with cream lace and tied her braids into a chignon with a matching ribbon. There was a knock on the door just as she finished; it was one of the servants.

"Mademoiselle Alexandra Julianovna? First Lieutenant Eminof is here, Mademoiselle."

Shura grabbed her cloak, muff, and tiny velvet bag and dived into Valentine's room for a hasty kiss. She was skipping down the stairs when she spotted Seyit waiting in the entrance hall and slowed down. More calm and composure were called for—composure betrayed by her radiant face.

Raising her hand to his lips, Seyit helped her into her cloak and whispered, "You are so beautiful."

Tatiana and Celil had been waiting in the carriage. She returned their cheerful greeting and sat down next to Seyit, musing that this was a first in her life being out with a male admirer. The carriage wended its way through the city along roads flanked by elegant residences of two and three stories. It had been snowing heavily since the early morning. As they crossed the Krasnaya Ploshchad, Shura admired once again the sight of the snow-covered square, the Kremlin Palace, the bell tower, and the bright and colorful domes of the cathedrals reaching into the sky. Pointing at some of the landmarks, Seyit ran an intermittent commentary. "This edifice resembling an Indian temple is the Uspensky Cathedral, where the tsars were crowned. It collapsed in 1472 and was rebuilt by an architect from Bologna. It's meant to be Byzantine in style, but I personally could never make head nor tail of those Indian domes." In a short while, they were facing another iconic building. "And this is the Blagoveshchensk Cathedral, the one with the nine domes. It was finished in 1489, and the architects were from Pskov. That's where Andrei Rublev's famed sacred paintings are housed. The bones of all our tsars, from Ivan Kalita down to Ivan V, are all interred in the Archangelsky Cathedral. Except for Boris Godunov."

Unfamiliar as she was with most of the names he reeled off like a history teacher, Shura proved to be a rapt listener.

"This is the Spasskie Vorota, the middle gate between the square and the Kremlin. There are two more on either side. Immediately behind the square stretches the central residential area of old Moscow. Do you know what *Kıtai Gorod* means?"

Shura shook her head.

"Means *fortress* in Crimean Tatar. That's where the merchants lived, to the north of the River Moskva. The other districts of the city were called Byely Gorod, meaning White City, and Zemlyanov Gorod, East City. And that's the bit to the south of the river. Russia's first university was founded in 1755 in Moscow..."

A street photographer waved. The sparkle in Shura's eyes prompted Seyit to stop the carriage, and the sightseers bustled out for several quick photos.

Before long they were at the junction of the Mokhovaya and Herzen Roads. With a stab of disappointment, Shura mistook this for the end of the trip, thinking they were on their way back now. But then the carriage turned around and headed south of the Moskva. Now they were driving past residences set well apart inside spacious gardens. As the snowfall thickened practically into a blizzard, the young passengers chatted merrily. Before long, the carriage drew to a halt; Tatiana touched Shura's hand to point to the house in the middle of a garden.

"Here, this is my home. Come on, I can't wait to settle by the fireplace. We got here just in time."

It wasn't big, but it was exquisitely and expensively appointed. Every single room and hall resembled a stage set. What might have looked somewhat incongruous in the hands of anyone else was the perfect setting for Tatiana's personality. Shura liked the house as much as she did its owner.

After drinks in front of the crackling fire, they settled down at the table. Shura had quite forgotten the age gap and had overcome her shyness by this time. Lunch was an opportunity to get to know one another better. She spoke of her family and life back in Kislovodsk; the more she spoke, the more she relaxed. True, she wasn't keeping up with the others in wine consumption; two glasses had been sufficient to make her quite tipsy. The family home back in Kislovodsk, her mother and siblings, her father in the hospital, and even Valentine were now all far away, miles and miles away.

They moved to the music room after the meal. A silver samovar stood on the table between high-backed burgundy velvet sofas flanking the fireplace. Tatiana poured the tea and moved to the piano. She started with a theme from Alexander Borodin's *Prince Igor*. The reckless fight between the Crimean Tatar Khan Kontchak and Prince Igor, the sand- and snowstorms of the north and the steppes of Asia, the sinuous oriental dances of the Tatar girls intended to seduce Prince Igor, the brutality of the warriors, and the pounding of their steeds' hooves all seemed to come to life on the keys. Shura joined in the cheers when Tatiana had finished. Celil's grin narrowed his slanted Tatar eyes into slits. "You know, Tatya plays this piece so well because she's in love with me!"

His outburst drew happy laughter from the rest.

Tatiana's next offering was a jolly tune called "Chupchik" in a lively rhythm that sounded as though it had been composed to flatter the pianist's nature. The officers accompanied the song that filled the room, which cheered them all up even more.

When she launched into the fourth and final scene of *Swan Lake*, a profound silence fell over the room. Shura was reliving the sad tale they had watched only the previous night. Skirting the back of the piano, she stood by the French window that invited the garden into the house. Despite the early hour, it was as dark as evening. All that kept the snow clouds in the sky from descending to the earth seemed to be the tall trees. The blizzard concealed what lay beyond them: the wrought-iron garden furniture immediately outside the window, the broad marble planters, and the tiny pond.

Shura crossed her arms, shivering at the scene and the sorrowful tune.

She turned her head when an arm hugged her shoulder and felt safe again at the warmth of Seyit's lips on her forehead. She laid her head against his chest without a protest. That peculiar sensation, like when they had just met, was back: a cramp in her stomach, the racing of her heart, and an inexplicable thrill. Just like that time. A feeling that something new was about to happen, something that would change her life.

They never even noticed the other couple's silent departure. Locked in an embrace, they watched the snow rapidly filling the garden, pondering what to do next. Shura was alone with a strange man for the first time in her life. As concerned about losing him as being mistaken for a loose wench, she waited in his arms, frozen to the spot, fearful of saying or doing anything that might be interpreted as an invitation. As Seyit's lips wandered on her thick blond braids, he too waited, reluctant to frighten her off or receive a rebuff and conscious of her innocent complaisance.

They enjoyed each other's warmth in silence for quite a while.

He was amazed at himself; he had never experienced such serenity in a relationship to this day. What could he possibly expect of this little girl, at any rate? Yet he had never felt this degree of peace and thrill with anyone else. An utterly unexpected desire washed over him, a desire to hug her tight and cover her hair and face with kisses. Gently stroking her under the chin, he lifted her head. Now he could see the quivering twinkles in her large blue eyes.

Her resistance crumbling before his passionate gaze, Shura closed her eyes in a sign of submission and parted her lips. The taste of that unpainted, fresh, and plump mouth—too timid to respond as yet—whipped his ardor. Tender as his hold was, he recognized his growing impatience to discover the delicate curves concealed by the folds of fabric. Shura's feet left the floor as he gripped her waist tighter. She wrapped her arms around his neck and laid her head on his chest, afraid of opening her eyes. He lowered her onto the sofa without releasing the embrace. By wrapping her arms tightly around his body, Shura made it obvious that she was not oblivious to Seyit's fiery kisses and caresses. The warm breath wandering on her ears, throat, and neck was as intoxicating as the wine she had drunk.

All she had to do to stop him, to save herself from this sweet slavery, was offer a single sign—a fleeting thought she waved away equally swiftly. She had no wish to lose this stranger who proffered such ineffable pleasure. She had to get to know him better, experience all the love he could give. The warmth from the fireplace stoked their bodies. Shura half opened her eyes for a glance at his face, where shadows played in the half light of the fire, curious about his intentions. She sensed that look in his eyes again, the look that made her feel half naked. Dreadfully self-conscious, she turned her head to the side.

Seyit rose on his elbow and placed a palm on her cheek. "My beautiful darling, look at me. I want you to look at me. Don't look away."

Shura did as he asked, in response to his impassioned, albeit tender, plea. The lust in his eyes made her blush furiously, as did the appellation of *darling*—a magical word that made her heart flutter. Seyit held her gaze as he kissed her palm and slipped his lips toward her wrist. Shura trembled from head to toe. Timidly, and ever so slowly, her right hand reached out to his head. Her fingers ran through his straight sandy hair in a touch that shook them both. Freeing her left hand from his hold, she touched his face, now painted a different color by the light of the flames. Her fingertips tentatively followed the line of his forehead and prominent cheekbones. Her index finger settled in the deep cleft in his chin for a while before moving back up to the forehead to resume caressing his face, as if to memorize his features.

Seyit knew he had never felt such singular pleasure in his twenty-four years. He was astonished at this gentle, warm, and calm love that had such power to arouse him. The innocent and affectionate caresses of a girl eight years his junior, a virgin, had invoked a tenderness whose absence had been freezing his heart, a tenderness he had been missing for years. She was different from all the women he had ever known.

First they had gotten used to each other's touch in that earlier embrace, and now their hands and faces were exploring each other's bodies. Before long, Seyit felt an overwhelming desire to possess this inexplicable love lying in his arms, body and soul. Loosening his hold, he drew back. Shura regarded him quizzically. Stroking the blond curls falling on her brow, he spoke, his voice betraying the intensity of the desire he was trying to restrain. "Shura, I want you so much... more than I have ever wanted anyone. But I must be honest with you: I can offer you no promises."

For the first time ever, Shura felt she could look directly into those flashing eyes, as if this young man had been a part of her life for years. She was no longer intimidated or afraid. Quite the opposite: now she could see beyond the confident rake's seductive gaze, into the woeful loneliness—the loneliness she wanted to dispel. Wasn't it going to happen one day anyway? Why not experience it with the man she loved? Seyit was her destiny. She wanted to make him happy until such a time as fate would tear them asunder. The last thing she wanted to worry about now was the aftermath—what would happen once she was on her own or how it might change her life. She responded by locking her arms around his neck, closing her eyes, and snuggling her head against his throat. At this reply, much more eloquent than any flamboyant verbosity, he stood up and held his hand out. Fully aware there would be no return beyond this point, she laid her hand in his and rose from the sofa. Words would have served no purpose other than destroying the magic of this moment. She followed, still holding his hand. The only noises in the room were the crackling of the burning logs and the swish of her skirts.

She wondered where Tatiana and Celil might be. Total silence ruled the house; there was no sign of the servant who had lit the fires and served the meal.

All those thoughts vanished when Seyit picked her up. Like a newlywed bride, she let him ascend the stairs with her in his arms. She shut her eyes, determined to experience it all like a dream—one she would always recall down to the last detail whenever she closed her eyes. When she sensed she was being laid on the soft bed, she knew she wouldn't be the same young maiden afterward. But she did not have the slightest desire to run away. Instead, she longed to hasten this unfamiliar union and spend time with the man she loved. A voice inside lifted her inhibitions and promised to teach her to enjoy this adventure.

Seyit shut the door. Shura lay motionless, staring at the gray whiteness outside the window. Snow lashed at the window and settled upon the sill. The wind shook the snow-laden branches of the spruce immediately outside, now in view, now gone in an eerie sigh. The tiled fireplace by the bed, to the left of the door, had evidently been lit a while back: the logs were charred, and the fire was now mostly embers.

Shura watched Seyit's unhurried moves as he removed his jacket and knelt by the fire. He took a log from the marble ledge, placed it on the embers, and stoked the fire with spruce twigs. They caught and set alight the dry log in the middle. He rubbed his palms together, rose, and walked toward the bed calmly. He knew that all his efforts to restrain his intense desire would merely delay the inevitable. Sitting at the edge of the bed, he took Shura's hands in his own. Their fingers interlaced. Careful not to touch her body, he leaned down to her lips, lest she suddenly want to get away. Patiently, taking his time, he kissed her cheeks and throat until she indicated she too wanted to make love.

Their bodies entwined in the yielding hollows of the bed knew there no longer was any obstacle to their union. Even at that stage, Seyit was determined to prepare her gently until she was absolutely certain. He gazed at her face as he undid the top button of her dress. Shura's pupils were ablaze like the fire in the grate. Coy, yet passionate. When he had removed her dress, she crossed her arms over her chest; no one had seen her in her chemise other than her big sister and her nanny until now. Seyit sat down on the floor before the bed. Conscious of her hesitation, he picked up one of the hands on her chest and kissed the palm. Turning to the fire, he murmured, "I don't want you to do anything you might later regret. Nor would I wish you to blame yourself or me." He turned back to look at her. "I want you very much, but this doesn't mean possessing you. You're very special for me, my little Shura. Do you understand? You're different from everyone else. You will always be the most beautiful ever, even if I never see you again."

Drawing her knees up, Shura turned to her right as her free hand reached out to his hair. The mention of the possibility that they might never meet again was a reminder of reality. Perhaps their paths would never cross after leaving this place. No, she wasn't going to miss out on his love. She leaned down and presented her lips for a kiss. Seyit grabbed her and pulled her close.

They now sensed that when their bodies joined, it would be forever. He removed the pins holding her chignon, and her hair tumbled down her back, all the way to her waist. The fireplace cast dancing lights and shadows on her naked body.

"God! You are so beautiful!" Seyit trembled as he embraced her blushing nakedness again, yanked the bedspread off, and tucked them both in as he covered her with kisses. "My beautiful little darling, my dear, my darling..."

The first naked touch confirmed the depth of longing their souls and bodies had for each other. On inviting his kisses to the most intimate folds of her body and the parts never seen by anyone, she felt as though she were floating. Her shyness vanished in his warm, muscular embrace. Her cautiously affectionate caresses slowly responded to his summons. When he was convinced she was ready, he covered his sweetheart's body with his own. Their eyes met again; Shura saw again the unforgettable glint that hid in the darkness. It was as if they had always belonged to each other. Light played on their locked bodies in the darkened room. Seyit kissed her hair, the dip between her breasts, and the rounded alabaster shoulders as he breathed in her fresh, innocent scent. Shura felt she was no longer a baby. She wanted him with her body and soul as she lay in his arms. Wrapping her arms around his neck, she drew his weight over her to signal consent. This was a first for them both. She stifled an inaudible scream that took nothing from the pleasure. The duvet had long since been kicked off. All that wrapped their naked bodies now was the warmth of each other's embrace—and the fire. They continued making love like a couple who had been apart for years. With infinite patience and passion, Seyit held her, watching and listening to her eyes, movements, and breathing until his sweetheart reached her first climax. It was as if he had found the missing half of his own body—and she thought of him as the man who would complete her life.

Still holding her tight, Seyit spoke softly, "I never want to let you go, my little sweetheart." They lay in front of the fire, locked in a silent embrace, knowing full well it was impossible. "I wish I could take you to Petrograd," he added. Another impossibility. He continued, "Not that it would solve anything."

The first thing that popped into her mind was that he was married. She waited in silence.

"We're due to set off for the Austrian front soon. Where would I leave you in Petrograd?"

"When are you going?"

It was the first time she had spoken for hours; she had forgotten the sound of her own voice.

"I'm not sure, but it won't be long."

"When will you return?"

He forced a smile. "I have no idea."

Shura felt like crying for the man she now thought of as her own. She'd been worrying about him going away, but knowing he was going away to war made it far worse.

"Now do you understand, my little sweetheart, why I cannot make any promises?"

Shura want to hide the tears in her eyes but let go all at once. Hugging him close, she tucked her head under his arm and wept in silence. Seyit lifted her head, brushed away the damp hair, and cupped her tearful face in his hands. His heart was breaking as he gazed at her. "My God! How can I possibly leave you?"

They embraced again in a prelude to another bout of passion.

Shura sensed something new: an impression that her life would always be marked by melancholy from now on, an impression powerful enough to bring her to silent tears even as she made love.

***

The day after they became lovers was the day they had to part: Seyit and Celil returned to Petrograd, and one week later, the Verjenskys left for Kislovodsk. Although Julian would never regain his old health, at least the progress of the disease had been checked for a while.

Shura was no longer the same old Shura. It was as if the physical change that had taken place that afternoon with Seyit had spread to her soul. She could have been sleepwalking—such was her longing for him from the moment they parted. True, they had exchanged addresses with promises to write, but she had no certainty of claiming space in his heart in those turbulent times. The distances were great, and the front was in such disarray that for the past year virtually no news had come from her two big brothers.

Seyit was on her mind day and night as she tried to settle back in Kislovodsk. She resumed school and joined in the family's daily life, but she couldn't wait for dinner to be over so that she could retire into her room to daydream. She wrote letter after letter. At first they were quite bashful, but soon she gathered sufficient confidence to use a bolder lover's tone. Yet there was still no reply.

At long last a letter came from Tatiana. That had to be news, and a letter from a girlfriend she'd met in Moscow would not raise suspicion. Shura ran upstairs to her room, her heart beating hard. She opened the envelope once she was sure she was on her own. There was an extra sheet inside; spotting the signature, she pressed the letter to her chest with a muffled scream of joy. She sat down on the bed and started reading, Seyit's words warming her heart as if he were there, beside her, holding her hands. He had entrusted his letter to Tatiana before setting off for the Carpathian front.

Staring at the name at the bottom of the letter filled with words of love and longing, Shura thought she had lost Seyit for good. The postmark indicated he had not received her letters as yet. She felt infinitely sad. He had gone to war before reading her words. She was desperate to get in touch with him, to send word somehow. Then she wondered how she had come to devote herself to, and trust, a man she knew so little about. Did she regret what she had done? No, she regretted nothing. She would make the same decision again today. She read and reread his letter, memorizing every word. She went to bed clutching it, unable to dispel the pain in her heart or restrain the tears filling her eyes as she stared at her lover's words. Pressing his letter to her chest, she closed her eyes and murmured, "I love you too, Seyt Eminof. Love you very, very much."

The Eminofs, Alushta, Crimea

CRIMEA IS THE fertile peninsula stretching between the Sea of Azov and the Black Sea, the chestnut soil of its northern steppes lush with cypresses, a thick cover changing to oleander, oak, beech, alder, and silver birch as the slopes rise in the lee of the high Krymskie Gory range—a bulwark against the bitter mainland northerlies.

Golden wheat waved on the plains. Terraced vineyards stretching between the vast forests and the rocky cliffs above the shore overlooked the sea from lands blessed with the longest sunshine hours in the Russian Empire.

Mirza Mehmet Eminof was justifiably proud of his lands. The best wheat grew in this Crimean nobleman's fields; the finest wines served in Saint Petersburg and Moscow came from his Zabel and Muscat grapes, which ripened on double rows of wire, now almost ready for harvesting. He wandered among the vines, checking the quality of his produce and thanking God for his bounty. What wonderful lands were these—fruitful fields and vineyards! Not that they had come easily. Their ancestors had settled in Crimea long ago, although his father had never been certain quite how many generations it had been. As for his grandfather's tales, they went way, way back.

***

In 1475, when Ottoman Turks from the south annexed Crimea, the Crimean Khanate established by the Tatars, who had settled there hundreds of years earlier, became a vassal state of the Ottoman Empire. Its capital was named Bakhchisaray, from *bahçe* and *saray*: garden-palace. For nearly three hundred years, the Black Sea remained a Turkish lake as Ottoman authority secured peace in Crimea, and the Khanate offered a vantage point into the Russian front.

The Russians never renounced their aspirations concerning the Black Sea and Ottoman lands however—aspirations only stoked by Peter the Great's ascension. Having trained in shipbuilding in the Netherlands and England, he subsequently founded a mighty navy, joined the Holy Alliance against the Ottomans, and attacked the Fortress of Azov, which he took on the second attempt—this was the first step in securing a foothold on the Black Sea.

His next dream of opening a way to the Baltic Sea triggered a war with Sweden, a disastrous engagement, as it turned out. It took eight years and an ill-advised campaign by Charles XII to venture deep into Russian lands for Peter to have his first taste of victory. The wounded Swedish king sought shelter in the Ottoman Empire, and the Russians in pursuit entered Turkish territory, which they promptly ransacked and torched. The Ottoman army eventually surrounded the Russians at the Pruth Marshes. Terrified of annihilation, Peter sued for peace. His plea was acceptable to Grand Vizier Baltacı "Halberdier" Mehmet Pasha, who had no appetite for a much more extensive foray into the depths of Russia. The only Ottoman demand in the 1711 Treaty of Pruth was the return of the Fortress of Azov. Before long, however—in 1736, in fact—the Russians joined forces with the Austrians to declare war on the Ottomans once again. They entered Crimea and retook the fortress. The Russian scorched-earth policy did not spare Bakhchisaray either. The Ottomans prevailed once again, and the Russians withdrew from Crimea once again. The treaty signed in 1739 handed Azov to the Russians, provided the fortress would be demolished.

Crimea was not destined to enjoy an extended period of peace after all this blood and war. When the next grand vision emerged a mere three decades later, its scope reached far beyond the annexation of Crimea and the Caucasus. Empress Catherine the Great also had designs on the Bosphorus, the Dardanelles, and the Balkans. Averse to the prospect of direct confrontation with the Ottomans, however, she set about extending her influence over the Balkans first. Next, she attacked Poland, chased Polish nationalists all the way to Turkish lands, and crushed the town they had sought shelter in, civilian and resistance fighter alike. That action was treated as a *casus belli* for a war that would humiliate the waning Ottoman Empire. Russia overran Wallachia and Moldova, crossed the Danube, and entered Crimea. The Russian navy sailed south from their Baltic Sea base, entered the Mediterranean through the Strait of Gibraltar, and set fire to the Ottoman navy at anchor in the Çeşme Harbor on the Aegean shore of the Anatolian Peninsula. This time, it was the Ottomans who sued for peace, and they had little choice but to accept the harsh conditions of the Treaty of Küçük Kaynarca: Although Russia was forced to return territorial gains to the Ottomans, it now had the right to keep a navy in the Black Sea and gain protectorate of the Orthodox population on Ottoman lands. Most importantly, the Ottomans had to concede to the creation of an independent Crimea—which had been Catherine's primary objective all along. That devolution and the permanent presence of a fortresslike Russian navy in the Black Sea precipitated the inevitable in 1783, when Russia at long last annexed Crimea. The hitherto turbulent destiny of Crimea and the Crimeans finally lay in Russia's hands.

Her insatiable objectives fueled by this appropriation, Catherine turned her eyes southward, over the lands beyond the Black Sea, with dreams of establishing a vast Orthodox empire in the Middle East, one she would rule with her grandson Constantine. Such was the extent of her long-term ambition that a six-month visit to Crimea, ostensibly to prove her power and authority over the lands she had conquered, took four years of planning. The architect of the visit was Gregory Alexander Potemkin, victorious general of the first Russo-Ottoman War (and later, lover to the formidable empress herself); he left not a single thing to chance in his plans, which he designed to impress Western diplomats and to please his beloved tsarina.

In January 1787, three thousand guests departed from Saint Petersburg in luxuriously appointed troikas to reach the Dnieper in May, where a fleet of eighty vessels awaited. Throughout their cruise hugging the Crimean littoral, the guests were treated to one wondrous scene after another: young people singing and dancing in their Sunday best, shepherds playing merry tunes on their flutes, Cossack and Tatar horsemen in razor-sharp uniforms drilling and staging mock battles in Sevastopol and Bakhchisaray, English gardens on the slopes of artificial waterfalls, and village choirs illuminated by firework displays.

Making no secret of her intentions, Catherine referred to the Dnieper by its ancient Greek name: *Borysthenes*. Battleships at anchor in Kerch were emblazoned with the inscription *This Way to Byzantium* in Greek. The grand finale, a reenactment of the crushing defeat wrought upon Charles XII by Peter the Great, was so realistic that the sailors in the Sevastopol fleet burst into a cheer of "Long live the empress," much to the delight of the empress and her guests watching from the Heights of Inkerman.

This magnificent display accomplished its purpose of impressing Catherine's guests, a splendid show whose memory they would relish for a long time to come, but few could have been deceived into mistaking the jubilant display for genuine affection. The suffering of the past seventy years had to be still fresh in Crimean minds, after all.

Only Potemkin and the Crimean Tatars would ever know the truth.

Potemkin's Crimean spectacular might have been an act of love; in time, however, the peninsula became his passion. In 1784, he established a big naval base in Sevastopol—a city he had founded. The addition of a second one in Odessa ten years later equipped Russia with the wherewithal to set sail on the Black Sea at the drop of a hat. Impressed by Crimean horsemanship and military prowess, he also established the Imperial Life Guards, whose regiments consisted of Don Cossacks and Crimean Tatars.

A Turkic tribe from Central Asia, Crimean Tatars had braved a long trek to Crimea that took several generations, terrorized the principality of Muscovy with their raids, joined forces for a while with the Ottomans—descendants of yet another tribe from the same lands—and ultimately were assimilated into Russian society.

Kurt Seyt,
Alushta 1892

Mirza Mehmet Eminof, a member of the foremost aristocratic Crimean Tatar family in the Yalta region, had started his military training in Moscow at a very young age. He served in the Cavalry *Polk*, a regiment drawn from the leading Crimean, Azeri, and Caucasian Muslim families, and eventually rose to the post of tsar's adjutant, a full major by that time.

He always spent his leaves in Alushta in order to oversee the family vineyards and orchards, plan the sale of crops, or issue instructions for planting, depending on the season. Much as he enjoyed the military life between Moscow, Saint Petersburg, and Livadia, his lands were never far from his mind. He longed for the vineyards, the briny Black Sea breeze, and the house shaded by the plane trees—until, after a highly active bachelorhood, he got married. Thereafter, it was his exquisitely beautiful wife who commanded his mind and heart.

Zahide was the precious youngest child and only daughter of the Parterofs, distant relations who had settled in Poltava, from Prussia, several generations earlier. Like most rich landowners of their class, they spent the summer near Yalta; Zahide would have lived in Alushta all year long if she could. Her pale skin, slender figure, and sparkling blue eyes may have captivated every young man for miles around, but ever since she'd been a mere slip of a girl, she'd had eyes for only Mehmet Eminof. The handsome officer spent most of his time in Saint Petersburg, however, and returned to Alushta only on festive days or furlough. Whenever he appeared in the town square, she thought her heart would stop at the sight of the young officer, riding his black charger with a white star on the forehead. She wept in secret, believing he would never notice or love her. Goodness knew how many Russian mistresses he must have in Moscow; goodness knew what his life must be like. What would he do with a young, gawky, inexperienced girl like her?

She was mistaken. Struck by her graceful figure two years earlier at a family wedding, Mehmet hadn't been able to get her azure eyes out of his mind. His father had counseled patience—"Let's wait awhile; she's too young to be wed"— but too many hopefuls hovered in the wings, many of whom were Mehmet's friends. He could wait a little longer—and lose her forever.

What he didn't know was that this young beauty had steadfastly refused every single suitor on some pretext or other. When the Eminofs came to ask for her hand, she couldn't believe her ears. Realizing this was the prince of her dreams, the one she'd been waiting for, her parents gave their blessings to the match. At any rate, a better son-in-law than Mirza Mehmet Eminof would have been hard to find. The newly seventeen Zahide and the guards officer were betrothed straightaway, and the wedding followed a brief period of preparation.

Letting a handful of soil run between his fingers and crouching by the ripe bunches of grapes, Mehmet cast his mind back to the years since then. His darling Zahide was as fertile as this soil. She'd given birth to Hanife, a beautiful, healthy girl, nine months after the wedding and had fallen pregnant with a second before the infant had turned one—and was due any day now. He wanted many more yet. He would grow fields full of wheat and tobacco and vineyards full of grapes, and his children would throw roots into these lands like the beech trees in the forest. His grandchildren would grab fistfuls of this cornucopia just as he was doing now. Brushing the dirt off his hands, he rose to his feet, straightened on his head the kalpak that had caught on the grapes, and strode slowly away.

His musings were interrupted by a shout: his steward had appeared at the other end of the vineyard, waving his cap as he ran. Fear gripped Mehmet's heart on his way to the panting Cemal: Had something happened to his Zahide?

"Quick, tell me: What news?"

The steward answered as he tried to pull himself together. "Good news, sir— good news! You have a bouncing baby boy!"

Mehmet took a deep breath. "Thank God. How is she? How's my wife?"

"Both Zahide Hanım and your son are fine, says Hacer."

Cemal's wife, Hacer, was the midwife who had attended the birth of Hanife. Hacer had "a way about her," a perpetually unflustered knack for reassuring both the expectant mother and the family crowding the house.

His eyes beaming with gratitude, ecstatic at the news that he was a father twice over, Mehmet drew out some money to tuck into Cemal's shirt pocket and patted his steward on the shoulder. Repeating "Thank you...thank you," he hastened home.

***

Forty days later, in the large two-story home, a muezzin spoke the baby's name into his ear: "Seyit Mehmet, Seyit Mehmet, Seyit Mehmet."

With further prayers, *Kurt* came to prefix *Seyit*: According to centuries-old Crimean belief, distant baying of wolves frightened some babies, and facing that fear was the only way to overcome it. Hence *Wolf* Seyit.

Whether there was any substance to the custom or not, baby Seyit stopped crying but would be known as *Kurt Seyit* from that day on.

Alushta, 1904

THE EMINOFS CONSIDERED themselves to be the happiest couple in the world, blessed with several children in the house shaded by plane trees: Mahmut had followed Seyit after two years, an Osman four years after that. They all enjoyed robust health that belied their graceful physiques. Seyit's eyes were identical to his mother's, with deep blue flecks. His effortless leadership among the siblings and rational behavior well ahead of his young age had earned him a special place in his father's heart, and Mehmet Eminof took pride in watching his children play at his feet. Seyit would take over when he grew old, and Mehmet's mind was at ease. This was a son who would manage the growing family and lands. One day he blurted out these dreams, to merciless teasing from Zahide: "Shame on you, Eminof! Would you listen to your plans for a little child? You'll make the others envious too, speaking as if we only had the one!"

She was right; Mehmet took her hand and seated her beside him on the sofa. They watched their children giggle and chatter in front of the fireplace. Seyit was telling a story, and Hanife, Mahmut, and Osman listened with eyes as wide as saucers, nearly choking on laughter. Hanife was a year older, but she treated Seyit like a big brother. And Mahmut and Osman adored their big brother. Whenever they went out, they flanked him at once and grabbed his hands. Holding his hands, they felt safe. They never argued. Seyit commanded an effortless authority that directed all their games inside and outside the home, an authority his brothers and sister appeared to have submitted to eagerly.

On finishing his tale, Seyit kissed his brothers and sister. "Come on—it's bedtime."

Hanife and the boys kissed their parents obediently and mounted the stairs, Seyit at the rear. Mehmet caressed his wife's cheek. "See what I mean? They're not envious—quite the opposite. They've already elected him *Han*. He's never unfair or harsh. If he manages the property, he'll look out for his siblings, make sure they're all well off."

"You may be right," said Zahide. "I must have been worrying needlessly. You're right—unless God has written a bad fate."

***

The children's care was in Zahide's hands whenever their father was away on duty in Saint Petersburg or Moscow. The one aspect entrusted to Cemal was Seyit's instruction in riding, that being a particular point of pride for Mehmet. Whenever he returned home—sometimes having been away for several months—he loved watching Seyit's new tricks on horseback.

During his latest furloughs, Mehmet had mentioned disturbances in the capital. But life in Alushta was so tranquil, so blissful, that Zahide was very happy to bring a fifth child into the world. Hanife was eleven; Seyit, ten; Mahmut, eight; and Osman, six when Havva was born. With pale skin and enormous deep-blue eyes, she was the child who resembled her mother most.

At barely twenty-seven, Zahide looked nothing like a mother of five. She still had the innocent gaze and ivory complexion of a fifteen-year-old. Still madly in love with his wife, only Mehmet knew the smoldering femininity ripening under that childlike exterior.

Seyit and Mahmut were scheduled to undergo circumcision that summer. Mahmut regarded it as an occasion for lavish presents, but for Seyit, it was much more of a milestone on the way to becoming a man. Feverish preparations swept through the household. An enormous bed made with starched broderie anglaise bed linens, pillows, and silk satin duvets was set up in one of the big ground-floor reception rooms. Zahide led a small squad of hardworking servants in cleaning the house from top to bottom. Guest rooms were made up for visitors from afar. Tables, chairs, and lanterns were arranged in the garden. Zahide wanted everything to be perfect to spare Mehmet from having quite so much to do when he did arrive. As it turned out, he made it at midnight the day before the ceremony was due to take place. She had been waiting anxiously. At the sound of approaching hooves, she grabbed a lantern and rushed to the door. Was it her Mehmet or some bad news? Wrapped in her shawl, she waited in the cool of the night.

She recognized at once the rider talking to the guard at the gate at the bottom of the path. It might be a dark night, and his voice might be inaudible at this distance, but she knew that imposing posture by heart. Filled with joy, she walked among the plane trees toward the path. Mehmet had spurred his steed on; spotting his wife in her long white nightgown and shawl, he reined the horse in and leaped off, concerned.

"Zahide! What are you doing outdoors at this time? What's wrong?"

Her fears now allayed, the young woman's face shone with happiness. Mehmet couldn't help but admire this slender fairy in the light of her lantern, hair blowing in the gentle breeze and adoring, sparkling eyes shining. A wordless embrace was the first step to make up for all that time apart.

"You're cold," said Zahide, stroking his stubble. Mehmet took the lantern from her hand, put it out, and placed it on the bench. Leaping up to the saddle, he held out his hand. She grabbed that powerful hand, placed one foot on his boot, and allowed him to fling her on his back in a single move. With a hug, she rested her head against his back. Mehmet started a slow walk home, halted, turned his head, placed a kiss on her forehead, and murmured, "You must have come from a snug place. Perhaps you'll warm me up too."

Zahide blushed furiously in the darkness of the night. As excited as a new bride, she closed her eyes, which welled up with an indescribable joy as they trotted home.

They got no sleep that night. Kept awake by the joy of reunion and the anticipation of the momentous ceremony ahead, Mehmet had only just dropped off when the first light of day came. Giving him a silent, fond kiss on the forehead, Zahide tucked him in. She tugged the curtains closed to darken the room, dressed in a hurry, and tiptoed to baby Havva's room next door.

Zahide stared at her daughter sleeping like an angel. Havva's skin was as pale as a doll's, and her cheeks were as rosy. She was sleeping deeply on her tummy, one thumb in her mouth, and Zahide picked her up gently to avoid awakening her. Settling into the sofa, she unbuttoned her shirt; her breasts were throbbing now. Softly she brought the baby's head to a nipple. At the smell of her mother's breast, the sleeping baby opened her mouth as widely as she could. Her head moving right and left and guided by her mother, she latched on. Zahide whispered as she watched her baby suckling hungrily, "My God! I'm glad I've had you; you're so lovely."

When the baby was full, Zahide laid her back down and shut the door. She entered the boys' room. Seyit was already up, trying to rouse his younger brother. "Come on, Mahmut; wake up! It's our circumcision today. Come on; it's nearly morning."

Mahmut sat up as if pricked and asked, rubbing his eyes, "When are we going to get circumcised? Right now?"

Zahide couldn't suppress a laugh. "Not right now, no. But we have lots to do still. You'll have your baths and go to morning prayers with your father."

The boys bounced over to the door to hug their mother, and Seyit bombarded her with questions. "Is Father back? When did he come? Can I go and see—"

"Calm down, calm down. Your father arrived in the middle of the night, and he's exhausted. Let him sleep a little. I'll have to awaken him presently, at any rate, so you can go to the mosque together. Let him sleep until then."

"Was Father circumcised too?" asked Mahmut.

"Of course, silly!" Seyit pinched his brother's cheek. "All males are."

"So what happens at circumcision then?"

"They snip the tip of your willy," replied Seyit with a knowing air.

Mahmut's sleepy eyes popped wide open, and he gave his mother a terrified look. "That's a lie, isn't it, Mummy? My brother's lying, isn't he?" He collapsed on his bed in sobs before she had a chance to gather her wits. "I won't have my willy snipped! I won't have my willy snipped!"

Zahide scolded the elder as she tried to soothe the younger with a cuddle. "See what you've done! Shame on you. Why would you scare your brother so?"

Mahmut's wails were just subsiding when Seyit resumed his precocious air. "Why should he be scared? Men aren't scared! And I'm not lying either! He'll know I'm no liar when his willy's snipped."

Mahmut burst into fresh screams on his mother's lap. Zahide was at a loss; Mehmet had to speak to his sons at once. She didn't know what to say. Her older brothers had all been circumcised, of course, but traditionally these were topics for men only; mothers usually stayed out of it all.

Worried about his brother's tears, Seyit was now trying to console him, stroking the tear-streaked cheeks. "It's not that bad, Mahmut; please stop, for God's sake! And look, you'll get such marvelous presents. And you know, when you're circumcised, it's just like being a big man."

Happier now that Mahmut was distracted for a while, Zahide left and hastened back to her room. Her husband had to get up and take charge.

Mehmet was about to rise when she burst in. He asked sunnily, "What's all the fuss, for God's sake? Even Saint Petersburg was more peaceful!"

"Eminof, there's something you have to sort out," she replied, addressing him by the patronymic, as she did when she was serious. "You must talk to these children straightaway."

Mehmet was in a good mood. "Which children? The girls? The boys? The three eldest or all five?"

"Not in the least bit amusing, Eminof; the time for their circumcision's come, and no one's yet told your sons what to expect. Seyit's heard a smattering, and from whom, and how much, God only knows."

Growing serious at once and cuddling her sheepishly, Mehmet admitted, "You're right; I'm not here for them enough. I do have to talk to them more and about much more. Don't worry; I'll sort it now. Then we'll have our baths and go to the mosque."

Mehmet went into the boys' room, and Zahide went downstairs to check the bath, her mind a little more at ease.

Soon the males were all bathed. Whatever Mehmet had told the boys must have worked; instead of crying, Mahmut had assumed grown-up airs in that one hour. The boys got dressed in their circumcision outfits, which had been ready for many days: white trousers and shirt, a red satin sash diagonally across their chests from one shoulder down to the waist, and an evil-eye bead on the other shoulder.

Zahide watched as they walked out of the house, holding their father's hands. *How quickly they've grown, my God!* she thought.

Excitement in the house reached a peak by early afternoon. The kitchen was a hive of activity; the staff had been cooking pies, vegetable dishes, a halva, saffron pudding called *zerde*, pilaf, and sherbets since early morning. As Mehmet took care of the boys, Zahide supervised preparations, rushing to and fro among the kitchen and larder and guest rooms and garden. Hanife was looking after Havva—except for feeding times, that is. She loved playing house with her baby sister.

Now that everything seemed to be in control, it was time for Zahide to get ready. She took a bath, plaited her damp hair, and picked the pale-blue printed chiffon dress that happened to be Mehmet's favorite. Around her waist went the thick silver Caucasian belt that had been a wedding present. She flicked her hair back, wrapped her plaits once around the belt, and let the ends dangle free. She fixed her silver-embroidered fez in place with the gauze kerchief hanging down her back and gave herself a quick look in the mirror: yes, she was ready for the great hustle and bustle. This was all the time she could allow herself.

She was skipping down the stairs when the steward's voice came from the entrance hall: Cemal had just admitted the hodja and the *sünnetçi* at the door, and Mehmet was greeting the arrivals.

He showed the cleric and the circumcision medic into the large drawing room and offered them lemonade. The boys were waiting in one of the nearby rooms, their hearts in their mouths. Mehmet brought them over to kiss the cleric with the pure-white hair and long white beard. In a soft, gentle voice, he invited Seyit and Mahmut to sit beside him. "*Maşallah*, praised be God's will! Strapping boys they are; *maşallah!*"

The hodja faced Seyit first. Under Mahmut's avid gaze, he opened one hand in supplication and placed the other on Seyit's head. His eyes half open, he murmured something, circling his head every once in a while before blowing on Seyit's face. Every time he did, a lock of hair on Seyit's forehead fluttered in the faint breeze, making the boy blink furiously. Terribly amused by this sight, Mahmut finally broke into giggles when he spotted the fly circling the cleric's turban—and swallowed them back at his father's warning stare.

Seyit's prayers were done with a resounding *Amen*, and the hodja pulled his hand away from the older boy's head. "May you grow up to be a good son and a strong man, by God's will!"

Seyit felt as if he was halfway through a big test. He settled into the armchair next to his father and watched Mahmut's blessing.

His tools ready, the sünnetçi waited in the room set aside for the procedure. A small and quiet man, he had quelled the boys' trepidation somewhat with his unhurried and gentle manner: surely such a man couldn't harm them!

Now he appeared at the door, shirtsleeves rolled up to the elbows, hands washed and disinfected. "Yes, sir; I'm ready. Who's first?"

Mehmet had considered putting an end to his younger son's torment without delay, but Mahmut was already clutching at Seyit's shirt. Seyit stepped forward and held his breath to prevent his voice trembling as he said, "Me first." Mahmut rewarded him with a grateful look; Seyit had watched out for him once again. Mehmet grasped his elder son's shoulder fondly and followed the medic into the room. The door shut. Mahmut was left outside. But he'd wanted to watch Seyit's procedure so that he'd know what to expect! This was precisely why the sünnetçi never had more than one boy in the room at once: the first one might scream and scare the others. Cemal took Mahmut for a stroll around the house.

Meanwhile, Seyit tried to look away from the instruments laid out on a towel on the table in the corner. The thought that a piece of his body would be cut out made him feel woozy and a little sick, but he pulled himself together. No one must think he was scared. Feeling his father's hands on his shoulders, he lifted his gaze.

"Bravo, son; I'm so proud of you. Come on now; get ready."

"What should I do?"

"This way—remove your clothes and stretch out on the sofa."

"Wasn't I going to lie on the circumcision bed though?"

"Afterward. Once it's done, you'll move to the fancy bed."

Seyit rose on tiptoe to whisper, "Am I to undress before this stranger?"

"Well, since he's the one who'll circumcise you, yes."

"Why don't you do it, Father?"

"Why don't I do what?"

"Our circumcisions."

Mehmet burst out laughing. "Because I'm not a sünnetçi; I'm a soldier."

Refusing his father's offer of assistance as he undressed, Seyit asked, "I'll be a soldier too, won't I, Father?"

"Of course you will. That is why you must get ready for a little bit of pain. And you'll be surprised at how quickly it will all be done and dusted."

When Seyit sat down facing the sünnetçi, he thought time had suddenly come to a stop. He held his breath as he looked at the man and the instrument. He had to avoid screaming at all costs. He gritted his teeth so hard that he bit into his cheeks. The hand his father was clutching was slick with sweat now, and he was gripping the hem of his shirt with the other hand. The pungent smell of disinfectant assailed his nostrils as the liquid poured over his groin ran down his legs in a cool stream. He wouldn't make a sound, no matter what happened, for the sake of his brother waiting outside. He heard a roaring sound in his ears. The sünnetçi's "Bismillah!" came from a distance—*in the name of God* must be the signal then. Seyit clenched his fists. He took a deep breath and shut his eyes, and the deed was done. It hurt and dwindled into a dull ache.

"All done. Well done—*Maşallah!* Get better soon now," exclaimed the sünnetçi.

"See, nothing to it!" said his father. "Now get into that big bed. Well done, my brave boy. Your brother's next."

His wound dressed, Seyit allowed his father to help him with the circumcision nightshirt and stretched out on the bed. Mehmet kissed his son, stroked his hair, and asked, "Did it hurt?"

The boy shook his head and then spoke so that he'd sound more convincing. "No, not really."

Mehmet kissed him again and straightened up to go and fetch his younger son, grinning to himself and murmuring, "You little liar!"

With no screaming or crying from Seyit, Mahmut's fears were allayed somewhat, which made little difference when his turn came. Feeling awful that he couldn't alleviate his brother's pain or screams, all Seyit could do was wait for Mahmut to be brought next to him. When Zahide entered to hug her sons, Seyit was wiping Mahmut's tear-streaked cheeks and admonishing him. "That's unworthy of you, Mahmut, and look, it's all done now. And don't you want to become a soldier anyway?"

Mahmut stopped crying and faced his big brother. "Yes, but when I'm big."

"Well then, are you going to cry like this whenever you're hurt when you're a soldier?"

Zahide withdrew; she was racked with sobs when her husband returned after seeing the hodja and the sünnetçi off.

"What's wrong?"

"Nothing."

"Are you crying for nothing?"

"I don't know; perhaps I'm crying with happiness. May God spare me the pain of my children; I couldn't live with it, Mehmet."

"Well, Zahide! What are you like? If that's what you're going to think of when you're happy, deliver me from being anywhere near you when you're sad! Come on, love; pull yourself together, and we'll join the boys."

Soon guests flocked in, surrounding the bed with presents that helped the boys forget about the pain. Their shoulders and chests were thick with gold sovereigns and ruble notes as the room filled with colossal boxes they were dying to open. Every new arrival visited with them first, asking how the circumcision had gone. Echoing his big brother, Mahmut's happier "Didn't hurt at all!" elicited approval as the boys lay showered with good wishes. Both boys were pleasantly surprised at the attention that followed the initial pain.

Lambs were being roasted on spits nearby for the lavish feast under the plane trees in the garden. Zahide went upstairs from time to time to nurse the baby. Cemal's eldest daughter, Leyla, would look after Havva during the night, but nursing was Zahide's job and delight.

After laying the baby down, she stepped out onto the balcony and cast a look at the garden. A warm, still summer evening was settling on Alushta. The lanterns had long since been lit. The musicians were taking their places on the veranda. Mehmet had selected the wine from his own produce years ago and had allowed it to mature in barrels. Taps now filled cup after cup. It might have been just the start of the party, but many were already quite tipsy. Her eyes sought her husband in the crowd: there he was, arms slung over the shoulders of two male guests, laughing and chatting. She gazed at him, a woman in love. He was the handsomest man in that crowd. She was very happy, very happy indeed. Leaning on the railing, she closed her eyes and took a deep breath. The briny breeze from the Black Sea mingled with the fresh green of the vines in the vineyard and rustled the century-old plane trees' leaves in the garden. "Thank you, God," she said in gratitude.

Leyla was laying out the baby's nappies; hearing Zahide, she asked, "Say something, madam?"

Zahide stepped in, beaming. "What a wonderful evening, I said."

Downstairs once again, she entered the circumcision room first. The boys were sitting up against puffed-up pillows, clearly enjoying the crowd around them. Little Osman envied all this pomp, impatient for his own circumcision party. Taking Zahide's arrival as a sign to leave, the visitors succumbed to her cheerful guidance. Once they had all left, she sat down at the edge of the bed. The boys looked tired but happy.

"How are you? Are you well? Is there anything you want?"

"I'm fine," said Mahmut. "And so's Seyit. Aren't you, Seyit?"

Her younger son's hurried affectation of ignoring his pain made her laugh.

"All right, all right; I see everyone's fine then. That's wonderful. Your father will be delighted to hear it too."

"Will Father come here again?" asked Seyit.

"Of course. We'll take turns to check up on you." She walked over to the wide window facing the bed, drew the curtains and the netting aside, and pushed the shutters out. "There now: all the fun's in your room. You may watch until it's time to sleep."

The lights, sounds, and music in the garden flooded the room at once. The boys tried to sit up straighter. Zahide plumped up their pillows, made them comfortable, and left after kissing them both. Exhausted by a highly charged day of anticipation, fear, and worry, the boys soon fell into a deep sleep.

The next morning, Seyit awoke well before his brother. He was struggling to get out of bed when his father appeared at the door.

"Wait, wait! Where do you think you're going? It's only been one day!"

Seyit wanted to go to the toilet, so Mehmet helped him down. Racked by the pain in his lower body, Seyit opened his legs wide and waddled in his long nightshirt to prevent anything from touching his bare legs and still-open wound.

All this time, however, his eyes never left the huge, beautifully decorated parcel his father had left by the table. His curiosity didn't escape his father's notice. "You may open it when you get back."

Seyit couldn't wait to find who had sent this last gift and what it was.

Before long he was settled into the sofa by the window again, with his father's help. Dragging the obviously heavy parcel toward him—a task that required both hands—Mehmet asked, "Aren't you going to ask who sent it?"

Wondering what weighed so much and admiring the glossy wrapping paper and huge, colorful satin ribbon, Seyit was about to ask, "May I open it?"

Mehmet sat down next to him and repeated, "Aren't you going to ask who sent it?"

"Don't you know?"

"Of course I do! Who do you think carried it here all the way from Saint Petersburg?"

"Did *you* bring it from Saint Petersburg?"

"Of course. But because it's so special, we've not placed it with the rest. I wanted to give you this one on its own."

Seyit's curiosity was rising. "You bought me another present?"

Last night, the boys had been told of their father's gift: a horse each. So Seyit couldn't understand why he merited another present, unlike his brother, and therefore took pains not to rouse Mahmut, who still slept like an angel. Even if Seyit deserved such a privilege, he wouldn't want to upset his little brother.

"No," replied his father. "This is very special. You have to open it to understand why. To be honest, I am as curious as you to find out what's inside."

No matter how much Seyit racked his brains, he couldn't figure out who had sent him—and him alone—a circumcision present from Saint Petersburg. He started unwrapping it, removing first the ribbon and then the glossy paper. His curiosity urged him to rip it all off at once, but another voice suggested he might want to enjoy this lovely surprise—and therefore prolong the pleasure. It would have been a shame to tear up this nice paper anyway. Whoever had sent the gift might have intended to test his patience though: the wrapping paper exposed a thick cardboard box. Seyit lifted the lid. The mysterious gift was now wrapped in tissue paper; by this time, Mehmet's eyes were no less curious than his son's.

The surprise was finally revealed as Seyit crumpled the tissues with a childish impatience. Mehmet stood to help his son, whose eyes were now wide in astonishment. As he pulled away the last of the wrapping, he couldn't suppress a long whistle of admiration.

It was a small trunk, about half Seyit's height. It was no ordinary trunk, however: The black lacquer body was delicately adorned with colorful landscapes that looked ready to become real. The brass cockerel on the lid placed above the brass lock was even finer. So realistically crafted were its cockscomb, feathers, and claws perched on a tiny rod that Seyit exclaimed, "How lovely! It looks real, like it could crow any minute now, doesn't it, Father?"

"Yes, and it will..."

Mehmet put a hand into his pocket at his son's questioning gaze, pulled out a bright golden key on a black silk cord, and handed it over. Seyit's eyes were still wide in amazement as he took it. "It's wonderful, Father! Who could possibly have sent me such a lovely present?"

Unwilling to torment his son any longer, Mehmet replied, "You've got the key; why don't you unlock it and see?"

Seyit slid forward, placed the key into the lock with trembling hands, and turned it. The brass cockerel gave a convincing crow and started spinning; it fell silent after three turns and stopped. The lock sprang open.

His father lifted the lid gently and secured it open with slats. That was when Seyit saw the inscription in brass lettering on the inside of the lid. He slapped a hand to his mouth to suppress a cry of delight.

The tsar's gracious message of good wishes and success was topped and tailed by his coat of arms and a seal, all in brass, all embedded into the wood.

"From Tsar Nicholas! Father, I can hardly believe it! It's fantastic! How does he know of me? How did he hear of my circumcision? Does he send such gifts to everyone?"

Amused by this breathless stream, Mehmet rubbed his son's back; the boy would soon settle. Seyit had slid down to the floor, all pain forgotten, crawling around this masterpiece on his knees, stroking the glossy lacquer, and peering at the paintings close enough for his nose to touch the surface.

"I explained the importance of your circumcision when I requested a pass. His munificence indicates that I must have done a reasonable job. It's a great honor to receive such a present from the tsar, son—one I'm sure is granted to few twelve-year-olds. Make sure you appreciate it. I'm sure you'll safeguard it all your life and proudly tell your children and grandchildren about it."

"May I tell my friends too? I mean, until I have my own children."

Mehmet chuckled; for all his precocious airs, Seyit was still a child at heart. "Of course you can—until you have your own children, anyway. Except you're not going to have much time to do that."

"What? You mean you marry immediately after your circumcision?"

"No, son, you still have lots of time before you marry. But you don't have quite so much time around here."

His attention dragged away from his fabulous present, Seyit cast his father a somber look. "Why? Where are we going?"

"I've got some things to attend to in Livadia first. Then I'll welcome the tsar and his family in the summer palace. But I'll return in three weeks to collect you, and we'll set off for Saint Petersburg together."

"Great! Really, Father? So I'll come with you now?"

"Yes, son. The time has come for the education you'll need for the rest of your life. Make sure to look after yourself really well now; don't catch a cold or anything. Once you've recovered, practice your horsemanship diligently. You will eat well and ride every day until my return. No crazy capers now—save them for later. All right?"

Seyit nodded, eyes glistening with excitement. He stayed kneeling on the floor by the trunk long after his father kissed him on the forehead and left.

One of the pictures depicted a beautifully dressed young man in a red cape offering a flower to a girl with a lovely face under a weeping willow, its branches curling down to the ground. Her hair flowed from under a gold crown, fell over her shoulders in waves like the branches, and was gathered into a braid. She was so beautiful! Would he see such lovely girls in Saint Petersburg when he grew up? Lost in a reverie, he imagined himself as the young man holding the flower.

Saint Petersburg, 1904

ONE MONTH AFTER the circumcision, Seyit prepared for the first great journey of his life. So thrilling was his father's surprise announcement that the boy had barely slept a wink for several nights afterward. He was now twelve; it was time to enroll in the military academy in Saint Petersburg. It was finally beginning to dawn upon him why his parents had taken such a close interest in his education: regular Russian lessons from a former Kiev secondary-school teacher who had retired in Alushta, as well as riding skills on par with an experienced adult, and countless tricks known to few riders—all thanks to his father's and Cemal's expert instruction.

No amount of warning that they faced a long and arduous journey could dampen his spirits. He still couldn't believe he was going to see places he'd never seen before: great cities, the Imperial Palace, and even the tsar himself. His imagination was working double time.

Leaving home was a sad affair. Accustomed to seeing her husband off Zahide might have been, but she couldn't hold back the tears when she had to bid her son good-bye. Her other children stood mutely wretched, lost without Seyit.

Mirza Mehmet was in uniform. Seyit wore riding trousers, boots, and a lightweight white summer shirt with baggy sleeves gathered in snug cuffs and buttoned all the way up to the neck. He had taken leave of his siblings and his mother and mounted his horse; Zahide remarked how much he'd grown. *He looks the picture of health—and so handsome!* she thought. Her chest filled with pride. She allowed herself a wry smile. One of these two men about to leave was her husband, and the other was her son. How could she possibly *not* feel proud?

Father and son rode to Odessa and boarded a train. It took two changes—one in Kiev and the second in Moscow—to reach Saint Petersburg. All through the journey, Seyit watched the train and the stations, astonished at the sheer numbers and variety of humanity, trying to etch into his memory the noisy, crowded platforms teeming with passengers and porters, and the chimneys spewing that coal-rich smell—almost as though all this detail pertained to someone he had just met. Everything looked so different from Alushta. It was all a far cry from the greens of the forest and vineyards, the blue of the Black Sea, and the briny breeze he'd grown up with, but he wasn't complaining. Quite the opposite: he was having a great time.

They traveled first class, in a carriage of immaculately dressed passengers. It was another story entirely when it came to the masses crammed into the rear carriages, however: unshaven men with filthy faces, weary women with untidy hair escaping from faded old scarves or shawls, snot-nosed children in torn shoes and ripped shirts, and young girls clutching wicker baskets like their most valuable possessions, girls who had never learned to smile. They clambered over one another to board as though this were the last train that would ever stop at that station. Fights broke out between alighting and boarding passengers as one group blocked the other's way, invariably attracting whistles from the station staff, who promptly issued cautions that sporadically degenerated into curses, stuffed passengers into already overflowing carriages, and locked the doors before the train could resume its journey. Leaning out of the window, Seyit marveled at it all as only a twelve-year-old could.

It was nearly evening by the time they arrived in Saint Petersburg. With a protracted squeal of its wheels, the train shook, groaned, and drew up to the platform to discharge hundreds of people. Mehmet helped his son down the stairs with a caution. "Better hurry, or we'll never get a carriage outside!"

Progress toward the exit was a stop-start affair, and they broke into a run whenever they could, keeping an eye on the porter carrying their luggage.

Seyit's amazed eyes took in the colossal doors of the station and the soaring ceilings as he clutched his father's hand. Every time he turned his head one way or the other, he ended up treading on a lady's long skirts or banging into a suitcase carried by a porter; every time he did so, he apologized sheepishly without breaking a step and continued to trail in his father's wake.

Families, friends, or lovers of the arrivals flooding the concourse created a secondary flow of traffic that painted an astonishing panorama of noisy embraces; sad, disappointed gazes; and passionately silent embraces.

Countless carriages lined up outside the station, certain of rich pickings in the falling darkness. As soon as one picked up a fare and moved out, another took its place.

Father and son had sped through the crowds, partly helped by the relatively modest amount of luggage they had. The coachman threw the reins the moment he'd pulled up to the curb; he leaped down, dutifully picked up the cases, and placed them next to his seat. In the meanwhile, the Eminofs took their seats in the rear.

"Tsarskoye Selo," Mehmet called out. With a nod, the coachman whipped the horses, and they shot off like an arrow.

"What did you say, Father?"

Mehmet chuckled at the curious gaze and tone. "That's where our home is."

"Isn't our home in Alushta?"

"I spend half of my life here, son. That's why we have a house here too. And from now on, it's our home together."

"Where's this Ts...arsk...ye..."

Mehmet corrected him with a smile. "Tsarskoye Selo is just outside Saint Petersburg. It's more of a resort, really. Our place isn't as big as the house in Alushta, but it's very nice; you'll like it."

"Are we to stay there together all the time?"

"Sadly, no. We'll stay there tonight. Perhaps tomorrow too. We'll rest a little. And then return here. Once you're enrolled, we might be able to spend a few more days together. Saint Petersburg is one of the finest cities in the world. I want to show you around and introduce you to my friends; I'm sure you'll enjoy it."

"Afterward?"

"Afterward...afterward you'll go to school, and I'll return to my regiment."

Seyit's eyes and voice clouded over. "Are we never to meet again then?"

"Of course we shall! Whenever your school and my duties allow us, that is."

"But I'll miss you."

Mehmet hugged his favorite, the child he missed most whenever he was away. Seyit had lived with his mother and siblings until now, but he was going to be on his own in a totally new environment of discipline, where he would have to endeavor to shine. Concerned as he was about his son, Mehmet had no doubt that Seyit would succeed.

"Son, you only miss people you love. This ought to make you happy...so long as your nearest and dearest aren't too far to ever meet again. That kind of missing would be too hard to bear."

Nodding, Seyit looked up. He couldn't quite make out whether his father's eyes were welling up or his own eyes were tricking him.

The carriage proceeded along a broad thoroughfare lit by gas lamps and flanked by splendid buildings.

Seyit was happy; how could he complain, sitting in the rear of this carriage pulled by swift-footed horses, sitting next to his father, speeding on the roads of this magnificent city adorned with lights? True, he was beginning to miss his home, his mother, and his siblings. But hadn't his father said you had to be happy you had people to miss? Soon he'd be missing his father too. So he might as well enjoy what little time they had now.

After a while, the bright lights of the main city roads fell behind as they entered a dim, tree-lined road. Lulled by the rocking of the carriage, the whirling of the wheels, the jingling of the horses' bells, and the all-enveloping velvety darkness, Seyit's eyelids dropped, and he fell into sweet slumber.

Mehmet wondered just how much longer he'd be able to cuddle his son. Gently, so as not to awaken Seyit, he removed his own jacket, hugged the boy again, and tucked him in against the noticeable damp.

The horses had already halted when his father's gentle voice awakened Seyit; rubbing sleepy eyes, he looked around. The first thing he noticed was the gigantic wrought-iron gate in the fence; it was flanked by enormous lamps, like the ones illuminating the roads they'd passed. Emulating his father, he leaped down from the carriage. In the flickering light, he saw a couple running over from the house. On reaching the gate, they halted and clasped their hands deferentially.

The man was quite tall and skinny, hunching as if ashamed of his height. The voice that issued from the smiling lips virtually hidden among the thick beard and moustache sounded far too soft for his physique. "Welcome, Major Eminof."

The woman was shorter and much heavier, as if to make up for it. Her white hair was gathered at the nape. A broad forehead, lively pale-blue eyes, and full lips permanently on the verge of a smile gave her a gentle and cheerful aspect. She repeated the man's greeting as she repeatedly dried her hands on her apron.

Mehmet held his son's shoulders. "This is the guest you've been expecting. My son, Seyit Eminof."

He addressed Seyit. "Seyit, meet Ganya and Tamara Karlovich; they look after this house."

Warming up to them at first sight, Seyit held his hand out. His greeting was a flawless *Zdrastvuyte* that surprised Mehmet: he'd never imagined Seyit would be so quick to adopt the language he'd have to speak all the time now.

The Karloviches took the suitcases and drew aside. His hands still on his son's shoulder, Mehmet entered through the gate and walked toward the house along the trellis enclosed by ivy and trees.

The place in Tsarskoye Selo was a typical Russian summer house, equipped with fireplaces on the ground floor as well as in the bedrooms upstairs to guard against the long winters that raged from early November to the middle of April and the relentless damp that clung throughout the brief springs and summers. A large entrance hall opened to the kitchen, library, and dining room; a staircase rose to the second floor, hugging a wall display of weapons. Exhausted as he was, Seyit was fascinated by this new place, a colossal new toy. Mounting the newly polished stairs (if the smell and the slipperiness were anything to go by) in his father's wake, he was filled with a new emotion. He felt older and much more mature now. The prospect of sharing a house with his father was wonderful: two men on their own, a house he would enjoy as its master on school holidays, a house he would have a key to.

Yes, he would miss Alushta and his family, but this new life held the promise of being something entirely different and thrilling.

The second floor landing was a large hall leading to three bedrooms. Gas lamps with brass feet and pink glass stood on tiny consoles between each door.

His father opened the middle door. "Here, this is your room. No one else has slept here before. All yours now."

It was all very different from his room in the Alushta house; instead of plain white broderie anglaise bed linens and crocheted window netting that spoke of a woman's gentle touch, everything was in heavy dark-red velvet. A Kazakh carpet in reds, burgundies, and browns all but covered the entire floor. Pleased by the plain, somber elegance, Seyit smiled at his father. "It's smashing!" He opened the window to look out.

"I don't think you'll be able to see much in the dark, Seyit. Leave it until the morning. Best have a bath and go to sleep now."

Ganya arrived, holding both suitcases. "Which one shall I leave here, sir?"

Mehmet pointed to his son's suitcase as Tamara appeared at the door.

"The bath's ready, sir; we've been keeping the water hot for quite a while."

"Thank you, Tamara," said Mehmet. "A bath is the best remedy for weary travelers. Come on, Seyit. Pick up your clothes and have your bath first."

"I've prepared supper too, sir," continued Tamara. "Would you like to dine after your bath or before?"

"Let's wash off this grime first. We'll be ready by the time you lay the table."

Flashing a smile of bright white teeth, Tamara gave a courteous nod and descended to the ground floor wordlessly. Ganya took the other suitcase to his master's room.

Mehmet turned to his son. "You couldn't find more loyal servants even if you were to search all Russia with a fine-toothed comb."

Seyit was beaming. "I like them too," he said. A thought popping into his mind blew away the sleep. "Which is your room?"

"Here, take a look. You can come over if you're scared at night."

The teasing tone hadn't gone unnoticed. "Father! Really!" Seyit followed.

They entered the room next door. Ganya was hanging Eminof's clothes in the big mirrored walnut wardrobe that took up the entire wall behind the door. Seyit's delight grew the moment he stepped in: the wide walnut bed, the bed-spread, the curtains, and the carpet were all identical to those in his room. The only difference was a stack of books in Russian on the ottoman at the foot of the bed. His thrill knew no bounds. So he was old enough to have a room just like his father's—except for the uniforms hanging in his father's wardrobe, the glossy boots lining up at the bottom, and the ceremonial swords hanging neatly on the wall. Many more years would pass before he could truly be like his father. He felt no resentment, however; he was only at the start. All he had to do was to work very hard.

The third room was set aside for guests. The upholstery and furnishings were in cream velvet, and two runners in green and cinnamon on a beige background flanked the bed.

"Who stays here as a guest then?" asked Seyit.

"Occasionally a friend stays if his furlough's too short to go home or if he has no one to go to."

"Will I have such friends too?"

Mehmet burst out laughing. "You'll have all sorts of friends. And so many that you'll astonish even yourself." He grew more serious. "But you will try to pick people who will make the best friends. And that, my son, is much harder to learn than soldiering."

Seyit's murmur revealed his appreciation of the gravity of the things that awaited him at this major turning point in his life. "It looks like I'll have much to learn."

***

Exhausted, and cocooned in the deeply silent darkness ensured by the thick velvet curtains, Seyit slept until quite late. It was nearly noon when he was roused by the sound of approaching hooves. Bounding out of bed, he dashed to the window, drew back the curtains, opened the window, and pushed the shutters apart. The view was breathtaking: a forest of tall trees in a myriad of greens all but charged into the room. About twenty yards to the right, a small stream flowed in a gentle incline, carrying south twigs and leaves shed by the trees leaning away from the wind. Birdsong filled the fresh air redolent of earth and trees as hundreds of nests hidden inside trees chirped with the joy of a bright, happy summer day.

Reluctantly taking his gaze away from the intoxicating view, Seyit looked down where his father and Ganya, now dismounted, were walking toward the house.

"Good morning!" he called down to them.

His father looked up and replied cheerfully, "Isn't it a bit late for good morning now, Seyit Eminof? Have you rested well though?"

"And how! I could set off on a new journey now!"

Mehmet laughed. "No need! We're staying here today. Go on—wash up, get dressed, and come downstairs to lunch." He walked toward the kitchen door at the rear.

With a deep breath, Seyit looked at the forest again and thought about the woods surrounding their home in Alushta. The smell was different here, as if the trees had just been rained upon. Throwing open all the windows, he made his bed. He whistled cheerfully throughout his morning toilet. Feeling an inexplicable thrill, he knew that in the course of one single week, he had left childhood behind and grown into a totally new person.

Tamara's lunch was a feast of borscht soup, roast duck, baked potatoes with sauce, and a cherry tart. Mehmet offered his son a glass of his vodka. Seyit felt an unfamiliar warmth and light headed, but he couldn't finish it.

"If you start to drink with your father, you'll learn to drink like a man. Start with a stranger, and you'll make a fool of yourself," said Eminof Senior.

He then said they were going for a ride. Mounting the horses Ganya had brought over from the stables, Seyit realized this ride wasn't just about the surrounding countryside. His father wanted to prepare him for what might and what would definitely happen from now on, and no environment could have been more reassuring or calmer for the advice and cautions to follow.

That ride winding in and out of the trees between the stream and the sky turned into a dream for Seyit, who was still partly woozy. The things his father spoke of were hard to believe at times, and he was astonished at himself for listening to such shameful talk with such ease.

Once he had covered what to expect in boarding school, Mehmet turned to the matter of girls and women. The more he believed Seyit took it all in, the deeper he went, stealing a sideways glance from time to time to judge the reaction. That was the reason for the vodka in the first place; the boy had to relax a little first. The result was much as he'd hoped for.

Blushing from time to time and blinking feverishly, Seyit listened with an expression of mature comprehension well above his age. He could never have imagined growing up into a man would cause such cataclysmic changes in one's life. It all sounded like a tale—nothing, however, like those told by his mother.

"If there's anything more you need me to explain, feel free to interrupt and ask," said Mehmet.

Seyit wasn't sure what more he could learn; he'd already heard quite enough. He looked at his father, shaking his head. Mehmet had to turn his face toward the road to suppress a smile at the sight of his son's bewildered, flashing eyes and pink cheeks.

That night after supper, they sat facing the fireplace in the library. Flicking through his books, Mehmet occasionally took a note. Seyit, on the other hand, could think of nothing but his father's words, trying to visualize how the things he'd heard could actually happen. Mehmet had told him it was all right to enjoy pursuing Russian girls until he was thirty, but he would have to marry a Crimean Tatar, a girl of Turkic origin, when the time came.

"Why thirty?" he asked all of a sudden.

Mehmet knew at once what Seyit meant, lifted his head, and chuckled. "Are you asking why one marries after thirty? Because that's when a man finally calms down and mends his ways. Tires of bachelorhood. None of this might make much sense now. Just pay attention for now, and engrave my advice into your mind. Learning is one thing, understanding another. No matter how well you absorb my lessons, true comprehension only comes with experience. And that takes time, son."

"When does all this happen?" persisted the boy, still gazing at the flames.

Pleased by this willingness to openly express curiosity and happy at this new bond between them, Mehmet moved over, sat facing Seyit, and replied in the same calm tone, "There's no definite time for any of this, son. That's why I told you about it all in one go. Everyone takes such things in his own time. Nature's laws governing birth, life, and death are immutable. But everyone's timing is different. This is as true of men as it is of women. What you have to watch out for is what humans do; we can't do anything about natural events, after all. You will appreciate in time that the greatest harm comes from our own ill-judged acts."

"What about friends?" asked Seyit.

"Isn't the friend who might harm you also your own choice?"

"I suppose...of course." A thoughtful nod.

"That is why you can't be too careful in your choice of friends. In the meantime, of course, never forget who you are and where you come from."

"You mean from Alushta?"

Mehmet laughed, resting his head against the high back of the armchair. "Yes," he said. "Yes, precisely. That you come from Alushta, that you're the son of Mirza Eminof, that your ancestors have been living on these lands for hundreds of years, that you own fields and vineyards, and that your children will also ride on these lands. We're Crimean Tatars, proud of our Turkic origins. But we are also proud Russian subjects. Your mission, son, is to top your class, like I said before, and thereby merit this privilege conferred upon our family. I shall retire in a few years. It's no mean feat to rise to the post of adjutant to the tsar. There will be many who will place obstacles in your path. You will have to be careful and cautious. Nothing, I repeat nothing, must distract you from your first priority, which is school. I trust in you."

"Very well. What about...when you mentioned 'a time to choose,'" what did you mean?"

Mehmet was glad Seyit had the spirit to ask all that was on his mind; the moment they parted, the boy would be left alone with those questions.

"That time might never come. Everything might be a bed of roses. But it would be remarkably optimistic to imagine such a stable future for Russia. You've been spared all this in Crimea, son, but trouble's brewing in the big cities. People are restless. Many are starving, and many more are unemployed, and as cities grow and factories open, those half-starving people confront rich city folk. And neither side likes the other." He paused to ask, "Do you understand what I mean?"

"Yes," said Seyit. This was easier to understand than the things he'd been told during the day, but it was also much gloomier.

Mehmet carried on. "Tsar Nicholas is a kindly man, a gentle soul. But his power-hungry entourage is busy turning the people against him. From what I know of Russia and Russians, I can safely assume some momentous events are in the offing and in the not-too-far future at that. When that happens, your place is beside your tsar; however, should you ever have to choose between Russians and Crimean Tatars or between Russia and Crimea...I believe I don't have to tell you which side you must take."

"I understand, Father." Seyit sounded pensive, feeling tired again: too many ideas to take in all in one day. He nodded several times as if to fix it all in his mind.

Mehmet stood up, came over, and placed a hand on his shoulder. "Enough lecturing for today. I suggest you go to sleep now." Guiding Seyit toward the staircase with an arm over his shoulder, he asked with a smile, "It feels like you lived through several months instead of one single day, right? And I'm sure you're exhausted."

"Yes."

"I know; I felt the same about the days I had with my father before starting in the academy. Trust me though: There's no need to worry. You might never have to confront the dangers I spoke of. And those that you do may spread over a long time period. So keep all this in a corner of your mind and carry on with your normal life—so long as you stay on the safe side."

He sent Seyit up to bed with a kiss on the forehead.

That night, Seyit's dreams veered between wonderful scenes he would love to see again and hellish nightmares. He saw himself graduating from the academy in a smart uniform, his chest covered in medals like his father's, surrounded by a bevy of Russian beauties. There were so many that he didn't know which one to pick; some lifted their skirts to display their ankles, and others caressed his face with their hair, expecting a kiss. Then they morphed into an obnoxious mob in filthy rags, dragging him off his horse with shrieks of "Death to the tsar's man!"

He woke up bathed in sweat, freshened up with a handful of water from the pitcher in the china bowl at his bedside, and lay back down. Perhaps he could avoid the same nightmare by keeping his eyes open, he thought, but eventually he succumbed to a deep sleep.

At the end of two days of riding, chatting, and resting, father and son packed again to return to Saint Petersburg. His father sympathized with Seyit's regret at leaving this lovely place and the Karloviches. "That's the job, you see. You can never settle anywhere, not really."

Early in the morning of the third day, the carriage arranged by Ganya took them away. The loyal couple waved respectfully until the Eminofs vanished out of sight. Seyit waved back, feeling he had reached a turning point in his life in the past two days. "Now I have two homes I want to return to."

"You'll have many more yet!" Mehmet chuckled. He added in a more serious tone, "But your real home's always in Alushta. Never forget that, no matter what happens or how far you are."

The return journey was fun. It was lovely day, warm but not oppressive. A gentle breeze brushing over the leaves licked their faces and hair. Brought closer by the intimate conversations of the past couple of days, they felt like friends now. During the long ride back, Seyit heard advice on how to avoid getting girls into trouble.

"Is Mahmut going to learn all this too?"

"Yes, of course...when the time comes. But perhaps not as young as you."

"Why?"

"He won't have to leave his mother's skirts like you, which means he can afford to learn a little later. You, on the other hand, have to know everything much earlier, since you're on your own at the age of twelve; you have to grow up more quickly and avoid making mistakes as you do—or at least, you should make as few as possible, which means you have to learn some things at a younger age." Turning to Seyit, he said, "It might sound unfair..."

"No, no, I'm not worried about growing up quickly."

Mehmet stroked his son's head and then placed a hand on his shoulder. His mind was at ease: Seyit would cope—and probably more easily than anticipated.

The day held many more wonders. When Mehmet pointed to the majestic block rising on the south bank of the great River Neva and said, "There, that's the Admiralty Building," Seyit felt an irrepressible thrill at the prospect of frequenting such places one day. Riding past the Winter Palace on the same bank, he was rendered speechless by the splendor, an impression reinforced by the ride down the Nevsky Prospekt that dominated the city between the Admiralty and Alexander Nevsky Square.

The Neva and a multitude of canals gave the city an archipelagic aspect, weaving as they did between islets connected by bridges of all lengths. The embankments were built of pink and gray granite.

"The Neva freezes for five months of the year," said Mehmet as they crossed one of the bridges. "Winters here are so long and so bitterly cold that you'll be missing Crimea's winters!"

They chuckled. His father had described much greater terrors; who'd worry about snow or winter instead?

Mehmet was determined to show Seyit the sights and speak about their histories and how and when they'd been built: the ministries on Vasilievsky Island, the Fortress of Peter and Paul, and the cathedral where Russian tsars had been buried since Peter the Great, Peter the Great's Summer Palace, and the Fortress of Kronstadt on Kotlin Island. They even toured the port.

"Over fifteen hundred ships call here every year. The city's population is around one and a half million and grows by the day. Nearly a third consists of workers coming to the port and the factories in the vicinity."

"Are the workers Russian too, Father?"

"Yes, of course. But just like us, there are also people of all sorts of origins, like Finns, Estonians, Jews, and Poles...any nation you can think of."

Seyit thought they'd never reach the end of the city; it looked so immense. At long last, directed by his father, the coachman drew up outside a house in one of the narrowing streets off the main square. It was a two-story wooden building with an exterior wooden staircase leading up to the first floor, virtually identical to all the others in the street. Minor details distinguished individual houses, such as the curtains in the small narrow windows and the begonia or geranium pots on windowsills. Children playing in the street flocked over to stare at the arrivals.

"And this is a middling Russian neighborhood," said Mehmet. "Well, not even middling, if I'm honest."

"Who are we visiting?" inquired Seyit.

"This is Yevgeny's home. The late Yevgeny's."

"Who's that?"

Mehmet instructed the coachman to wait and explained as he moved toward the staircase. "He was my equerry for many years. Very sad—the fellow died of tuberculosis. His widow and three children live here now. The poor woman works in a factory by day and does whatever else she can by night—cleaning, washing dishes, whatever—to make ends meet."

"Don't the children work?" asked Seyit. He regretted it immediately at the sight of the children shooting out of the door. The oldest of the screaming boys looked to be five or six—perhaps a little older. Too puny and scruffy, at any rate, to prevent a more accurate guess. Two more boys tumbled down the staircase, their legs almost too short to span the treads. They had to be a year or so apart.

It was obvious they knew Mehmet from the way they grabbed his legs. All three barely reached the tops of his boots. All three were barefoot. All three had corn-silk blond hair and huge baby-blue eyes. But for their heights and ages, they could have been mistaken for triplets. Under Seyit's astonished gaze, Mehmet kissed and lifted each boy up into the air. Seyit's heart fell. Could the blond woman waiting at the door upstairs have something to do with his father? The idea would have been utterly alien until the other day, after his father had pointed out that anything was possible when a man was far from home. His rapidly developing imagination filled in the blanks, and Seyit suddenly wanted to safeguard himself against this woman and her children. The idea of her and these children—whoever they were—making demands on his father aroused an imperceptible jealousy.

Hugging the two youngest in his arms and followed by the eldest, Mehmet walked toward the stairs. "Come on, Seyit; come along. Come—I'll introduce you to Yevgeny's family."

Seyit climbed obediently, hiding behind his father's shoulder to sneak a look at the woman who waited at the door with a huge, happy smile and a bashful expression. She looked very young. Her hair, braided by her ears and piled on her head, was the same color as her children's, and her eyes were an equally pale blue. Her threadbare dress, patched at the elbows, looked scrupulously clean. The bright yellow roses with green leaves on her red apron served to emphasize the reddened, cracked state of her hands, which hung at her sides.

When Mehmet reached the top step, she drew aside deferentially and invited him in. Her Russian sounded different from Ganya's and Tamara's. "Welcome. You make us very happy, Major Eminof."

Her words were all but inaudible, as if she was too shy to speak. As soon as Mehmet stepped into the small, cramped room, he lowered the children, pulled Seyit to his side, and turned to the still-bowing woman.

"This is my son Seyit. He'll be living in Saint Petersburg from now on. Seyit, this is Anna Verochka, Yevgeny's wife; remember me telling you about him?"

He moved to the armchair by the window without waiting for an invitation, accustomed to the space.

She asked in the same low voice, "Would you like a drink?"

"No, thank you. We're a little pressed for time, and we've been on the road for quite a while. We just wanted to call in briefly."

A baby cried in the next room, and Mehmet whipped round. Anna bowed her head bashfully, blushing furiously, still cringing at the door. Biting her lip, she stole a glance at Mehmet without lifting her head.

Mehmet got up, and Seyit followed him next door. There was barely enough room for one person between the two wooden bunks on either side of the bedroom. At the far end was a makeshift cot, a single sheet on a few sacks between the bunks. The baby lay prone, face red with crying, turning its tiny head from side to side, little fists pressing down and falling back, and thin screams drowning in the unyielding, shapeless mattress. The woman rushed over to pick it up. The baby looked like a small red bundle with a few strands of blond hair, pale enough to look white on the bald head.

Anna calmed her baby down and carried on patting the bundle as she spoke in a barely audible voice, too frightened to look Mehmet in the face. "Erm... Believe me, Major Eminof; it's not like you think..."

Mehmet walked over to stroke the happily gurgling baby's bare feet; gone was the crying infant of a moment ago. "How do you know what I think? At any rate, does it matter what I think? Will you be able to manage though?"

Her gaze slid to Seyit, indicating her unease at this discussion within his hearing. Mehmet gave his son a surreptitious wink. "Don't worry. His Russian isn't that good yet; he won't understand."

Seyit retreated to the front room quietly. Feigning ignorance wasn't difficult, but he couldn't stop overhearing. The rooms were so close and so small that he was sure he'd hear even if he plugged his ears.

"I'm afraid you might misunderstand, Major Eminof," she said, on the verge of tears. "But what I make is just not enough to feed the children or clothe them. Her father...I've known him a long time. He'd always treated my children kindly. He's a cook at the equipment factory in Putilov...you see...I mean...Do you understand me, Major Eminof?"

"Yes, of course. All right now...don't cry. I've not said anything, have I? And in any case, I can't interfere in your decisions concerning your and your children's lives! All I can do is look after you in Yevgeny's memory. That's all."

"I know, Major Eminof; bless you. Thanks to you, we're over the worst now."

"But you're not exactly in the money either, Anna Verochka."

"I know, Major Eminof; I know. We're not rolling in it. But I've sworn to spare my children the same hardships in the future. I've been saving every last kopek you've given us. I'll put them through school. It may not be the best one, but they will go to a school—no matter what. Yevgeny would've wanted it too. Believe me, I still love him...and miss him so much..." Bursting into tears again, she carried on talking between sobs. "But it doesn't make me a fallen woman, does it? Please tell me you don't think any less of me."

Seyit regretted his earlier nasty suspicions about Anna, her poor children, and his own father. His eyes misted at his father's gentle consolation.

"Please don't cry, Anna Verochka—please. Believe me; I've never entertained the slightest uncharitable thought about you. I know you and fully understand your reasons. I...it's just that...I was surprised at hearing a baby. That's probably why I looked astonished. I mean, I was concerned at how you would manage to look after another one. At any rate, you don't owe me any explanations about your private life. And you know what? I'm delighted that you want to put your children through school. I'll do my best to help."

Anna rocked her baby to sleep, lay her back down, and spoke hesitantly. "He wants to marry me."

Mehmet turned around on his way out of the room. "Do *you* want to?"

"I don't know; he has nowhere to live. He sleeps in the factory and sometimes takes night watch. If we marry, he'll have a home to come to. And then he can bring something for the children every night."

"Does he treat you kindly, more importantly?"

She perked up in defense of her new man. "Oh, Major Eminof, you won't believe how kind he is! He treats Yevgeny's children like his own. Of course he can't replace my Yevgeny, but believe me, he's a really good man."

"Anna Verochka, no one's expecting you to be buried with Yevgeny. You're still very young. You have children to raise. You're intelligent enough to know what's best for you and them. My only concern would have been if he roughed you up—or the children. But if he looks after you and loves you and is a good father to your children, don't hesitate—marry him."

On returning to the front room, Mehmet patted his son's shoulder. Seyit was relieved that Anna had brightened up; now he berated himself for his earlier mean thoughts. *Could I have made her cry so soon after our arrival?* Suddenly he noticed how pretty she was. Yes, she was truly beautiful—a beauty that had resisted poverty, pain, loneliness, and life's trials. The timid persona seemed to have gone too. Mehmet observed the sense of guilt vanishing after their talk. Seyit, still a child, just saw a new woman. The more closely he looked, the more he berated himself for having failed to notice her loveliness earlier. Her chafed hands were long and slender. The wrists that showed at the cuffs of her old dress were so delicate and pale that she must have been working very hard to get her hands into that state.

Anna Verochka grabbed Mehmet's hands with both of hers. "Thank you, Major Eminof; thank you! Thank you for your understanding; thank you for everything!"

She was still thanking him profusely when Mehmet freed one of his hands, drew a plump parcel from an inner pocket, and handed it to her. "Don't mention it; don't mention it! Come on now; stand up, Anna Verochka."

Seyit was sure the package contained money, which explained her attempt to vindicate herself—his father had been looking after them until now.

Anna burst into tears once again. "God bless you, Major Eminof. God spare your children!" She was clutching at his hands again.

Moving toward the door, Mehmet extricated himself. "Now that's enough thanks! Promise me one thing though: never give up on this idea of educating the children. I'll call in from time to time to see if there's anything you need, all right?"

It was a much more cheerful Anna Verochka who opened the door now. "I promise, Major Eminof. They'll all go to school and make something of themselves." Then, as if she'd forgotten something, she added, "I'll pray for your health every day. And I'll pray for your family too." As her visitors descended, she called out more bravely, "And you might meet him next time you come."

Mehmet waved silently without turning around on the step, placed his hand on his son's shoulder, and boarded the waiting carriage. The screaming and laughing boys waved good-bye from the bottom of the stairs. Seyit was astonished at their capacity for happiness in such poverty.

The horses galloped away from the wooden houses leaning upon one another in the poorer districts. Seyit stared at his father's face wordlessly for a while. How calm he looked, how gentle—yet so resolute too! Feeling immensely proud of his father, this man he was getting to know better by the day, Seyit turned back to look at the Verochka house shrinking behind them as the carriage drove toward the broader streets.

Poor Yevgeny, he thought. *Poor Anna Verochka...and their poor children!*

Silence reigned for a while, as if something was weighing them down. Mehmet called out to the coachman with a new address and preempted Seyit's question with an explanation. "We're now on our way to Sergei Moiseyev's place. You could say we grew up together; we've been friends since our earliest years at the academy. He joined the navy later. His fleet was engaged in the Japanese war from the very beginning. The Japanese bombed us on February 8 in Port Arthur. He returned injured not long before I set off to Crimea for your circumcision."

"Was he very badly wounded?"

"I believe he was; he's unlikely ever to return to action now."

"So who is right: us or the Japanese?" asked Seyit.

"Son, war means that no matter the actual cause, both sides believe themselves to be right. Only history will show who is right."

"And you—are you going to this war?"

"Soldiers go where they're ordered, Seyit. And no one ever knows quite what's going to happen beforehand."

"Where do the Moiseyevs live?"

"A nice house in a road parallel to the Nevsky Prospekt. He comes from a wealthy family. He'd never notice the difference in his lifestyle if he stopped working, truth be told. His father and grandfather owned nearly half the land where the city's factories now rise. Sergei went into the military because he's such a daredevil. His father's still alive. When he returned from Port Arthur, wounded, burly Sergei barely escaped a good hiding from his father!"

"Why?"

"Because he spurned all this wealth and risked life and limb just to go to sea."

"Why did you call him 'burly Sergei'?"

"You'll see for yourself; he's a giant of a man—not that it spares him a lecture from his father!"

Father and son howled with laughter in the moving carriage. Seyit had already warmed to Sergei Moiseyev; he couldn't stop grinning at the idea of a great hulk of a man still scolded by his father.

"Mind you don't laugh when we get there; it's rude," warned Mehmet and joined in his son's laughter before issuing another caution. "Also, you must address him as Lieutenant Commander Moiseyev." He winked. "As you know, military men like being addressed by rank."

Seyit completed his father's advice. "And noblemen."

Mehmet roared with laughter. "Where did you hear that?"

"You said it once."

I wonder when I did that, mused Mehmet, still smiling.

Resisting the temptation to burst into laughter again, Seyit shook hands politely when his father introduced him to the truly gigantic Sergei Moiseyev: the man just dwarfed Mehmet Eminof—no runt himself! Moiseyev wasn't fat, but he was big, with a thick moustache that joined his sideburns and beard. His sparkling coal-black eyes couldn't conceal the warmth behind the feigned stern gaze. The child within was clearly alive and well inside the huge man, who grabbed Seyit's hand, picked him up, and lifted him into the air. Despite the earlier warning, Seyit giggled at the image of this burly giant in a lieutenant commander's uniform receiving a talking-to from his aging father.

In a voice that suited his frame, Moiseyev boomed, "Must have tickled him," and gently lowered Seyit to the floor. Seyit stumbled a little as he slipped out of the hold and landed on his feet. Just then he noticed a raised eyebrow: his father knew precisely what had caused the giggles, and it wasn't ticklishness.

He's still a child, after all, Mehmet thought; it would have been unfair to expect him to grow by two decades at once. His expression softened once again.

"Are you going to stand here forever?"

Their host invited them into the drawing room through the broad frosted-glass door. Seyit couldn't figure out why this hale and hearty man with such an upright walk was unable to return to the front. Perhaps Moiseyev had recovered since his father had last seen him.

The drawing room had floor-to-ceiling windows and French doors to the veranda and was scattered with several sofas and armchairs upholstered in Gobelin and silk. The soft red dominating the furnishings and rugs was reflected in the curtains. A sweet afternoon breeze blew in through the open French door, rustling the netting and the silk-velvet curtains. In the bay window by the French door stood a grand piano, displaying an array of family photographs in silver and crystal frames. The gas lamps and vases all echoed the same red.

"You've made some changes since I was last here; it looks lovely," said Mehmet.

Moiseyev poured liquor into tiny glasses from a crystal decanter on a silver tray that covered a dainty console, as he replied, "You know what Olga is like: it would be a miracle if she could manage to live with the same furniture for an entire year. I've stopped interfering. I simply let her get on with it. The best way for us both..." He handed Mehmet a glass. "Welcome! *Na zdorovie,* my dear friend."

"Na zdorovie!" said Mehmet as he raised his glass. Taking a big sip from his drink, he resumed the earlier thread. "Thank God your wife has good taste. I'd suggest you put up with it—and without complaining too."

The lieutenant commander roared with laughter as he showed his friend over to the Gobelin suite. "I've grown accustomed to putting up with the change in the decor, Eminof; it's my pocket that's struggling to follow suit!"

"You of all the people in Russia!"

Mehmet chuckled at the thought of Moiseyev powerless before his wife. Lieutenant Commander Moiseyev called out to the butler standing at the door, "Pavlov, have we got nothing to offer this young man?"

The gray-haired Pavlov, possessor of an inscrutable face that offered no clue whatsoever to his state of mind, was experienced enough to recognize a command even when it was posed as a question. "As you wish, Lieutenant Commander," he said as he slipped out.

"Go out into the garden if you like, Seyit."

Seyit liked the idea; he complied with thanks.

"I do like your son, Eminof," said Moiseyev, cocking his head at the boy walking down the lantern-lined path toward the pool. "Mature for his age."

"He's come along in leaps and bounds in the past few days, Sergei. But he's always been quite mature."

Moiseyev's eyes misted up, and with a heavy sigh, he spoke in a barely audible murmur. "How I wish I had a son like that! I envy you, Eminof. You're very fortunate."

Sensitive to Sergei's profound sorrow, Mehmet offered some consolation to his childless friend. "But Sergei, surely you know we all envied you when you carried off the most beautiful girl in Moscow?"

Cheering up at once, Moiseyev grinned and slapped his friend on the shoulder. "Of course! You really were envious, were you?"

"And how!"

Sergei cheered up and giggled like a child; Mehmet gave him an affectionate look, accustomed to these unrestrained mood swings. The man would still be a child at heart at sixty.

The next topic was old times. Roaring liberally at stories they both knew by heart, they retold these tales as if they didn't.

Seyit wandered in the garden, holding the cold glass of lemonade Pavlov had given him. As he watched these two old pals, he wondered if he would ever have such a close friend, someone he'd like that much, and stay friends with for such a long time.

The liquor bottle was half empty, and the two men were engrossed in memories when the drawing-room door opened. They both sprang up at once.

Olga Tchererina Moiseyeva appeared at the door, and everything faded. All the precious objects, paintings, cut flowers in vases as tall as a man—everything. Seyit stopped dead in his tracks just as he was about to part the net curtain to return to the drawing room.

Her black hair had been gathered into a big chignon, and her head was adorned with tiny curls. Her black eyes were slightly slanted. The emerald silk dress exposing her shoulders was trimmed with cream lace at the yoke; frills in the same lace decorated the forearms. The large emeralds surrounded by diamonds on her neck and ears emphasized the whiteness of her skin.

She paused with a look of utter surprise at the company, a brief look that intimated her delight, and strode in gracefully, holding out her hands to the advancing Mehmet. "Eminof! Welcome! But why are you so late?" She offered him her cheek for a kiss.

"You look ravishing, Olga Tchererina—stunning as ever," was the admiring response.

Suddenly noticing Seyit, Olga walked over with a second exclamation of delight. Being quite tall for a woman, she had to bend her knees and lean to plant a kiss on the cheeks as she held his shoulders. Straightening again, she spoke, still holding his hands. "My God! He's a wonderful boy, Eminof. How adorable. Nearly the same age we were when we met you, isn't he?"

"He's twelve now," conceded Mehmet, delighted at the praise for his son.

Somewhat self-conscious at this probing stare, especially at the way a strange woman looked deep into his eyes, Seyit blushed.

"Yes, we were the same age when we met. And thirteen when we met you, my dear Olga," said her husband, sitting back down.

She might not have been a classical beauty, but she seemed to possess a secret power that instantly warmed wherever she went and commanded all attention, a vitality that outshone everything and everyone around her. The twelve-year-old boy was bewitched by this woman with the blazing eyes whose hands and arms danced gracefully as she talked. He noticed his father liked her too. As for her husband, it was obvious he was still in love with Olga Moiseyeva. There wasn't much of an age gap between them, but a face covered in a thick beard and moustache, coupled with his large size, made Sergei look at least ten years older than his wife.

As Olga settled into one of the armchairs in the corner the men had picked, her long slender white hands stroked the stones in her necklace.

"Tell me, Eminof—how was your journey? How is your family? How is the new baby? Tell me everything; I'm dying to know."

Her warm and lively tone indicated that she genuinely wanted to know. They had been friends long enough to regard each other as brother and sister, and Mehmet relaxed into telling her everything in great detail.

"And Zahide sends her love to you both."

Olga and Sergei had braved all that way to celebrate Mehmet's wedding in Crimea. Afterward, they had all spent ten wonderful days in Olga's family's summer house in Livadia, south of Yalta, a holiday all four remembered fondly whenever they got together.

"You two have yet to bring us ladies together again. Shame on you!" Olga's reproach sounded cheerful enough that the men took no offense.

"Don't worry, my dear Olga," said her husband. "Since this colossal body is no longer of any use to the navy, I can spend the rest of my life traveling. We'll go wherever you want from now on. I promise you. If you like, we'll never call in Saint Petersburg; we'll just drift here and there."

Saddened by that melancholy, she left her seat, moved in her customary grace, reached over the back of the armchair, and hugged her husband. Bending down, she gave him a kiss on the forehead. "Sergei, please stop worrying. You've done your best. Thank God you came back to me. What if something had happened to you? What would I do then?"

Sergei's sad gaze brightened up at her touch. Paddle-like hands stroked her embracing arms. "Don't mind me. It'll all be forgotten the moment the wounds and stitches stop aching," he said. He added sunnily, "And I've not reneged on my promise to travel either."

Dinner was quite late, and it turned into a small-scale feast. There was so much to tell, so much to laugh at, that Seyit was beginning to think they might sit up until daybreak. Olga entertained the party with imitations of Saint Petersburg society's latest *arriviste* wives, caricatures punctuated with facial expressions and her hallmark graceful gestures. Seyit missed some of the nuances but joined in the laughter nonetheless. It was really strange that a woman could be so attractive and striking and so funny at the same time. His own mother was very beautiful, but she'd never attempted such comic parodies.

They retired to the drawing room after dinner. As the gentlemen refilled their wine glasses, Olga walked toward the piano. Smoothing her skirts with both hands, she settled onto the velvet cushion of the piano stool and took a substantial sip from the tiny liquor glass her husband had offered.

"Thank you, darling," she said and placed the glass next to the tall silver candlesticks illuminating the piano. Suddenly she stilled; gone was the earlier exuberance. She paused, hands clenched among the folds of her dress. She lifted her head and closed her eyes. Seyit realized the other two men were also spellbound. He might be young but not so young as to miss her extraordinary quality. Even her wordless, silent movements drew his gaze. She looked as if she was getting ready to pray. In the light of the candles, her face bore a confident expression, as if aware of her admirers. The fingers she gently placed on the keys started playing something that grew in volume. Glasses in their hands, Sergei and Mehmet leaned on either side of the piano. Seyit was all but engulfed in the cavernous sofa. He felt overcome by melancholy all of a sudden. His mother also played some evenings, especially when his father was back. They must feel really lonely now. He felt all alone despite his father's presence. He stared at Olga, wishing his mother was playing instead. But it was impossible. His mother was left far behind, and it would be a very long time before he could see her again. It was hard to stop his eyes misting. Thank God no one was looking, and the room was quite dim. Olga could have been the only living creature in the room, surrounded by candlesticks, the piano, and music. The candles flickered, the music was sad, and the boy in the soft sofa was overwhelmed by weariness. He closed his eyes to stem the tears. Soon he was fast asleep.

The moment the music stopped, Olga silenced the applause with a finger to her lips and a telling glance at the sleeping boy. That she was the focus of attention never impaired her mindfulness of everyone and everything around her. Her eyes might have been half closed, and she might have appeared to have abandoned herself dreamily to the music, but she had been watching Seyit from the corner of her eye as she played. She missed nothing—neither the hand wiping his eyes nor the heavy sigh that followed. Standing up quietly, she whispered,

"Poor child—he must be exhausted. How inconsiderate of me! We forced him to sit up all this time."

"I'm sure he was delighted," replied Mehmet, making a move to rouse his son with a tap on the shoulder.

"Don't!" said Olga, grabbing his arm. "Don't awaken the child! They'll carry him up to bed now."

"No need, dear Olga. He's a big man now: perfectly able to wake up, walk to his room, and go back to sleep again."

Olga's voice resumed its amiably authoritarian tone. "Shame on you, Eminof! As if you were never a child. Don't you remember just how sweet sleep is at that age?"

Sergei summoned the butler, who was waiting outside the door. With a silent chuckle, he teased, "How could he? Mehmet's well past that age!"

"And you?" teased Mehmet back.

Olga replied, tracing her husband's cheek with a dainty hand, "Him? He never grew up. Isn't that so, husband?"

Sergei Moiseyev replied with another silent, yet hearty, laugh. "How droll: friend and wife in cahoots!"

Pavlov entered with a footman, and on the lieutenant commander's sign, they took Seyit in their arms and left.

"Dress him in his pajamas without awakening him, and put him to bed," said Olga softly.

Mehmet slapped his forehead.

"Good God! You're having a strapping lad carried. No one's going to carry him in the school. How's he ever going to be a soldier if you indulge him so?"

Squeezing the last few drops from the crystal carafe into his glass, Sergei let out another belly laugh. "Now do you understand why I'm no good at this martial stuff, Eminof?" He was doing himself an injustice, judging by the way his wife and friend laughed. "And this carafe just never stays full!" said Sergei. He called, "Pavlov! Pav—"

Interrupting him gently, his wife took the carafe from his hand and placed it back on the tray. "That's enough, darling. I think we all need sleep. Just because our guest is too polite to complain, we can't keep him up all night, can we?"

The lieutenant commander glanced at Mehmet, expecting him to take sides, the glance of a child looking for an accomplice for some mischief. Mehmet would have given in to temptation.

"We could have a glass..." Olga's raised eyebrow prompted a retreat. "But it probably does make sense to call it a night."

Moiseyev adopted a comical expression of helplessness at his friend cowering before his wife. "Oh, well! My dear Olga's terrified you too! There's nothing for it; we might as well go to bed," he said. "I'll swear on the saints, Eminof; sometimes I wonder which requires more discipline: staying in Port Arthur with Admiral Yevgeny Alexeyev or living here with Admiral Olga Tchererina Moiseyeva."

"I hope that's not the only difference between Admiral Alexeyev and me," teased Olga.

Accompanied by peals of laughter, they crossed the wide marble entrance hall toward the staircase leading up to the bedrooms, Olga between the two men, her arms through theirs. It had been a wonderful night.

When Seyit awakened in a bed of dazzlingly white sheets and rose-scented pillows, he had a fleeting sense of being in his own bedroom back in Alushta. He had no recollection of coming to this room or getting into this bed. He sat up and looked around. No, his memory held no images of this room. The last thing he remembered was that huge velvet sofa. The rest was a blank. Suddenly racked by the thought of having been abandoned by his father, he leaped out of bed and looked for his suitcase. He found it; it had been emptied. His clothes were already hanging in the wardrobe, and his boots were polished. He got dressed in a hurry, impatient to go and find his father.

There was a knock on the door when he was combing his hair. Olga called out softly, "Seyt, are you awake?"

An unusual pronunciation of his name, although not at all unpleasant. He called as he moved to open the door, "Yes, Olga Moiseyeva."

Olga's smiling face greeted him. She was in a pale pink dress, much simpler than last night's outfit. Her neck and ears were adorned with pearls this time.

"Good morning, Seyt. I'm glad you're up. It's wonderful outside, and I don't want you to miss breakfast in the garden."

Enchanted by her energizing personality, Seyit took the extended hand as they descended the stairs.

"Have you rested well?"

"Yes, ma'am," replied Seyit bashfully.

"You must have been exhausted, the way you fell asleep on the sofa last night. Do you remember?"

Mortified that he'd fallen asleep in a house he was visiting for the first time—and in front of people he'd just met—Seyit asked slowly, "Erm...Was it my father who took me upstairs?"

"No, Pavlov and Yuri helped you up."

How tactful she was! Too tactful to say he'd been carried upstairs like a baby. Seyit warmed to this kindly and vivacious lady who was holding his hand tight. Relieved, he started asking the question on his mind. "Olga Moiseyeva—"

Olga stopped, placed her other hand on his shoulder, and interrupted, looking him in the eye. "Not Olga Moiseyeva, Seyt. Please call me Auntie Olga. We are very old and very good friends of your parents. Sergei and Mehmet have been friends since they were twelve. They're like brothers now." She threw her head back in a tinkling laugh. "Closer than brothers, even. Do you have any idea what little secrets these two big men have? Secrets even I don't know. And I'm sure Zayde doesn't either."

That must be my mother's name.

She remembered she'd interrupted him just now. She stopped on the step. "Sorry; you were about to ask something, Seyt. What was it?"

They were at the French doors by then. Relieved at spotting his father talking to the lieutenant commander in the garden, Seyit knew his unasked question was now unnecessary. "It wasn't important, Olga Moiseyeva..." A raised eyebrow, a reminder to him of what they'd just agreed upon, and he corrected himself with a smile. "I mean, Auntie Olga."

Olga stroked his head. "That's better. Don't forget we—your uncle Sergei and I—are your nearest and dearest here in Saint Petersburg...after your father, that is. We're your second family, and this is your home. Deal, Seyt?"

More than happy to accept the warmth and attention offered by the Moiseyevs, the beaming boy nodded. "Deal; thank you, Auntie Olga."

As they descended the veranda steps, the two men at the table on the grass under the trellis stood up to greet Olga.

"Yes, it appears my wife has conquered another man's heart." Moiseyev laughed.

"My heart bleeds for you," replied Mehmet. "You'll have to contend with this jealousy all your life."

Olga asked as she approached, "What manner of mischief are you two chuckling over now?"

"We're discussing how you captivate men of any age," replied her husband.

Olga showed Seyit to the seat next to her and sat down in the chair Mehmet was holding. Picking up the china teapot, she began pouring. She spoke without lifting her gaze from her task. "Just you wait for a few years. You'll be astounded at the heads this handsome young man will turn."

Blushing self-consciously and glancing at his father, Seyit bit his lip.

Sergei turned toward his wife. "My dear Olga, you're embarrassing young Eminof."

Olga put down the cup in her hand and addressed Seyit. "Being handsome and stealing hearts is nothing to be ashamed of, Seyit." Tilting her head at the men, she added in a steady, yet playful voice, "Ask these two handsome fellows if you don't believe me just because I'm a woman."

"Well, thanks to you two, I've joined the ranks of the good-looking!"

Sergei's self-deprecation elicited chuckles all around, and Seyit's initial awkwardness vanished. These topics all had to be part of growing up, even if they weren't ever broached at home. If there was anything wicked or shameful, his father wouldn't allow him to be present where such conversations took place, would he?

The next day, Seyit wondered where the time had gone; he was having such fun here. The Moiseyevs always had something nice to say or something to make him laugh—a joke or a funny story. It had none of the dreary gloom of a childless house; instead it rang with the chirpy laughter of a big family.

On their second night, Seyit learned he was to enroll the following day. "Will I be staying there, Father?"

"No, son. Tomorrow we submit your application. You'll also have to pass a medical exam."

"But I'm not sick!"

"They don't know that though."

Lieutenant Commander Moiseyev joined in from his seat, a perennial glass in his hand. "The healthier you are, the better you'll serve the army, Seyt. That's why the unsound are rejected at once."

"What if I get sick later?"

"Then you'll get thrown out. No mercy. If you fall sick, you'll be sent home."

Olga chided her husband. "Shame on you, Sergei Moiseyev! The things you tell a boy who's not even donned his uniform yet! At any rate, no one threw *you* out. You left of your own volition."

The lieutenant commander looked crestfallen again. "What difference does it make?" he asked bitterly. "Whether they told me to leave or I chose to resign? I left nearly half my ribs and a kidney behind in Port Arthur." With a belly laugh, as if he'd just cracked a joke, he added, "Never mind; my head's still here. My feet carry me. My arms work. In actual fact, Olga is right: I am one of his blessed servants."

Giving him a kiss on the cheek, Olga adopted a soothing tone. "Me too, Sergei; he has similarly blessed me and sent you back to me." Then, in an attempt to lift the mood with her customary sparkle, she added, "Come on now; enough of this doom and gloom! Tell this young man about the fun side of soldiering now!" She reassured Seyit next. "Ignore them, Seyt. All military men are like that: trying to make out they've got the toughest job in the world. You've seen with your own eyes how much fun they have reminiscing! Uncle Sergei's just testing you, believe me."

Seyit was certain the lieutenant commander was telling the truth, but Auntie Olga's gentle, warm, teasing voice had dispelled speculations on what someone might feel as his organs were ripped apart.

The conversation turned once again to the girls of Saint Petersburg and Moscow.

"Make sure to come here on your breaks," said Olga. "Promise you won't trek all the way to Tsarskoye Selo, all right? Spare yourself the journey when you have family here who can't wait to see you. All right, my darling?"

Seyit glanced at his father, not knowing how to reply.

Mehmet spoke for him: "Thank you, dear Olga. We're grateful. Of course, this is one of his homes. But he will occasionally go to the summer house too. He'll be here for many years yet. He'll have time to go everywhere."

"Yes," said Sergei wickedly. "He'll have time to go everywhere."

The adults chuckled, but Seyit was mystified. He was bubbling with excitement about the following day. "Will I really see the tsar?"

"We'll order your uniform first. There's a time for everything. Then, once I know when he wants to see me, I'll take you along."

Seyit couldn't sleep a wink that night. When his father stepped in at daybreak, he felt as if he'd only just fallen asleep; his eyes stung, and he had a headache.

"You couldn't sleep, could you?" asked Eminof Senior.

Half asleep, Seyit only shook his head. All he could think of was laying his head back down on the pillow and falling asleep. He fell back onto the bed...and pulled himself together at his father's exclamation. "Seyit Eminof! Might I remind you that you are a soldier as of this morning?"

Still groggy with sleep, Seyit shot off, stumbled, lost his balance, and banged against the foot of the bed. Mehmet chuckled, hugged his son, and spoke fondly.

"I hope this clumsiness won't carry on throughout your life in the military. Come on then; get ready at once; we'll have to leave in half an hour."

Seyit hurried to wash and dress. In his haste he put buttons through the wrong holes and dropped his comb; his boots seemed to reject his feet. He was covered in sweat. His father and the Moiseyevs were already at the breakfast table when he went downstairs and sat down with apologies for his tardiness. Fresh as a daisy, Olga greeted him with her usual energy and cheer, as if it had been someone else who had sung and played the piano until the early hours.

"Come along, young Eminof. You must eat better than ever this morning. You've got a long day ahead of you."

She gestured Pavlov to serve Seyit. The youth was far too sleepy and excited for food though. He couldn't face the crêpes, muffins, and sausages heaped on his plate. Seeing Seyit's anxiety, Sergei exclaimed, "Olga, darling, I don't think our young friend can eat much on such a momentous morning. Best not to force him."

Seyit sent Sergei a look of gratitude that prompted Olga to take charge.

"Of course, darling. He can eat as much or as little as he wants." She soothed the child who might alleviate her own heartache, reluctant to jeopardize his affection. "Don't eat anything if you're not hungry, Seyt. A little fruit perhaps?"

A cup of tea and an apple were all Seyit could manage.

Mehmet was astonished at his friends as they contested how to parent his own son—without bothering to consult him!

To Seyit's surprise, they weren't required to take leave of their hosts this morning. The lieutenant commander had decided to join the Eminofs on this important occasion. Olga, meanwhile, planned to visit a couple of friends before doing some shopping.

The carriage turned into a high, arched entrance a little beyond the Winter Palace. The guards drew aside at a sign from Mehmet. The carriage halted at the end of a big courtyard, by a high marble staircase leading to a door, and Sergei and Mehmet leaped down. Seyit made a move to follow, but Olga held him back by the arm and kissed him on the cheeks. "There's no need to worry, Seyit; keep calm. Today's a very special day. I want to hear everything down to the last detail in the evening."

She kissed him again and watched him descend; the Moiseyevs felt as though they were sending their own son to school. She waved at the men as her carriage drew away. Sergei's adoring gaze following the receding carriage suggested he was missing her already.

"Don't know who she thinks she's going to chat to at this hour!" He chuckled.

Passing through a second gatehouse, Seyit, his father, and Moiseyev arrived at the magnificent entrance of the main building.

Major Mehmet Eminof and Lieutenant Commander Moiseyev were obviously no strangers to this building as they strode in without asking for directions. Their dignified gait and the flawless salutes they exchanged with other men in uniform countered the image of the two men who'd been downing one glass after another, joking, and bellowing with laughter for the past couple of days. Their boots echoed on the marble floor, the only sound in the colossal building. Seyit thought his breathing was loud enough to be heard in this stillness. They mounted a broad staircase wordlessly, strode down another long hallway, and halted outside a door near the end.

Eminof rapped and entered; Moiseyev followed, nudging Seyit forward.

It was a large room. A fat man in uniform sat at a big desk diagonally opposite the door. He raised his head from a pile of papers. His gaze changed into one of recognition, and he exclaimed, "Eminof! Moiseyev! Come—come in!"

He stood up to approach the guests. Despite being nearly as tall as Sergei Moiseyev, he looked much heavier. Wondering if he had arrived in a land of giants, Seyit was bewildered; he had no idea what to do, where to stand, or what to do with his hands. It was best to seek guidance in his father's movements and keep his eyes peeled for some indication or gesture.

"Hello, Valery."

Mehmet's vigorous handshake indicated they were close friends. *But not as close as Uncle Sergei*, thought Seyit.

Mehmet drew Seyit close for an introduction. "This is your new cadet, my son Seyit Eminof."

He turned to his son. "Seyit, Major Valery Paustovsky is the head of your department. Don't forget though: the moment you don your uniform, you're just a new cadet like any other. I mean, expect no special treatment if you misbehave."

Seyit's eyes opened wide in astonishment; he was fumbling for something to say when Lieutenant Commander Moiseyev intervened. "I'm sure Seyt will have no such problems. Will you, Seyt?"

The boy shook his head. He had no idea what sort of problems he might face here. What else could he have said?

"Welcome," boomed Major Paustovsky in a voice that suggested no leniency.

"Thank you, sir," replied Seyit.

"Sit down; sit, sit." Major Paustovsky beckoned them all and addressed Eminof next. "I'll have the forms brought over. You can fill them in, and we'll have a bit of a chinwag too," he said, pushing the chair between the desk and the wall; he had to squeeze into it by pressing down on his belly with both hands. He rang a bell on the desk, leaned back, and replaced the bell on the desk, when a very young soldier appeared at the door and snapped to attention. Seyit stared, speculating unsuccessfully about the difference in their ages. These outfits changed the wearer so much! Would he also grow up to be tall and well built like this soldier?

"Yusupov, bring me the year one application forms."

Seyit stared after the young soldier, at the way he clicked his heels and saluted. Before long Yusupov returned to hand his commander the required forms and left to resume his duties elsewhere. Checking that he had the full set, Major

Paustovsky handed the sheets over to Mehmet and cleared a space at the corner of his desk.

"Come, Eminof; pull your chair here so that you can write in comfort."

Mehmet Eminof did as he was told, scanned the forms, dipped the pen on the desk into the inkwell, and started writing in a neat hand. Moiseyev and Paustovsky chatted in low voices.

Seyit's mind was on those bright white sheets. Too shy to stare openly, he watched his father's hand as if the movements would help him decipher the words.

"There, I think that's all complete now, but just check it, Valery. Let's make sure we've missed nothing," said Mehmet as he signed the final sheet at the bottom.

Taking a break from the heated discussion, the major scanned the forms from top to bottom. "It's all there, Eminof. I suspect it makes sense to get the medical examination out of the way too, seeing as you're already here."

"Best to get it all done as soon as possible; I'm unlikely to get much more time off. I'll have to return to my regiment tomorrow or the day after at the latest."

"I'll write a note for Dr. Karloff to take you to the front of the queue."

"That would be a great favor, Valery."

"I thought there was going to be no special treatment! You're asking for favors from day one!" interjected Moiseyev.

They all laughed even as Major Paustovsky withdrew an ornate letterhead from a drawer, wrote a few lines, and handed it to Mehmet. This had to be the letter for Dr. Karloff.

"Give him my best regards. It's been a while since we last met." Then, extricating his enormous body from the chair, he settled into an armchair near his visitors, crossed his legs, and resumed speaking. He sounded much more somber this time. "This war with Japan...doesn't seem to be letting up any time soon."

"What's the latest?"

"Not that great," replied Paustovsky. "The worst of it is that we keep deluding ourselves that we're making gains."

Mehmet, who had been away from things for quite a while, had no doubt Paustovsky knew something he didn't. "What do you mean, Valery?"

"I don't want to worry you, Eminof. Let me just say this much, strictly between us: it's Bezobrazov, the very same head of your Imperial Guards, who's mostly responsible for the outbreak of this war."

"I don't understand; what's the connection between heading the Guards and holding sway over such a momentous decision?"

"The real connection is this: In their patriotic fervor, Bezobrazov and Plehve advocate that the western bank of the Yalu River ought to be Russian territory. At least they did until, as you know, July—when Plehve was assassinated by a bomb thrown at his carriage. A fate that might await any of us, actually, given court credentials of any sort or closeness to the tsar in any way could earn you as many enemies here as on the front. And Plehve's closest crony was Pobedonostsev."

"Is he still adviser to Tsar Nicholas?" asked Mehmet.

"There're no obvious grounds for him to leave. In the tsar's eyes, I mean. And what matters to Pobedonostsev above all is distracting the people with war. That's how he's hoping to suppress the voices on the streets."

"Yulyevitch put up quite a resistance though..."

"Yes, he did," replied Paustovsky with a wry smile. "Until August, when he lost the seal of finance minister. In other words, mess with Pobedonostsev at your own peril."

"You mean he manipulated Plehve and Bezobrazov's ideals to his own ends?"

"That's precisely what I mean. And if I'm overheard, I'll start shoveling snow in Siberia tomorrow."

His guests quickly allayed his fears with promises to keep his secret.

"In actual fact," Moiseyev offered, "this war's misfortune seemed to begin with the sinking of the *Petropavlovsk*. The poor souls of Admiral Makarov and six hundred sailors will never leave us alone."

"Thankfully Kuropatkin plays a more circumspect game. He's stringing the Japanese along until he feels he can overpower them."

Major Paustovsky had the look of a man with something he didn't dare articulate, but guessing correctly, Mehmet gave him a reassuring smile.

"Come on, Valery—tell us: Are we also due to set off? Since you know so much, you must know this too."

"I'm not entirely sure; I've just heard of a possibility. Nearly every week a new regiment sets off to join those already in Yalu or Vladivostok. At any rate, you're likely to get more reliable information today."

Seyit caught his breath at the suggestion that his father might go to war, a prospect Eminof Senior seemed to receive with astonishing nonchalance.

"Thank you, Valery," said Eminof, rising to his feet and extending his hand. "You've brought me up to speed as if I'd never been away. I'm certain that you're party to even our departure date, not that you'd tell me!"

Valery and Sergei exchanged smiles.

"Oh! I can't believe it; Sergei, you knew? All that time we ate and drank in your house, and you never said a word! Shame on you!"

"There was no point in putting the dampers on, Mehmet. You would hear today anyway."

"Thank you, friends; thank you!" teased Mehmet, and he shook hands with Major Valery Paustovsky as they took their leave.

"Call in before you leave, Eminof," said Paustovsky, sounding gentler than usual.

Walking between his father and Lieutenant Commander Moiseyev, Seyit felt even more bewildered now than when they'd arrived. His earlier worries about being on his own and having to live with strangers had been overshadowed. Just when he was coming to terms with the idea of an imminent parting, he now had to contend with the prospect of his father going to war. He would have sought safety in his father's warm hands if he weren't too shy to do so in public. *How embarrassing for someone who'll be a uniformed cadet in a fortnight to be clutching his father's hand now,* he thought and resisted the temptation.

All the way to the military hospital in the carriage, Mehmet and Sergei carried on the earlier debate. Seyit tried to follow along, despite the plethora of unfamiliar names.

It turned out to be a long and tiring day. After countless trips up and down hospital corridors and laboratories and with the tailor still to visit (a call that would take at least another hour), Moiseyev invited the Eminofs to a lavish meal in a sophisticated restaurant patronized by elegant ladies and gentlemen. Lunch was late, but since the evening meal would be closer to midnight than not, it was time for a break.

On leaving the restaurant, they dispatched the carriage ahead to the tailor's and set off on foot. True, they had all been hungry enough to eat for two, but a brisk walk would do them good now. They crossed one of the smaller bridges over the Neva in the warm breeze and proceeded to another district. Moiseyev exchanged greetings with a happy young couple walking arm in arm. The woman was holding a little girl of six or seven by the hand. Long blond hair tied with a blue silk ribbon matching the child's dress fell over her shoulders.

They walked past.

At first unnoticed by Mehmet and Sergei, Seyit stood nailed to the spot, staring at the girl walking away. She'd thrown him such an unforgettable glance that he wanted to see her face again—something he'd never felt before. He didn't want to lose this perfect stranger. He admired the blond hair swinging above her waist as she walked. As if she'd sensed she was being watched, she turned her head to give Seyit a half-bashful, half-mischievous look and carried on her way, chattering to her mother. He berated himself for failing to gather his wits in that brief moment and smile back; surely he could have waved at least!

It was his father's voice that brought him back to his senses. "Hello, Seyit? Have you lost interest in coming along?"

Even as he rushed to catch up, and later, when he was being measured for his uniform, all Seyit could think of was the little girl in the blue dress. Was this what they meant by love? Would he see her again? Even the idea of seeing her again quickened his pulse. Yes, this had to be what was meant by love. So what if both were far too young? Wasn't he going to grow up anyway? Would they recognize each other when they were grown up? Time seemed to fly past as these thoughts raced through his mind.

Evening was approaching when the Eminofs and their host set off to join Olga. The Moiseyev carriage was waiting outside a grand building in an elegant road. Olga might have spent the entire day chatting, but she didn't seem to be in the least bit tired. She led the conversation as soon as she settled in, impatient to hear about everything that had happened during the day—down to the last detail. One thing she didn't need years of experience and powerful feminine intuition to notice was Seyit's half-dreamy silence. He was staring at the cobblestones vanishing under the wheels; indicating him with her eye, she asked her husband, "Anything else? Anything exciting or mysterious?"

Sergei's gentle smile suggested she lay off. "That really is all, Olga darling. That's as much as we know."

The adults laughed, but Seyit heard nothing. His mind was on a girl he might never see again—a prospect that made him want to see her all the more.

His mind was in turmoil that night. It had been a long day, and one that had flown by—a day of many firsts, a day when he'd learned so much. Folk here spoke of different things and had other concerns and ways of having fun from those in Alushta. The realization that the enormous Russian Empire his father had shown him on the map was actually losing the war with the Japanese, that some people hated the tsar, and that starving folk marched on the streets tainted rose-tinted visions of several years of school, training, and having fun in Saint Petersburg. That night he barely spoke at all—with the exception of a few sentences Olga had to drag out of him—and went to sleep immediately after supper. He dreamed of the little girl in blue: they were grown up, and Seyit was offering her flowers under the branches of a weeping willow.

The next few days passed as if in a dream that had everything, from anticipation to joy, anxiety, and sorrow. During this week as a guest in Saint Petersburg, he had been officially admitted into the academy and had obtained a dashing uniform and glossy boots. He even, together with his father, had an audience with Tsar Nicholas II!

The gentle and placid personality behind all those titles, medals, and decorations was quite impressive. The man Seyit met was nothing like the stern and roaring despot he had envisaged. Quite the opposite: a mild and kindly looking man, Nicholas seemed willing to do anything to avoid hurting anyone. He didn't look like a man with a single malicious bone in his body. Tsar Nicholas was attentive, his eyes shone when he spoke of his children, he stroked the potted flowers gently, and he spoke in the unassuming tone of close friends. Seyit was utterly charmed into offering undying loyalty.

The tsar might be known as the sole authority of this vast empire, but his eyes were plagued by the melancholy of some incurable ailment. Thinking of the nasty things said behind his back, Seyit couldn't help but pity his emperor.

After a visit that lasted for half an hour, they strolled down Alexander Nevsky Square, chatting as they did so.

"Is he always this sad?"

His father knew whom Seyit meant. "He has many reasons to be unhappy."

"Doesn't he have reasons to be happy?"

"I'm sure he does. But the others possibly tip the scales."

"But God has given him so much! Shouldn't he be happy?"

"You're right; God blesses some of us more from birth. Titles, palaces, and wealth might just be waiting for you. But all that doesn't make you ready to rule, son. And under adverse conditions, sometimes what you possess might bring grief instead of joy."

"Is that what happened to the tsar?"

"Only time will tell. I am sure, however, that at times he wishes he was just a grape picker in Alushta."

"How do you know?"

"He must have been having a really bad day. He told me himself."

Seyit grinned at the image of the great tsar picking grapes in their vineyard. The conversation turned to more pleasant topics as they boarded the carriage to meet the Moiseyevs for dinner.

In the brief time since he'd left Alushta—and it wasn't a big part of his life—Seyit had learned far more than he had in his entire life. There was something else he had recently noticed: joy and grief alternated with remarkable pace in the adult world—a world he felt he had entered, despite being still only twelve. Just when he was enjoying the thrill of something good, something else came along that upset him or weighed on his mind.

It was yet another happy day when he packed his suitcase for school and began looking forward to the next morning. Earlier, citing some errands, his father had left on his own. Mehmet's announcement, when he finally did return, cast a pall over the household: he had been ordered to join the regiment departing for Yalu on the first train in the morning. This meant leaving before daybreak. Seyit struggled to check his brimming eyes. Feeling wretched on what had been such a special day for him, with no idea when he'd see his father again and afraid of crying in public, he shot up to his room.

Olga would have followed to console him but for Sergei's intervention. "Let him go, Olga. Let him cry in peace. We'll go up later."

"Yes," said Mehmet. "It'll do him good to cry a little and let it all out. He's been through so much that crying might offer a bit of relief."

"You're right."

Olga dabbed at her own eyes with a silk handkerchief and sat down at the piano to let her fingers dance on the keys.

It wasn't long before Mehmet left the Moiseyevs to join his son. Silent and pensive, Seyit was perched on the edge of his bed in full uniform and boots. Swollen eyes and a red nose said it all. It was enough to make Mehmet's heart ache; how young the boy was still, and how helpless! He would be on his own from tomorrow morning onward, virtually all alone in this struggle called life. He sat down softly next to his son. "You look great in uniform."

No reply. Disinclined to insist lest Seyit burst into tears again, he carried on slowly in a gentle voice. "Come on; get changed if you like. Hang your clothes, and we'll go down to supper. Olga's prepared a wonderful meal as usual."

"I'm not hungry." Seyit nearly choked, his voice tiny.

"Even so, we still have to sit down together. As you know, tonight is very special. In the morning, we're all going our own ways. And you know Auntie Olga; she's taken such pains that she'd be very upset if you're not at the table. Come on; let's not break her heart."

"When...when are you going?"

"We still have lots of time. Strictly speaking, we should all go to bed early tonight; but just for this once, we can forget this clock business. I suspect we'll all chat for a couple of hours after supper and then say our good-byes. You'll all be asleep in the morning when I leave."

"Not me...I'm coming with you."

Mehmet hugged his son and planted a kiss in his hair. "That's impossible, son."

"But why?"

"Why? Because if everyone took his son or wife along on his way to war, there'd be no end to it; that's why."

"But I'm a very good rider!"

"Of course you are. But you need to know more before you can join in battle. At any rate, war is not what it might appear from a distance. Most people fight only because they are ordered to do so. Very few actually know what exactly they're doing or why they're there."

"I know why: I want to be with you."

Cupping Seyit's face, Mehmet stared into his eyes. "Look, son, you belong here. You will go to school. One day, when the time comes, you will look after your mother and brothers and sisters. I have one more piece of advice for you: never, ever do something you don't believe in just because you want to stay with your loved ones. From tomorrow morning onward, you will have to make many of your decisions yourself. Never forget this. You are now on the way to becoming a grown man."

"I thought I'd become a grown man when I was circumcised."

"Yes, but that was just one step on the way to becoming a man. One event alone isn't going to make you a mature man, son. You will grow up with every single day, every single pain and trouble you face. Maturity takes time. Don't rush; learn from everything that happens. And always keep your elders' advice close to your heart. It'll all come in handy one day."

Knowing this was their last chat before they had to part, Seyit threw himself into his father's arms. Locked in that hug, he cried—but silently. It was high time to stop showing his feelings like a baby. Blinking back his own threatening tears, indescribable anguish in his heart, Mehmet buried his head in his son's soft hair.

The household barely slept that night. Instead they sat up chatting, sad at times and winding one another up at others.

Early next morning, Mehmet realized his plans to leave without disturbing anyone had been thwarted. Olga had given strict instructions that all the servants awaken and that she too be roused. Tea was ready not long after supper had been cleared. Mehmet was astonished to see Olga and Sergei waiting in the dining room, which was ablaze in the light of the gas lamps.

"What on earth are you two doing at this ungodly hour?"

"Shame on you, dear Eminof. Think we'd let you get away to war without even a cup of tea?"

"Thank you, Olga, but you really needn't have. You've had no sleep at all."

"We can sleep whenever we want; don't you worry about us."

Her sweet tone failed to disguise the concern she felt for this close friend. "And please don't worry about Seyt. We'll take him over to the school in the morning. And we'll keep an eye on him afterward. We love him like our own son, and we'll look after him as if he were."

"Yes," agreed her husband enthusiastically. "Don't you worry about him. I can't take your place, but I'll do my best so that he doesn't miss you too much. We'll also let Zayde know and do our best should she need anything. Rest easy."

"I've written a long letter. I'll leave it with you; I'd be grateful if you could post it. It will be quite a nasty shock for her too. She wasn't expecting it. I wish I could have seen them once more."

"Good morning!"

Three heads turned at the voice: Seyit stood at the door in full uniform. His features seemed to have sharpened since the previous night. His expression belonged to someone several years older.

"Come, Seyt; come, darling. Good morning."

Olga invited him to the table cheerfully, hardly believing this was the same child who'd run away on the verge of tears the previous night. What she was certain of, however, was that the stiff mask of dignity would slip and the eyes well up the moment he was alone again.

After a fairly gloomy and brief breakfast, it was time for good-byes. They all stood at the door at a loss for something to say, until Mehmet broke the silence. He kissed his friends and faced his son, standing at attention like a soldier awaiting orders. He opened his arms to hug his son as Sergei swallowed and Olga dabbed at her eyes. They stood, as if to freeze the moment and breathe in every last atom of that hug. Seyit looked like a miniature of his father. Drawing away reluctantly, Mehmet planted a kiss on his forehead and said, "Good-bye," when their eyes met. "I'll write at the first opportunity. Look after yourself and be a good student. Pay heed to what we've discussed. God bless you, son."

"You too, Father," replied Seyit in a barely audible voice.

He could speak no more, not that his father expected it. There was no point in dragging it out. Mehmet stepped out through the open door and boarded the waiting carriage. The coachman galloped toward the station, away from the hands waving and surreptitiously wiping away tears at the door.

The cool, damp air of predawn Saint Petersburg already bore a hint of autumn. Seyit suddenly felt very far from everything: his big family, his father's affection and friendship, and the laughter-filled new life of the past few days. Even the warm, cheerful sunshine of summer seemed to have vanished into the distance. How quickly everything changed! Feeling forlorn, shivering at a chilling desolation, his mind echoed with his father's words. Mehmet Eminof had said as they left Tsarskoye Selo, "You'll have to grow up more quickly than your brother, since you'll be left on your own at the age of twelve." This might have been the moment he was referring to. No, not *might have been*—had to be.

All Seyit knew was that he had never felt this lonely. What he didn't as yet know was that the same sense of loneliness would enslave him in later life too.

Saint Petersburg, Christmas 1904

I T WAS A cold, snowy day, an ordinary mid-December day in 1904. Swaddled in snow in the week before Christmas, Saint Petersburg looked like a fairy-tale illustration. Main roads, elite residential districts, and entrances to exclusive shops and restaurants indicated that the wealthy enjoyed a much merrier anticipation of the approaching holiday. The snow muffled the sounds of carriage wheels, the swish of troika runners and clip-clop of horses' hooves, but the bells rang clearly as everything scintillated in the light of lamps lit one by one. Street musicians huddled near wood fires in tin boxes by shop fronts or street corners where main roads narrowed toward the side streets. Their accordions, balalaikas, and violins harmonized with the magic of the descending night as they dreamed of the smattering of kopeks—or a ruble or two if they were really lucky—and played with eyes half closed, transported into another world.

A child carrying a small suitcase descended from a carriage that halted at the corner of the road. He lifted his coat collar up and started walking at a leisurely pace, watching everything around him, apparently enchanted by these sights and sounds. That was precisely the reason he had alighted well before the Moiseyev house: his wish to be closer to this vibrant street life. He peered into the window of an antiques shop full of Christmas decorations and the musical instrument shop next door. They had to be quite expensive if the outfits of the clientele inside (and the shop assistant's demeanor) were anything to go by.

Berating himself for staring so long when he had no intention of spending money in that shop just then, he moved away. A young man was playing a poignant folk song on his balalaika; the singer, who had a similarly moving voice, had to be none other than the musician's sister—they looked so alike. Framed by a floral scarf covering nearly all her hair, her face looked snow white in the light of their fire. Her eyes sparkled with the shadows cast by the flames—or perhaps tears. Seyit watched her for quite a while, worried she might burst out crying any moment. She had stoked his loneliness again with her song, the loneliness he'd been forcing himself to forget for such a long time. When she finished singing, however, and heard a few claps along with the tinkle of coins, her face broke into a smile sweet enough to lift Seyit's gloom. He extracted a few coins from his pocket; dropped them into the box next to the fire; and thinking he ought not to tarry any longer, strode off toward the Moiseyev house.

It was only his second break since starting the academy. He could have taken out weekend passes, but he had waived that entitlement in order to expedite his adaptation to an unfamiliar environment and a totally new curriculum. He was receiving private lessons in Russian Classics, French, and German as Major Paustovsky had arranged upon Mehmet Eminof's request. Success demanded working harder than, and learning before, all his classmates who spoke Russian as a mother tongue. It was quite an exhausting program, not that he complained. He had already distinguished himself academically, and his horsemanship skills raised his marks in sports. There was little time for homesickness with all that study and exams. Whenever he had a free moment, he dived into books until his weary eyelids fell—lest loneliness envelop him like an incurable ailment. For all their yearning to take him under their wings like their own child, the Moiseyevs had wisely agreed it was best for him to stay at school as much as possible. His tenacity and accomplishments were impressive.

There had been no news of Eminof since he'd gone. Many families preferred to write a few lines expressing love and longing rather than wait for news. These messages were entrusted to the kindness of others on their way to war.

Seyit's determination to keep himself occupied in his waking hours could do little to control his dreams. He missed his father in a different way from his family in Alushta. His mother, brothers, and sisters were all together, safe and secure in their own home. But he didn't have the slightest idea where, or under what sort of conditions, his father was...or whether he was still alive. The mere possibility that his father might never return compounded the nightmares. Seyit missed his love, friendship, and advice. He knew he'd miss his father all the more the moment he was in a home environment and would depress everyone around him—another reason he'd delayed visiting the Moiseyevs for so long. But now it was the time of year when no one should be alone; the academy would empty as all the cadets took Christmas leave to join their families.

As a Muslim Crimean, Seyit wasn't accustomed to celebrating Christmas, but he now lived among people who did. He would never offend Auntie Olga or Uncle Sergei, and he was going to enjoy this special occasion and make sure they wouldn't regret inviting him. For the first time in months, he waited at their door, shaking the snow off his boots.

Olga and Sergei's warm welcome said they couldn't have been happier if they'd seen their own son. The great hall itself and the giant fir tree by the staircase in the grand entrance hall had obviously been decorated with loving attention. The handrail rose in a profusion of massive red satin ribbons and flowers. Preparations appropriate to the occasion were clearly well underway as servants hastened hither and thither. The Moiseyevs beamed, flanking him with hugs as if he were still a little child, and led him into the hall.

"Oh! Seyt, I can't tell you how happy we are that you're here," said Olga. "No one should be alone on these occasions. And I promise you'll have a great time. We're also expecting a few young people your age." She gave him a wink. "There are few lovely young girls too. Yes, yes, I'm sure you'll have a great time. Now come, sit down, and tell us about school. How is it all going? Who's in your class? Who are your teachers? I know Uncle Sergei always brings news from your school, but I want to hear about it from you."

Seyit turned his eyes to see Sergei Moiseyev's cheeky gaze—the gaze he'd nearly forgotten—and beamed at this kindly man. So dear Uncle Sergei had been following his life closely and had done so on the quiet. Seyit allowed himself to relax, feeling tremendously secure, as if he were back home. He was blessed with affection here, and he was certain he loved them back. Casting aside his timidity and languor like a jacket, he launched into an account of the academy. He told them everything, from the very first morning Lieutenant Commander Moiseyev had delivered him to the school; he spoke about everyone he'd met and all that had happened. There was no danger of omitting anything as Olga listened, all ears, occasionally asking a question or two to clarify every last detail. Throughout the conversation, which carried on well past dinner, Seyit felt his place in this house was no less important than his father's. His hosts were pleasantly surprised by the maturity and resolve of this youth—indisputably more impressive than those of many adults.

Later that evening, Sergei gave Seyit the happy news: a mutual friend returning from the front had brought an envelope from Mehmet Eminof. It contained three letters: one for the Moiseyevs, one for Zahide, and one for Seyit.

Eyes sparkling with joy, Seyit read it over and over again; it felt like hugging his father in person. It wasn't very long. Eminof wrote that they were constantly on the move. He said the war continued unabated, and he had no idea when he was coming back but was in good health and spirits, missed his son a great deal, had received one of Seyit's letters, and rejoiced in his accomplishments. The letter concluded with an affectionate *I have full confidence in you, son.* Gazing at the handwriting as if trying to decipher something quite unfathomable, Seyit read the letter once again. It was the next best thing to a real reunion. That night he slept more soundly than he had for a long while.

Two nights later, the Moiseyev mansion was heaving with Christmas guests. Their Christmas party had, for many years, been *the* occasion for the crème de la crème of Saint Petersburg society. The city made merry with countless gatherings, but Olga's skill ensured that hers was the most successful. Thanks to a remarkable mastery of human nature, her guest list would be a perfect balance of aristocrats and celebrated artists, thereby bringing wealth, beauty, titles, and talent together as no one else could. It also meant that anyone who'd received more than one invitation accepted Olga's without hesitation. Every Christmas she announced the following year's party and secured commitments from favored guests. Consequently, while others were still posting *their* invitations, the Moiseyev guest list—and the plans for the food and drink—would be fixed.

Seyit met too many people to remember all their names or titles. Every time Sergei or Olga introduced him as Eminof's son, the reaction indicated that his father was known to most of these guests. Intimidated by the attention of an exceptionally flirtatious redhead, he was trying to sneak away into the crowd, parting the guests with repeated apologies in an effort to disappear from her sight...when he was forced to halt by a youth of about his age.

"Good evening! You must be the boy who is the lieutenant commander's guest—the one they call Kurt Seyt."

Seyit looked him up and down, trying to recall if they had met earlier. No, he had never seen him before. They were about the same height. Sun-bleached highlights shone in the boy's dark-blond hair, which was cut short in a style similar to Seyit's own. A reassuringly broad forehead was countered by pale-blue eyes set too close. Seyit was about to speak after this brief inspection when the boy continued affably, "My name is Petro Borinsky. We're in the same school."

"How do you do, Petro?" Seyit said and extended his hand. The two boys shook hands warmly.

"Were you sneaking away?"

Seyit had no intention of explaining to his new friend the reason for his haste, but it was evident that Petro missed little, if at all.

"You can't conceal it from me." With a wink, Petro pointed to the redhead dancing with a young man several years her junior. "You wouldn't happen to be running away from Svetlana Nicholayevna, would you?"

Seyit felt embarrassed; if this boy his own age had noticed it, then so had everyone else.

"Erm...I..."

"Come on; don't be shy! I've been trying to come over to introduce myself all this time since Uncle Sergei asked me, but she wouldn't leave you alone!"

"So why didn't you come over and rescue me?"

Taking his arm genially and glancing around to make sure they weren't over-heard, Petro leaned over to whisper in Seyit's ear, "I was caught by her once...and once was enough."

They burst into laughter, and lamenting the lack of a single girl attractive enough to keep them in the dance hall, they moved into the relatively quieter piano room.

"Who told you I was called Kurt Seyt?" asked Seyit. "Not even Uncle Sergei calls me by that name."

"Major Paustovsky is my uncle on my mother's side. And as far as I can make out, he and your father are close friends. I've just come here from the school in Moscow. Uncle sorted out the transfer. We might even be in the same class."

"I hope so; that would be great!"

"I hear you're a very good cadet though; I'm not."

"I don't mind; I suspect we'll get along well."

"My uncle says you're a great rider."

"I'm not too bad."

"Not too bad? I heard you had top marks."

"It's early days yet. No one can tell who's going to rise above the rest."

"One thing's sure though: it's not going to be me!"

There was an instant bond between the two youths; they laughed again. Chatting throughout the night, they decided they had much to learn from each other. Seyit would help Petro out in written French, and Petro would tutor him in little escapades away from family homes in Saint Petersburg—namely, how to relax when studies got too much to cope with. A very agreeable pact was thus made before they finally called it a night.

In those final days of 1904, Seyit missed his family enormously. All the same, he felt a good deal better than of late. He'd heard from his father for the first time since they'd parted, experienced his first Christmas, and made a new friend.

In the early hours of Christmas Day, he wrote to his father. He had no idea when his message would find its addressee, given his father's letter was dated three months previously. By his reckoning, therefore, his letter would reach his father at the same place in the spring. But he realized something else as he wrote. It felt as though his father was there, listening, as every line issued from his pen. Even if the letter would be read months later or never reach its destination at all, it brought them closer. Seyit resolved to write every week.

While the Moiseyevs and Russians of similar social standing welcomed the arrival of 1905 with jolly celebrations, preparations of a different sort were taking place in the poorer neighborhoods of Saint Petersburg—preparations whose foundations had been laid by the small-scale rumblings of the past year. Minister of the Interior Plehve, who had advocated war for the sole purpose of diverting public attention from long-awaited expectations of reform and modernization, had been fabricating news of nonexistent victories to appease the same public opinion, and he had been assassinated five months previously. Not even his death and the appointment of the far more popular Prince Svyatopolk-Mirsky to the post sufficed, however. In December and at long last, Tsar Nicholas II offered little more than a few vague promises in response to demands for certain rights. It was too little, too late. Thus were sown the seeds of the revolution that was still years in the future.

Christmas decorations had been barely taken down when a mass rally took place in Saint Petersburg, one of the first in a frequent series of bloody events. Murmuring hymns and holding up icons, thousands of workers marched to the Winter Palace behind Father Georgy Gapon. All they wanted was to petition their tsar face to face, instead of through the intercession of some official, as had been the case up to then. But the tsar was away. Panicking at the sight of the increasingly noisy ring around the palace like an iron chain, the guards opened fire on the defenseless crowd. The front ranks fell, initially unnoticed by the crushing crowds at the rear. On realizing what had happened, the demonstrators raised their icons higher and shouted louder; it was only when they recognized the ineffectuality of icons and hymns before armed cavalry that they dispersed. By the time the rear ranks scattered helter-skelter into nearby streets, it was far too late to save the front. Rifle shots, equine whinnies, and human screams rang in the air. An innocent rally had turned into a bloodbath.

Several hours later, when the plaza outside the Winter Palace had finally cleared, it wasn't cleared at all, contaminated as it was by sin: a lake of blood and a pile of human misery, victims of rifle rounds, and bodies trampled into a pulp under escaping feet or pursuing cavalry hooves.

Prince Mirsky resigned immediately after that Sunday of horrors, which had left one thousand souls dead. Hatred of Bulygin and the protest response to the tsar's actions manifested as murder: Grand Duke Sergei was bombed in the Kremlin, assassinated by a revolutionary called Ivan Kalyayev.

While the capital seethed in a time of rising unrest and Seyit collected unsent letters to his father in a large envelope, Major Mehmet Eminof battled on in blizzard conditions, one of thousands in Russian uniform fighting against the Japanese thousands of miles from Saint Petersburg. Russia was still dispatching thirty thousand extra troops to Mukden every month. Minister of War Kuropatkin rearranged his forces, which numbered three hundred thousand, into the commands of Linevich, Grippenberg, and Kaulbars. Eminof and his troops fought in the seven-division army under Grippenberg that attacked Sandepu, then defended by only two Japanese divisions. They battled for two days with the blizzard and the Japanese forces, winning the most significant Russian victory to date in the war. Certain of an imminent counterattack, however, and concerned about further casualties, Kuropatkin ordered his forces to halt.

Despite the routs in Mukden and Tsushima, the Russians held out until July. Japanese forces crossed Korea, captured Sakhalin Island, and advanced toward Vladivostok. Opinion in Saint Petersburg might have urged fighting until certain ultimate victory, but defeats and news of retreats only supported the revolution in preparation. The peace negotiations that started in August pointed to a Japanese victory.

The trains that for the past year had been taking away proud soldiers striding to the squeaky tempo of glossy boots, dreaming of peace, now brought back disconsolate multitudes, wretches too weary, infirm, and weak with the cold and malnutrition to be grateful for having survived. And those were the men fortunate enough to return.

Saint Petersburg's only contact with the war to that point had been distant rumors, except for those with family members at the front. That group sought solace in lack of bad news: their loved ones might still be alive and well and return one day.

Seyit had no way of knowing whether his letters reached his father; the only thing he'd heard back was a brief note written on the eve of the Battle of Sandepu, and *that* had arrived only shortly before the end of the war. Every weekend since the start of the return of troops, a hopeful Seyit had been going to the station. It was usually packed with the disconsolate, waiting in vain for their loved ones—or at the very least, news of their loved ones. Many stood in floods of tears. Women were seen to run to men they mistook for their husbands and slump to the floor at realizing their mistake; others, more determined, called out for sweethearts, running to and fro among the heap of wounded and crippled masses in uniform. Seyit would walk away with his head down only after the platform was deserted.

It was the end of August. Despite all that inner turmoil, he had passed his final exams with flying colors and qualified for year two with marks high enough to elicit an invitation to Major Paustovsky's office for a commendation. Quite sensibly, he attributed such indulgences to the continued absence of news from his father. He wouldn't let it go to his head.

One day he heard that the last train from the front was due. His father had to turn up now, or the shoots of hope he'd been nurturing for months would wither. He didn't even want to think about that possibility, but fear did not alter reality. He was left all alone on the platform once again.

It was getting darker. He shivered just as he had the morning he had parted from his father, as though in the clutches of a fever. *It's unfair*, he thought. All through the year, only one thing had helped him cope with loneliness: the thought that sooner or later his father would return. But now? His father wasn't there. Everyone who was coming back had done so. Only the dead were left behind. So he had been deceiving himself for months.

He grabbed the little suitcase at his feet and, squeezing it tightly, as if to take his anger out on it, strode toward the exit with tears in his eyes.

He had no wish to stay here any longer. Nor did he want to return to the Moiseyev house. He wanted to run away from everyone, from everything—to be on his own and cry like a child. No matter how grown-up he might be, every man should have the right to cry at his father's death. Leaping into the last carriage waiting outside, he said "Tsarskoye Selo" in a feeble, trembling voice. He wanted to go home, to the home he shared with his father. He would wander through every room and shed tears for his father and the dreams they'd never be able to share now. He thought of his past throughout the journey. Memories flashed past his eyes one by one: his father taking him a ride on his back when he was still a tiny child, then seating him on a pony for his first riding lesson, hugging his father tight every time he came home, the circumcision party for Mahmut and him, opening the tsar's gift together with bated breath, their journey to Saint Petersburg, and the days that had followed their arrival.

He pulled himself up when the carriage halted outside the house in Tsarskoye Selo. He paid the coachman, alighted, and plodded through the gate. It occurred to him that he wasn't so sure of entering this house either. His change of location did nothing to alleviate his pain.

He wasn't yet at the door when it opened to reveal the anxious Karloviches, holding lamps, surprised by the figure approaching the house. Ganya peered watchfully and exclaimed in delight, "Good God! It's Master Eminof!"

They ran toward him in a race to take his suitcase. Tamara's greeting was no less surprised than her husband's.

"By the Holy Ghost! Where have you been all this time, Master Eminof? Ages since you last came! And *Guvardia* Eminof has been absent too; what's going on?"

Tugging at her arm for silence, Ganya held the door deferentially.

Seyit knew he couldn't talk much. He started for the stairs, replying to the apprehensive servants without looking them in the eye. "I'm back. My father's not here...didn't return...didn't return from war...didn't..."

The words trailed off by the time he was upstairs. His door opened and promptly closed, muffling the sobs. Tamara sought comfort in a stream of prayer.

"Oh Lord, oh Holy Mary, have mercy on this child; have mercy on us!"

Ganya stood, nailed to the spot at the door he'd just closed. "No," he said. "No. He will surely return; there must be a mistake."

They couldn't speak any more. Tamara entered the kitchen in floods of tears to prepare something. Presently Ganya took a tray upstairs; knocked on the door; and hearing that Seyit wanted neither food nor company, had no choice but to go back downstairs. All the same, the loyal couple resolved to stay up and check on the young master frequently.

Seyit cried as he hadn't for years; he cried until he was exhausted. He rebelled at God for the injustice. He thought of his mother, brothers, and sisters. What would happen now? What was he going to tell his mother? Thinking of his little sister Havva, who would never remember her father, he decided God had treated her even more unjustly. All of a sudden, he felt guilty. He, a tiny child smaller than even a dot on the surface of the earth—who was he to judge God's mind? To accuse him? He opened his palms to pray for forgiveness and sobbed until his stinging eyes closed of their own accord.

It was well past midnight when a light drizzle started. Ganya would turn in only once he had reassured himself that Seyit was asleep; even then, he dozed off in the armchair at the entrance.

He shot up at hearing whinnying of horses and snatches of conversation. Peeking through the netting in the window of the room next to the hallway—reluctant to open the door straightaway—he saw someone wave at a departing carriage and turn toward the house. The other passenger apparently still had a way to go.

"By all the saints!" uttered Ganya. Yes, he would know this man anywhere in the world, no matter how old he might get: it was *Guvardia* Eminof. Hastily opening the door, he shot outside and grabbed his master's hands. Mehmet looked anxious.

"Hello, Ganya; hello. Tell me; is Seyit here?"

"Yes, sir, he is, but the poor boy is devastated. He arrived in the evening. Locked himself up in his room with neither food nor drink. Devastated, he is." Ganya felt the need to explain further at Mehmet's puzzled expression. "Erm... Sir, he thinks you're dead. The way he spoke, that's what we thought too."

Handing Ganya his kalpak, Mehmet bolted upstairs and softly opened the door. At first he saw nothing. It was only when he had fetched a lamp from the hallway that he spotted Seyit curled up in his daytime clothes on the bedspread. Incredible how much he'd grown since they'd parted! Placing the lamp on the bedside table, he knelt to watch his son. The poor boy looked dreadful. This was no longer a child, yet his face was the same as it used to be when he cried. Mehmet recalled the silent tears when tiny Seyit had thrown an occasional tantrum, tears that ended with the same rage and unbowed gaze from between swollen eyelids. So his little son hadn't changed at all.

He had missed Seyit so much and longed to cuddle him—but he didn't want to wake him. Instead, he gently brushed the boy's tearful eyelids. Seyit had been in a deep sleep, but the fond touch he'd been missing for so long awakened him at once. He opened his eyes and thought he was dreaming. But then he reached out to hold his father's hand; his eyes opened wide, and he flung himself into his father's arms. "Father! It's you, Father! You're not dead! You're here!"

"I'm here, son; I'm here right beside you."

They hugged in silent tears of joy. Seyit spoke about waiting for the last train at the station and then arriving in Tsarskoye Selo. Mehmet could hardly believe this adolescent was the same boy he'd brought here a year ago.

"How you've grown!" he exclaimed, stroking his son's hair.

Seyit felt the cold that had made his insides shiver dissipate. His father emanated a sense of security that nothing else would offer. Then he noticed several decorations on his chest that he'd not seen before, and Mehmet didn't miss the look.

"Thank God I brought them back personally!" he explained. "I lost a close friend a week before returning. He was too seriously injured to hold out for much longer. He had been decorated too, so it fell upon me to hand his personal effects to his family, which is why I alighted at the previous station to discharge that duty first and returned to Saint Petersburg on a later train. Went straight over to Sergei's home, and when I knew you weren't there, I set off for Tsarskoye Selo at once. And found you here, just as I had assumed. See, you worried in vain; here I am. I'm healthy, and I'm very happy to be with you."

"Me too, Father—I'm very happy too. But I couldn't stop worrying. When you didn't alight from that last train..."

"Son, never rejoice or worry in haste, all right?"

Tsarskoye Selo, 1906

IN SEPTEMBER 1905, a brief period of calm appeared to return in the wake of the Portsmouth peace treaty with Japan. Russia ceded half of Sakhalin Island, which it had taken in 1875, as well as the Kwantung Peninsula and Port Arthur. It also agreed to a total retreat from Manchuria and conceded Japan's area of influence over Korea. All these terms clearly indicated Russia had lost. Nonetheless, the public were pleased when the government in Saint Petersburg sued for peace, finally reining in that seemingly limitless appetite for war. Everyone was prepared to forget the routs of Mukden and Tsushima in the closing weeks of the war, the thousands of dead soldiers and sailors left in a land on the other end of Asia and in the waters of the Pacific, and the sunken and burned ships—provided, that is, the news they'd been waiting for came from the palace, but it never did. Workers organized a variety of delegations to petition the tsar directly. On October 26, Trotsky became the spokesman for the recently formed workers' soviet. The Constitutional Democratic Party was founded only two days later; popularly referred to as the Kadet Party, it embraced the moderate members of the independence union as well as the radical wing. Its aim was parliamentary rule based on universal suffrage.

These developments ran parallel to frequent demonstrations on the streets, rallies, and strikes. Tsar Nicholas II signed a manifesto on October 30; while it fell short of using the word *constitution*, it still promised civil liberties such as freedoms of speech, the press, and assembly, as well as human rights to dignity. Sadly, there would be no time for the delivery of these promises; pogroms planned by the police against the Jews and counterrallies organized by the royalists tested the revolutionaries' patience.

Popular as he was, thanks to the peace plan and manifesto he'd drawn up in the tsar's name, Prime Minister Count Witte was struggling to maintain ideological harmony in his United Cabinet, and it was the direct consequence of continued fragmentation that had its origins in the idea of equality between the nobility and the workers. The aristocracy closed ranks to protect their titles and rights. The revolutionaries stood on divided platforms: the moderates were prepared to collaborate with the aristocracy in the cabinet, whereas the radicals pushed for a definitive revolution; meanwhile, farmers' demands for land reform added a new dimension to political rallies.

Supported by Lenin he might have been, but Trotsky had thoroughly antagonized both the socialists and the ruling class with his radical vehemence. On October 16, the leaders of the revolutionary wing were arrested, a move that sent its armed supporters onto the streets in Moscow. The suppression of the occasionally trigger-happy revolutionaries by the guards deployed from Saint Petersburg started an irreversible process. All hope of mutual understanding, patience, and trust was gone.

On a break from school near the end of October 1906, sitting with Petro in the Tsarskoye Selo home, Seyit's mind was on his father, who remained in Moscow.

Mehmet Eminof longed to see his family, but he'd had no opportunity to go to Crimea after returning from war. He had managed to send a letter to Zahide by Olga's hand, when the Moiseyevs went to their summer place in Livadia. Desperate for news of her husband and worried sick for months, when Zahide saw Olga, she nearly fainted: What if it was bad news? Thankfully it was not: Mehmet's affectionate letter, redolent of his longing for home, reassured Zahide that both he and Seyit were in fine form and in good spirits. She burst into tears of joy.

For hours Seyit and Petro had been engaged in a heated debate on the war and the riots, based on what they'd heard from their elders and managed to learn for themselves. Seyit was particularly worried about his father, and until Eminof returned, neither boy would know much about what was happening in Moscow.

"You know," said Petro, "we've been saying the same things over and over again for hours. And none of it makes the slightest bit of difference. There's nothing we can do right now."

"Even so, we're only talking, but many actually have to live through all this. Who knows? We might be battling on the streets one day. I wonder what's going to happen by the time we finish school."

"Who knows? We've got a fair way to go before we find out."

They sat, lost in thought, until Petro broke the despondent silence. "You know, sometimes I have to agree with my father. He never wanted me to go to military school."

"What did he want for you instead?"

"Become a lawyer, like him."

"Why didn't you want to?"

"I grew up on Uncle Valery's tales of military derring-do. I was in awe of him—and his uniforms too." He chuckled. "He was really trim then, not like the man you know now! At any rate, I always found him far more impressive than my own father. So when the time came to choose a school, and both Mother and my uncle supported me, all Father could do was sulk. But like I said, I can understand his present concerns, with everything that's going on."

"But you could give up if you wanted, right?"

"Yes, but that would place my uncle in a difficult position. Father's just waiting for a chance to gloat—'Haven't I told you so?' I have to finish school, at the very least."

"So you're going to become a soldier to make your uncle happy."

"Partly. He never had children of his own and wants to raise me like his own son."

"And your father? Does he have other sons besides you?"

"No, you know I'm an only child."

"Which is what I've been trying to say, Petro. You're trying to keep your uncle happy, but who's going to make your father happy?"

"You're right; I never thought of that! I guess I thought having me as a son should make him happy enough."

"How magnanimous of you!"

Their relaxed laughter dissipated the last of the tense atmosphere. Petro leaped to his feet as if suddenly hitting upon a fantastic idea. "Come on, Kurt Seyt—enough of this idle chatter. How about doing something different, a bit of fresh air, for instance?"

"Petro, it's already dark, and it's really cold out. It's too late to go to Saint Petersburg. Stay put, for goodness' sake!"

"Who said we were going to Saint Petersburg? You can have fun wherever you want! Even in Tsarskoye Selo."

"You're out of your mind! Are we just going to knock on doors until we find a party to crash?"

With a wink that Petro thought made him look like a man of the world, he bent down to his chum's sofa and whispered, "I know a house that will definitely have a party when we knock on the door, and they'll be delighted to entertain us. Come on; get dressed, and we'll go."

Seyit's eyes opened wide in realization. True, Petro had embellished tales of such houses before, but so far, they had remained nothing more than tales. That such diversions might be available in this elegant summer resort had never occurred to him either.

"Are you sure, Petro? Who are we going to? Not many stay here at this time of year."

"Have no fear, chum. We're not going to a house of ill repute. Quite the opposite—we're going to call upon an aristocratic lady."

"An aristocratic lady?"

Petro burst out laughing. "You heard right. Aristocratic, beautiful, and lonely. She'll be delighted to see us; trust me."

"Petro, I'm grateful that you want to entertain me, but I don't think this is right."

"Don't be so bashful! You're going to do it sooner or later. At least take your best mate's recommendation; then your initiation will be plain sailing."

"And what do we say to Ganya and Tamara?"

"Well, you don't have to tell them everything, do you? Just say we're going for a bit of a ride; that should do the trick."

"And you? What are *you* going to do?"

"Don't worry about me; there's always a girl for me in that house."

Soon the two youths were dressed. They'd decided to ride rather than ask Ganya for the carriage, more to spare their blushes than anything. Seyit didn't dare voice any of the questions on his mind, even though he was dying to know whom they were going to visit and what aristocrat would choose this line of business. Moreover, he had no idea what he would be expected to do or what would happen. Perhaps it was best to let things take their own course. Petro was right; he would inevitably be initiated into this aspect of life sooner or later. It was a natural part of being a man. And again, perhaps it was a stroke of luck to have his best mate along in this out-of-the-way place.

They had barely ridden for fifteen minutes when Petro halted outside a gate in a high garden wall. He was clearly familiar with the man walking toward the gate. "Good evening, Niko."

A silent nod in greeting. The gate opened, and the man drew aside. Taking his cue from Petro, Seyit dismounted. Niko took both reins as the youths ascended the stairs. The house was similar to the Eminof place, if a little larger; an exquisite conservatory adorned with spectacular stained-glass windows extended from the steps toward the garden at the side.

In contrast to the composure of Petro, who was knocking on the door, Seyit was anxious and tense. *We'll go away if no one opens*, he thought, but open the door did, and a servant welcomed them with the air of someone greeting a familiar visitor. The elegant opulence suggested this was more of a permanent residence than a summer place. Music accompanied the tinkle of laughter both female and male. They were shown into a drawing room separated from the conservatory by net curtains. Seyit tried to relax; this might be a normal soiree similar to many in the Moiseyev house, and nothing suggested otherwise at first sight. Petro obviously knew there was a banquet here and knew the hosts. He'd probably made the rest up to tease Seyit. There was nothing out of the ordinary in the group seated around the large fireplace.

As soon as Seyit and Petro entered, a woman seated between two men rose and sashayed over. "Petro, darling! What wind brings you here?" Then, embracing and kissing him on the cheeks as if they were close relatives, she asked, "And who's your handsome friend?"

She sounded foreign. Seyit felt intensely self-conscious under her scrutiny and question.

"Baroness, allow me to introduce you to my friend Seyt Eminof. We all call him Kurt Seyt."

Seyit was floundering when the woman offered him as familiar a greeting as she had given Petro: she placed her hands on his shoulders and touched his cheeks with hers. Dizzy at the décolleté that bent down and the warmth emanating from her heavily perfumed skin, he barely heard his friend's words: "Baroness Maria von Oven Starova."

That informality only compounded Seyit's awkwardness. Her perfume clung; it was all he could smell at each breath now. That she was extremely attractive was beyond question, but one had to travel a fair way back in time to describe her as anywhere near young. If her coquettish manners, the tantalizing slits in her gown, and the young men sitting around the fire were any indication, however, age clearly did not present her with much of a problem. Briefly setting aside whatever hilarity had been occupying them, three men in their early twenties stood up to be introduced to Petro and Seyit. They shook hands without letting go of their crystal vodka glasses.

Accepting a glass the baroness pressed into his hand, Seyit toasted their introduction like the rest of the party. The warmth relaxed him somewhat.

Their hostess handed out flattery to all her guests evenly, but she did seem to single him out. The talk that dominated the party, as though this were another world outside Russia, had veered toward women, love affairs, and racy tales. Somewhat light headed after several swift drinks, Seyit no longer felt awkward at the course the conversation was taking or his own relative youth and inexperience. His inhibitions were lowering. It was a wonderful atmosphere. There was no pressure. No one expected him to speak or asked unnerving questions. His glass was refilled again and again as the baroness sitting next to him emanated more warmth than the fireplace. Every once in a while, she slipped a little hors d'oeuvre into his mouth—a sliver of something with caviar or salmon—before clinking their glasses once again to invite him to take another sip. Seyit was wondering whether this would be the sum total of the evening's amusement when a few more ladies entered, laughing. So the party was only just beginning. The baroness stood up to greet the newcomers. Petro's amiable, tipsy gaze asked a silent *What news? How's it going?* Seyit responded with a wide grin. He now knew talking wasn't essential to have fun this evening.

Throughout the introduction ceremony, the men rose to their feet, gallantly lifted to their lips the ladies' hands, and lavished flamboyant compliments upon them all. Seyit, who only an hour ago would have cringed, found himself quite happy in this company. With one exception, the ladies were all around the same age as the baroness. And as if by design, the male-female ratio was now equal. They all sat down in pairs as if by chance. Seyit appeared to be under the baroness's wing once again. Petro was with the younger woman, whom he clearly knew. Despite his curiosity about what lay in store, Seyit felt that everyone else took it all for granted. He had no choice but to fall in.

Sensitive to his diffidence, the baroness avoided overfamiliarity; instead, whenever she brushed his shoulder or knee as she chatted to someone else, she behaved as if the contact was perfectly normal intimacy and avoided catching his eye. Softly, ever so softly, she chatted in a hushed and hoarse voice that made her risqué topics and light touches increasingly more arousing to the cadet.

As the evening progressed, the lamps were dimmed, and the couples snuggled more cozily. Seyit was the focus of the only one-sided courtship in the room now. He stole a glance at his chum's intimate embrace. The dim light seemed to have doubled up the effect of the vodka. His heart was pounding out of his chest. He was nailed to the spot just like the times when he'd been petrified by a nightmare as a child, silent and motionless in his bed.

Couples began leaving the drawing room one by one with murmured excuses. Where were they going? Oh no, Petro couldn't leave him on his own! He made a move to sit up, but a soft, warm hand held him back. He looked up: the baroness was already on her feet, waiting. He rose to face her before he knew it. Well developed for his age, he looked taller than her. The gaze that guided him in a way he'd never experienced before was daunting. With one hand she stroked his face and gently tugged him out of the room with the other. They mounted

Kurt Seyt & Shura

the stairs wordlessly. The youth followed like a good child, happy to be spared the others' looks, happy to let her take charge.

They entered a delightful bedroom in dusky-pink and bright-green silks. The wide ivory lacquer bedhead was adorned with figures of naked men and women, enchanting depictions despite the artistic license taken in the women's floor-length hair waving luxuriously in the breeze and the musculature in the men's shoulders and legs. The room had a familiar smell, the same cloying perfume he'd been inhaling for hours. It suited the room as perfectly as the paintings did. Amused by his silent inspection, the baroness approached slowly. Leaning toward his ear, she asked in a husky voice, "Do you like it?"

That hot breath in his ear flooded his muscles and bones all the way to his marrow. Seyit shuddered in the clutches of a sensation he'd never felt before. He couldn't respond—not that a reply seemed to be expected in the first place, since she kept probing and leading him.

"Are you cold? Come, darling; you'll soon warm up. Come now."

Seyit was in her hands like a windup toy. She dragged him toward the bed, made him sit, and knelt to help him with his boots. Recoiling at the prospect of being undressed by a woman, he tried to get up, but she eased his fears with a single move: she stood up and turned down the bedclothes.

"Come on, Seyt; get into this bed and tuck yourself in. Until you stop shivering. Remove your clothes if you like; I won't look."

Seyit was of two minds; there was this new pleasure he wanted to see through to the end, yet the softness of the bed was tempting him to sleep. One way or the other, he was sure he'd spend the night here. He forced himself to shed his inhibitions, or she might later regale others with tales of this night. That would be even more embarrassing than undressing in front of her. Making his mind up in a flash, he stood to remove his clothes.

"Are you sure you want me to stay?"

She stood absolutely still when she asked this question. The last thing she wanted was to frighten him. She could wait until she was certain of his self-confidence and desire. But the alcohol she'd consumed all evening and her own anticipation got the best of her. She sashayed toward him. Placing her hands on his still downy, yet muscular chest, she spread her own warmth into his whole body. Seyit was afraid; his inner trembling and heartbeat were audible. Another kind of drunkenness he had yet to define had replaced the vodka's effect. His head was roaring, his stomach was knotting up, and he was on the verge of collapsing to the floor, standing with his hands down at his sides.

The baroness walked around him, her hot hands touching his body as she viewed him like a nude statue. Every time she touched him, his body felt on fire. He couldn't stand it any longer. He wasn't entirely certain what a man might feel about a woman at such a time. Her identity hardly mattered now; she was all but cloaked behind a veil of mist in this dim light. He had little doubt that he was equally unremarkable as far as she was concerned, that this was nothing more than one of many such nights in this house.

No, he wasn't going to be tormented by the curious stares of a woman as his breath quickened with his arousal.

She was patting his back with her bare nipples. He swung around roughly and gripped her. There was no stopping him now. Startled by the abrupt change in this shy, inexperienced youth, now an aggressive partner, the woman who'd entertained so many in this room attempted to quiet him, but her words failed. The tables had turned. Seyit was now taking revenge on the woman who'd dominated him for hours. He no longer heard the seductive voice beckoning him to a calm and gentle lovemaking. Things would now go his way. He laid her on the bed on her back. Her hair mussed, her expression lost behind the heavy makeup, the baroness was shocked. It was the first time anything like this had happened. She had always held the reins when it came to how much pleasure every guest offered and took. But this time she'd picked someone who marched to his own tune. She turned her head to stare at the paintings as she let him have his rough way.

The youth rose from the bed, feeling far more relaxed, as if he had just passed a crucial examination, and aware he no longer was the same bashful Seyit of old. As he grabbed the clothing he'd removed under such duress only an hour ago, he knew that nakedness was not only natural but also—even—beautiful. A satisfied smile on his lips, he looked at the woman watching him quizzically from the bed.

"You'll be back again, won't you?"

"Don't know," replied Seyit, secretly pleased with his response. *A much older man might also respond in the same way.* He got dressed and descended to the ground floor, where Petro was waiting.

"Where the heck have you been, for God's sake? Tell me you weren't intending to stay here all night!" He peered closely. "All right? Is everything all right? Tell me, how did it go? She's wonderful, isn't she?"

Pulling the door shut as he left, Seyit laughed in reply. "Why don't you ask her?"

"We-hey! Will you look at our Kurt Seyt! I see you're terribly magnanimous too!"

"Oh yes, Petro: Who is this person you call the baroness?"

Petro burst out laughing. "Haven't you figured it out? Didn't you even speak?"

"You didn't bring me here for a chat, did you?"

The two youths mounted their horses, feeling as free and light as birds. Yet they must also have been exhausted with all the vodka, perfume, logs burning in the fireplace, cigarettes, women...in short, the entirety of the evening's smells. They rode slowly over the fresh snow that had been falling for hours, snow that now softened the lines of the road and cleared their heads as they inhaled the chill air of the descending whiteness. They didn't feel the cold at all in their happy exhaustion.

"Oh yeah!" enthused Petro. "Didn't the baroness tell you her story?"

"Trust me—she didn't. Does it matter?"

"Not particularly, but she normally tells every newcomer, which is why I mentioned it. She's German, a baroness by her first German husband. He died on a trip to Saint Petersburg. Rumor has it she might have helped him along. Anyhow, she liked it so much here that she stayed and then she met a Muscovite merchant as rich as Croesus. Can you imagine what she must have looked like twenty years ago? Must have been fabulous. Before long she took her place in the highest circles of Moscow as Mrs. Starova. Whatever she did to convince her new husband, it worked: everyone calls her the baroness instead."

"Doesn't the new husband mind?"

"Don't think so. Mother says the poor wretch didn't actually have the time to make an issue of it anyway: he died two years after they got married."

"Almost enough to make you wonder if she didn't dispatch them both."

"And you wouldn't be alone. That, my dear fellow, is how our darling baroness graduated into the upper echelons of Saint Petersburg gentry."

"Does everyone know about her lifestyle?"

"Of course."

"So...how come she's not shunned then?"

"My dear chum, one of the reasons is her aristocratic credentials, and the other *is* her lifestyle."

"Excuse me?"

"All parents of boys feel they can breathe easy, thanks to her. No one needs to worry about their son's transition into manhood. Somehow they're all certain that the baroness is the best teacher."

"Incredible!" Seyit said, bursting into laughter. They laughed all the way back.

A week after this major rite of passage in Seyit's life, Mehmet Eminof returned to Saint Petersburg. As usual, they had a lot to talk about. A proposed visit home in the middle of the winter raised Seyit's hopes briefly, but taking leave of school was out of the question. Eminof enjoyed a brief family reunion in Alushta on his own.

As 1906 piled trouble after trouble on Saint Petersburg, Seyit maintained his successful progress in the academy and collected several addresses similar to the baroness's Tsarskoye Selo home.

He had a trip home in the summer to look forward to, hopefully with his father, by which time he would have been away for two years. His heart ached at the thought of his mother, brothers, and sisters—an ache that nothing would alleviate until he saw and hugged them all.

Alushta, 1916

LONG AFTER THE southern slopes facing the Black Sea had welcomed spring's colors and scents, bitter northerlies continued to lash the high hills of Krymskie Gory.

Four galloping horsemen appeared between the fields of earing wheat and halted one by one on the slope surrounded by vineyards. A verdant skirt of land descended to the sea in terraces below the lush forest of fir, plane tree, silver poplar, beech, and alder.

All four riders wore uniforms. Judging by their confident and upright seats, they didn't appear in the least tired after their journey. One rode his horse slowly to the edge of the hill, drew the reins, and removed his hat with his right hand. Assuming an air of introduction, he turned back to his friends and gestured toward the frothing waves lashing the shore. "There it is: the Black Sea!"

Closing his eyes, he inhaled the briny sea air rising up to the hills. His brown hair, which glinted in honey highlights in the sun, was cut in a fringe. The eyes staring at the Black Sea were in practically the same shade of blue. His straight nose emphasized the faint prominence of his cheekbones in a narrow face. A sardonic air danced on his full lower lip even when he wasn't smiling. A moustache as neatly trimmed as his hair exposed a thin cupid's bow. A deep cleft in his chin seemed to complete that fine oval face.

"This is paradise, Kurt Seyt!" The biggest man in the group was a blond officer, who looked quite impressed with the view; he rode up to halt beside his friend. The others followed suit as the blond man continued, "If were you, I'd settle back in my own lands and enjoy this beauty instead of rotting in Saint Petersburg."

As Seyit beamed at this compliment, the smile of a host delighted at his guests' approval, a third officer spoke, one who looked as though he might have been the slimmer brother of the blond man.

"Mischa! Mischa! You know it's not Saint Petersburg any longer; it's Petrograd!"

"You know something, Vladimir? I've not taken to this new name at all. What was wrong with Saint Petersburg?"

"Nothing. Other than being German."

"So what? Never bothered anyone before!"

"We're at war with the Germans, in case you'd forgotten."

But Mikhail—Mischa to his friends—seemed quite insistent on the matter of the capital's name. He stuck to his guns. "No, I've not forgotten. I do not want to hear the word *war* now, in these last few days before we go to the front. I simply don't understand why, just because we are at war with them, we need to Russify a name we've been using for years and years."

Seyit, who had been following the debate with a smile, joined in. "What if someone worried that a German name would tempt the Germans just that little bit more?"

Laughter broke out and ended the debate. Shaking off his calm—almost lethargic—air, Seyit turned his horse on the spot and called out to the fourth man. "Come on, Celil; how about welcoming our guests in our own style?"

With a wide grin, Celil winked in response. His hair was as coal black as his eyes framed with long lashes, his coloring a distinct contrast to Mischa and Vladimir.

Seyit and Celil rode toward each other ceremonially and then trotted in a slow turn around each other. Seyit drew a handkerchief from his pocket, raised it in the air, spurred his horse, and galloped into the forest. Celil burst into an equally fast chase, surprising Mischa and Vladimir, who stared at each other and decided to follow. Seyit emerged from the trees and placed his handkerchief on the ground. On his heels, Celil tilted to the right on his saddle, reached out, and picked it up. He settled back into the saddle; spurred his horse; and a few seconds later, overtook Seyit. He dropped the handkerchief after leaving a gap. This time it was Seyit's turn for acrobatics: he rode toward the bushes where the handkerchief rested, but he rode on the side of the horse with only one foot in the stirrup. Soon after, he passed his friends, waving the handkerchief in the air, and vanished into the beech thicket. Engrossed in this handkerchief race, Mischa and Vladimir were galloping to catch up, whooping and yelling wildly as they tried to join in this tough, thrilling game that they could only watch in a crazy blur of motion.

The four young men rode for a little longer, their course weaving between the slopes parallel to the shore, disappearing in the thick tree cover from time to time, only to reemerge on level ground. After turning inland, away from the shore, they slowed down when they came to the top end of Sadovi Road, a broad expanse flanked by high trees and elegant houses nestling in large gardens. Seyit led the way through the big gate in the high wall. All four felt refreshed by the warm spring breeze in the shade of the trees after that gallop.

"I'll say it again; this is paradise, Seyt." Mischa inhaled the spring air.

"You're welcome to stay any time. Even if I'm not here, my family would be delighted to host you."

"I'll keep that in mind."

Vladimir interjected, having remembered something, "Why didn't Petro come along?"

"I don't know," said Seyit. "Said he had to go to Moscow."

"He's been going there far too often recently. I wonder what he's up to." Suspicion shone in Celil's eyes.

"Yes, he's been quite odd for a while now. He's changed toward us."

Vladimir agreed heartily with Mischa. "That's right; there is something odd. I felt it too. We used to be inseparable. Especially with you, Seyit; you were like brothers. It's like he's grown cold—not just his attitude but even his gaze."

Seyit felt the need to defend his absent friend. "Come on, chaps; you're being unfair. If you ask me, he regrets leaving the military. He's not happy in his father's business. Perhaps being around us reminds him of the life he now misses. Then there is his new life; it doesn't exactly give him the opportunity to be as close to the four of us now."

The others looked unconvinced. Celil sneered. "All the same, I see something quite unfriendly in his eyes. There's something about Petro, something we can't work out."

Seyit was reluctant to pursue the matter, no matter how concerned he might have been about the change in Petro. He'd even heard rumors of Petro attending meetings at the harbor, but there was no point in worrying the others any more just now.

The treelined path ended in a wide clearing; rose bushes flowered in the center of the pebble paving. Pink aloe vera blossoms flourished in carved marble planters flanking the broad marble staircase. Ivy and honeysuckle rose to the upper stories. A tall wooden front door was decorated with stained crystal panes in geometric shapes. In the gloaming of the spring day, the house and garden offered a calm respite, a warm welcome. At the rear, trees much higher than the house signaled the start of the forest.

The riders were dismounting when Cemal's voice rang out. "Well, well, see who's here! Welcome, welcome! We've missed you. Everyone's been looking forward to your arrival."

Arms open wide, Seyit walked toward the smiling steward for a hug. Celil received an equally warm hug, but a more deferential welcome met the two first-time guests. The years seemed to sit lightly on the steward, who handed the reins over to two young stable lads with instructions: "Come on, quick; the horses need sponging down, watering, feeding, and brushing! Quick, quick!"

Throwing an arm over Cemal's shoulder, Seyit walked toward the house as his friends followed. "Well, Cemal, tell me: How is everyone? How's everything?"

Cemal couldn't have been happier if his own son had returned; Master Eminof had grown up in his hands, after all. They were close enough for him to address Seyit by name.

"Everything's fine, Kurt Seyit; everyone's fine. Your father is older, of course, but then who among us is not? Look: even you are getting older!"

By the time they'd reached the door, still chuckling, the whole household was gathered at the entrance: Seyit's father, mother, brothers, and sisters; Hanife's husband; Mahmut; his wife, Mümine; and Osman. Seyit was covered in hugs and kisses; he'd been away for far too long. It was like a festival, and Celil was clearly no stranger. Mischa and Vladimir were introduced to the family, and they all passed through the veranda to the rear garden.

Zahide couldn't take her proud eyes off the son she'd been missing for so long. She might have been forty-one, but with the exception of a few silver strands barely visible in her hair, she showed no outward signs of her age. Slim and elegant, she looked like a big sister to her eldest, Hanife.

In the prime of her beauty at twenty-five, Hanife gazed adoringly at her husband sitting beside her. Little Havva was barely fourteen and as beautiful as the full moon in the Turkish metaphor: huge soft navy-blue eyes gazed happily like lucky evil-eye beads on her clear, pale face. She didn't talk much, but her gaze showed her joy at her big brother's return. Thrilled at the presence of Celil and the other two young men, she was blushing to the roots of her hair.

Mahmut's wife was a willowy Circassian beauty with pale skin and long dark hair. She and Seyit's sixteen-year-old brother, Osman, sat side by side in the garden chair, looking like two young children.

Leaning back in the wrought-iron garden chair, Mirza Eminof proudly watched his big family around him. Now fifty-eight, he had a head of white hair, and an equally white beard framed a face that showed the beginnings of crow's-feet and a few wrinkles on the forehead. He looked in the prime of health, youthful, and agile. He had dedicated himself to his lands, wife, and children since his retirement. He was happy, finally able to do everything he had been longing to do and finally united with his precious wife and children after years of missing them. Except for Seyit. He'd missed his eldest son so much! He had a few things to ask once he'd chatted briefly with each of his son's friends.

In order to avoid offending their guests, Mehmet and Seyit took pains to speak in flawless Russian, indistinguishable from any of the Saint Petersburg nobility. Mischa and Vladimir followed the conversation between father and son in astonishment.

"Why hasn't Petro come, Seyit? He always used to accompany you."

With a warning look at his friends, Seyit answered, "He had to go to Moscow, Father. You know he's working with his father now. I suspect he's been unable to take time off to coincide with our furlough."

Petro was forgotten when pastries and cold lemonade were served. Eminof inquired about the friends he'd not seen for quite a while. "What news of the Moiseyevs, son? Are they in good form?"

"They send you their warmest regards. I believe they're coming to Livadia in the middle of the summer, and they intend to call upon you. Auntie Olga mentioned she was about to write to Mother about the time we were due to leave."

"Petrograd's going to be deserted at this rate," said Vladimir, helping himself to a second glass of lemonade.

Leaning forward tensely, Mehmet's white eyebrows rose. "Are things going that badly then, boys?"

"They don't look that hopeful," replied Mischa. "Petrograd's simmering, as is Moscow."

Settling back in his chair, Mehmet shook his head. "Those fires were lit long ago and have been stoked for years." A smile brightened his somber face. "But nothing's ever managed to empty Saint Petersburg. That city has always had its own appeal—and addicts too."

Seyit winked at his friends, pointing at his father. "And my father is one such!"

"See, Kurt Seyt, your father's not adopted *Petrograd* either!" said Mischa, happy to have found a supporter.

Mehmet laughed. "I'm done with that magnificent city. For me, it will always remain Saint Petersburg. But you, you all have a long life there ahead of you. You are now *Petrogradians*."

Soon everyone had relaxed into a chat, and later they all filed into the dining room. The conversation at the table was deliberately kept light to avoid boring the children and the women. Mischa and Vladimir couldn't praise Zahide's cooking enough. The lamb *tandır* and vegetables would have tempted the fussiest eater with a full stomach. Although he had long since forsworn alcohol, Mehmet happily served his guests vodka. As the party moved to the drawing room facing the garden for their postprandial coffee, he gave Seyit a fond tap on the shoulder.

"It's wonderful to see you here, son. Don't be such a stranger again." He laughed, recalling his own younger years. "Ah, never mind me! I know you can't do anything about it. Don't forget I've trod the same path myself; I know what it's like." He seemed to be wavering. Eventually he couldn't stand it any longer and blurted out the question that had been plaguing him: "Anyone in your life, Seyit?"

"Who do you mean, Father?"

"I don't mean anyone in particular. I'm asking you. You're now twenty-five... around the same age I set my sights on your mother."

"No, Father, there is no such person as yet."

"But you do have liaisons?"

"Erm...of course. I mean, there are some, yes."

"Anyone special?"

That wild affair in Moscow popped into Seyit's mind out of the blue. How he missed his little sweetheart! She was the only woman he could think of. But how was it possible to yearn for a romance he might never experience again?

His silence was as good as an affirmative reply for his father. "Who is it? Do I know her father?"

"I don't think so. She's from Kislovodsk, the daughter of Julian Verjensky."

"Military man?"

"No, he owns mines. Shura's older brothers are in the army. And her maternal aunt's husband is General Afrikan Petrovich Bogayevsky, the ataman of the Don Cossacks."

Mehmet Eminof looked impressed. "An important man...a very important man. One of the most reputable people in the empire after the tsar himself." He changed the subject. "What's she like?"

Even the recollection of their time together filled Seyit with a thrill. Was he falling for her? "Shura? She's beautiful. Her name's Alexandra, but she prefers Shura. She's very young yet."

"You're not thinking of marrying her, are you?"

"Marrying? The idea hasn't even crossed my mind yet, Father. Wouldn't it be madness, thinking of something like that, just when I'm about to go to the front?"

"Very well...and when the idea *does* cross your mind, you'll pick a girl from around here. Don't forget: Russian women are ideal to teach men about life and love, but you will eventually have a wife, and she will be a girl from here."

Seyit nodded wordlessly. Somehow his tongue refused to issue the promise his father expected. Eminof placed his hand on his son's shoulder. "Come along then; doesn't do to keep our guests waiting for much longer."

When they rejoined the others in the drawing room, the young men stood to offer him their seats.

The bright-green leaves of the great plane tree in the garden shimmered in the breeze, rustling softly against the window. Seyit recalled lying in the circumcision bed, watching the party in the garden; now he stood here as an adult and a lieutenant to boot. How long ago it all was! He recalled how innocent he'd been then, how daunted at the prospect of things to come. Was it any different now? No. A week from now, they would set off on yet another adventure into the unknown. No one had mentioned it yet, as if reluctant to spoil the evening.

"How does it feel to be back home, Seyt?" Vladimir spoke slowly, exhausted at the end of the day, relaxing in this warm company and the vodka he'd consumed at the table.

Seyit seemed to inhale everything in his field of vision as his gaze wandered over the house, the garden, and the branches of the plane tree soaring into the sky above their heads. "Feels wonderful..." he mused. "Wonderful."

Having lost his parents at a very young age, Vladimir had been raised by his sister, who was ten years his senior, and her husband, a landowner from Moscow. He might not have been particularly handsome, but he was a very good husband, who had willingly taken his wife's younger brother under his wing and raised him as his own son. Affectionate as they were, however, Vladimir had always missed having a real family. On that invigorating spring evening, his yearning surfaced in Seyit's family home. Years in the military had taught Mehmet Eminof that people without parents missed home most. His heart went out to the young man facing him.

"This is your home too, Vladimir. I hope you share Seyit's feelings."

"Thank you, sir; we'll never forget it," replied his guest gratefully.

The conversation deepened and eventually came to the signs of revolution in Petrograd and Moscow. Eminof was profoundly troubled at the prospect of these bright young men going to the Carpathians to war and possibly even to their deaths. They looked so young, so wet behind the ears! He did his best to conceal his worries.

"What I can't understand is," he said, "how they could even bring themselves to divide the nation in the midst of a war!"

"At the outset, everyone seemed to be united. But I suspect the government failed to capitalize on that. Instead, they tried to disenfranchise the Duma. Losses at the front, of course, also divided opinion further."

The others nodded as they listened to Mischa.

"And worst of all is the fragmentation in the army, Father."

"Witte would have prevented all this if he'd been around. This Goremykin fellow...what's his attitude?"

"Regretfully, sir, Goremykin's only stoked hatred of the tsar," Mischa said. "He is responsible for the dismissal of the liberal ministers who'd supported the National Cabinet. And neither is he particularly popular with the aristocracy. Thankfully he was forced to resign in February."

"Is that so? I had no idea. Moiseyev's latest letter referred to him."

"Father, resignations in Petrograd move faster than letters to Alushta!" Seyit leaned back with a booming laugh, and the others joined in.

"So who's the lucky fellow now?"

"Stürmer, sir."

"Stürmer...Master of Ceremonies Stürmer?"

"Yes, sir, the very same."

Eminof shook his head, lifting his eyebrows and curling his lips in an unmistakable expression of disbelief. "I'm sure Saint Petersburg has men capable of rational decisions in such times. Where are they all?"

"Rationality and capability no longer appear to be prerequisites for advancement in court these days, sir."

Mischa's apparent vehemence elicited a cheerful explanation from Vladimir. "Mischa's mother's quite close to the tsarina. That's how he gets to follow all this so closely."

But Mischa was incensed all the more.

"These fools will upset the whole system; can't you see? Things that could have been checked a few years ago are now out of control. The people on the streets are divided like never before. You can't tell friend from foe any longer. Even the academy student body is breaking up into factions, I hear. Ultimately it will be the man on the street who gets the blame. It all stems from bad government. The venerable empire is crumbling. There is a war on, and people are dying. It's our turn to step into the breach. We may die too, but for whom? The tsar or Lenin?"

"What difference would it make once you're dead?" asked Vladimir.

"A lot. It matters a lot if some scoundrel living in Switzerland's gonna rule the Russia I die for." The more Mischa spoke, the more he worked himself up. His face was bright red. Combing his hair back from his forehead with his fingers, he continued, "As a matter of fact, they'll never let us live, even if we survive the war." Suddenly weary, he rested his head on the chair back, took a deep breath, and murmured, "How peaceful and calm it is here! Like the safest place on earth."

"I'm not sure any such place exists." Mehmet stood up. "Boys, stay up if you like, but I must take my leave now. I'm not as young as you; I need my rest. We'll talk again to our hearts' content tomorrow."

They all stood up to wish him good night.

"Forgive me, sir," said Mischa guiltily. "I've bored you. I'm afraid I got a little carried away."

Mehmet gave his shoulder a fatherly pat. "You don't need to apologize at all, young man; I had a great time. At any rate, getting carried away is the most natural thing for people of your age. It only becomes dangerous at my age. Never regret your passions, son."

He left, and the young men sat back down. They were exhausted and sleepy, yet the idea of going to bed was the farthest thing from their minds. Before long, Mahmut and Osman also left but not before hugging their brother tightly, as if they'd only just got together.

"It's great having you here, Seyit. I wish we could always be together."

Knowing Mahmut meant it, Seyit gave him another hug. "I know, Mahmut; I know. So do I."

Vladimir teased to hide his own emotions at this display of fraternal affection. "They're quite crowded even without you, Kurt Seyt. Don't think anyone needs you!"

Chuckling, they sent the younger men off.

"You know, lads," said Celil, who'd been silent for a while, "I wish I could swap places with one of those young men. Wouldn't it be lovely to hug my pretty wife in bed instead of tossing and turning with the nightmare of the Carpathians?"

"Need a wife to hug first," Mischa pointed out.

"What about Tatya then?" interjected Vladimir.

Celil objected in a murmur. "Not the same thing at all."

"How would you know? Have you ever been married?"

"And by the way, how long have you been together?"

Seyit's question made him think. "Three years, I think...perhaps a little longer."

"Has she never wanted to marry you?"

"Tatya? I don't know; I never got that impression. I guess we're both satisfied with things as they are."

Mischa slouched a little deeper, extended his legs, crossed them, and looked at Celil. "Just in case you ever break up, remember to let me know, all right?"

"No!" exclaimed Vladimir. "You've had your eye on Tatya, eh? I can't believe it, Mischa."

Laughter dispelled the tension of the recent topics of discussion.

"Not just me...so many men have their eyes on her. As if you didn't know!"

Untroubled by the turn in the conversation, Celil just chuckled, until Seyit teased him into a semblance of possessiveness. "Why don't you say something? Our chum's quite liberal in his expression of admiration for your sweetheart!"

"Don't get any ideas, Mischa; I'm not about to let her go."

"But you're not going to marry her either, are you?"

"Who knows? We might," replied Celil with a smile that left the others wondering.

"Then make sure you don't die at the front. Because I'm not going to. The one who gets back wins her."

"You're both in cloud-cuckoo-land," Vladimir pointed out. "Every night, hundreds of men will admire her long legs until your return. One of them is certain to win her favor."

"Is it true that she has the longest legs in the Bolshoi?"

Mischa's question amused Celil so much that his eyes disappeared altogether.

"Don't know; I've not measured them all!"

Remembering there was more to life than war, they had all cheered up.

Prompted by this talk of women, Vladimir asked, "So how do you have fun around here, Kurt Seyt?"

Seyit and Celil exchanged glances and grinned.

"Really, Seyt—isn't there anywhere around here where we can have a couple of hours of fun before we go to the front?"

"Have a few days of fun, if you like," said Celil.

"Stay until the summer, even," added Seyit.

Throwing his head back and raising his arms, Mischa gave a heavy sigh. "I'd love to oblige, but we have no time. Two or three hours on the outside ought to do the trick."

"In that case, let's call it a night and rest a little," said Seyit.

The young men all sat up.

"But you've not told us anything yet, Seyt! Where are we going? What are the girls like? Is there a beautiful brunette among them?"

Mischa received a friendly punch on the shoulder from Seyit, who had joined Celil in a chuckle.

"To be honest, Mischa, I'm not going to be able to help you there. You'll just have to take whatever you get. All right, gentlemen, time for a little rest. We'll need our strength tomorrow night. Come—I'll show you to your rooms."

Taking care not to disturb the sleeping household, the young men ascended the stairs in the gaslight. Seyit showed Mischa and Vladimir into their rooms; each door he opened revealed a bed made up with lavender-scented broderie anglaise linen, inviting the guests to sleep.

"If you want to take a bath before bed, the hamam downstairs is hot. Let's see how you like a Crimean-style *banya*! I'm going there with Celil now."

"My eyelids are beginning to droop, but I wouldn't say no to a hot bath," admitted Vladimir.

"We're on our way!" added Mischa.

"Fine; get your stuff. We'll wait for you in the hall, under the stairs."

The size of a large room, the Turkish-style marble bathroom in the Eminof house was the ideal place to wash away the exhaustion of the day: polished cop-per bowls rested on carved marble bath bowls called *kurna*, and snow-white towels lay stacked on the marble shelf behind the door and low wooden stools.

Steam rose from the kurnas, and the young men were soon filling their copper bowls with cold water from the brass taps to rinse away the journey.

"Aaah!" said Mischa. "This is wonderful! I'm going to have one built in my own place one day!"

"I could just fall asleep here, chaps," purred Vladimir, already stretched out on the hot marble, eyes shut.

"Come along then; it's time to go upstairs. I'm sure you'll be more comfortable in bed," urged Seyit, tugging his arm.

By the time they had wrapped themselves in thick bathrobes and trundled upstairs silently, thoroughly relaxed, faces flushed from the heat, all they could think of was a soft bed to sink into and a night of undisturbed slumber.

***

Yalta was home to much more than fertile lands stretching along the shore; a sunny, warm climate; and forests of ageless trees. Elegant houses along the forest near the shore, set far enough away so that no two overlooked each other, usually belonged to the wealthy and the aristocracy who chose to spend their summers away from their Moscow or Saint Petersburg homes. Designed with no concessions to the short-term occupancy, every house gave sufficient clues to the social standing and financial situation of its owner.

These summer residences would start to fill from the middle of May onward. The gardens and windows burst into life as the servants arrived first, threw open the shutters and thick curtains to invite the sunshine in, and set about cleaning the rooms, which had dozed in the dark throughout the winter. Occasionally, younger children and their nannies and governesses also arrived in this first wave.

On this cheerful spring morning, Yalta's forests were waking up to birdsong and sunshine that warmed seasonal visitors to the bone.

Early in the morning, the previous day's exhaustion long since forgotten, the four young men went for a ride in riding trousers, casual shirts, and jumpers. The sun was so warm that as soon as they reached the terraced vineyard, the jumpers came off. Weaving among the burgeoning vines, they reached the lunch table under the trellis of the vineyard house shaded by beeches and alders.

The two-story house was a delightful, cozy structure in stone and furnished quite simply. It commanded a fabulous view on the crest of the hill that seemed to reach out to the sea. The trellis was thick with vines and honeysuckle, a green frame to the blues of the sea and the sky.

The young men tethered their horses, washed their faces in water drawn from the well, sat down, and downed their *ayran* in one go. Once the chilled yogurt drink went down, they attacked the food like hungry wolves.

"You're so lucky, Kurt Seyt. What a blessing to have such lands to come back to! I'm green with envy."

"Thank you, Mischa. But these lands have also witnessed such desolation that it's difficult to say what the future might hold."

"Never mind the doom and gloom; what are we doing tonight? Where are you going to take us?"

"Vladimir, can't you think of anything else, for God's sake?"

"No, Mischa; I *can't* think of anything else. I even dreamed of women all night long. Come on; tell me now: What's the plan for tonight?"

"Who says we have to wait for the night, Seyit?" asked Celil with a wink.

Tapping the cleft in his chin ostensibly in contemplation, Seyit dawdled deliberately to tease his friends, who waited on pins and needles. "Absolutely not! The days are ours, as are the nights!"

"Yippee!"

Vladimir leaped up from the table, swinging his jumper in the air, and the others followed. The servant bringing the fruit platter out spotted his charges leaving the table; he burst into profuse apologies for his tardiness, but thankfully Seyit knew how to soothe him with compliments and an enormous grin. "Don't worry, Ismail Efendi. We've got to go on an errand now; we'll have the fruit some other time. Thank you."

Before long they were back in the forest, merry as children on their way to a fairground.

On a path too narrow for anything wider than a single carriage, they drew aside to make way for the coach they heard approaching. The suitcases piled up next to the coachman obscured the passengers from view; it was only when the coach passed them that Seyit spotted the young woman sitting between two little girls. A wide grin broke out on his face. She smiled back with a faint nod. As soon as the coach passed, three young men whistled.

"Who else could find a lady to greet in the middle of the forest? Fortune went past in a coach, Seyit."

Mischa's tease elicited a laugh.

"Not fortune, Mischa. An old friend—a very old friend."

"Do we get to meet her too?" asked Vladimir.

"No," said Celil, patting his mate's horse on the head. "Sadly, that belle's not going to have any time to meet you."

"Why not?"

"Because whenever she comes here, Seyit makes her acquaintance anew and commandeers all her time!"

"Who is she, for God's sake?" insisted Vladimir, still laughing.

Closing his eyes as if sniffing a delicate flower, Celil replied, "Larissa, lovely Larissa, governess to the Arkadiev children. Daughter of a Frenchwoman who originally came here as a governess before marrying a wealthy Russian and settling down in Moscow. Aristocratic families were vying to hire her." Cocking an eye at Seyit, he carried on, "And until the Arkadievs arrive, she takes good care of a handsome friend of ours whenever he's around."

As they chuckled, Seyit shook his head. "I can't cope with you lot, so I'll be making my excuses soon."

Mischa was worried they might have gone too far. "Don't go, Seyt; we were going to have such a good time! Where are you going?"

Without a word, Seyit turned his horse's head toward the garden of the big house they were passing.

Celil's chuckle allayed any concern the others might have. "Don't worry, Mischa; he's not leaving because he's cross. This is the Arkadiev house. Our Kurt Seyt's stop, in other words. He's going to call upon his governess."

"What about us?" asked Vladimir. "Seyt's sorted out!"

Seyit turned his horse back to the crossroads and trotted back. "Celil, you know where to take them." And he cautioned the others. "You're in Celil's capable hands now, chaps. I'm sure you'll have a great time. Let's meet back in the vineyard house; it would look strange if we straggled back home separately. Have a good time."

"You too! Mind your governess doesn't lay you down to sleep."

"You too; mind you're not caught by the master of the house!"

They parted, still chuckling.

Seyit saw the coach outside the house as the luggage was removed. Larissa stood on the steps, holding the two children by the hands, but her eyes were on the forest road. Knowing she was looking out for him, he emerged, rode toward the house, and bowed when he came to the door. "A very good day to you."

Larissa replied with a bashful smile. "And a very good day to you too."

"I was wondering if Mr. Arkadiev had arrived; I wished to present my respects to him."

Watched curiously by the housekeeper and the footmen, the young woman replied in a highly formal tone, "No, not yet. Mr. and Mrs. Arkadiev are expected in ten days' time, I believe."

Seyit tugged on one rein to turn his horse's head around. "Thank you; I shall call then."

Bowing once again, he went into the forest, dismounted, and waited. The governess handed the children to the housekeeper, grasped her shawl in one hand and the skirts of her pink chiffon gown with the other, and vanished inside the house.

Seyit tethered his horse away from curious eyes, skirted the garden in a broad circle, went to the rear of the house, and carried on waiting. The shutters were still in place. Soon a French door in one of the rear rooms opened a crack. Seyit snuck through the flowerbeds, slipped in, and shut the door behind him. Not a single ray of daylight penetrated the thick curtains. His eyes would need to adjust, but the room was familiar enough. A warm breath on his face brought him to the person who was waiting. Without a single word, they were locked in a passionate kiss. The young woman's skin glowed with an internal heat that defied her clothes; at any rate, the flimsy chiffon offered every curve to the touch generously enough to arouse even the stoniest of men.

Slipping from his hands, she whispered, "Wait, Seyt; wait a little. I have to see to the children. I had no idea I'd be seeing you as soon I arrived! Give me half an hour. I must feed and put them to bed."

But Seyit pulled her closer, grasping her by the waist, unwilling to release this soft, warm creature in his hands.

"And what do you expect me to do with myself in that half hour?"

Tantalizing fingers mussed his hair; reaching up to his neck, she breathed. "I can take you upstairs to my room without anyone noticing. No one will dare go in there. And I'll come up just as soon as I'm done."

Slipping out of his arms, she tiptoed to the door, opened it a little, looked out, stepped into the hall, and came back a few moments later. "Quick!" she said. "Follow me before anyone else turns up. Go through the door under the stairs to your right as soon as you're out."

Whipped up by this childish thrill, he followed her to the imperial staircase. The governess tugged at the gilt frame of the enormous mirror hanging between two planters to reveal a secret door.

"Quick! Through here. The stairs are quite narrow; take care. First room on the left upstairs. I'll go upstairs and unlock the door."

She shut the mirrored door behind him without waiting for an answer. Seyit patted the cramped, dark void until he located the handrail and began ascending the spiral staircase, silently chuckling as he watched his step so that he wouldn't trip. The stairs ended in a door; this had to be the door she'd mentioned. Holding his breath, he waited for a signal, his ear on the door. No one came. He tried the knob; it was locked from the outside. He was stuck on a dark staircase between two closed doors. Just when he was about to berate himself, he heard soft footsteps. Then a key turned in the lock. Seyit waited with bated breath. The idea that it might be someone other than Larissa was chilling. Far better to have come through the front door and announced he had come to make love to the governess than to be caught ignominiously on a back staircase.

He had worried needlessly. No one entered once the door was unlocked. This had to be Larissa's sign. He could step outside now. Sticking his head out slowly, he saw that the corridor was safe and bolted out, making for the first room on the left as instructed. It was empty; Larissa must have been busy with the children. Her suitcases were open, and some of her belongings were placed at the foot of the bed. Settling into the big armchair behind the screen that shielded the bed from the door, Seyit started waiting. He was no stranger to this room, and he had to admit he'd missed coming here.

His mind went to Shura. He tried to compare the two women. It was no good. There wasn't a single point of comparison. They were like chalk and cheese. Larissa exuded passion. Everything she said or did evoked a carnal association—be it a word, a seemingly innocent touch on her own body, or the permanently languid gaze. Seyit couldn't figure out for the life of him how such a woman could be employed as a governess. Perhaps she minded her behavior when she was with children.

Any man would regard Shura, on the other hand, as an ideal life partner. She had everything going for her in addition to her father's social standing and wealth: an excellent education and a patrician beauty that would turn heads even on the street. Shura would never stoop to any wiles like Larissa's. That she knew she was the focus of attention and admired was indisputable, but she acted as though it didn't matter to her in the least. And that made her even more attractive. Her warmth offset her inexperience and lack of any sexual overtures. Seyit had, all the same, discovered the woman latent underneath her quiet and dignified purity. He recalled their lovemaking when they were alone, the hours of unbridled passion that had started with soft, romantic kisses.

He'd been astonished and flattered that he was her first. Shura was the first woman who truly belonged to him—a maiden who had offered him her most intimate side, her innocence. He delighted in the thought that only he knew the storms hidden beneath that serene and mild nature. Only he knew she was made for love.

But what would happen next? Such a lovely girl could have her pick of suitors. Even the idea of all those men he didn't know was enough to trigger a highly unwelcome emotion, another first for him: jealousy. How he wished she were here with him now! His pulse quickened at the mere thought. His throat dried, and he felt feverish. He recalled their passionate lovemaking, hiplength blond hair swishing over their bodies, when they'd both known that was the first and last time. He didn't feel at all well. He needed her now, a sick man desperate for his medicine—which was miles away. He stood up and washed his face in the china bowl on a stand. Patting his neck, he tried to cool down.

He must have been lost in a daydream when the door opened. He hid behind the screen once again; fortunately, it was Larissa. "Are you here, Seyt?"

Seyit emerged as she locked the door and dashed over to hug him tight. Clasping his head between her hands, she opened her lips and pressed them on his, kissing him as if she would suck his blood and life while she wriggled against his body.

The ideal partner for a man pressed for time! thought Seyit. Then he thought of Shura. How different it would be if Shura had stepped into the room just now! She wouldn't have dashed over like this woman now writhing in his arms. No. She would walk in slow, confident steps, her gaze locked on his—a deep gaze full of love, whispering of the pleasure she was about to offer him—close her eyes, snuggle up, present her lips for a kiss, and wait. Seyit would happily take his time for the hours of passion that serene embrace promised, at the end of which they would both be thoroughly sated with each other's bodies, from the ends of the hair on their heads to the tips of their toes.

My God, he thought, *I'm holding a woman desperate to satisfy my every desire, and here I am dreaming of another miles away.*

Larissa could never take Shura's place but used her allure, experience, and insatiable desire to make Seyit forget what was on his mind for a few minutes. Once the man in her bed was temporarily sated, she fell asleep in his arms. Seyit lay musing, his free arm under his head when he was awestruck at recognizing something for the first time. He had come here for Larissa, yet he'd felt as if he were with his little Shura throughout. It was the thought of her that had aroused him, the recollection of making love to her that had taken him to bed. He had actually made love to the Shura of his dreams. Another woman lay beside him now, a woman who evoked a sense of guilt at having betrayed his lover. He now knew he belonged to Shura. Yes—he had made love to Larissa as a substitute for Shura.

Good God; I never knew I was in love! he thought, instantly regretting how he'd missed it all this time.

He had no wish to stay here any longer. He withdrew his arm gently lest he awaken Larissa, rose, and dressed in total silence. He darted through the door to the secret staircase and descended furtively. There was no one to watch out for him this time. The hall seemed to ring with the hurried footsteps of the servants; another coach must have arrived with more luggage. He sat down on the bottom step for what turned out to be quite a long wait. Eventually the noises died down, and he heard the front door close. All was quiet at long last. The household must have all retired to their rooms. He left the same way he had entered. It was growing dark. He untethered his horse, mounted, cast a final look at the house behind him, and smiled at the time he had spent there. He didn't think he would ever be back.

***

The others had not yet returned to the vineyard house when Seyit arrived. He was tethering his horse to a tree outside the house when Ismail Efendi charged out, surprised at seeing him back after all these hours.

"What's the matter, sir? Is everything all right?"

Seyit spoke as he strode toward the trellis. "Remember I said we'd have the fruit later? Here I am!"

Somewhat bemused, the servant rushed back into the kitchen.

Seyit called out as he sat down, stretching his legs up to another chair, "Lower a bottle of vodka into the well to cool it; my friends will be back soon."

"Very well, sir, at once." Ismail Efendi dashed back inside.

In the feeble light of the gas lantern hanging from the side of the trellis, the colors of the descending night and the sea blended. He could hear crickets in the vineyard. Seyit shivered in a sudden chill wind. He lit a cigarette and rested his head against the back of the chair. He felt an indescribable disquiet, as though he was and yet was not here. He had no idea where he wanted to be just now. He recalled their arrival in Saint Petersburg together with his father, the days they'd spent in Tsarskoye Selo, meeting the Moiseyevs, enrolling at the academy, and sending his father off to the Japanese war. He had felt the same inner shiver that morning too. Many years had gone by since then. He was no longer that callow, timid boy. He now knew both Petrograd and Moscow like the back of his hand and had countless friends. The house in Tsarskoye Selo was an escape for them all. And all his family here in Alushta were in fine form. So where did this disquiet come from? Many houses in many places, different people and different customs. Where did he belong? Where would he settle down? Whom would he love enough to marry? His father had told him to sow his wild oats until the age of thirty and then marry a girl from around here. Yet today Seyit had realized he wanted Shura and no other. What about marriage? What would happen when it was time to marry? What would his parents do if he wanted to marry Shura? His brother had married a Tatar girl. She was beautiful, came from a great family, and made her husband very happy. Wouldn't his father hold them up as an example? If his father were to give his consent, would Shura come here to live? Perhaps yes, perhaps no. What about him? Where would he like to live for the rest of his life? Since the age of twelve, he'd spent more time with the Moiseyevs in Petrograd and the Tsarskoye Selo home than here in Alushta.

"Where do I belong?" he asked himself under his breath.

Ismail, who was laying out the cheese, fruit, and roasted chickpeas, thought Seyit was addressing him. "Did you say something, sir?"

Lowering his gaze from the stars twinkling above, Seyit gave a dismissive wave. "No, no, I wasn't speaking to you, Ismail Efendi. Is the vodka cool now? Bring me a glass then."

He looked at his pocket watch. It was nine o'clock already. Stroking the crystal, he gazed at the watch again, a present from Tsar Nicholas II after Seyit had won an equestrian competition two years ago. Seyit usually did well in these events held between members of Moscow's Manezh Riding School and cavalry officers and was already the proud owner of several decorations pinned by the tsar himself. But this watch was something he could also wear in mufti, which made it doubly special. It was a round gold case on a long golden chain, and the lid was engraved with his initials in enamel and tiny rubies. The warmth in his palm reminded him of life in Petrograd. Yet the briny breeze, the scent of the green vine leaves surrounding him, and the yielding fertility of the soil under his feet all seemed to repeat, "You belong to us."

He filled his tiny glass with ice-cold vodka, downed it in one, and took a deep drag of his cigarette. Instead of calming his restlessness, contemplation had proved to be all the more confusing. How he wished little Shura were with him now! All he wanted was to cuddle her and sleep for hours and hours. Just knowing she was there would have been enough. Suddenly overwhelmed by a desire to be reunited with his love, he wanted to drop everything and go to her. He got up and paced under the trellis.

This has to be the vodka! What on earth was I thinking? He was due to leave in three days' time, perhaps never to return—and here he was, trying to decide whether to live in Alushta or Petrograd!

The sound of galloping hooves brought him back to his senses. His friends were back. And clearly tipsy, if the laughter and chatter were anything to go by. They flocked to the table like so many merry children.

"We didn't think we'd find you here," chimed Celil, before noticing his friend's pensive expression. Leaning down, he inquired, "Is something the matter, Seyit? You don't look well."

Seyit filled the empty glasses with vodka. "Nothing's the matter, Celil—just thinking a little."

"You should have come along, Kurt Seyt," said Mischa. "We had a great time. My God! What a bevy of angels. So unfair. Them hiding in this forest, I mean!"

Well oiled by this time, eyes shut, swaying to the back and sides as he chuckled, Vladimir was murmuring a song.

"I bet Seyt's had a great time too. Right, Seyt? Come on; tell us: What'd'ya do? How was your governess?"

Seyit couldn't suppress a smile that shook off the earlier gloom. "Never mind me; what about you three? You must have more to tell, seeing as you've had so much fun."

Mischa swallowed a slice of apple and chased it with his vodka, teasing Celil all the while.

"Go on, Celil—tell him!" Unable to remember what he wanted to say, he paused and carried on. "Where was it...whose house was it?"

Celil drew up a chair next to Seyit. "The Ulyashins' place."

"Aha! Now I know what kept you so long. Which of the girls were there?"

"All three. And a cook's assistant too. A peach." Pointing to the two drunken Russians, Celil chuckled. "And she was the one who brought these two young bucks to heel. She's quite something, they say."

When the bottle of vodka was gone, Seyit stood up. "Come on, chaps; it's midnight. Time to get back."

Mumbling a song, a half-sleepy, half-drunk Mischa grasped the table he was resting on and grumbled, slurring his words. "You're not taking me anywhere. Gonna lie down right here. You lot can go."

The others helped him up and placed him on his saddle. Seyit called out to the servant sheltering in the porch, "Good-bye, Ismail Efendi; thank you. I'll be seeing you."

"Good-bye, sir; safe home now."

The young men started out, chatting about their evening escapades. Halfway to the house, Seyit left the narrow path, turned into the depths of the forest, and called, "Come on—this way!"

"Where's he taking us now?" asked Vladimir.

"To the lake," replied Celil.

"To the lake?"

"Only way to sober up after a night like this."

"You're crazy," objected Vladimir. "It's cool, and it's midnight; bet the water's icy."

"Too bad! It's all part of the fun. Better get used to it if you want to live like us here!"

Soon they reached a little lake on level ground, fed by a forest stream.

"Nothing like it to clear the head after women and vodka," said Seyit. He stripped and dived into the icy waters of the lake. Celil followed. Dragging their feet, Vladimir and Mischa undressed reluctantly and shivered on the spot as their eyes gradually adjusted to the darkness.

Then the moon emerged above the treetops and transformed the scene into a breathtaking tableau: they were standing on the banks of an enchanted lake in an enchanted forest. Moved by this singularly lovely night, no longer aware of his chattering teeth, Mischa whooped and launched his impressive body into the lake. Startled at the splash breaking the gelid calm of the surface, birds perching nearby flew away with a frenetic beating of wings. He emerged a fair way down and called to his chum standing on the bank. "Come on, Vladimir! What are you waiting for? They're right; it's marvelous! You'll feel like a new man; come on now."

The water was ice cold—cold enough to revive bodies after hours of passion; all that vodka; and despite the feigned bravado, all thoughts of war gnawing at their minds. Icy needles gave every single nerve a new lease of life.

They climbed out, refreshed, shivering naked in the cool, damp forest air... and thoroughly sobered up.

"*Now* we're in a fit state to go back," said Seyit, putting on his shirt.

"Is this a regular thing, Seyt?" asked Mischa.

"Yes—the only way to end these little escapades."

"You're lucky; it's mild now. Then there's winter, see."

"Nooo. Celil? Don't tell me you come here for a swim in the winter."

"You'll see. If it's written that we should come back, we'll do so in the winter and give you a swim in the ice."

"It's good to return home sober." Seyit chuckled. He turned to Celil to ask, "Remember the night we slept in the snow?"

They both burst out laughing, and Celil launched into the story. "How could I possibly forget? One night, we were thoroughly soused. Snow lay knee deep. Barely made it to the lake. We must have taken our time to sober up; when we got home, all the doors were locked. Major Eminof must've decided to punish us. There wasn't a single window or door left unlocked."

"We were only seventeen at the time, mind!" added Seyit.

"And? What did you do?" asked Vladimir curiously.

"Had no choice but to lie down on the bench under the trellis!" Seyit was laughing so hard that tears were running down his cheeks. "Can you imagine? It was snowing on us! We were too blotto to stay indoors anyway."

"So what did you do in the morning?"

"Steward Cemal awakened us in the morning. We snuck in through the rear door, went up to our rooms, brushed up, and went down to breakfast as if nothing had happened."

"Didn't your father figure out you were late?"

"'Course he did! First thing he said was, 'You were too late last night.' Then he added, 'When I looked in the morning, there wasn't much snow on you'—all while staring us down, mind you!"

"I was mortified like never before," said Celil, "but now I look back, and it's quite funny."

"I'm sure we'll laugh at the memory of these days—many years from now, I mean," said Mischa.

Looking at one another, they repeated, "Many years from now..."

It sounded more like a question than a pledge. They halted and hugged.

A smattering of birds fluttered past, breaking up the melancholy descending over the forest. The crickets around the lake sounded weary. The moon slipped between the beeches and vanished behind the hill.

Thus ended another night in a Yalta forest.

The Carpathian Front, 1916

THE FRONT WAS a living hell.

For months the Russian army had been stationed on the flatlands leading to the Hungarian plains. The field guns and the explosions of the sixteen-inch German shells sounded no more distant than if they had landed in the middle of the encampment in the forest. Every shell shook the ground in a man-made earthquake. Night was transformed into day by flames that lacerated the skies between plumes of smoke rising from the gouged soil. Troops who had been trudging field guns forward not so long ago lay pulverized, their remains strewn over those gouges and charred debris of bushes, peppered with shattered pieces of their gun carriages. A scene painted in a grim color, one single color defined the garments on the bodies covered in blood, sweat, and soil and everything around them: a coal-black gray.

Some of the bodies were still on fire. Some of the living lay heavily wounded. Some lay in comas as others prayed for a merciful death.

It had taken an interminably tough struggle to repulse the Austro-Hungarian troops back beyond the plain. The only difference between the men at the front and those in the encampment was that the latter didn't actually engage in hand-to-hand combat.

The medical team in the village a little farther back consisted of two military doctors and a handful of volunteers. Ramshackle lean-tos of locally felled timber and a number of tents augmented the pathetically inadequate emergency and surgery facilities in what was little more than a small house.

A heavy stream of casualties flowed day and night on the narrow road between this corner of the forest and the front in wagons, more patch than solid coachwork, and on weary horses. Medical volunteers had long since regretted their decision to forsake their soft beds in towns and cities. It was too late by the time they had realized they had come to inhale the breath of death in this far corner of Russia. No one therefore voiced any complaint or fear, seeking solace in a frenzied tempo of work instead. That tempo was ubiquitous. Volunteer nurses did all they could to save the wounded, but in the majority of cases, all that effort proved to be futile. Supplies were running low. No provisions had arrived from behind the lines for a few weeks now. Stitching back torn organs or cutting off a part that would turn gangrenous had become unbearable torment for the doctors. Anesthetics had run out. Young men tried to brave it out at first, too proud to scream or moan in pain, but bodies riddled with shards of shrapnel or half taken away by a shell knew no pride when the surgeon's knife cut through nerve and muscle, when the saw bit into bone. They cried at the top of their voices and screamed until they fell unconscious. Some mercifully never regained consciousness and expired on the table from loss of blood; they were relatively fortunate.

The corpses left on the battlefield were burned, smashed into pulp, and scattered by a new volley of gunfire. These poor wretches were destined for more than one grave; in the fullness of time, covered by new soil, bushes and weeds would sprout over the pieces that had once comprised a complete human being.

Two officers covered in dust from top to toe galloped down the road from the encampment, leaped off their horses outside the hospital hut, and bolted up to the door. A nurse bending over a new arrival drew aside to let them pass.

"Where's the doctor?"

Momentarily speechless at the sight of the gaping hole in the casualty's belly, her eyes as wide as saucers, she pointed to the tent at the side. The officers ran into the tent, where the wounded were all but stacked. The doctor, who was checking an amputated leg, raised his head at the sight of the men dashing in.

"First Lieutenant Eminof, Doctor. We're looking for a friend."

"Who is it? When was he brought here?"

"Lieutenant Vladimir Savinkov, cavalry. Must've been among the casualties rescued after the latest battle."

The doctor lowered the leg back to the bed, the look on his face saying he wasn't holding much hope for the amputee's chances. He took a deep breath.

"Too many casualties come in too fast to keep track of names. Ask the matron, though; she might be able to help you from the register. Then there are patients who arrive unaccompanied or in a coma. We only learn their names if they survive and come to. Occasionally others come looking for their mates, like you, and that helps with identification. Feel free to look around. I'm sorry I can't be of more help."

"Don't worry; we've taken up too much of your time as it is. Thanks."

Outside the tent, Seyit looked around, hesitated, and turned to his friend.

"Celil, you take the tents, and I'll look in the building. That might be quicker."

"Very well, Seyit."

Staring at the occupants of the beds between wooden pillars, Seyit was horrified. He had seen far worse sights on the battlefield, where such scenes somehow belonged. Behind the lines, though, the horror was far too stark. There weren't enough beds, so casualties had been lined up on stretchers alongside the walls. It stank of blood, pus, and disinfectant.

Seyit couldn't see Vladimir anywhere. Some of the faces were mutilated beyond recognition, and he had to peer again and again. It would have been almost impossible to recognize Vladimir if he were among them.

He kneeled next to a soldier on a stretcher by the far side of the wall, whose face was completely covered with bandages. They were red, soaked in blood throughout. Only the mouth area of the young man had been left unwrapped. It appeared deep as a well through which he was trying to gasp for air with great rasping sounds. He had no lips or teeth. Seyit shot up to his feet, with his hands on his stomach, barely holding back the onset of nausea.

He cast a glance at the nurse by the next bed; she was cradling the head of a dying man. The poor fellow, who couldn't have been much older than twenty, managed to swallow the first mouthful when she tilted the glass to his lips. The second sip frothed and ran back into the glass and over his chin. His dying wish granted, his body tensed and quivered. His eyes were still open when his head rolled onto her chest. She laid his head down on the pillow and closed his eyes without bothering to wipe herself own. With a lump in his throat, Seyit watched her draw the sheet over the dead young man. This golden heart evidently came from a good family, as suggested by her manners; she had slender, neatly manicured hands and a graceful gait. Like her fellow idealists, she must have volunteered for Princess Tatiana's charity. A profound compassion for the young woman he would never see again swelled in Seyit's heart.

She stood up to attend to her living patients and caught his eye. "Did you know him?"

Seyit shook his head. "No...never saw him before. I was actually looking for someone else..."

"You didn't find him here?"

"I can't see anyone who looks like him. His name is Vladimir Savinkov. Lieutenant Savinkov." Pointing to the soldier on the stretcher, he asked, "That soldier on the stretcher, the one with the bandages over his face...I wonder if you know his name."

The nurse replied, her face full of pity, "Oh, that poor wretch! He's unlikely to last long. We don't know his name, but as far as we can make out, he's a gunner. Is that the man you're looking for?"

Relieved that the casualty in such an awful state wasn't Vladimir after all, he tried to smile. There was still hope that Vladimir might only be lightly injured.

"No, it isn't. Looks like I won't find him here. Thank you. God bless you."

"It's good to see some people still believe in God." She hastened to explain when confronted with Seyit's quizzical stare. "Don't misunderstand—my own faith is unshakeable. But I've seen so many casualties rebelling against God..."

"Perhaps because they're so close to him," mumbled Seyit as he strode away.

Outside the door, Celil was rushing back and forth, asking anyone who passed by if they'd seen Vladimir.

Having failed to find him in the medical center, they decided to search the battlefield instead.

"Are we are doing the right thing, Seyit? How are we going to find him in that vast place? What if they start firing again?"

"I remember where I saw him last, Celil. A little beyond Mischa."

Spurring their horses, they galloped down the same road at breakneck speed. Mischa spotted them going past the tents down to the plain and called out to Rüstem, who was dunking a rusk into the pale liquid that passed for tea.

"Rüstem! Kurt Seyt and Celil are going to the battlefield! Are they insane or what? What's got into them now?"

Like Mischa, Vladimir, and Celil, Rüstem was a lieutenant under Seyit's command, a Tatar from a good Alupka family. Placing his cup on a rock by the tent, he shot off as he said, "Come on; we're going too."

"Where? Are you out of your mind?"

"I'm off; come along if you like."

Rüstem would happily die for Seyit. *If he's speeding to the plain, he must have a good reason*, he thought; as he mounted his horse, he was glad to see Mischa do the same.

The battlefield was as silent as the grave when they reached the spot where Seyit had seen Vladimir's horse felled by a shot. They walked among the bodies, turning over anyone lying prone and dragging anyone caught under a wreck; it was during this thankless task that Seyit noticed movement in the bodies heaped on the Hungarian side.

"Quick, Celil! Quick! There's someone there—must be wounded."

On emerging from the tree line, Rüstem and Mischa gaped as Seyit and Celil galloped over to the wounded man. A soldier was crawling among the dead; at the sound of the hooves, he darted up and broke into a run.

"Bloody hell!" exclaimed Seyit. "That's not one of ours; that's a Hungarian!"

Celil thought Seyit would stop and return—mistakenly, as it turned out. Seyit was galloping toward the running soldier. Celil paused for a moment and looked back. They had to go back. They were now in the enemy's range. Did Seyit have a death wish? There was no way Celil would abandon Seyit though; he shot off after his commander.

Panicking at the approach of the foe on his tail, the Hungarian soldier ran as fast as he could. Every time he turned his head for a look, he stumbled over a dead body or a chunk of a shell. For hours he had waited for nightfall so that he could make his escape in the dark; this was a totally unexpected piece of bad luck. He was running for his life. Certain his pursuers wouldn't dare advance any closer, he'd believed salvation lay a few steps away. But he was wrong. All too soon, horses were breathing down his neck. Before he knew it, he was hoisted up by the armpits and held dangling between two horses. As this strange three-some shot off toward the Russian line, his eyes were nearly popping out: if one of the riders let go, he'd be smashed into a pulp. And what would happen to him when they reached the Russian encampment? By the time Seyit and Celil handed him to Mischa and Rüstem, the Hungarian soldier had fainted.

"Take him to the encampment; we're going back for one more look," said Seyit.

"Be careful!" shouted Rüstem.

They did find Vladimir this time. His legs must have been broken, judging by the way they were twisted, and his left cheek and shoulder were shattered. Lifting him gently, Seyit cradled his head. "Vladimir! Vladimir! Answer me! You're alive! You must live!"

Vladimir was alive, but only just.

"Celil, let's take him back at once; God willing, we found him in time."

They lay Vladimir on Seyit's horse, in front of the saddle; Seyit cradled him in his left arm as one would a small child, and they set off for the encampment. Darkness was falling.

Mischa and Rüstem, who had been waiting at the end of the road, ran over at once, carefully lifted Vladimir off, and laid him on a stretcher. Disjointed bones slumped down, and his head slipped to the side. Mischa tried to place the bloody arm dangling from the left shoulder along the body.

"Is the ambulance here?" yelled Seyit at the troops waiting ahead.

His eyes fixed on the horrific wound in Vladimir's face, Mischa whispered, "No need. He's already gone."

They rushed to the stretcher, checked his pulse, and leaned down in the hope of hearing a single breath. All in vain. Lieutenant Vladimir Savinkov was no longer among the living. Mischa crossed himself as Seyit knelt down by the stretcher, his face twisted in grief. "Oh, Vladimir, my dear friend! Forgive me; I was too late." Biting back his tears, he bent down to kiss Vladimir's forehead and bloodshot eyes. With a bitter smile, he murmured, "Winter's nearly upon us, chum. If I survive and make it back to Yalta, I'll have a swim in the icy lake for you too, I promise."

They buried him in a grove near the encampment with a wooden cross to mark the mound of his grave. As Mischa crossed himself and prayed to the Holy Ghost and Virgin Mary for forgiveness of Vladimir's sins, Seyit, Celil, and Rüstem opened their palms up to the skies and said prayers beginning with a *Besmele*.

That night when Lieutenant Vladimir Savinkov was laid before God's mercy accompanied by Orthodox and Muslim prayers, a rare honor for most warriors, northerlies blew away the seemingly relentless stench of blood and gunpowder.

A harsh winter was in the offing, slamming down what had been a lingering, mild autumn. The days grew short and dark. Clouds scudding on a ferocious wind brought the smell of the first snow somewhere nearby. Daytime's chill turned into a bitter cold at night. Food and fuel were in short supply, regular supplies to the front now a thing of the past. The uprisings and social divisions that had started in Moscow and Petrograd were spreading around the land.

Frontline combatants had long since lost contact with their families and loved ones. The grapevine between regiments was the only conduit for news about the progress of the war—or the revolution, for that matter. It was predictably difficult to ascertain its veracity, but the revolutionaries were on the verge of making peace with the Germans, if the rumors were anything to go by.

Men who had been fighting the Hungarians in the Carpathian front for such a long time, men who had worried whether they would survive the next few minutes, might be forgiven for temporarily dismissing the political realities behind the front as distant dreams. What remained a mystery was where and under what conditions they would find their families if the revolutionaries took over the country. Such were the thoughts on their minds during the brief respite whenever the field guns fell silent or the bullets stopped whistling.

It was evening. The corpses that hadn't been gathered, dead horses, and shattered gun carriages that had smoldered all day long on the plain lay under the snow that had been falling for hours, a gentle blanket over the vast plain as though it was not the same earlier inferno where death outpaced rider and bullet alike. All the soldiers could hear was the crackling of fires outside the tents spread between snowy mounds. Soldiers huddled inside cloaks or blankets, sitting spellbound by the flames. Anyone who wanted to talk did so in whispers, as if scared of his own voice.

It was going to be another sleepless night for Seyit and his friends. They were due to descend to the other side of the plain in the morning. Encouraged by the recent rise in the number of enemy prisoners, Russian forces had gained a new lease on life, and a new attack was in the offing. Seyit stared at his weary troops huddling on the snow, wondering how far they could penetrate into Hungarian territory without facing annihilation.

Mischa was drawing long lines of crosses in the snow with a twig. At the warm touch of the mug of tea, he lifted his gaze. "Thank you, Celil."

Celil added a few drops of vodka to the mugs. No matter how hot the drink, it wasn't going to do the trick on its own. Mischa took an enormous gulp, closed his eyes, and swallowed slowly, letting the alcohol warm his body to the marrow. He must have scalded his throat: his eyes opened wide, and he shook his head. Twisting the metal mug into a snug hold in the snow between his feet, he asked, "Remember, Kurt Seyt?"

Seyit brought his gaze back from the other side of the plain to his mate. "Remember what?"

"Remember we were going to swim in the icy lake? What was it called, anyway?"

"*Karagöl. Kara*: black, and *Göl*: lake, you see? Well, we're not in Yalta, but we're doing roughly the same thing anyway. Life here's not much different from swimming in ice," replied Seyit with a bitter smile.

"You've not heard from your family at all, have you?"

"No, Mischa, it's been about four months. Perhaps even longer."

"You think the rebellion's reached that far south?"

"I haven't the foggiest, to be honest. The disturbances in Petrograd and Moscow never spread to our part of the world, but I have no idea what's happening now."

"You know they'll never let us live if they win, don't you?"

As Mischa carried on drawing crosses into the snow, Seyit made an attempt to set his friend's mind at ease. "Don't be so despondent. I'm sure reason on both sides will prevail, and I'm sure they'll find common ground. It might even be happening now—who knows?"

Mischa's family was much more than merely very wealthy; his mother was very close to the tsarina, which placed them at the top of the Reds' hit list. Seyit sympathized only too well—his own heart was filled with dread for his family back in Crimea. Reports of brutal massacres by the Reds raiding farms and vineyards were commonplace; a titled Mirza family, close to the tsar to boot, would most certainly mean the Eminofs were on the same hit list.

He gave a deep, troubled sigh. Worries about their families shoved thoughts of the next day aside.

Rüstem and Celil carried on cleaning their weapons as they listened in silence. A balalaika rang out from a far corner, spreading a melancholy tune under the slowly falling snow in the stillness of the night. A deep voice rose from another corner. Soon the entire camp was humming the same song, singing of the vast Russian steppes, icy rivers, a spirited troika flying over the snow...a song of lovers and a lament for lost beauty too. Fleeting as it was, beauty reached everywhere. Sorrow, on the other hand, was never absent.

At dawn, Seyit's unit was ready to set off. Letters to their families—in case they failed to return—were entrusted to friends who were staying back. Certain the Hungarian forces had been pushed well behind the plain in the last attack, they took the shortest route over open ground. That total stillness offered the momentary illusion that the war was over. But they knew it was a passing fancy the moment they crossed the plain and entered the woods; danger lurked nearby. The enemy had obviously abandoned the camp only a few hours previously. Death lay no farther than hopes of heroic deeds.

Seyit halted his unit when he spotted the returning scouts, riding as fast as they could on the snowy ground. They drew to a halt before him, still panting, and saluted. One of them announced excitedly, "We've spotted the enemy, sir."

"How far away?"

"About half an hour's ride, sir."

Of course they would eventually meet, but this sounded closer than anticipated.

"Are they numerous?" Seyit asked in a pensive tone.

"Not really, as far as we could make out, sir. Most appear to be wounded."

Peering deep beyond the trees as if he could see the enemy, Seyit rode next to Celil.

"They must be waiting for reinforcements. Otherwise they'd have pulled back deeper." After pausing to think, he added, "It'll be easier for us if we surround them before their reinforcements arrive. Let's hurry. Celil, you and Mischa take your men and carry on. Rüstem, you take the left flank." Tilting his head up toward the wooded hill on the right, he said, "I'll move over there; the road to the plain is behind that hill. I might be able to spot any new developments."

Mischa, Rüstem, and Celil gathered their men to wait at their positions. Seyit ordered them to attack even if he had not returned within half an hour.

He turned Socks to face their new direction, patting the handsome black head adorned with a white star. "Come on, son; come on, Socks—this might be our last ride yet."

Socks nodded as if he understood.

The snow that had been falling uninterrupted since the night hinted at a blizzard. They were all chilled to the bone as they ascended. The plain was no longer visible from the flat hilltop surrounded by tall plane trees. Whiteness reigned supreme. The trees, the sky, the ground, the horses, and the troops—everything was cloaked in white. The road down to the plain fell away from the flat ground. *Pointless to ride all the men to the edge just to take a look at the road*, thought Seyit. He ordered a halt and rode toward the cliff on his own. Visibility was down to almost nil in the snowstorm. On reaching a hundred-year-old pine, he spotted the cliff a few yards ahead, pulled back the reins, halted, and breathed a sigh of relief; one careless step, and they could have easily tumbled off the edge. He dismounted and secured Socks to the formidable trunk of the ancient tree. He took a few cautious steps forward, shielding his eyes to peer at the narrow road at the bottom for signs of activity. It was impossible to see anything other than snowflakes scudding about. Swaddling his face all the way up to his eyes with his scarf against the snow now lashing at exposed skin, he stretched out on the snow in the hope of hearing something. He waited grimly until his ears got accustomed to the noise of the wind whipping up the snow.

He heard a new noise, one that gave him a start, one he recognized well: the creak of gun carriage wheels and the pounding of boots—weary carriages and wearier feet crushing the fresh snow.

He leaped up and brushed his greatcoat off. Socks looked tetchy in the snow covering his legs up to the markings he was named for. With a soothing pat to the horse's head, Seyit untied him and mounted; there was no time to lose—he had to get back to his friends.

He spurred Socks. Cannon fire exploded just then, echoing up from the plain. Alarmed, Socks reared up, turned around, and bolted. Seyit couldn't recognize the horse he had personally trained; Socks had gone berserk, running toward a certain death despite the uneven snow cover slowing his progress. Seyit drew back the reins, murmuring soothingly to no avail. Jumping off was out of the question; he couldn't leave Socks to die. He had to find a way of stopping the animal. Another idea flashed into his mind: as they reached the last tree before the edge, he grabbed a thick branch, still holding the reins, and dug his spurs in. Socks protested against the pain in his mouth, neck, and belly; neighing angrily, he did halt.

They stood barely a few yards from the edge. Seyit was about to shake himself up to relieve the pain in his palms and shoulders when, instead of calming down, Socks reared up out of the blue and threw his rider off. Seyit raised his arms to protect his face from the raised hoof—it slammed into his arm. Pain and warmth exploded at the same time. So much pain that he missed his footing as he fell on his left leg. It crumpled under his weight, and pain shot from his ankle up to the hip, far worse than the first one in the arm. He sank into the snow facedown, lifted himself up on his right elbow, and screamed in anguish as Socks leaped over the last mound of snow. "Socks! Sooocks! Come back, son! Come back, Socks!"

Handsome coal-black Socks of the white markings vanished where the snow did. A helpless neigh fell away. His heart aching far worse than his body, Seyit punched the snow with his right hand, tears streaming from his eyes. He yelled until he was exhausted. His eyelids fell. Colors swirled before his closed eyelids now, as though snow were falling inside his eyes.

The last thing on his lips when he lost consciousness was his horse's name.

***

He couldn't work out whether it was his pain-racked body or the pungent smell of medicine in the air that had awakened him. The one thing that was certain was he wasn't dead yet. It took a lot of effort to open his eyelids; they felt unbelievably heavy. He could make out blurred figures in white bustling around. Or were those snowflakes again? He tried to recall where he'd been last and in what state. His vision cleared a little, and he shook his head incredulously, recovering from an unwelcome nightmare. His beloved horse had fallen down the precipice, and he had collapsed in the snow. What about the cannon fire? What about his friends and his troops? Who had found him and brought him here? How long had he been here? Racked with questions, he felt a little more awake. He tried to sit up, but it hurt too much, and the dressings held him back.

His left arm was covered in thick bandages from the shoulder to the fingertips. Excruciating pain shot up his left leg hidden under the blanket, and it felt quite numb in places. He couldn't figure out what they might have done to his leg. The possibility that it might have been amputated chilled his blood. A legless man was no good for anything, never mind the cavalry. His eyes darted around, seeking someone to ask—then he recognized this place. This was the same ward where he had looked for Vladimir all that time ago. Or *was* it all that time ago? He seemed to have lost all sense of time. His head felt far too heavy for his eyes to stay open.

Seyit learned all the answers when he came to next time. He had been lying half unconscious for a fortnight. His troops had brought him here. Socks's kick had torn off a piece of flesh from under the left arm and dislocated the left shoulder. The fractures in his left leg had been pinned. The doctor said the arm would heal completely, but getting back up to his feet would take quite a while. And how well the leg would heal was up to his own constitution.

Seyit was more concerned about his men though. Thankfully the doctor, a young fellow with a bright face and cheerful disposition, seemed to be on top of the news—a veritable war correspondent happy to share all he knew. Seyit watched in awe as the doctor examined the fresh dressing on the arm wound, chattering and illuminating his patient blithely, as though gazing at a flower blossoming in the snow.

"You're very lucky, First Lieutenant, very lucky indeed."

"Am I healing rapidly then?"

"Yes, but you also made it here in the nick of time." He explained without prompting, "You were the last of the Russian troops on the battlefield. Retreat began as soon as your cavalry were back. If they hadn't found you and brought you back, you'd have been taken prisoner—if you had survived in the first place. All that's left now are a few casualties like yourself and medical staff. And as soon as our patients are able to travel, we'll all leave."

"Have they signed a treaty then?"

"No, not yet. We're withdrawing, that's all. Should've left the Carpathian front long ago, if you ask me," he said, opening his hands out in a gesture that said "Well, whatever!" He carried on, still beaming, "Not that anyone asks me. My job is to patch, stitch, and chop, not plan attacks and retreats. That's your job, First Lieutenant. All the same, like I said, you're very lucky." He suddenly slapped his own forehead. "Good God! Here I go, forgetting your letter. Your friends were quite concerned."

A table next to the glazed cupboard for dressing supplies held a few of the doctor's personal belongings. He carried on talking as he picked up an envelope from the drawer and walked back to the bed. "No need to worry, First Lieutenant; they were in the pink of health when they left you the letter. A little tired, obviously. But then again, who isn't? They'd captured the Hungarians beyond the plain. Oh yes! There are some enemy casualties in the camp too. Hungarians, Germans, and Turks..."

Seyit had been opening the envelope as he listened with half an ear. He froze at that last word. His expression stopped the young doctor in his tracks; bending down anxiously, he asked, "Are you all right? Is the pain back?"

Seyit just shook his head wordlessly.

"You must be tired. Such excitement is not great in your condition. You'd better rest now."

"Where are the prisoners?"

"In the other hospital hut. Thankfully none of them is seriously injured. Otherwise they'd never survive the journey."

"What journey?"

"I believe they're being sent to a camp in Siberia. I hope the poor wretches can recover well enough for the march by the time the escort party's here..."

Remembering he had other patients, the doctor hastened away without completing his train of thought.

Seyit's eyes welled up reading Celil's letter, as though the two friends were together now.

***

A few days later, Seyit started walking on crutches. *If you can call this walking!* he thought. What he actually managed was to stand on his right leg and drag the left. His left arm, still in stitches, ached intolerably when he used crutches, but he'd been determined to get up ever since he'd heard of the prisoners in the next hut. He went outside. Incredulous eyes scanned the encampment against the dazzlingly bright snow melting in the sunshine: what he remembered as a military site complete with tents, troops, guns, and horses now had a few wrecked gun carriages, some supply crates, and a scattering of tents.

A guard stood outside the prisoners' infirmary hut. He saluted and opened the door as asked. Seyit stepped in.

The wounded prisoners of war turned anxious eyes toward the young officer on crutches at the door. Seyit looked at every face one by one. It was difficult to connect these faces lying racked in pain with the terrifying enemy of a few weeks ago. Turning to the guard, he asked in a low voice, "Which ones are the Turkish prisoners?"

"There are two, sir: the bed on the left and the one next to it."

Seyit took a deep breath, as if unsure what to do, swallowed, and moved toward the patients in those beds. One was barely out of childhood, no older than thirteen or fourteen. He looked shell shocked, an impression reinforced by the enormous dressing on his head. He kept rubbing his interlaced fingers, a mechanical gesture that seemed to demand all his attention. The other man was in his thirties, apparently unbowed by captivity if his haughty expression was anything to go by. He had a luxurious head of black hair and a moustache; and his most striking features were enormous watchful eyes and an aquiline nose. He was quite thin but then, his cheekbones might have become more prominent in captivity. The sight of the deep cleft in his chin drew Seyit's hand to his own. It was as if he were seeing his own determined face. He felt an inexplicable affection and compassion for this Turk who watched him silently, lost in his own thoughts. Seyit approached the bed slowly, unable to trust himself to speak.

Stirring restlessly against the pillow at his back, the prisoner asked glumly, "Are you sending me away now?"

His Russian was flawless. Seyit, who had been of two minds about speaking Turkish, felt relieved. He swallowed and answered, "No, no, I don't know when or where you are due to go."

An inner voice was telling him to leave without delay, and another insisted he talk to this total stranger who felt so much like an old friend. Realizing all eyes were on them, Seyit continued cautiously. "I only thought you resembled someone I know. May I ask who you are?"

Still in the dark about the nature of the punishment that awaited them and riveted by this exchange between their Turkish brother-in-arms and the Russian officer, the unfortunate prisoners tried to follow, fearful and uncomprehending—since none spoke Russian.

The captive officer leaned back against the pillow once again, marginally comforted by the answer, yet intrigued by his interlocutor's interest.

"Major Ali Nihat..." He paused, as if to continue, which he did in a more sarcastic tone. "Turkish prisoner of war Major Ali Nihat..." The pain was unmistakable—not a physical one, but rather, the pain of captivity.

"Whereabouts in Turkey are you from, Major?"

The staunch dignity gave way to yearning; Ali Nihat's voice was barely audible. "Istanbul...Istanbul..."

"Are you married?"

"Yes."

The young officer's barely concealed affable interest shone through, prompting Ali Nihat to talk freely for a little longer. "Yes, I am married. And I have a four-year-old daughter." He paused and pulled out a few photos. "Here, my wife and daughter. They must be waiting for me. I consider myself fortunate to have hung on to their photos. Not a luxury for those captured on the battlefield."

Seyit was perched on the edge of the bed, staring at the photos in his hand. "Where were you captured?"

"I'm in the Engineering Corps; I was deployed immediately behind the front. What matters is my present location, of course, isn't it?"

Major Ali Nihat's eyes seemed to demand an answer. Seyit rose on his right leg, using his right side to bear the weight of the injured left. Grabbing the crutches and deliberately glancing away, he mumbled, "I guess so..."

It was hard to think of anything else to say. The mere idea of admitting his Crimean Tatar background was daunting. With a final look at Major Ali Nihat, he tried a smile. "Look after yourself; I hope you're reunited with your family and country soon."

The captured engineer asked as Seyit walked to the door, "May I ask your name, First Lieutenant?"

Seyit hesitated. His courage failed, and he dragged his leg as he left the hut.

Perhaps it was God's will that had spared him the ignominy of capturing people of his own race.

One week later, orders came to abandon the encampment. Rickety, broken, useless or not, what few belongings remained were loaded on carriages and horses. It was a sunny, dry day. Seyit stood outside an empty hut, waiting for the carriage. It was all over. Days of snow and ice, blood, the smell of gunpowder, death, agony: it was all a nightmare they were leaving behind. A dreadful nightmare. Yet now, not knowing what lay in store seemed far more terrifying.

His little black bag packed, the cheerful doctor greeted him on his way out of the hut. "Good day to you, First Lieutenant Eminof. Isn't it a wonderful day for travel? Couldn't ask for better." Pointing to the prisoners gathered outside the headquarters building, he lowered his voice. "For the sake of those poor wretches, in particular. Now they're about to set off for that horrific cold."

The prisoners of war were posing for a photo with their Russian nurse. Smiling at the camera, wearing a thick black gown, white pinafore, cap, and unpolished black shoes, the pale young woman with chubby cheeks might well have been the only friend those twenty-nine prisoners had. Her heavy bone structure made her look heartier than she was; in reality, she was no less malnourished and ill kempt than her charges.

The Turkish, German, and Hungarian prisoners had lined up on the stairs outside the headquarters and offered her the only chair. The young Turkish soldier standing by her left shoulder wore what had to be a bespoke military jacket. Seyit gave a wry smile, wondering how this youth had ended up on the battlefield and watched him standing to attention—ramrod straight, legs together, and arms stiffly held at the sides like a mature soldier. Except for the four civilians, the prisoners were all in uniform and boots. Seyit knew all too well neither heavy shoes nor boots would last through weeks on foot. The thought of Siberia's vast snow-covered steppes and the bitter wind that would slice through to the bone was enough to make Seyit shiver. How many would actually survive the journey? Anyone who fell on the way would be abandoned on the spot. That little boy and the elderly German civilian at the rear would be unlikely to greet the following summer.

The shutter clicked.

Every pair of eyes stared at the lens, except for Major Ali Nihat's, whose gaze was fixed at a point beyond the camera's reach. Spotting the major standing in the center on the third step, Seyit realized the engineer was watching him.

When Seyit's carriage drew up, he took leave of his doctor and was helped up to the carriage by a soldier. The prisoners were lining up. Seyit asked the coachman to stop for a moment when they drew close. Resentful faces filed past, apprehensive about the journey ahead. Seyit gave a courteous salute when he locked eyes with Major Ali Nihat. "God bless you, Major."

Ali Nihat stared after the carriage trundling away from the quagmire that was the Carpathian front. He stared until it passed from view. He didn't think they would ever meet again. And he would never know who it was.

Back from the Front

THE TRAIN SEYIT had boarded at the station nearest the abandoned encampment grunted in a world of horrors beyond imagining. The bucolic scenes, blushing village flirts, and strapping lovers of song were no more. The reality was a heaving mass of humanity that howled and elbowed at random, swarming the carriage doors as soon as the train ground to a halt in a scene that was repeated at every station, each of which was crammed with people waiting for hours on end. There was hardly enough air in the carriages crammed beyond capacity. With the exception of a few returning soldiers like Seyit, the passengers were all from the countryside. Some of the children were clinging to their mothers' hands; others were on laps, but all seemed to carry their own share of luggage in bundles tied to their necks or hands.

Not even in his worst nightmare could Seyit have envisaged the squalid chaos around him. A group of farm laborers—if the cracked, sun-scorched faces and large, calloused hands were anything to go by—exchanged raucous vulgarities as they tore bites out of a stale loaf of black bread and passed it around. The old woman sitting next to him had a filthy bundle covered in patches; it toppled over his bad leg with a jolt of the train. Grimacing in pain, he tried in vain to free the leg. She didn't care. Never mind help, she glowered at him for daring to touch her possessions—an impudent and spiteful glare.

He leaned back. He might as well grin and bear it; he didn't have far to go, at any rate. Ignoring the ache in his leg and the heavy, acrid stench of sweat, he extracted a couple of letters from his inside pocket to pass the time.

Celil's letter trusted to the doctor informed him that several regiments, including the cavalry, were recalled at once on the tsar's orders to quell the commotion in Petrograd. Wishing him a speedy recovery by the will of God, Celil hoped they would meet there soon.

The second had come from Shura some eight months ago. Five pages of neat handwriting said she didn't know if he had received her previous letters; she had heard nothing back and was concerned. There was no reproach, simply the words of a worried woman in love. Their warmth had coursed up his palms into his heart and belly even on the bitterest night. Her letter had been his only connection to visions of life beyond the war, and he longed for her. He had probably reread it hundreds of times, drawing solace from the sheets handled by his sweetheart, sheets that conjured her warm, tender, and feminine snuggles. Every night, as Mischa knelt before his tiny icon and Celil and Rüstem read their Korans, Seyit had sought comfort in her words as much as in silent prayers.

The full stop was a sentence of terms of endearment and kisses. He was beaming, engrossed in the letter, when he sensed his neighbor staring brazenly over his shoulder. He folded and replaced the sheets back in the envelope, annoyed at this intrusion into his privacy. Even if she was illiterate, which was highly likely, gawking was unwelcome all the same.

Then again, she might have envied his smile. There had been so little to smile about for such a long time! Still staring, she wiped her nose with the back of her hand in a silent, spiteful curse. *No, we will never be friends*, thought Seyit, and he turned his head away to watch the fields as the train sped past.

On arriving at Petrograd Station, Seyit waited for everyone else to leave first. The restlessness on the faces was palpable in the thronging crowds. He disembarked only when he thought it was safe to descend to the platform without being jostled. Handing his suitcase to a porter who had materialized out of nowhere, he took a deep breath, as if to open the nostrils he would have gladly blocked on board. It was hard to believe he was back; he wanted to take his time and prepare himself for the idea that he was indeed back—and safe and sound too.

He gave his address to the coachman and settled into the carriage, suddenly filled with dread: How would he reach his sweetheart? She lived fifteen hundred miles away; how could he find her at a time when families were torn asunder?

Was there any reassurance that she was still waiting for him, after all this time with no word? Another man might have entered her life by now, or she might have left Kislovodsk altogether. He indulged in anticipation of some news or a message as he alighted outside the house.

He ascended the marble steps, hesitated briefly, and knocked on the door. A deep silence echoed in the big hall. There was no movement inside. After a second and equally fruitless attempt, he inserted the key into the lock. It responded to the familiar touch. Seyit felt instantly enveloped in the cozy and tranquil atmosphere of home. He shut the door, leaned against it, and scanned his surroundings: everything looked just as he'd left it.

He was certain a long hot bath would take away his exhaustion. After lighting the fire that had been prepared in the bedroom, he opened his suitcase. The wardrobe and cupboards held his possessions. He looked at the picture in the silver frame on the marble mantelpiece: his photograph with Shura. Picking up the memento of the afternoon in Moscow, he kissed her image. His heart swelled with love. It was quite strange that he missed the young girl he'd shared a few hours of love with instead of all the women he'd been entangled with for weeks or months on end. That was the reality. No other woman or finer love came to his mind. He felt an irrepressible longing to see and embrace her, even as an ache inside his rib cage pointed out it was an impossible dream.

The next morning Seyit was awakened by the bells of Saint Isaac's Cathedral. It was nearly noon. He left the bedroom in his dressing gown. The house was still as silent as it had been the previous night. His housekeeper wasn't at home. Had he slept through her knocking? No, she had her own key. Perhaps she was enjoying a sneaky holiday while he was away? Seyit shaved and got dressed, hoping to drop in at the Guards Headquarters to see his friends. Medical leave or not, he had been out of action for so long that he was impatient to catch up.

He'd walked for only a couple of blocks when he spotted the woman running toward him: it was Ilona Vetrovna, his loyal, kind-faced housekeeper. She looked delighted to see him, but there was something else on her face. After greeting him respectfully, she burst into an excited account. "Oh! Seyt Eminof, it was God who sent you! Thank God! You have no idea how worried we were."

Stealing a glance at the cane and Seyit's leg, she hesitated. "In the name of the Holy Ghost, Eminof! What's happened to you? Not a single line, no message, no nothing!"

Seyit rubbed her shoulder to calm her down as she burst into tears. "Don't cry, Ilona Vetrovna; don't cry, for God's sake. Look, here I am. It's not that bad. I should be able to discard the cane soon."

She carried on crying, holding a handkerchief up to her nose. Seyit realized it wasn't just about him.

"What's wrong, Ilona Vetrovna? Why are you so upset?" Her lateness and uncontrollable tears didn't bode well. Had she received bad news from his family? "Is everything all right, Ilona Vetrovna? News from home?"

"No, no, please don't worry—no bad news from Alushta, but..." Looking back, she asked anxiously, "I hope you weren't planning to go to Nevsky, Eminof?"

Seyit failed to suppress a smile at her anxious mothering. "Indeed I am; how did you guess, Ilona Vetrovna? I thought I'd walk a little and hail a carriage when I got too tired."

Ilona Vetrovna turned back toward the house with a light touch on his arm.

"The roads are terrifying, Eminof. I beg of you, let's go back. See how many hours it took me to cover such a short distance!"

They fell in step.

"What is going on?"

"Oh, Seyt Eminof, the roads are full of crazed mobs. They're attacking everything with stones, sticks—whatever they can lay their hands on."

Seyit wondered if she wasn't exaggerating, but it still made sense to avoid such altercations in his present condition.

"If only you knew, Seyt Eminof, sir. I was terrified I'd be trampled or get my head smashed in!"

"Calm down, please, Ilona Vetrovna—calm down and start again. Who are those crazed mobs?"

"Oh! Of course, you have no idea what's been happening here, Seyt Eminof. Striking workers were sacked, as were the women factory workers who participated in the Women's Day March. So they all flooded the streets, shouting, 'Bread! Bread!'" Thank God I met Aktem; he took me round the back to the top of the street. He says the crowds go all the way back to the pier. And they've been looting and ransacking bakeries along the way. Lord in heaven! Whatever next?"

"Don't worry, Ilona Vetrovna; it's nothing new. It'll go on for a couple of days and peter out soon enough."

He didn't believe it himself but knew he had to calm the old lady down. He was even more eager to go to his garrison for news, but standing on his pinned leg for an hour had taken its toll.

She hastened toward the kitchen as soon as they entered. "It's wonderful having you back, First Lieutenant Eminof. I'll make you tea straightaway."

Nursing his aching leg as he sipped tea by the fire she'd lit in the sitting room, something else occurred to him. "How will you get back in the evening, Ilona Vetrovna?"

"Aktem's going to collect me. I'd have to stay here tonight otherwise."

"Well, you still can if you like."

"That's very kind, sir, but my husband would worry. I would have told him I'd be staying over if only I'd had any idea when I left."

Placing his teacup down, Seyit peered at her. "Since Aktem's going to take you back...perhaps I might ask for a favor."

She was delighted to be of help. "Of course, First Lieutenant Eminof—whatever you wish. You know I'll do anything I can for you."

"I know, Ilona Vetrovna; I know. That's why I feel I can ask you. On one condition though: If the roads are still chaotic on your way back, please forget it. Just hasten home without delay. Is that understood?"

"Just as you wish, Seyit Eminof."

"I'll give you a letter. Swing by the Mariinsky and hand it to Miss Tatiana Tchoupilkina. Make sure to hand it to her in person."

He recalled hearing about Tatiana's transfer from the Bolshoi; it was in one of her letters Celil had received at the front. Given his own present condition that confined him indoors, this was as secure a way as any to send word to his friend.

"Of course, sir—with pleasure. Would you like me to wait for a reply?"

"No, no, just make sure my message gets through."

"Mademoiselle Tatiana dropped in several times to ask if I'd heard from you. God bless her. And Lieutenant Sorokin and the others called round the day after they returned. They explained how they'd had to leave you behind and what a sorry state you were in." He asked if she meant Mischa, Rüstem, and Celil when she glossed over the unfamiliar surnames. "Yes, them; they'll tell you everything far better than me. I'm just an old servant, after all. All I can tell you is what I've heard on the tram and what my husband tells me. One thing I do know though: this isn't going to end well, Seyt Eminof. May I offer you another glass of tea?"

"Thank you, Ilona Vetrovna. Yes, I will have another. Add a few drops of my medicine as well, will you?"

The housekeeper grinned all the way to the kitchen, knowing precisely what he meant. She rinsed the glass with boiling water, filled it halfway with tea, and topped it up from a bottle of vodka she took from the cupboard.

"I suggest you don't leave it too late; set off as soon as Aktem's here. I wouldn't want you to be late home."

"He said he'd be here at six, but I wouldn't be surprised if he doesn't make it."

Coachman Tatar Aktem did turn up as promised and brought them up to date: the crowds had dispersed quite close to the city center but were expected to resume their action the next day; several bakers had been killed resisting the looters, and the streets were said to be deadly quiet for the time being.

Seyit handed them a brief note for Tatiana and watched their departure from the window. He could trust them both implicitly. Since there was nothing he could do other than wait, he decided to have a little of Ilona's borscht soup. The smoked fish platter—that at any other time would have been his favorite—he left untouched. He picked up the bottle of vodka and sat back down before the fireplace with a heavy heart, pondering how, if the riots continued, he could meet Shura again or even get back home. He was hoping the disturbances hadn't yet spread so far south. Perhaps a book would help ease his mind.

The only wall not covered from floor to ceiling with books was the wide window looking over the back garden. Two Borovikovsky portraits flanked the pilasters framing the window; the stately poise of the models perfectly complemented the sobriety of the heavy tomes filling the library.

Staring at the family photos in silver frames on a bookshelf, Seyit yearned to see his parents, brothers, and sisters. If he could go to only one place when he left this house, would he go to the woman he loved or back to his family? A dilemma that had no place in his mind.

He had read and reread most of the books lining the shelves. What he needed now was something to cheer him up. After a brief hesitation between Pushkin and Nikolay Yazykov, he picked up Nikolay Nekrasov's *Komu na Rusi zhit horosho?* The four-part epic chronicled the journey of seven peasants in search of a happy person. Seyit recalled how much he'd enjoyed the cutting wit in the folk song–type verses of *Who Is Happy in Russia?* and how some of the descriptions would have fitted people of his own acquaintance to a tee. He settled into the sofa facing the fireplace in the sitting room.

A knock on the door awakened him; the fire had long since gone out, and the book lay on the floor. His bad leg had gone to sleep. It took a while to reach the hall on his cane, but the impatient voices outside were instantly recognizable. He opened the door without delay and hugged Celil, Tatiana, and Mischa. He needed no cane on the way to the sitting room, supported on either side as he was by his brothers-in-arms. Tatiana followed in light, graceful steps as befitted a dancer, surreptitiously dabbing at her eyes.

The fire was stoked again and the vodka and the glasses placed in the middle. It might have been two in the morning, but for the four young people, it was merely the start of a wonderful day they'd been longing for.

"Where's Rüstem? Couldn't you get hold of him?" asked Seyit.

"On duty in Livadia. I guess he'll be back soon," replied Celil, staring at the good friend he'd missed so much. "You know something, Kurt Seyit? We did wonder if we'd ever see you again!"

"I wasn't particularly confident I'd make it back either!"

Tatiana had no wish to join in the gloomy conversation. She interrupted, twirling her glass delicately as if stroking a flower. "How on earth did you figure out to find me at the Mariinsky, Seyt?"

"Fortunately I'd read your letter to Celil before falling off my horse."

Unruffled by the revelation that her passionate letters had fallen into Celil's friends' hands, Tatiana giggled provocatively and reproached the culprit in mock exasperation. "Oh, Celil! If only I'd known you couldn't keep secrets! I wouldn't have written a single word!"

"All I read was that one line, Tatya—I swear," said Seyit. "Nothing else."

She waggled her right index finger as though scolding naughty children. "You great lying lumps!"

That relaxed good cheer dissipated when Seyit inquired about his family. Celil tried to answer as best as he could, which wasn't saying much; he'd had no opportunity to go to Crimea yet. "There are fears that the riots will close in on the palace, Seyit. Guards are on constant duty in Petrograd and Tsarskoye Selo. All leaves are canceled. And no one knows what's in store after what happened today."

"Ilona Vetrovna was horribly distressed about today's horrors."

"It's bound to get much worse tomorrow," said Mischa pensively. "The government refrained from any intervention today, apart from keeping the crowds out of the city center. I'm afraid things could get out of hand at this rate."

"Are they so many then, the rioters?"

"Hard to tell, Seyit. Ostensibly it started out as the reaction of a hundred and thirty thousand striking workers, but not everyone in the crowd today had been sacked, and there were plenty of ne'er-do-wells too."

"Aren't they getting what they're asking for?"

Mischa replied, "At first all they wanted was higher wages, or at least that's how it seemed. The real objective is different though. I'm sure it would make no difference today if their salaries were raised. Frankly, it's revolution they're after. They think they'll be happier if the tsar was gone."

"General Khabalov—he's the chief of the Petrograd military district now—is a highly cautious man. He could have dispersed today's crowds brutally if he wanted. He'd much rather bide his time and wait for things to settle down."

"He would have to intervene if a direct order came from the palace though."

They carried on chatting in this vein until daybreak. Exhausted or not, Tatiana also stayed up. Celil warned Seyit as the party broke up. "Don't leave the house at all unless you have to, Seyit; if revolution does break out, you might find yourself in a stickier position than us. We'll try to keep you posted. But it's best nobody knows you're here. You can send me messages through Tatya. I've stayed away from home for quite a while now. Whenever I go on leave, we stay at her aunt's place."

"Thanks, Celil. I won't forget your help. God be with you."

They hugged; Seyit beckoned Celil closer before the others descended the stairs. "Did you know Petro's been about?"

Celil's outrage over their former friend's treachery was unmistakable. "Don't know where to begin, Seyit; he's a lost cause. Best to stay away. He knows our lives inside out. You've not seen him, have you?"

"No, I have not, but I hear he called round several times while I was away."

They would have carried on talking, but Celil had to report for duty. With yet another hug, they shook hands and parted.

After seeing them off, Seyit sat at the desk in the study. He listed various possibilities based on all he'd heard through the night and contemplated what course of action he ought to take in each case. His position was precarious not simply because he was an Imperial Guards officer—any land, property, or title was enough to attract the enmity of the marauders on the streets. He thought about his family in Alushta; they must have been desperate for news. He shoved the list aside to write them a letter instead.

The next day, it was nearly noon when Ilona Vetrovna arrived, and she was much more agitated this time. "I'd like to stay here if that is acceptable to you, Seyt Eminof," she said. "The roads are far too dangerous now."

"Of course, Ilona Vetrovna; consider this your home. Stay as long as you like."

Thanking him profusely, she went to work.

On the second day of the riots, a much bigger crowd of demonstrators descended upon the city center. Their ranks had swelled with university students as well as nearly a third of all the workforce of Petrograd. The workers were still chanting "Bread," but now the occasional anti-autocratic or antiwar slogan rose in the noise. Aggressive splinter groups terrorized the city.

By the third day, things had spun out of control. Police officers were slaughtered in the sacked stations throughout the industrial district of Vyborg. The rioters were now armed. The earlier innocent rallies for fair pay had given way to armed massacre. Yells and fists waving in the air inflamed the crowds, who had forgotten their demands of a couple of days earlier. Bread was no longer the issue. Now they wanted to spill blood. Oppressed and vindictive, they set about punishing all social classes except the proletariat to make their dreams come true. Bloodthirsty mobs emboldened by the sheer magnitude of their numbers were now armed after razing police stations to the ground.

Seyit was pacing like a caged lion between the sitting room and the study. The crowds had to be near Alexander Nevsky; the noises were quite close now. There wasn't a single soul on the road. The houses opposite his looked deserted. Inhabitants had to be seeking safety behind closed doors, the furtive twitching of a net the sole indication that an anxious glance attempted to estimate how close the riots were.

In the evening of a day that just wouldn't pass, Seyit was exasperated by a growing unrest and uncertainty over his own predicament. He was unable to return to duty. Goodness knew what sort of trouble his best friends were in or getting ready to tackle. The woman he loved was far away, and he had no idea about her circumstances. He might never see his nearest and dearest again. All he could do was to sit and wait. Other than Ilona's steady supply of tea and the vodka he'd been imbibing for the past couple of hours, he had eaten nothing all day. The old woman's entreaties had fallen on deaf ears: he hadn't been able to face the roast duck she'd prepared with such care. The enormous lump in his throat and a churning stomach prevented him from touching a single morsel, never mind enjoying a feast. Restless—he felt so restless...

He darted to the window at the sounds of hooves and carriage wheels that broke the stillness of the night. It was Celil, and he was in a hurry, judging by the way he leaped off the carriage and charged up the steps two at a time.

Seyit called out, "Ilona Vetrovna, Lieutenant Kamilof's here; please open the door at once."

Celil was already at the door by the time she'd dashed out of the kitchen; he burst in. "The worst has happened, Kurt Seyit. The tsar has wired General Khabalov from his headquarters at the front. We are under orders to suppress the demonstration. The rioters are about to set off for the city center; they're carrying torches, and they're armed. Mischa's just led his unit to confront them. I'm to be stationed near the palace. It's not good news, Seyit—not good news at all. It's going to be awful."

Lashing his bad leg with his cane, Seyit gritted his teeth. "God damn it! And all I can do is sit here nursing my leg!"

Celil patted his shoulder with a tender smile. "Don't worry, Kurt Seyit; you'd feel better if only you could see the crowds on the streets. Even people staying home might be expected to do their bit. This mob's got no mercy for the old, the infirm, or anything." He carried on more gloomily, "Wish it had never come to this..." He hesitated and fidgeted with his hat. "Seyit, give me your blessing. I've always looked upon you as a brother. Hope you'll think of me the same way."

They hugged as they parted. Seyit murmured, "You have my blessings, Celil, my brother; please give me yours..."

They had grown up together, ridden together, laughed, and cried together. Had gone womanizing together and fought side by side at the front. Their lives could have been two halves of a single unit.

Seyit stroked Celil's shoulder like a fond big brother. "Take care of yourself. God be with you, brother. I'll pray for you."

Celil's eyes regained their cheeky expression at once. "Wasn't God with us from the off, Kurt Seyit? Just look at us! Who had more fun than us, eh?"

They hugged again with a choking laugh and broke apart.

"You're right, Celil; you're right."

Celil turned back once more at the door. "Erm...If I don't make it back, Seyit? Give my love to my parents. Ask them for their blessings."

Seyit couldn't reply. All he could do was to swallow, raise a hand, and wave. The wave turned into a fist that flopped to his side as the carriage departed.

On the morning of March 12, Aktem turned up in quite a state, only to face a volley of questions from Seyit, who was hungry for news. The flustered coachman gave the best account he could, given he'd been without a decent fare for days and unable to go home in the harbor district for six days now. "Thank God I have no wife or children!" he exclaimed. Imperial forces were decimated by the revolutionaries. "They're like mad dogs, First Lieutenant Seyt Eminof—I swear they are!" Nicotine-stained fingers shredding an ancient flat cap, he cringed as he added something in a polite voice that belied his rough looks. "I have something to ask of you, Eminof..."

His mind still churning, Seyit asked, "What is it?"

Aktem's uncertainty was evident as he continued to cringe. "Erm...sir? If it's not too much to ask...I mean...Do you think you could give me a job, Seyt

Eminof, sir?" The final words tumbled out as if to put an end to his misery. He fell to his knees and continued, still twisting his cap. "I beg you, sir! The streets are terrifying. I'll ask for nothing. I'll sleep in the car—do everything you want just for a bit of food. And I won't eat much. I beg you, First Lieutenant Seyt Eminof..."

With a pat on the shoulder, Seyit silenced the coachman. "Very well, Aktem, very well! Get up. We'll do whatever we can."

Aktem rattled off his skills to secure this unbelievable stroke of good luck. "I'll do anything, Seyt Eminof. I'll be your loyal slave. I'll fetch wood, keep your stoves clean, and lay the fires. I can make repairs. I'll carry messages."

Seyit laughed, throwing his head back as he lowered himself into the armchair. "So you want to become a spy? God bless you, Aktem; you're scared of running your carriage in a riot. How on earth are you gonna run messages?"

Flustered at the prospect of losing his new position, Aktem stumbled over the words. "That's different, Seyt Eminof; that's different. Believe me—I'll do anything you want."

Now weary, longing to be left alone with his thoughts, Seyit seemed to wave at some invisible object. "All right, all right, got it. You don't have to be a spy or sleep in your carriage. Take one of the storerooms in the basement; Madam Vetrovna will tell you what to do with the stuff you've cleared out."

"Thank you, Seyt Eminof—God bless you. I will never forget your kindness."

Aktem walked backward, bent double in gratitude, as Seyit asked himself what on earth had prompted him to take in someone who'd never done anything other than drive a horse carriage.

That was the day the Duma convened to debate possible solutions, the radicals took the next step they'd been planning for a long time, and most of the city fell to the revolutionaries.

Later that night, the strike stewards who had led the riots for the past few days met with the committee chiefs responsible for arming the workers, as well as 250 sitting socialist representatives in the Duma.

This, the first soviet, was riven with discord, with vastly varying approaches to the revolution and degrees of permissible violence. Their first priority was a powerful committee, they decided; imminent hunger would otherwise jeopardize the revolution anticipated by swiftly growing numbers. Any ideological differences could be dealt with later. Moreover, the present regime must be denied any opportunity to resist or react. The first priority was control of food stocks, and that was just the beginning.

Amenable as the Duma might be to a possible republic, abolishing the dynasty altogether was out of the question. One thing was certain though: Tsar Nicholas II's position was now untenable. The Duma pressed for abdication; Grand Duke Michael could serve as regent until Tsarevich Alexei Nicholaevich came of age. But Guchkov and Shulgin, two right-wing Duma delegates, came back empty handed from the ringleaders in Pskov, and the dynasty that had been ruling Russia for three hundred years was abandoned to its destiny.

Later still, Tatiana turned up at Seyit's door, more distraught than he could ever imagine. Aktem ushered her in; her stage makeup had run in a mess of eye shadow and rouge, and her hair stuck out in big curls from under her lopsided hat. Like a little girl whose toys had been taken away, she collapsed into Seyit's arms in floods of tears. "Oh, Seyt, we can't stay here any longer. You'll never believe what I've been through!"

Before long she had composed herself, washed up, and accepted a cup from Ilona. Sipping her tea, she recounted what had happened as she'd been about to leave the theater.

"The audiences had been dwindling for quite a while, anyway. And tonight was like performing for a cemetery. We'd just taken a bow and were off to changing rooms when we heard yells from the stage door. Poor Boris! I can't forget the poor doorman's screams..." She burst into tears again, dabbed her nose with a handkerchief, and continued, "That rabble had come to raid the theater. We all bolted out in a panic, audience and all, but some people fell down. My God! What's going on? I can't go back there ever again, Seyt!"

"Perhaps you could go back to your family in Moscow? You might be safer there. You'd have to wait for things to settle down first though."

"I have no idea how things are there, Seyt."

"You're right. Moscow's hardly likely to be much different."

She rose; trouble shared was trouble halved. Patting her hair, she pecked him on the cheek. "Oh! What a fool am I! I can't believe it. Please forgive me, Seyt. You have a letter from Shura. I don't know when it was posted, but I only received it this morning." Placing a tearstained handkerchief back in her bag, she drew out a folded envelope. "I do hope everything's fine. Do let me know if there's anything I can do." She pivoted back toward the door. "Seyt...have you heard from Celil at all?"

"No, but I'm sure he'll be back. Rest easy."

Aktem earned his keep for the first time when he drove Tatiana back.

Seyit had a new lease of life, the exhaustion of all those sleepless and anxious nights washed away by Shura's letter. He tore open the envelope impatiently. It was a brief note, written in haste, either because she wasn't sure it would reach him or because she might not get a reply. Thankfully it was written in her customary affectionate style.

> My darling,
>
> I don't know if this letter will reach you, just as I don't know whether the others ever did. I miss you more every passing day. I hope that we shall be reunited one day.
>
> Life in Kislovodsk's not the same as it was either. It's no longer the peaceful, fun little Kislovodsk of old. Wounded soldiers are sent here for treatment. My mother's friend Anna Ivanova Tcherkosova arranged several rooms in a hotel for their care.
>
> The other day I was so overwhelmed by longing for you that I even indulged in the hope that you might be among the injured soldiers. But believe me, my love, I would much rather you were in good health and away from me than see you wounded.
>
> All my love,
>
> Shura

Smiling at the artless, innocent confession, he reread those lines on his feet until his throbbing leg brought him back to his senses. It was in a bad way, swollen and more painful than usual. He swallowed two of the tablets the surgeon had given him after the operation and lay down. How long had it been since he'd last lain without a woman by his side for so long? He tried to recall every woman he had made love to. Baroness Maria and the middle-aged redhead at the Moiseyevs'—he had to call on the Moiseyevs at the first opportunity. His mind strayed back to caress the faces and bodies of scores of alluring women, redheads, blondes fair and honey, and brunettes, slim and full busted. His eyelids grew heavy. The last thing he picked out from between a narrow slit was Shura's letter. He fell asleep, dreaming of his true love.

Late the next night, there was a knocking on the door. One hand on the wall, the other holding his cane, Seyit passed down the hallway; Ilona was already up, staring at the door with trepidation. She raised her lamp, saw Seyit, and drew aside.

The knocking was repeated, followed by Aktem's reassurance. "He's home, sir—just asleep, I guess. Please wait awhile."

Seyit recognized the other voice at once and called out, "Ilona Vetrovna, let him in, quick! It's Lieutenant Kamilof."

It had only been a couple of days, but Celil might as well have been away for years. He looked weary and exhausted, as though he'd just come back from battle. With a hug, they proceeded inside, arms over each other's shoulders, and Seyit could no longer contain himself.

"What's happened, Celil? For God's sake, tell me what's going on."

Celil slumped into the nearest armchair in the sitting room, held his head in his hands, elbows on knees. He stared at a point between his boots and rubbed his forehead miserably. He didn't seem to hear Seyit's question. When his mouth finally did open, a stilted stream of words poured forth. "Finished, Kurt Seyit— it's finished. It's all finished..."

Drawing up a chair, Seyit sat down beside him and lay a soothing hand on his shoulder. "Hold on, Celil; hold on. Calm down and tell me from the beginning. What's finished? Why are you in this state?"

Celil sat up, threw his head back, opened his hands out as if in prayer, and lowered them back to his knees again. His gaze was filled with anguish.

"Oh my God...what now?"

He paused, hands hanging at his sides. Seyit waited until he composed himself. Celil spoke, avoiding his friend's gaze. "Mischa...Mischa's dead, Seyit...died right before my very eyes..." The voice that had started so firm and determined petered out, and he burst into sobs. "He died...right before my eyes...and I...I could do nothing."

Seyit couldn't believe his ears. Return from the Hungarian front only to die in Petrograd! It was unthinkable. Celil must be mistaken—even a little unhinged perhaps?

"You only got away if you swung your sword, Seyit. Anyone who slashed indiscriminately, maiming and killing, got away. It was apocalyptic. But he refused to wield his sword. He was trying to talk sense into the rabble surrounding his horse..." He couldn't hold back the tears any longer. "You know? He didn't believe his fellow citizens could ever harm him. They were crazed, Seyit. They shot him first and then dragged him off his horse. None of us could reach him, neither his own men nor me. They tore him apart on the ground. It was horrible. Oh, God, it was horrible..."

Seyit frowned in anguish. He placed one hand on his friend's shoulder. The two young men sat in silent tears, as if seeking strength from each other's contact in what was effectively a silent funeral service for Mischa.

That night, Seyit lay tossing and turning for hours and resolved to discuss plans with Celil first thing in the morning. At a loss as yet about how to include Shura in those plans, he fell asleep dreaming of their eventual reunion.

During those same hours, Russia's history continued to change as Tsar Nicholas II and his family was arrested.

On March 14, the number-one *Prikaz* of the soviet summoned a representative from each military regiment in Petrograd to the Taurida Palace. The same edict included changes to the administration of the military; there would be no more saluting other than on duty, formal terms of address such as *Your Excellency* or *Sir* were banned, and aristocratic titles were forbidden outright. Officers could no longer address their men in the second-person singular. Orders would be guided by the committees appointed by the soviet, and the officers would merely convey those orders. Through these ostensibly special privileges, the soviet intended to suppress any opposition to the revolution from the armed forces.

Meeting a few close friends in secret confirmed Seyit and Celil's earlier fears. Their chances here were now blown. They needed to decide what to do and get on with it. After extended discussions, they agreed to return to Crimea, plans they intended to keep secret for the time being.

On a bright, chilly April morning, Aktem drove Seyit and Celil over to the Moiseyev house for a farewell visit; the two young men were in mufti—just in case. Ilona Vetrovna had gone out to restock the larder. Tatiana was waiting for Aktem to take her shopping.

A carriage halted outside. Tatiana looked out of the window and recognized Petro Borinsky as he alighted, instructed the coachman to wait, and turned toward the stairs. *An odd time to call*, she wondered but offered her childhood friend a warm welcome nonetheless.

Petro failed to conceal his nervous tension.

"Goodness, Petro Borinsky. Whatever brings you here at this hour?"

He leered. "Perhaps I've missed you, pretty Tatya." He strode over and issued a command. "I want you to pack at once. I'm taking you away."

She tilted her head quizzically and sat down on a sofa. "What on earth are you talking about? What does that mean, 'You're taking me away'? What is the meaning of all this?"

Petro sat down beside her. "It's all for your own good, Tatiana Tchoupilkina. You have to leave. Nasty things are in the offing in Petrograd. Listen to me. I'm off today, and I've come to take you away."

Tatiana was even more confused. "What on earth are you saying, Petro? Where could I go? This is my home. My work, my life: it's all here."

Petro flared up when his sketchy explanation failed to sway her. "Now listen. If I say it's dangerous for you to stay here, that's because I know something. Listen and do as I say. There'll be no place for the likes of you soon."

Shrugging his hands off, she moved away on the sofa, her eyes open wide. "'The likes of us'? And you? Who are the likes of *you*?"

"Does it matter? But since you ask, dear Tatya, let me tell you…" He walked to the middle of the sitting room, hands in his pockets, like a condescending school-teacher trying to recollect his notes. "The likes of you, lovely Tatya, are the owners of money, land, and vineyards." He was sneering now. "You, the aristocracy, the gentry. The chanters of 'Long live our tsar!' You, the masters of Russia—until now."

She gaped in undisguised astonishment: Petro, born with a silver spoon in his mouth, had never accomplished anything other than spend money and womanize! This had to be a nasty joke. "You're not exactly different from all that either though, are you?"

"It's different for me. It no longer matters how I lived up to now or who I am. A new era begins in Russia, my love—a brand-new era." He talked with animated, expansive gestures like a commander promising a great victory. "I have decided to join this new era. How I lived up to now doesn't matter; nor does what I've done. I've been very useful to them, which is why I'm not going to compromise my standards much."

This arrogant, presumptuous man before her was unrecognizable. This couldn't be her childhood friend, the boy she had picnicked with, the boy whose nanny and hers were such good friends, the boy she'd danced with for the first time. Incensed, she sprang to her feet. "How did you secure this concession then?"

Unmoved, Petro struck a nonchalant pose, one arm on the mantelpiece and one leg crossed over the other, and shrugged. "Frankly, explanations are quite pointless. Far be it from me to tax your head with stuff beyond your grasp, dear Tatya. What I want you to do is trust me and come with me. More specifically, I want you beside me from now on."

He strode toward her with deliberately slow steps, staring at her eyes wide in revulsion. Realizing she was about to flinch away, he grabbed her arms. "Hey! What's the matter? Scared of your old friend? You know I'd never hurt you. Quite the opposite—I want to take you under my wing. I'll see you right, you'll see. No one will be able to touch you. Not even my father gets the same treatment, in case you were wondering."

Remembering the old man, Tatiana asked, pity evident in her voice, "Does Uncle Andrei know what you're up to?"

"Like he would, Tatya! Absolutely not. Wouldn't he blame me if something nasty were to happen to him?"

Struggling to free herself from the clutches of the foe she'd looked upon as a friend all this time, Tatiana screamed without bothering to hide her disgust, "You are a beast, Petro Borinsky! Good God! What's happened to you? How could you change so much? Didn't you enjoy rolling in wealth simply because you were born a Borinsky? If it hadn't been for your father's fortune, you'd have been destitute. You're a traitor. Bastard! Traitor!"

Petro shook her shoulders violently to silence her. Unused to such rough handling, her delicate body collapsed onto the sofa. He pounced before she could gather her wits; she struggled in vain to push him off. He latched on to her lips.

"You should have known it, lovely Tatya, should have guessed all these years. I've always loved you, always wanted you. Waited patiently all this time, even when you never gave me any hope. And look, it's me beside you, just when you need me most."

Tatiana was incandescent and terrified by now. "Whatever gave you the idea that I might need you? Petro, pull yourself together and leave at once. Only then might I forget all this."

Still crushing her, Petro kissed the slender wrists in his clutches and murmured, "The worst of it is, my lovely darling, you've no idea just how much you're gonna need me. Just take my word for it. Not even your Crimean lieutenant could save you. Or? Or are you with the other one now? Of course, seeing as you're settled in his house now. I've had you followed for a while. Knew I'd find you here. Couldn't have known which prince enjoyed your favors, of course." .

Tatiana chose not to reply. Petro presented an enormous danger to them all. Misinterpreting her silence, Petro threw his head back and guffawed. "So you're with him now! You little fool! They're all done for now. No tsar, no Imperial Guards—don't you get it? The moment they show their faces, they're done for. Their names are all on the list."

She punched his face repeatedly, yelling in outrage. The idea that Celil and Seyit could suffer Mischa's awful fate was heartwrenching, but she had no intention of letting Petro sense her fears.

Planting his mouth over hers to silence her, Petro set about forcibly lifting her skirt. Praying for Seyit or Ilona Vetrovna to return as soon as possible, Tatiana spotted a vase on the coffee table next to the sofa. It was within reach.

Petro's face was still buried in her neck. She grabbed the vase and brought it down. It slammed heavily at the spot where his neck met the shoulder. The surprise worked where the blow didn't: her dazed assailant leaped back. She grabbed her chance, slipped from the sofa, and ran into the bedroom, her hair messed up, her lips swollen, and her neck and chest covered in blossoming bruises.

Petro chased her, growling at the pain in his shoulder. Tatiana picked up the little pistol concealed in the desk drawer and waited in terror, her back against the wardrobe. Petro was still rubbing his neck when he appeared at the door. There was no love on his face now. Close-set blue eyes glared like shards of ice. This was the first time she'd seen his real face; this wasn't her old friend Petro. She spoke with extraordinary composure. "Leave now; don't force my hand. I swear I'll shoot if you take one single step. Don't force me, for the sake of our childhood memories, if nothing else."

The wind taken out of his sails, Petro swung his arms with a sneer. "Suit yourself. You'll regret it though. The wolves will soon get your precious *Wolf* Seyt—unless he's scuttled away first, that is. I can't say what your fate would be. You'll be left on your own sooner or later. One day, if I ever see you again, I swear you'll receive no mercy from me, Tatiana Tchoupilkina."

He went to the door, followed at a safe distance by the young woman holding the pistol. He paused to turn on his heel, as if he'd just remembered something. "Oh yeah! Tell your Crimean prince this thing doesn't end in Petrograd. I do know the way to Alushta."

With a taunting look, he walked out. Tatiana slumped into the nearest chair and dropped the weapon. It took her quite a while to compose herself. She had no idea how to tell Seyit and Celil. Her lover and his best friend had to get away—that much was certain. But how would she tell them? What would she do?

She decided to wait instead of going shopping. Time wouldn't pass. Petro's words kept echoing in her mind: *You'll be left on your own sooner or later...You'll be left on your own sooner or later...*

No, she couldn't bear to lose Celil. Come what may, they would stay together. If he chose to stay, so would she. If he chose to go away, then she would go with him. She couldn't live without him.

Celil was her fate, and she was ready to embrace her fate.

Farewell to Petrograd

O N April 16, 1917, as the sealed train carrying Vladimir Ilyich Ulyanov, who was now known by his revolutionary pseudonym Lenin, arrived at the Finland Station in Petrograd, another train groaned out, whistled, and picked up speed on its way south.

Reassured by the concessions he had obtained from the Germans, Lenin was happy to return from Switzerland. The environment he had been waiting for since 1905 was now ready, and Russia was about to become the country he had been dreaming of.

Several of the passengers on the Odessa train, on the other hand, could be excused for not sharing his confidence. Seyit, Celil, and Tatiana pretended to be complete strangers in their compartment, careful to avoid attracting attention until they reached Crimea. Each carried no more than a single suitcase.

Ilona Vetrovna and Aktem had been entrusted with the house in Petrograd, as were Ganya and Tamara with the one in Tsarskoye Selo. Celil had overruled Seyit's intention to go there, saying it might be too risky. Instead, Seyit had sent the Karloviches their instructions in a brief note.

All three young passengers sat silent and preoccupied. Revolutionary officials questioned passengers at every station, and they waited with their hearts in their mouths at every station. *Wish we'd get there as soon as possible!* Tatiana's eyes seemed to plead.

The train stopped at a village station, waiting for an oncoming train to pass and clear the tracks. Seyit, Celil, and Tatiana spotted a pitiful wretch between three revolutionaries on the opposite platform. Barely able to stand up, the poor man's face was covered in blood, and he was crying openly like a child.

From the snatches of exchanges they could hear, the man appeared to have been arrested for refusing to hand cornmeal over to the revolutionary committee. He fell to his knees, wiping his nose with the torn sleeve of his filthy jacket, slobbering plaintively. "Only two sacks…and you took them; please, let me go… I'm just a poor peasant. Please…"

One of his captors twisted the long moustache mingling with his beard, spat an enormous gob into his palm, and grabbed the rifle in the other hand. He whacked his detainee on the head with its butt and, as the poor man lay sobbing on the ground, said, "Cut it out, you fucking son of a bitch—enough of your whining!"

Unused to such foul language, Tatiana blushed to the roots of her hair. Horrified at the sight of the collapsing peasant now beyond moaning or sobbing, she darted to the window with a scream. Celil dragged her back to her seat and patted her head against his chest to calm her down.

The other train arrived. Their train blew its whistle; the engine's noise grew louder, and billowing out smoke, they left the miserable little village behind.

Things improved as they moved south. Sacked and burned villages and plundered fields seemed to give way to a different world. It was warmer. A gentle breeze redolent of forests and fields came through the open window, all of which lifted the passengers' moods. Breathing in the smells of spring in this unfamiliar land, Tatiana grabbed Celil's hand. With a smile, she gazed into his eyes in a silent rush of love. *We are together,* said her beaming face. He responded by planting a tender kiss on her hair. She rested her head on his shoulder, watching the verdant hills and golden fields through half-open eyes. It felt as though they had escaped from hell and were on their way to heaven.

It didn't last long. The train screeched to a halt unexpectedly.

They hung out of the window to see what the matter was.

"That's all we need. Bloody hell!"

The soldiers who had stopped the train wore red armbands, marking them as deserters who had joined the Bolsheviks.

"Celil, we must leave the train at once."

Tatiana inquired, her eyes wide, "Here? Where would we go in the middle of nowhere, Seyt?"

Celil put a finger to his lips and whispered into her ear, "No choice, Tatya; they'll scour the train. We must leave."

"Well, not without me then. I'm coming along."

There was no time to argue, even if the men could object. Grabbing their luggage, they filed toward the last carriage in what could be mistaken for an utterly nonchalant attitude, not that anyone showed the least bit of interest. All eyes were on the soldiers swarming into the carriages, swearing profusely, and ordering everyone about. Not a single person knew what they were looking for or wanted, and everyone felt vulnerable—any passenger could be picked on at any moment. Although no one actually had anything more other than the bundles in their hands—they had no animals or grain—they were still terrified. Having a name similar to that of some fugitive could be sufficient reason for punishment, as could coming from the same village...or the soldiers might simply take a dislike to someone.

While the other passengers on the train were petrified with fear, Seyit and his friends knelt to wait on the rear deck of the last carriage. The soldiers must have settled into the train by now. With a shriek of the whistle, the train shuddered on the rails. Seyit threw his valise down first, and the others followed. Celil jumped down at a run behind the train in order to catch Tatiana when she jumped. Fear would serve no purpose in this utterly unexpected situation, she knew. She gathered her skirts and let herself go. She would have landed on her knees if Celil hadn't grabbed her first; together they collapsed onto the tracks. Seyit leaped off the step and landed on the gravel alongside the track.

The train sped away with a grunt. Certain they wouldn't be seen now, the three fugitives collected their suitcases. They were standing among wheat fields that stretched as far as the eye could see.

"Any guesses as to where we are?" asked Tatiana, voicing their thoughts.

"No, but if we follow the train tracks, the next station will tell us."

"I'm not sure this is such a great idea, Celil. The deserters who stopped the train just now were also following the tracks, don't forget."

"You have a point."

They kept the track in view as they walked in the fields. Later, when the track reached open ground, they had no choice but to move into the woods.

Toward evening, after having failed to spot a single intact building all that time, their sagging spirits were lifted by a horse-drawn carriage on the forest road. They waved eagerly; the driver pulled the reins with a silent, guarded look. Their neat city-folk outfits and bearing must have allayed his fears, but he still looked watchful. You never knew with anyone these days.

"Is there anywhere we could stay the night around here?"

"My village is not far, sir; if you're looking for somewhere to stay, you could come to my house." When they hesitated, he offered a little reassurance. "Don't worry, sir; you'll be safe. Trust me."

There wasn't much choice other than sitting in a row alongside the logs in the rear. "Not far" turned out to be an hour's ride away. Grateful for the descending darkness, no one spoke throughout the journey. The peasant remained equally quiet, a man riding a cart on his own to all intents and purposes.

What he called a village consisted of a scattering of no more than eight or ten huts in the middle of the forest. He drew to a halt in front of the farthest one, nearly hidden by tall trees. Tethering his horses to a tree outside, the peasant spoke for the first time since they'd climbed into the cart: "Don't worry, sir; no one will disturb you here. I don't have much to offer, but at least your lives will be safe."

They followed him in. A big hearth covering an entire wall projected into the single room. A thin mattress above the fireplace obviously served as a bed. There was nothing else, other than a broken chair and a few old pots and pans hanging on the wall. Tatiana had never seen such poverty before.

The three travelers looked around as the peasant lit the fire and placed a cauldron of water over it before speaking apologetically. "I'm very sorry, sir; I've got no seats to offer you...Oh, wait! Perhaps if I were to place this mattress on the floor, you might be more comfortable."

Seyit laid a hand on the man's shoulder to indicate he was worrying needlessly. "You've already helped us tremendously; more is not required. Please don't worry...sorry; what's your name?"

"Stepan, sir—Stepan Milovich."

"Can you tell us where we are, Stepan?"

Scratching his thick beard, Stepan broke into a smile. "I don't think this place is on any map, sir, and you must be the first strangers to ever come here. But if you really do need a name, we're somewhere near Ryazan."

"How near?"

"A full day's trek by cart, sir, until sundown."

Despite the generous offer of hospitality, the travelers might still be wary, thought Stepan, and gathered his courage. "Where did you want to go, sir?"

Seyit and Celil exchanged glances; Stepan's answer had been unexpected. If he was right, they were miles off course.

"Why do you ask, Stepan?" asked Seyit cagily.

Stepan bowed his head and stroked his beard timorously. "I might be able to help if you're going south."

"Where?"

Stepan hesitated. It was his turn to worry about speaking frankly. He stared at the attentive faces of these—clearly—fugitive gentlefolk. No, they couldn't harm him. "Can I trust you, sir?"

Seyit replied, "You can, Stepan. We won't hurt you. We are travelers too and had to change course. Perhaps we can help one another."

"We're clearing out tomorrow, sir," said Stepan, relaxing. "We're off to Rostov with my mates."

The penny dropped as Seyit listened; how on earth had he missed it all this time? This was no peasant. The thick beard was clearly a disguise. His hands were far too neat to belong to a woodman. Seyit visualized Stepan in an officer's uniform. The meek, timid rustic in threadbare clothes was a highly successful persona that no longer deceived the Crimean.

"Would you tell me where you're from, Stepan?" he asked with a smile.

"From Sheptukovka, sir."

"And the others too?"

Stepan scratched his beard, staring quizzically. Seyit tried to explain. "I mean, are they also back from the front?"

Tatiana and Celil were no less surprised than their host, who slumped onto the logs next to the fire. He asked in flawless Saint Petersburg Russian. "How did you guess, sir?"

Seyit laughed, shaking his head. "Firstly, the way you address us has to be a military habit!" Drawing the broken chair and looking much more grave now, he sat down facing their host. "Yes, Stepan...or is Stepan as fake as the beard?"

"No, no, that's my real name."

"What did you do at the front, Stepan?"

"Artillery at the Prussian front." He paused. He didn't want to say more. His guise was gone, but he knew nothing about his guests.

"It's all right, Stepan," sympathized Seyit. "Don't be afraid of us. That's where we're coming from too. We must have so much in common. You may speak freely, I assure you."

"I'm sorry, sir. We no longer know whom to trust. I've seen the treachery of my own troops at the front. Only one first lieutenant and four lieutenants managed to get away. The others were torn from limb to limb—not even the enemy did that."

His guests knew he was speaking the truth. Seyit asked, "What was your rank, Stepan?"

Habit took over, and Stepan sprang to attention, looking somewhat incongruous in peasant garb. "Lieutenant, sir."

"Welcome to our regiment, Lieutenant Stepan Milovich."

The ice was broken. The three former officers exchanged salutes. Now they could speak freely, knowing they were all in the same boat.

"Since you're from Sheptukovka, you must be a Cossack."

Stepan nodded.

"Is something up in Rostov then?"

"Yes, sir. We're going to join General Bogayevsky. Our only hope is to stop the Bolsheviks before they reach the Caucasus. We might be able to save the south at least."

"Are you gathering in Rostov then?"

"No—that's where we'll meet the others before we move to Yekaterinodar. One group will stay in Novorossiysk. Where were you headed, sir?"

"We were on our way to Odessa, but things didn't work out as planned. Now we'll try to cross into Yalta."

"Then come with us, sir. Train stations and trains are no longer safe. It will take longer, but at least we'll have protection."

Unexpected as it was, this hopeful development was accepted with alacrity.

The next morning, a group of rickety peasant carts left the depths of the Ryazan forests and headed south to the lands dominated by the River Don.

Not unsurprisingly, it wasn't an easy journey. The Bolsheviks were already penetrating into the south. Repeatedly forced to hide in forests and fields for days, sometimes even weeks, the fugitives stocked up on provisions at Cossack villages at every opportunity—but frequently went to sleep on an empty stomach. Despite being the only woman in the group, Tatiana was quite philosophical about braving the hardships of this life-and-death journey. She had already bid a mental farewell to her glory days on the Mariinsky stage and in Petrograd's exclusive salons.

It was December by the time they reached Rostov. Winter here might not be as bitterly cold as in Petrograd, but given Seyit, Celil, and Tatiana had set off in the spring, they felt as though they had been on an interminable journey.

Stepan wasted no time in making safe arrangements for the three travelers to reach Alushta following a deserted route over the Kerch Peninsula.

Seyit had changed his mind about going to Crimea immediately but was reluctant to influence his friends. They were sitting by the fire in a historic hotel in Rostov when he broached the subject. "Celil, take Tatya and make directly for Alushta. Find my father and settle in. I'll join you later." He sounded determined.

"What's on your mind now, Kurt Seyit?"

"I'm dying to see her. See where we are? How can I possibly leave without seeing her when I'm this close?"

Celil knew precisely whom his friend meant. "Seyit, we're in the midst of war and revolution. Don't do something crazy. You know how many days it'll take to get to Kislovodsk. We've been on the road for months. I'm sure getting there isn't going to be any easier."

"Save your breath, Celil. My mind is made up. It must be fate that altered our route and brought us all the way here. I must find her."

No stranger to Seyit's stubbornness, Celil gave up and leaned back. "Then we're all staying. Where you go, we all go together."

"No, Celil, you're responsible for Tatya. We can't endanger her further—"

Tatiana interrupted. She had been listening with her arms crossed. "Neither of you is responsible for me, Seyt Eminof. If a twist of fate brought us here, then this is our fate. I'm with Celil. We're coming with you."

"I give up then!" said Seyit with a grateful smile. "I'm not sure I'd be up to arguing with you both. Together it is, then."

Kislovodsk,
December 1917

O N THE NIGHT of December 30, the Verjensky home in Kislovodsk was in
darkness, unusual for the festive season. Only a couple of upstairs windows
glowed with a faint light.

Shura was bustling between her wardrobe, chest of drawers, and valises on
the bed, picking items her governess and mother thought were the most essential. With a pensive look at the valises, Yekaterina Nicholaevna removed the
largest. "No need for this one. The lighter you go, the better, Shurochka."

An hour later, Shura was ready: two cases and a small travel bag. Her sable
hat and muff waited on top of her luggage. When the carriage drew up to the
door, it was time for a sad farewell in the entrance hall. Shura hugged her mother tearfully, but Yekaterina Nicholaevna held her own tears back. Rocking her
younger daughter in her arms like a baby, she covered Shura's cheeks in kisses.

"Don't cry, Shurochka; don't cry. It'll all be all right soon, you'll see; we'll all be
together again. You'll be safer with your uncle."

Still in tears, Shura took her leave of Valentine; her eldest sister, Nina; and
her governess next. As her luggage was being loaded, she hugged her mother
and sisters once again. Artillery noises in the distance drew terrified eyes to the
sky. The clashes must be getting nearer: flashes of light ripped the deep blue of
the winter night.

Yekaterina Nicholaevna led her daughter to the carriage. "Come on, sweetie;
you'd better hurry, or you'll miss the train."

The carriage galloped away, and Shura watched her home vanish behind a
veil of tears. She was already missing her family; her happy childhood was already

a memory. If the coachman hadn't been around, she would have bawled out loud. Lifting her coat collar, she bit her lips. It was hard to control herself.

She couldn't believe her eyes when they reached the station. In contrast to the deserted streets and roads, Kislovodsk Station was heaving. Evidently she wasn't the only one leaving. The platform was a flood of people clutching suitcases stuffed with their most valuable possessions, waiting for the train of hope that would sweep them away from the approaching enemy. It dawned on her that the security of her father's home and her mother's love were left behind for good. She was now one of hundreds—nay, thousands—of terrified refugees desperate for a chance at life and with no idea where, or even what, they were heading for in a struggle that brooked no privilege.

At the distant sound of the approaching train, the station was transformed into an apocalyptic scene of masses dragging their children and elbowing one another out of the way that left Shura gasping. The stationmaster's warnings fell on deaf ears. The Novorossiysk train—nothing more than a glorified freight carrier—was already packed by the time it drew into Kislovodsk.

Shura hadn't expected such a melee; fortunately, the coachman had stayed on to carve a path as she clutched her luggage. He helped her up, and a gallant young man also assisted. Shura felt her life was now dragged by floodwaters, as if she no longer had control of anything. The faces stacked between sacks, bags, and heaps of wood and hay were dishearteningly devoid of any trace of a smile, pleasure, or happiness. Had they all been born with these gloomy and resentful expressions? What an uncharitable thought—it had to be war and revolution that had the power to alter people so greatly.

The young man who had helped her up beckoned from a relatively free corner. Relieved to note that he expected no reward, that this was the act of a gentleman who posed no threat, she tried to move, but her polite requests to pass were in vain. Eventually she resorted to the same tactics as everyone else and shouldered and elbowed her way through the choking crush. It was only when the young stranger grabbed her hand that she finally reached his side.

"Where are you going?"

"To Yekaterinodar."

"Unfortunately you'll have to put up with this throng all the way."

"How long will it take, do you think?"

"Who knows? Perhaps ten days, perhaps longer."

Shura's eyes opened wide in consternation. "Really? Is it that far?"

"Not really...at least, it wasn't before. But now getting there at all will be a stroke of luck in these conditions."

She peered in dismay, but he appeared quite philosophical, if not a little cynical, as if he were watching a stage play. Shura found his presence a secret comfort in this crazed crowd. He stacked her luggage in the corner and drew aside a tiny wooden slat at forehead height, more an air vent than a window. Shura gave him a grateful smile. She had warmed to him, an innocent emotion that had nothing to do with romance. All that she could offer in thanks for his kindness and courtesy was a friendly smile, anyway.

Their sporadic progress varied between speeding, abrupt braking that juddered passengers, and hours of standing still in the middle of nowhere. Rumors swept through the train: the Bolsheviks were on the tracks and would send them back. No one actually knew anything for certain. Every time Shura got worried, her companion just smiled. "Do you see? People would rather believe in their own depressing fabrications. That's what happens when all hope of a better future is lost."

Shura couldn't help but smile at the pontificating eccentric, a strangely comforting companion on this journey from hell.

On the third day, the gallant stranger descended to buy a few things at a station but didn't return. Shura waited with her heart in her mouth until the train set off but never saw him again. He had either boarded another carriage or had failed to board at all. Feeling totally alone and unprotected in this crowd, Shura decided to keep to herself until they arrived at their destination. The less she spoke or engaged with others, the safer she would be.

The journey seemed interminable. Shura pricked up her ears at every station, but she'd yet to hear the name Novorossiysk. Perching on her suitcases, she sought solace in daydreams. Her mother, Valentine, and Nina—what were they all doing now? Tears sprang to her eyes as she remembered her father. It was so difficult to get used to his death. And her brothers: Where were they, and whom were they fighting? Where was...Seyit? The thought of her sweetheart pierced her to the quick. She must have lost him for good now. Had he ever received her letters? With no reply in all this time, she had no idea. Had he returned from the front? Was he even alive? He might have been arrested along with the tsar and his family. Refusing to cry in public, she pressed her eyelids together and composed herself.

It took ten days to reach Novorossiysk. Lurching on benumbed legs, Shura parted the crowds. Relief at the end of this nightmare journey was tempered by anxiety about the immediate future; she wasn't certain of meeting her uncle after all this time—General Bogayevsky might have been forced to leave Novorossiysk. She stepped down to the platform apprehensively. What would she do if her fears were proven right? All she could do was to wait here.

It was getting dark. The snow had already erased all traces of the departing train. It wasn't the coldest night of the year, but Shura shivered in growing fear and despair. Raising her collar, she shielded her face with her muff. A deceptive silence had settled in the station. The platform still thronged with hopeful passengers who'd failed to board the train—hopeful, as they settled down to wait for the next train that would come they knew not when.

Shura was beginning to think she was destined to share their disappointment tonight when she heard firm footsteps beside her. A young officer flanked by two soldiers had sprung to attention.

"Mademoiselle Alexandra Julianovna Verjenskaya?"

Shura could have hugged him. She leaped to her feet. "Yes, that's me."

"Captain Rubin. I'm here to escort you to General Bogayevsky. Are you on your own?"

"Yes. Yes, I am."

At a sign from the captain, the soldiers picked up her luggage, and they boarded the automobile waiting at the exit. Shura was pleasantly surprised by the idea of a vehicle carving its way through the snow to take her to safety with her uncle.

Proceeding on the road running parallel to the tracks, on her way to General Bogayevsky's private train, her vision obscured by a scarf and the blizzard whipping at the windows, she missed the occupants of the carriage passing in the opposite direction.

Novorossiysk,
Winter 1917

T HE OCCUPANTS SPEEDING back toward the city were none other than Seyit, Celil, and Tatiana. That they had missed one another could be ascribed to the cruelest twist of fate: all four had traveled on the same train to Novorossiysk—except Seyit, Celil, and Tatiana had caught it at the next station after Kislovodsk.

Once in Shura's hometown, Tatiana had left the men in the hotel and proceeded to the Verjenskys'. The only person at home was Shura's aging nanny, who fortunately had recognized Tatiana's name from her correspondence with Shura. The moment she heard that Shura had left on a train to join her uncle in Novorossiysk, Tatiana had hastened back to fetch her companions, and they had sped to the next station in a hired carriage. For once fortune had lent a helping hand with the train's stop-and-start progress. Seyit had wandered between the carriages throughout the journey at every station in vain and somehow failed to spot Shura in her corner. It was only finding Lieutenant Milovich on the general's train that offered a glimmer of hope; their savior from Ryazan had promised to send word as soon as he heard anything.

Seyit, Celil, and Tatiana settled in to a roadside inn, reluctant to move too far from the train. Supper was nothing more than borscht soup and a bottle of cheap wine, but it tasted better than a feast after all this time on the road. Exhausted after months of tense, sleepless nights and drowsy after a second bottle of wine, they withdrew into their rooms as Tatiana consoled Seyit. "I'm sure

Shura will arrive soon. The niece of such an important man as the ataman? Of course she'll come—you'll see. Come on; try to sleep a little, Seyt."

He smiled back at her kindness, gave her a kiss on the cheek, and patted Celil on the shoulder as they exchanged good nights.

Seyit's swollen leg was aching. Anticipation or agony: one or both would clearly keep him awake all night. He took a couple of painkillers, lit a cigarette, and stared out the window. The snowflakes were the size of kopeck coins now. The wind tugged at the rotten shutters with rusty, broken hinges, squeaking in a nerve-racking persistence. Bogayevsky's train had to be somewhere beyond the snowy mound blocking the inn's view. In fact, it wasn't that far at all; but for the heavy snowfall, he could easily have spotted it between the trees. Yearning for his sweetheart made him forget the perils awaiting the whole of Russia and himself personally. The painkiller was beginning to work. He undressed halfheartedly, lay down naked, and fell into a troubled sleep as he did whenever he was weary or anxious. He felt as cold as he had that morning years ago at the Moiseyevs' door, when he'd sent his father off to war. He sweltered in the infernal heat of the front as he watched a parade of everyone he had lost, his dead friends, people he would never see again. The aching leg reminded him it was still there, as if his mind resisted the sleep his body longed for.

Then came other sounds that somehow didn't fit in. A door opening in the distance. Whispers. A door shutting. A sudden floral rush, like narcissus, like... daffodils—that's it. A familiar scent. What did this perfume have to do with the Carpathians? The warmth of slender fingers wandering on his face, as light as a feather. A hot breath on his lips...delights transforming his nightmare into a lovely dream. The touch of hands stroking his hair gently felt so real, as real as the scent enveloping him. Was that his name in a whisper? Cautiously, he opened his eyes lest the beautiful dream vanish. Light from the lamp beside him illuminated the face and the neck of a young woman sitting on the edge of the bed—a beautiful, fine face glowing with exhaustion, sorrow, anxiety, and joy. Weeping eyes that spoke of love above all.

This beauty in love was none other than Shura.

They embraced, a wild embrace without a single word—without even daring to speak or move. They wanted to believe that they were together, that they were touching each other, that this was no dream. Shura wept mutely, her head snuggled into Seyit's neck, warm teardrops falling on his bare shoulders and washing away the pain like an elixir. Ignoring his aching left arm, he cuddled her tightly against his chest and covered her tearstained face with kisses. Their lips found each other as if trying to quench the thirst of nearly two years. There was so much to speak of. But their hunger for each other came first, their passionate and spiritual hunger.

Shura looked at her lover's face: He had the same gaze as the first time they had met on that winter's night in 1916. His deep-blue eyes flashed greedily, gazing at her with the promise of the pleasure on offer. Shura felt her whole body tremble. Impatient to yield to her lover, she invited his extended hand to unbutton her shirt. Bringing his palm to her lips, she gave him a hot, lingering kiss and stood up. As Seyit watched her body turning into a nude statue in the light of the lamp, his aches vanished. Bones and muscles forgot the pain that had been their bane all this time. Now every organ, every nerve was alert; his blood pounded, ready to shake off the torpor. Shura undid her long hair, spread it out the way he liked, and stretched out over him, and Seyit tensed like a bow from the top of his head to his toes. As they rediscovered the bodies they had yearned for, their hearts beat hard enough to jump out of their chests.

They first made love in a breathless rush, desperate to satisfy their hunger and thirst. Then they made love again and again, this time inviting each other's nakedness to love with patient and tender caresses. Then, and only then, did they allow themselves to catch up, still locked in an embrace on the bed.

Lieutenant Milovich had passed Seyit's message on to Shura as soon as he could once she had been reunited with her uncle, and Shura had persuaded Milovich to take her to the inn the moment everyone had retired for the night. It was going to be dangerous, yes, but she would risk everything to see Seyit again now that she knew he was nearby—so long as she was back in her carriage before sunrise, that is.

Seyit and Shura had to plan what to do next and without delay.

"I suspect we'll be here for a few more days," said Shura. "My uncle's then going to send me to Crimea. He says we'll be safer there."

"To Crimea, eh? That's wonderful! So you'll be in the same place as us!"

"Us?"

"Yes: Celil, Tatya, and I."

Shura suppressed a scream of joy. "Really, Seyt? They're here too?"

"Yes, they are; we're all looking for my sweetheart!"

Shura hadn't felt so happy in a long time. She lay her head on his chest with a laugh and kissed the deep cleft in his chin, feeling at peace for the first time since leaving home.

As twilight began to melt away the darkness, Shura rose and got dressed. With one last passionate kiss, they promised to send word and parted. Seyit looked out of the window as his sweetheart vanished into the snowy gloom alongside Stepan, who had been waiting across the road. He wondered fleetingly whether this hadn't been a hallucination brought on by his persistent longing and desperate desire. No, it had not. The traces of the night were still with him. Her subtle cologne lingered in the air, and a hairpin lay in the folds of the sheet. He picked it up and brought it to his lips. Fate did move in mysterious ways.

They managed to meet a few more times in the brief time they stayed in Novorossiysk, thanks mainly to Tatiana, who regularly visited Shura in her private carriage and invited her out for a stroll—which was the perfect opportunity for the lovers to meet.

One morning, as Shura waited impatiently to stroll into the forest, Valentine turned up. The two sisters embraced with tears and screams of joy.

"Tinochka! Tinochka! I've missed you so much! When did you arrive? How did you come? Tell me; tell me!"

"This morning. And guess who else is here with me?"

"Mother?" asked Shura.

"Unfortunately no, sweetie, not mother. But someone you'll be really pleased to see. Constantine is here, as is Vladimir," said Valentine, stroking her hand. It worked. Shura brightened up immediately. Baron Constantine was Valentine's fiancé; the poor couple had found no opportunity to meet since their engagement. Vladimir was their elder brother, recently promoted to Princess Pavlovna's guard after rising to headquarters captain. They'd heard nothing from him for a long time; so he was back at the front then.

"Where are they now? When will I see them?" Shura clapped her hands.

Valentine threw herself on the bed and stretched her legs. "Hold on, Shurochka; don't be so impatient! You've traveled the same way. You know how exhausting it is! Uncle Bogayevsky's allocated them a carriage too. They'll have a bath and catch up on sleep first."

"I'm sorry, Tinochka; I was too excited. Did you travel together all the way?"

"No, sweetie, I only met them when I arrived here. There's no telling what tricks fate will play on us, is there?"

Shura blushed, wondering if her elder sister knew everything. No, she couldn't. "Yes, you're right."

Shura launched into an account of her journey to Novorossiysk, but exhausted after her trip, Valentine fell asleep. Tucking her in, Shura tiptoed out to give Seyit the good news and hasten back. For a whole week, the three siblings and Baron Constantine enjoyed their reunion on General Bogayevsky's stationary train.

Constantine and Vladimir returned to their regiments at the end of the week. The trysts were now much shorter and far less frequent, since Shura felt she could hardly leave her sister alone.

The fighting was moving south; Caucasia was on the brink of falling to the Bolsheviks. Within a week, Valentine was pleading with her uncle to see her fiancé again; she'd heard he was somewhere near. It was hugely risky, but Bogayevsky's heart melted at his niece's tears. You never knew in war; the last thing he wanted was for her to blame him for the rest of her life. Assigning her an escort of three guards, he sent her off for a couple of days.

That same evening, he had to leave for Novocherkassk. Shura's carriage was uncoupled from the train; entrusting his younger niece to several of his men, the general went away, promising to be back the following evening. Five days passed with no news from either Valentine or her uncle.

Seyit could see how desperately worried Shura was; he hugged her tight. "Don't cry, sweetheart. You know the clashes are very near now. The roads are far worse than when we were traveling. Perhaps their way back was blocked. We must be prepared for everything. And I'm here with you. Come on; stop crying. Let's wait for a few more days, and then we can take a decision. The sooner we reach Alushta, the better. There'll be lots for us to do there."

Shura resigned herself to the idea of never seeing her family again. All she could do was to pray for their health and safety.

Nothing much changed over the next few days. Seyit and Celil heard from other officers that the Bolsheviks were ransacking the country as they moved south. The Crimean coast was the farthest point from the fury of the revolutionaries. Seyit and Celil had to get there as soon as possible. Perhaps it wasn't too late yet.

Much as he was convinced they had to leave Novorossiysk, Seyit knew there was no way he could leave Shura here all on her own. But how was he going to explain it? Would she agree to leave her family behind to come with him? He returned to the inn in a state of perturbation. Shura was waiting by the fire in his room, her eyes swollen from crying. She leaped up to hug him the moment he stepped in, her anxiety all too evident even without saying a single word.

With a kiss, he held her hands and sat her down beside him. "Shura, my darling, I'm going to ask you something, like something I asked earlier. Think it over. I must return to Alushta. I don't see how we can save Greater Russia. But we might be able to save Crimea. At any rate, anyone getting away from here goes to Odessa or Alurga. I'm sure you can find many people you thought you'd lost there."

Wordlessly, Shura pointed to her cases behind the door. Her mind was already made up; she would stay with the man she loved. Wiping her eyes, Seyit embraced her. They were on the threshold of a new adventure now.

The following morning, before daybreak, they boarded a carriage to go to Yekaterinodar. Finding a boat that would take them to Feodosia was a stroke of pure luck. It wasn't the most comfortable voyage, to say the very least. But, and again at the very least, they were able to proceed without being stopped or searched on the open sea. This was a blissful journey in comparison to the awful train trip from Kislovodsk to Novorossiysk. The shared cabin was the height of luxury in comparison to the freight cars. But the ship was heaving; even the top-deck lifeboats served as beds. It snowed relentlessly, the wind slashed exposed flesh, and the Black Sea churned viciously. None of it mattered to the passengers though. No hardship could compete with the fear of death. A few rubles Seyit tucked into the steward's palm secured a cabin; cramped or not, it presented a degree of privacy.

It took a while for their land legs to return after docking in Feodosia, to stand upright without feeling dizzy. Thankfully a night in a decent hotel, a hot bath, a decent meal, a little wine, and a good night's sleep helped to restore their spirits.

Seyit resolved to ask Shura for nothing until she was utterly happy with her decision. He wouldn't even initiate lovemaking: What if she were to regret a decision made after a night of passion? She still had time to change her mind if she wanted, he explained.

"Don't you want me?" she asked, offended.

Seyit cuddled her. "Of course I do, my little dove. I just don't want you to regret anything when we get to Alushta."

Kissing the hand resting on her shoulder, Shura said softly, "Never did I regret a single thing I did with you, Seyt—not a single thing."

She nuzzled him like a kitten. Hugging her back, Seyit inhaled the delightful warmth in his arms. No more words were needed. They both knew what the other wanted.

Best of all, they both wanted the same thing.

Return to Alushta

FEBRUARY 1918 WAS drawing to a close when the fugitives from the Reds reached Alushta. Sensitive to the less than ecstatic reception that would greet the young ladies at the Eminof home, Seyit made directly for the vineyard house.

With a deep bow, the housekeeper, Ismail Efendi, kissed Seyit's hands and set his wife and daughter-in-law to work at once to prepare supper and bedrooms. His charges defied the evening chill to dine under the trellis, sipping their wine and enchanted by how the Black Sea turned to molten platinum as the sun set behind the hills. In seventh heaven in this peaceful corner of the world together with their lovers, Shura and Tatiana chattered merrily for the first time in quite a while.

Afterward, the men kissed their sweethearts and asked their leave.

"Don't worry about us, Shurochka," said Seyit. "My family might keep us there tonight. You're safe here. Enjoy yourselves; we'll be back tomorrow."

Parting on their first night there was a little disappointing, but the young women put on brave faces as they kissed the men good-bye.

Seyit and Celil mounted their horses and rode off, as in the good old days. And as in the good old days, they met with a rapturous welcome: the men bit back tears, the women allowed theirs to run freely, and everyone hugged everyone. Everyone asked endless questions to quell the longing of all these years. There were new additions to the family: Mahmut and Mümine had a baby, as did Hanife and her husband.

In the early hours, as the household finally retired for the evening, Seyit braced himself for the question that had been plaguing his father all night long. Mehmet Eminof stroked his silvery beard. "Why didn't you come home straightaway, son?"

Seyit's feigned ignorance failed miserably.

"You must have tarried a good while." Mehmet Eminof's powers of observation had lost nothing of their sharp edge; this was the man, after all, who had figured out Seyit's time of return from a night of carousal by the depth of the snow on his back.

Seyit bit back a chuckle; it wouldn't do to show disrespect now, especially as his father expected an answer. "We stopped at the vineyard, Father..." His father's inquisitive look forced him on. "We had some goods to drop off."

Mehmet took a deep drag and watched the smoke rise in the air.

"Since when do you drop off goods in the vineyard house? It must've been something quite extraordinary this time, too unusual to bring home."

Seyit was cringing. His father wasn't about to let go; it wasn't his way. He had never lied to his father before, nor would he start now. But before he could open his mouth, his father took a second puff and beat him to it. "These 'goods' you left at the vineyard; they wouldn't be live goods, would they? Like women?"

It was out in the open now. Seyit lowered himself into the armchair opposite his father and waited, acknowledgment on his face.

"I'm listening," said Mehmet, staring at his son. "I'm listening. You must have a reason to lug her all this way. I want to know why, not that it will make the slightest difference."

Seyit needed a cigarette more than anything just then, but he could never smoke in front of his father. *Candor is the only way*, he thought, brushing his fringe back. "I couldn't abandon her, Father. She waited for me for two years. When I returned from the front—a desperately lonely invalid—it was her love that gave me a new lease of life. She left everything behind to come with me— her family, everything." His father would never approve of this relationship, Seyit knew; all the same, he was hoping to soften that stance. "You'd like her if you knew her. Perhaps..."

Eminof Senior rose to his feet stiffly. "No, Seyit. You can't bring her here. I cannot allow a mistress to come into contact with my daughters and daughters-in-law."

"Would you rather I married her?"

"That's not what I said. Even if you were to marry, given her erstwhile lack of morals, she could never be welcome in our family. I told you years ago, Seyit, to learn about love from Russian women but pick a wife from around here. And I meant it. All this is part of our traditions. Do what you like in Saint Petersburg and Tsarskoye Selo. But it's different here. This is your family home; these are your lands. You can't live with your mistresses here." He sounded utterly calm, yet his tone brooked no debate. "Shame on you. Seems you forgot everything I said."

Seyit's heart sank. This certainly put a damper on the joy of homecoming. He loved Shura far too much to sacrifice her to custom. He made his mind up. "Very well, Father. I shan't impose upon you by staying here. I'll find somewhere else to live. Far be it for me to ever fail in my love and respect for you. But I am not sending her back. She is in as much trouble as I am. I must protect her. She's got no one else to turn to. I'd be deliberately throwing her into the jaws of death if I sent her back."

There was nothing more to say. Mehmet was no stranger to his son's stubbornness—Seyit was much the same as his own younger self, if truth be told. He wouldn't attempt to change his son's mind. But he was heartbroken. They were losing the son they'd missed so much, and for what? Some strange woman! He walked toward the door without a glance at Seyit. "Do what you like. You will get your share of the money, vineyards, orchards, whatever. But never bring her here or come here yourself so long as you live with her. I will pretend you never came back in the first place."

Seyit wanted stop his father, hug him, and apologize for the hurt he had caused. But no amount of regret would have made any difference, would it? His words would remain hollow unless he was prepared to change his life. His father's intractability was perplexing. Could it be just a test of strength? Would his father change his mind and turn toward him now? But Eminof Senior walked out without another word. It was all over. Seyit had offended his teacher, friend, and mentor; that loving and supportive father was now renouncing him.

Mehmet paused on the first step of the staircase in the big entrance hall, slowly turned for a look, and said, "Seyit, it would be best for all concerned if you're gone by morning."

Seyit wanted to run, but his feet were nailed to the spot. Dragging his bad leg, he took one step and halted. He would have shouted, "Father, I love you very much. But I love her too. Being with her doesn't mean choosing between you—please understand," but his lips refused. He gulped. "If that's what you want—"

"Not me, Kurt Seyit; it's what *you* want. And you're free to do what you want."

As he walked toward the door, Seyit turned eyes flashing with unshead tears at his father one last time. "You're wrong, Father; I've not forgotten anything you told me. You once said, 'Never rejoice or worry in haste.' You know, you were right..."

He pulled the front door shut behind him, feeling utterly drained. He was totally alone in his own land, in his own home. Alone with Shura. He couldn't, didn't want to, believe what had just happened. He waited, hoping his father would open the door and call him back.

Mehmet Eminof stood on the bottom step, still grasping the banister. It was a bad dream. How could he have possibly lost his own son, his favorite son, the offspring he had pinned his hopes on, just when they were reunited—and it had taken only five minutes of conversation! He waited for Seyit to knock on the door to apologize.

After a long silence, Seyit walked away heartbroken, convinced he was no longer wanted in the family home. Mirza Mehmet Eminof plodded upstairs, convinced his son wanted to repudiate his family. Suddenly he felt very old. A pillar of his life was gone.

Seyit had untied his horse and was leading it out of the stables when Celil dashed out. He'd overhead the final part of the conversation between father and son and hidden out of sight until Mirza Eminof shuffled into his own room. Since his own situation was no different from Seyit's, Celil knew he would be equally unwanted. The household would be shocked in the morning.

Celil couldn't believe any of it. How was it possible to forsake such love so easily? In his heart, he blamed Seyit for this turn of events; couldn't he have been a little more yielding? But he kept his own counsel. What Seyit needed most now was not a lesson but friendship and sympathy. A pat on the shoulder and a supportive look were followed by a leg up. Seyit threw his good leg over the saddle and settled on the horse. "Thanks, Celil."

Without another word, they set off at a slow walk, breaking into a trot at the end of Sadovi Road. By the time they'd entered the seaward road flanked by plane trees, they were galloping into the briny breeze.

***

Shura had been lying awake in this unfamiliar place. Once Tatiana had gone to sleep, she'd gone out to the sofa under the trellis. In the darkness, the fresh smells of the sea and the fertile soil mingled. The wind ruffled her hair and rustled her skirt and the leaves on the newly burgeoning vines. The sea pounded the rocks beyond the vineyard in a sporadic explosion that drowned out the wind. How much safer this wild landscape was, compared to the life she had left behind! She snuggled into Seyit's jacket and closed her eyes as she stroked the broad collar with her cheek. Imagining herself in Seyit's embrace and listening to the wind and the sea, she was lost in a reverie. Her earlier life was now as far as the distant seas. It had been wonderful. But those wonderful days had come to an end. There was no point in indulging in nostalgia for a life that was gone. Now she was somewhere new, among people she didn't know—strange people and their ways. When would she return to Kislovodsk, if ever? Perhaps Seyit wouldn't come along when that day came.

She berated herself for this befuddling speculation and opened her eyes. She had to live in the moment instead of daydreaming. Had even one single thing turned out the way they had planned? It was best to just leave it all to time and destiny. Had she not made love to Seyit that first night simply because she wanted to enjoy the moment? Had she not yielded to him without caring whether he would want her again the next day? Had she not shared his bed for the sake of a pair of blazing blue eyes? Now she had even more reasons to stay with him. And she would stay until fate tore them asunder.

She grew hotter at the thought of making love to Seyit. Slender fingertips wandered on her neck. Despite the chill wind, her skin was burning. She wanted him here, now—his embrace, kiss, squeezes, and hungry gaze. She was missing him already. Her heartbeat quickened at the thought of his imminent arrival. Tipsy with happiness, her body tensed with anticipation. Undoing the collar, she bared her neck to the wind. She shivered a little as the cool sea air stroked her burning skin. She threw her head back and hummed a song under her breath, a paean to the stars twinkling above.

Sensing she would soon freeze, she stood up; that's when she heard the sound of hooves approaching at a gallop. Thrilled as she was by Seyit and Celil's return, she was concerned too: something was clearly amiss, judging by the look in Seyit's eyes and the fact that it was still hours until morning. Celil lifted an eyebrow in a silent warning, so she bit back her question. Instead, she embraced Seyit and rested her head on his chest.

Seyit fleetingly wondered whether he should be cross with this woman who was the cause of the rift with his family. But he felt quite the opposite; he loved this graceful, gentle, and aristocratic beauty far too much. They walked toward the house together. Celil went into his room, leaving the lovers alone, and Seyit led his sweetheart up the stairs.

He sat back on the wide sofa at the window overlooking the sea and drew her close. They cuddled in silence for a while. Seyit stared at the cliff ahead, where land and sea met. He wouldn't have felt as hollow if he'd jumped off it. He was homesick in his home country, where he'd been born and raised, where he'd learned to ride—in his father's home. He was homesick. The warm embrace he had been longing for had been snatched away. He would have to give up the woman he loved first. And he had nowhere else to go. He'd be an even worse stranger anywhere else.

Even in the darkness, the sorrow in his eyes didn't escape Shura's attention. She lay on his chest, stroked his face, and waited patiently for him to open up. The furrowed brow and drawn cheekbones felt as unyielding and blank as a statue. But the tense mouth did not reject the touch of her fingertips. He grasped her wrist and kissed them one by one before lowering his lips to her wrist. He removed the pins holding up her chignon. Her light, playful fragrance rose from the freed hair. He kissed the blond waves cascading down his palms and then bent his head down and sought her lips. He wanted to forget his sorrows, loneliness, and endless yearning in the face, hair, and body of the passionate woman in his arms. Shura was ready to respond. This was what she had been dreaming of for hours. Seyit was here, and he was with her. She wasn't going to ask where he had been, or with whom, or even what he'd done when he was away. She wasn't going to ask anything until he was prepared to tell her. What mattered was that they were together now. Taking care not to press on his bad leg, she stretched on his body and started undoing the buttons on his shoulder, planting kisses on the sad face and eyes. Soon all inhibition was discarded. The body enveloped by his jacket was aroused, he knew, and he squeezed her tighter. Grasping her by the waist and shoulders, he drew her close. His eternal bane, that frosty loneliness was still there, and it would melt away only at the warmth of her love and her body. She was the only person in the whole of Russia who could offer him love—the only woman who offered it without demanding a return. His moves grew rougher still at the thought of losing her one day, as if by possessing her at once, he could ensure her undying devotion. Shura remained surprisingly untroubled by his abnormally brusque alacrity; if anything, she responded with kisses and caresses of equal vehemence. This Shura was a totally different person from the hitherto serene girl. This was an eager, wild woman thirsty for love. She was ecstatic. The night enveloped them like a spell. Every single sound seemed to be directing her movements: the wind, the waves down at the shore, the froth pounding the rocks, and the tinkle of the tiny marble fountain. Their lovemaking was as wild as the nature surrounding them in this corner of the world. When she threw her head back in a soft yell of pleasure, she noticed their only witnesses were the stars outside the window. She was drunk with joy. Stars and more stars, the lusty pounding of the waves, the frothing waves...she let the tears flow freely.

***

A week later, Celil and Tatiana left for Poltava. What Celil kept a secret from Seyit was the number of times he had pleaded with Eminof Senior—unsuccessfully, as it happened, since the father wanted a contrite son to come to make amends, whereas the son waited for the father to send for him.

Seyit knew they couldn't stay at the vineyard house forever. His father hadn't come to the vineyard once since their arrival, and this was the season when he would normally spend all day there. Seyit found a house for sale on a hill over-looking Alushta Harbor. Originally built as a summer residence for a merchant from Moscow, it was a lovely, large, single-story house nestled among the trees. Shura loved it at first sight. The bedroom commanded the best view she could have imagined; like the sitting room, its vast picture windows overlooked the sea.

One day, Seyit saw Cemal, the family's steward, in the vineyard and gave him a list of items he wanted from the house. A few hours later, Cemal turned up at his door with a young lad and started unloading the cart. Shura was bustling with the delight of having a place of their own; the old faithful greeted her politely before addressing Seyit in Tatar. "A bad business, sir—a bad business indeed. We'll all miss you."

Seyit patted the aging man's back.

"Don't worry, Cemal. Time will sort it all out, God willing."

"Zahide Hanım's crying all the time. *Guvardia* Eminof is upset too, but he is a father, isn't he? He wants his word to be law—what can you do?" lamented the steward in an avuncular tone warranted by having practically raised Seyit from childhood.

"I wouldn't wish to upset my father, Cemal, but what *can* you do? *Kısmet*."

Seyit's clothes and books were placed into walnut trunks. The black lacquer trunk with the brass rooster had also arrived. Seyit was delighted as he carried it into the sitting room; he had almost forgotten about this precious circumcision present from Tsar Nicholas.

In the evening, Seyit and Shura snuggled up on the huge floor cushions in their new home. There was little in the way of furniture. Their most precious possessions were the piano by the window embracing the Black Sea, a coffee table from Seyit's bedroom next to it, and the black trunk by the fireplace. Supper was Seyit's expertly baked pirozhkis and a bottle of vintage wine from the vineyard, after which they sat facing the fireplace. At first Shura was quite merry. She started singing. Then sorrow took over, and the tears flowed unchecked as she launched into a lament of unrequited love. Sorrow would catch up with them no matter what they did or how happy they might be. Sorrow, in fact, never left them alone.

That was the first night they slept without making love. Cuddling naked in the brass bed under a gossamer canopy, they watched the boundless sea from the windows in total silence. Their caresses and snuggles were tender and sensitive rather than passionate; they banished loneliness rather than sating lust. On a night that ought to have marked a happy beginning, they recognized instead that the future held no hope for happiness.

Life in Alushta was much the same as before. It all seemed so calm, so serene, that Shura finally accepted she was in a different corner of the same country. The occasional cautious, brief letter from Seyit's friends in Petrograd kept them abreast of developments. Rüstem, who had hidden in Livadia for a while, had come to stay upon his return to Alushta, and his accounts had verified the dreadful state of affairs. Everything had gone from bad to worse since they'd left. The revolutionaries had fallen out over ideological differences. Trotsky's return on May 17 with his supporters bolstered the Bolshevik faction, even as the Mensheviks and several generals thought their time had come. Revolts flared up on the streets throughout June, July, and August, mostly fomented by one group or another for domination. The suggestion that landowners would be overthrown and their land handed out to the peasants instigated unsanctioned riots as thousands of peasants ransacked farms and fields, massacring the landowners as the enemies of the people.

Promises of land reform, worker-run factories, and distribution of provisions allegedly stockpiled by the aristocracy and the bourgeoisie poured hundreds of thousands to the streets hell-bent on dreams of wealth and happiness. They wanted it all, and they wanted it now: land, factories, beautiful houses, everything.

Crimeans watched it all from afar, mindful that trouble would reach them sooner or later. The grapes in the vineyards and the wheat and tobacco in the fields had all been harvested. The earth was in slumber, ready to burgeon in the spring. With the exception of evergreens, winter reigned unchallenged over the earth, the sky, and the sea. The days were bright but short and chilly. It still didn't feel like proper winter to Shura, although she had to admit it was no patch on the lovely summer they'd just had. She was stuck indoors in the cold. She sighed, staring at the violent waves frothing on the sea.

I'm just being silly, she thought. She had to accept that things had changed—and not because she was here. Life in Kislovodsk wouldn't be the same either.

Dragging her index finger over the entire length of the keyboard, she walked past the piano and went into the bedroom. She sat down at the small desk to finish a letter to her mother. Having received no replies to her earlier letters, she was justifiably worried that something awful might have happened.

She took pains to keep her letter quite brief. A thick envelope might attract attention; it made sense to avoid offering too much information about their lives in case the letter fell into strange hands. She finished the letter, placed it in an envelope, and left it on the desk to be posted the following day. Just then she heard Seyit and dashed to the door, still as excited as a young maiden meeting a beau for the first time. They embraced as soon as the door was shut. They were learning to create their own little happy world in this fugitive life—or was she mistaken? All she could see in his eyes was misery. She drew back, anxious that he would leave her as she always did whenever he looked sad or hesitant. Then she noticed he was holding a letter. He plodded in broodily and collapsed into an armchair. She waited, nervously standing by his side, watching his face. She knew him well enough; he would open up in his own good time. It was only when their eyes met that she moved over and sat down beside him. Seyit handed her the letter. She took it apprehensively and started to read.

It was dated November 8 and was from Sergei Moiseyev to Mehmet Eminof. Shura read with bated breath, occasionally choking back a doleful sob.

It clearly had been scribbled in haste. The Bolsheviks had triumphed by November 7 from the front to quell the revolution, and the military academy cadets who supported them had been massacred in the city center. The city was in a nightmare. The revolutionaries had commandeered private residences. Sergei Moiseyev and his wife, Olga, now lived in the larder next to the kitchen, and food distribution was in the hands of a committee. He would send the letter through the most secure way he knew; they could be killed if it was discovered. He asked Mehmet to burn the letter once he'd read it and reassured his friend that they would always remember the good old days.

Seyit answered Shura's silent question. "Cemal brought it over once Father had read it."

Shura felt numb all over, body and soul. She stood up, went to the bedroom, picked up the envelope addressed to Kislovodsk, and stared. The envelope that would never reach its destination seemed to glow with the faces of her mother, sisters, and brothers. And she would never see them again.

She returned to the sitting room and threw it into the logs crackling in the fireplace. Spent, she sank to her knees, staring at the inky embers fluttering in the flames. Seyit sat down next to her. Cupping her face in his hands, he kissed her tearstained cheeks. Shura had the impression of looking at the last memento of her home city as she stared back. She sank into his arms and cried for a long time. The silence, when she eventually did stop, was one of acquiescence. Rocking the disconsolate and vulnerable young woman, Seyit sensed that destiny would not leave him alone. It would continue shoving him hither and thither. Just when he thought he could go no farther, he would be dragged away from here too. But where? This was the southernmost point of Russian soil. The sea lay a little ahead, beyond the cliff, and that was the end of the vast land that was Russia. How much farther would he run? *Where? Where? Where?* That single question pounded in his mind.

And Shura? Would he take her along every time he ran away? She couldn't go back any more. Nor could she live in Crimea on her own. What else would happen? What else would they have to cope with?

He sat motionlessly, his lips in the hair of his sweetheart, who had fallen asleep on his chest. It was well past midnight when the logs in the fire turned into embers. Seyit was still awake, and he would stay awake many a night yet.

***

The next year 1918, started inauspiciously and went from bad to worse.

Seeing no point in carrying on the war with the Germans, and under Lenin's instructions, the soviet regime signed the Treaty of Brest-Litovsk. Right Socialists in government were angered by certain concessions in the treaty; they regarded the Bolshevik offer to ship trainloads of war and food supplies, petrol, leather, and copper to Germany when Russia was starving nothing less than treason. The Allies, meanwhile, demanded an immediate stop to this blatant Bolshevik support of Germany.

Petrograd and Moscow teemed with multiple countries' spies. The Allies relied on the Mensheviks to halt the provisions shipped to Germany. Left Socialist

Revolutionaries were similarly dissatisfied by the performance of the soviet government: peasants might dream of the fields and vineyards they would soon get, but the Bolsheviks had developed an entirely different program intended to empower the proletariat instead. At any rate, land ownership had not been given to the peasants but seized by the soviet; any produce deemed surplus to field workers' needs would similarly be surrendered.

The Right Socialist Revolutionaries eventually took the bold step of acting against the Bolsheviks, with the sole aim of assisting the Allies by sabotaging the Brest-Litovsk Treaty. Freight trains destined for Germany were blown up, as were the bridges they would cross. The assassination of the German ambassador Wilhelm Graf von Mirbach-Harff on July 6 in Moscow was another act in this scheme. The Socialist Revolutionary leader Boris Savinkov took over Yaroslavl some two hundred miles north of Moscow, although Red Army regiments from Petrograd and Moscow regained control within two weeks.

Threatened with dwindling support of their earlier efforts to form a government and the revolt of the Czech Legion that had fought alongside the Russians in the war, the Bolsheviks were exceptionally frustrated with these diverse political factions. Helped by the Czechs, the Whites took control of Siberia all the way to Vladivostok. By July 31, most of Siberia was cleared of the Reds, and the Czechs continued their westward push. Then there was the additional danger posed by Admiral Kolchak's counterrevolutionary preparations in Omsk. Further triumphs in the White Army's advance and the endurance of a political body intent on overthrowing the Bolsheviks could easily reinstate the tsarist regime. If the ultimate objective of all these counterrevolutionary attempts was the revival of tsarism and the bourgeoisie, then there was only one solution.

Not a single soul was around to hear a call for help when Tsar Nicholas Alexandrovich Romanov; his wife, Tsarina Alexandra Feodoravna; and their five children were awakened and led down to the basement at 1:30 a.m. July 17. The imperial family had been imprisoned at Yekaterinburg for months. Sentenced to a summary execution by the soviet, the Romanovs were slaughtered by a hail of bullets in the course of a few minutes. Yakov Sverdlov and his men carried out the sadistic massacre, looted the bodies for the last few jewels, and doused them with acid.

"God Save the Tsar," the imperial anthem that had been sung for generations, had fallen silent. God no longer had a tsar to save.

The Whites were horrified by the news. Some refused to believe it, thinking it had to be a ploy to discourage the tsarists, but they were simply deluding themselves. The awful truth was too hard to accept.

Having regrouped after their defeat in Yaroslavl, Savinkov led a faction determined to revive the tsarist regime. On August 30, one of his agents, Fanny Yefimovna Kaplan, shot and wounded Lenin as he left a meeting in Moscow. The next day, the Chekist Uritsky was shot; Socialist Revolutionaries claimed responsibility for the assassination of the leader of the Petrograd region.

Founded in 1917 as an emergency committee, the Cheka had unrestricted authority to carry out mass arrests, trials, and executions. The Bolsheviks decided to retaliate after the wounding of Lenin and the death of Uritsky. That same night, firing squads killed five hundred representatives of the tsarist regime in Moscow and another five hundred in Petrograd.

Red terror now reigned in Russia.

By August 1918, all private trade was banned, and all private property was handed over to the soviet. Old payment methods were swept away, and workers were paid in coupons and vouchers instead of cash. The soviet sequestered all surplus produce, offering farmers little more than promises of future recompense. A chaotic distribution system paralyzed the transportation network, which had been hampered already by serious damage sustained during the war. Russia reeled in the clutches of one of the worst famines in its history.

Once the central regions were under their control, the Bolsheviks shot southward. A chain of committees acted upon orders to establish an absolute Bolshevik rule over these fertile lands as a matter of priority.

Certain they were on the Red Army hit list, Celil and Tatiana left Poltava at the end of July. Seyit and Shura were delighted when they came to stay. They were all happy to be reunited, especially under the circumstances.

News that a Crimean army had formed in Bakhchisaray against any possible Bolshevik invasion prompted Seyit to prepare for all contingencies. He contacted old friends who had run away to Alupka after battling the Bolsheviks in Omsk and arranged to purchase what weapons they still had.

Carts arrived at the vineyard, usually after midnight, in batches spread out irregularly to avoid rousing suspicion. As Seyit, Celil, and Ismail Efendi's son removed the weapons from under the sacks of manure and buried them one by one beneath the vine stocks, the old man kept a lookout. The slightest touch on the soil seemed to resonate in the stillness of the night, broken only by the chirping of crickets.

Shura asked no questions whenever Seyit returned home shattered and disheveled, contenting herself with watching him. Their love had not changed, but his unusually preoccupied mood and furtive disappearances late at night filled her with a terrified apprehension.

Mahmut and Osman frequently snuck away to visit their older brother. Seyit could do no wrong in their eyes, no matter what their father might say; they worshipped the ground he walked on. They had grown to like Shura too. At first she had waited patiently and kept her distance until the younger men cast aside their timidity and suspicions. In time, once they got to know her and learned how she had left everything behind and was prepared to put up with any hardship just to be with their brother, they came to respect and even like her. She was so different from their image of a mistress! Nothing in her character screamed *fallen woman*.

Cemal was the only person who knew about those visits, and he carried messages if they had to cancel for any reason.

One evening, Seyit was scribbling at the desk in the bedroom after supper as Shura's piano playing floated into the fresh, still summer night. They were on their own, as Celil and Tatiana were visiting with an elderly aunt in Alupka.

The spell was broken by the sound of a carriage speeding toward the house. Osman leaped out, glanced around apprehensively, and darted in, panting.

"Seyit *Abi*, they're here! You must hide—run away!"

At eighteen and barely out of childhood, Osman, who still used the honorific *Big Brother*, received a playful slap on the neck intended to pacify. "Hey, hold your horses! Catch your breath first and then speak."

"The Bolsheviks are here; they've taken over one of the buildings in the main square. And they're armed! Seyit *Abi*, please run away—run away tonight!"

Wringing her hands to hide her panic, Shura waited for Seyit's reaction. He remained surprisingly composed as he stroked Osman's shoulder. "Thanks, brother. I'll never forget this...but I can't go anywhere tonight."

"But—"

"Not tonight, Osman—not yet."

"Tomorrow morning then."

"Tomorrow's too soon too. I've still got a little more to do here."

Osman and Shura both thought he'd gone mad.

"Please, Kurt Seyit...they'll descend on our house first thing tomorrow. It won't take them long to find you. Please run; get away while there's time," pleaded Osman in a weepy voice.

Shura thought she might remind Seyit of her presence; perhaps that would convince him. Walking over, she murmured, "Seyit..."

Giving her a kiss on the lips, he gazed at the vineyards below, a man not prepared to listen. Shura waited in silence. Seyit stared at the harbor, scanning the rocks at the shore and the sea. An unfathomable resolve shone on his face when he looked back.

"Don't worry, Osman; please don't worry. We will go, but it's not yet time to leave Alushta. I need a few more days."

"What if they find you in the meantime?"

Seyit shrugged. He was ready to face his fate. "*Kismet*—whatever fate says." He turned toward his sweetheart and continued, "Get ready straightaway. Take nothing that isn't essential."

Shura hastened to the bedroom, relieved at the prospect of a plan of sorts.

Osman took this opportunity. "What are you planning to do now? Where will you go?"

"We'll stay in the vineyard house for a couple of days. I'll let you know when I decide what to do after that."

Osman stared at his big brother expectantly. "Seyit, I beg you: take me wherever you go."

With a fond smile, Seyit stroked his cheek; the boy's face stood on the threshold of maturing into masculine features.

"Osman, I have no idea where to go or what I will find there. You're still very young. All your family is here. You'd be wasted if you came along."

"But I've wanted to go with you ever since I was little. I was so envious every time you went away! Now I'm grown-up. Please take me along."

"Of course you are; you're now a young man, Osman. But you'd only get into trouble if you came along. I love you too much to place you in danger."

Cocking an eye at Shura, who was packing a small valise, Osman asked, "And you're taking her along...because you don't love her?"

His envy was understandable. Seyit ruffled his wavy dark-blond hair. "If I succeed, I'll go on my own. I'll be alone. It's me they're after. So long as you all stay away, you'll be safe."

They were speaking in Tatar, but Shura caught the occasional word. Her name hadn't come up, but she knew *yalğız* meant alone—*on my own.*

Seyit didn't want his brother to tarry. "Come on, Osman. Get back before it's too late. You'll get in trouble if you're caught on the road." He stumbled over the next part. "My dear brother...we might never meet again. Please don't try to see me off or anything. I'm sure they'll be on your tail. Thankfully we've been living apart for months. At the very least, you can prove you have nothing to do with me. Pretend you've not seen me at all and don't leave home."

Osman's objections fell on deaf ears. He burst into unapologetic sobs as Seyit gave him a good-bye hug.

Dousing the lights, they waited. Now in a plain dress, Shura waited for a sign from Seyit. She neither knew nor wished to know where they would go. Seyit kept peering toward the vineyards; there was no movement as yet. He had to check his cache as a matter of urgency.

The wind had picked up, and a silver moonlight slid over the phosphorescence in the sea; it all looked so lovely. Nature remained unperturbed by man's affairs.

The stillness of the night was shattered by the sound of boots stomping up the steps outside the front door. Seyit took up his place behind the door, holding a pistol he'd taken from the desk, and gestured to Shura to go into the bedroom. Whoever was at the door, it couldn't have been Celil. Seyit held his breath and waited for a knock.

He heard a cautious tap that contrasted with the stomping feet. Barely audible. Seyit tried to look out of the narrow window, but all he could make out was a tall male figure standing on the marble step. Another soft tap. After brief hesitation, Seyit called out, "Who's there?"

An anxious reply came in a whisper. "Seyt, open; it's me, Yasef—Yasef Zarkovich. Open up, Kurt Seyt—quick!"

Seyit was momentarily taken aback. There could only be one Yasef who knew his childhood nickname. His childhood friend Yasef. All the same, the pistol remained in his hand as he opened the door a crack. The man slipped in, shut the door, and leaned against it. Seyit drew back instinctively. He stared, hoping to recognize Yasef Zarkovich; he hadn't seen his friend since they were children, but he couldn't see much in the dark. Then moonlight flooded in from behind the trees. Seyit was horrified at the Bolshevik outfit and the red armband.

"Bloody hell!" he said, turning his pistol on the man. How easily had he fallen for the old childhood friend ploy! *It's all over now*, he thought.

The man whispered again. "Are you out of your mind, Kurt Seyt? Drop it, mate. Don't you recognize me?"

"It's been a long time," snapped Seyit frostily. He kept the pistol pointed at the man, but Seyit tensed at the prospect of attracting attention if he were to use it.

"Put it down, Seyit, please! I'm not here to hurt you. Look, I'm not holding a gun, am I?"

Yasef's pistol was indeed still in its holster.

"What's that on your arm then? What are you doing here?"

"If I really intended to hurt you, I wouldn't have knocked on the door, would I? I've come to help."

Seyit wasn't about to believe that a Bolshevik would help him. "What's your game, Yasef? What's on your mind?"

"There isn't much time, Seyit; they'll be along soon."

"Who?"

"They're doing a door-to-door search tonight. Do you have any idea what will happen if they find you?"

"So why aren't you doing the same?"

"Don't be like that, Seyt; weren't we friends? Just because I'm a Bolshevik doesn't mean I'm gonna renounce my old friends."

"You don't think like a Bolshevik at all."

Yasef chuckled. "Perhaps I'm not—who can say?" He hastened to add a more serious, "Seyt, listen. I was at the vineyard today; I know what's going on. I've not said anything to anyone. Run away at once. I'll help you get away."

Seyit stared incredulously. "I don't understand why you're doing this."

"Never mind the questions. If you tell me what you're planning, I will help you."

Seyit hesitated, his suspicions not yet allayed. "How can I trust you when you're wearing that armband?"

"Do you have a choice?"

He was right. Seyit had no choice.

Silence implies consent, thought Yasef, and he carried on. "Just tell me what you're going to do when, and I'll help you."

Seyit was struggling to share his escape plan with one of the enemy sworn to kill him, when he'd kept it a secret from his sweetheart and family all this time. It could all be a trick—a terrible trick that would cost him his life.

Yasef spoke calmly, trying one last time to reassure him. "I swear on the Holy Bible, Seyt; I'm here to help you. I'm not about to tell anyone about the weapons. I will help you wherever you're going."

Seyit was beginning to believe his childhood friend. "I'll have to get to the shore from the vineyard."

"You must move swiftly. I'm on duty tomorrow night. I'll look out for you."

Seyit took a deep breath. He left dozens of questions unasked. "All right... tomorrow night."

"Make sure you're in disguise, or you'll make it difficult for me. I'll stop by the vineyard in the early hours and give you a precise time." Peeking out of the door, he was about to leave when he turned back as if he'd just remembered. "Seyt, don't forget—only you. I can't help anyone else."

Seyit had no chance to say anything more. At the sound of riders between the trees toward the left, Yasef slammed the door behind him and skipped down the steps. Seyit felt his chest constrict as he watched the road from behind the netting. Shura had stood up at the end of Seyit and Yasef's conversation; she dropped down by the bed once again.

There were four or five horsemen, their boisterous yells drowning the clop of hooves on pebbles. A couple dismounted and started toward the house. *Now we're trapped*, thought Seyit. But Yasef stopped the riders.

"Don't waste your time, comrades; there's no one we want here. I've just been."

But the two Reds insisted on seeing for themselves. Feigning nonchalance to avoid suspicion, Yasef leaped up on his horse. "We're wasting time, comrades. Fuck knows where the bastards are hiding, and here we are, hanging about!"

Seyit wouldn't have thanked him for the insult, but Yasef's ploy seemed to have worked. The others finally mounted their horses again. "You're right, Comrade Zarkovich; let's check the houses in the forest. He knew them well, the tsar's dog!"

Seyit was beside himself. Grinding his teeth, he refrained from bursting out and walloping the owner of the voice he knew so well. He cast another glance at the mounted silhouette. The rider turned his horse around to face the way they had come, and Seyit was now absolutely positive.

Petro Borinsky. Comrade Borinsky, as he was now—complete with a red armband.

As soon as the horses' hooves faded into the distance, Seyit rushed over to Shura. The poor girl was nearly catatonic with fear and worry. Seyit lifted her to her feet and held and kissed her trembling hands. "It's all right, darling. We're safe for now. But we must move to the vineyard house first thing tomorrow."

"What about Celil and Tatya?"

Just then there was a tap on the sitting room window. Seyit crept up. It was Celil, peering inside from between the foliage. Seyit opened the door, and Celil and Tatiana dashed in holding hands.

"Where on earth have you been? We were nearly caught!"

"We hid when we saw a horse outside. No one came out, and we thought we'd wait a little longer. Then the others arrived. What an earth is going on, Seyit? What are we doing now? How did you shake them off?"

"A long story—I'll tell you later. We must get to the vineyard house first... and at once. Leave nothing that might lead them to us. Now pack, quickly!"

This time they took even less than the bare minimum that had been their luggage leaving Petrograd. Seyit had packed his decorations, photographs, and letters into a small bag already. His eyes kept straying to the trunk. It was too big to take along, but he wasn't going to leave it there either. He snatched it, went to the back garden through the kitchen, grabbed a shovel from the tools in the big basket, dug under the oak, and buried the trunk. He knelt to stroke the brass cockerel one last time. What he was burying here wasn't just the black lacquer trunk; it was his whole life. The generous donor of this fabulous gift now lay under the earth, hundreds of miles away; it might be his turn next.

He was wasting time. He hastened to fill the hole and level the soil over the spot. *Maybe one day*, he thought, as he turned for one last look before going back into the kitchen. *Maybe one day...*

Soon they were slinking through the woods wordlessly, their eyes and ears on the road, terrified of meeting anyone. It took nearly an hour of running, hiding, and walking to reach the vineyard.

Not a leaf stirred. Seyit still insisted they stay hidden until he gave the all clear. Yes, it was quiet...but danger might be lurking anywhere.

Ismail Efendi's small house looked quite normal. Seyit whistled their secret signal used on the nights they had buried the weapons. The old man materialized at the door, a jacket hastily thrown over his nightclothes. "Oh, Seyit Eminof, I wish you'd stayed away!"

Seyit drew him toward the house.

"I know, Ismail Efendi; they were here today. I need your help. I have to stay here until tomorrow night."

The old man was wringing his hands. "Erm, yes, sir; you're very welcome..."

Seyit thought he'd misunderstood. "Ismail Efendi, I'm talking of staying in my house. It's not like you think."

"Yes, sir, of course you can stay here. But you can't go into your own home. They came this evening and padlocked all the doors."

Seyit stamped his heel and gritted his teeth. "Did they leave a guard?"

"No, Seyit Eminof, they can't spare the men, I guess. They're looking for you, sir. They interrogated every single vineyard worker. God watch over you! What have we done to deserve this, Eminof?"

"If you could arrange somewhere for the ladies to sleep, we've got something to attend to first."

Seyit signaled to the others hiding behind the trees. Ismail Efendi's son and daughter-in-law offered their room to Shura and Tatiana, who gratefully stretched out on clean sheets, although sleep was the last thing on their minds.

All night long, Seyit, Celil, Ismail Efendi, and his son dug up the weapons, stacked them in grape crates, and hid them in the storeroom. Every time a leaf rustled, all four men fell flat on their faces under the vines and held their breaths. It was nearly daybreak by the time the last crate was sealed and the storeroom was locked. The women had waited up; whatever the men had been doing, it was undoubtedly crucial.

With the first rays of dawn, Cemal turned up to inform them that the Sadovi Road house had been commandeered. The entire Eminof family had been crammed into the ground-floor servants' quarters, he explained, on the verge of tears.

"Who'd have thought it, Kurt Seyit? Who'd have thought it, eh? How could Mirza Eminof sleep in the same place with the watchman or the gardener? Wasn't he out there fighting the Japanese so that we could sleep like babes? A great war hero, all those decorations and medals and everything! Disgraceful!"

The reception room and bedrooms had been padlocked and declared out of bounds until the Reds picked new occupants to move in. Seyit felt awful; he hadn't been there to help his family in their hour of need. Drawing the steward aside, he whispered instructions. "Cemal, please listen carefully. This might be the last thing I will ever ask of you."

"God forbid, Kurt Seyit—God spare us! The things I've seen in Russia all my life! This too will pass. Just keep your head down for the time being."

Neither man believed that this would pass or even change, but voicing the obvious wasn't going to be helpful. Seyit carried on. "Not a word to anyone else, all right?"

The old man visibly perked up, proud to share the secrets of the young man he had raised.

"Go down to the shore at once and find Tatoğlu Hasan. Tell him to wait offshore for my signal at midnight and at the same time tomorrow if I don't make it."

Cemal's eyes opened as wide as saucers. "What do you mean, Kurt Seyit? You're crossing the sea?"

"Got nowhere else to go, have I? I'll try to reach the other shore...if God wills it, that is."

"And *Guvardia* Eminof—what's he gonna make of it?"

"That's the other thing. Please tell him about my plan. He hasn't forgiven me, but ask my father for his blessings."

He lifted misty eyes to the first rays of the sun. Dark-gray vestiges of the night mingled with the golden crimson of early morning in the vineyard. The deep navy-blue gauze over the Black Sea changed color as frothy white clouds formed in the heavens.

All Cemal could say as he departed was, "As you wish, Kurt Seyit."

Seyit, Shura, Celil, and Tatiana spent the whole day hiding in the backroom. The women waited in silence, sitting on the narrow sofa, as Seyit and Celil debated in whispered Tatar. Soon it would be time to leave. Seyit had no idea how successful his plan would be, but no matter how badly it might turn out, he would still be far safer away from here. When he recounted spotting Petro, Celil slapped his knee furiously. "Blast and damnation! They couldn't have found a better person to put on your trail if they wanted! What if he's there tonight? He'd recognize us both in a flash. Nothing Yasef can do would save us—they'd tear us to pieces then and there."

"My thoughts exactly. They're likely to stick together, like last night, in which case, this would be nothing less than suicide."

Celil tapped his fists together reflectively. "What can we do? Can you think of anything?"

Seyit disclosed his own quandary very slowly. "There's only one thing, Celil, only one...I can't think of anything else either. My brain must have seized up; it can't be me thinking of this...this..."

Elbows on the table, he buried his face in his hands as if trying to hide his shame or looking for another way out.

He removed his hands and locked eyes with his friend, and they read each other's minds. Celil sat up, bringing his face closer. "You're not thinking what I'm thinking, are you?"

Seyit gritted his teeth, and his cheekbones seemed to quiver tensely. "We have to, Celil. There's no other way."

"But how?"

"If only I knew he wouldn't turn up..."

"He'd kill *you* without blinking an eye though."

"I know, I know; all the same, we're not like that—"

A knock at the front door interrupted the conversation. Seyit opened the door a crack for a look: it was Yasef. He dashed out as the others drew back. Yasef spoke, watchful eyes scanning their surroundings. "If you manage to get away tonight, you'll be fine. Otherwise I can't help you. Are you ready?"

Seyit nodded.

"Fine. Don't blame me in case something goes wrong though."

"Thanks, Yasef—I'll never forget your kindness."

"Great...then make sure you survive. Like I said, only you. You might attract attention otherwise. And I couldn't save you either."

"Yasef, I've got to take my friends along."

"Your call, Seyt. I can't save any of you then. Now they're used to the smell of blood, they live for the chase. Your house above the harbor? It's already been taken. They're waiting for you to go back. You're their sacrificial lamb."

"So they know I lived there?"

"There are ways of making people speak, you know, Kurt Seyt. Especially if someone has it in for you."

"Who are you talking about?"

"Borinsky, former bourgeois-turned-Bolshevik," Yasef sniggered.

"And you?" asked Seyit.

"Who would save you, unless I was among them, Seyt? Eh?"

Seyit hesitated, but curiosity overcame caution. "Where is he now?"

"Petro? He's taken your house. He's sure you'll go back. And he's determined to meet you," said Yasef, opening the door. "This morning I'm checking on all the properties we've padlocked. They all belong to the soviet now, as you know. Anyway, everything seems to be all right; I'm going back now. God be with you. Please forgive me should anything go wrong."

"God be with you too, Yasef."

Seyit came back in, pensively avoiding all eyes. How was he going to explain he'd have a far better chance of survival if he ran away on his own? Celil's voice broke into his dark thoughts. "Seyit, you know what? I've been thinking, and I've decided to stay here."

Seyit gaped. They'd been planning all this time, and now his friend was suddenly throwing in the towel? Celil carried on. "I'd like a fish out of the water there, Seyit. I don't know anyone. A strange land, strange people. At least here I'm in my homeland. Tatya couldn't cope either. We'd be too lonely. I'm not like you. I'm not as strong as you. And I'm not leaving her behind; she stuck around through thick and thin. I couldn't break her heart now."

"You know your fate isn't going to be much different if you're caught, don't you?"

"I know, Seyit. But what I was thinking was, if we settled in a tiny village and lived like peasants, we'd drop out of sight. They'd soon forget about us."

Celil was speaking sense, but Seyit was convinced he stood a better chance if he got away. Except for his responsibility to Shura...as Celil's speech about Tatiana pointed out. Had Shura not done even more than Tatiana as a woman, lover, and friend? Wasn't he doing her a dreadful injustice by leaving her with the servants in a vineyard house in Alushta? It didn't take a genius to know she was going to be devastated. What about him? He would never be free of guilt, would he? But if he were captured in the middle of the night with a cart full of munitions and a beautiful young woman—no, she would be safer here. He resolved to go alone.

"Don't worry about us," said Celil. "We'll take her along if she wants. It's not like these romances were meant to last a lifetime, is it? Our fault for deceiving ourselves they would."

Seyit threw his arm over his friend's shoulder and led him to the little window at the rear. "I thought our friendship was meant to last a lifetime?"

Celil's eyes filled up, and they hugged and stared at the vineyard and the hills behind the hazy veil of the net—but what they saw was their friendship through the years.

"Seyit, we'll remain friends even if we're apart, even when we die."

"I'm sure someone will tell the tale one day."

The exchange ended with a sorrowful smile.

Tatiana was lost in reminiscences of the good old days, perusing old letters she and Celil had exchanged, as Shura lay on her side, ostensibly asleep.

She wasn't asleep at all. She had figured out Seyit's plan, based on the snatches she'd been hearing over the past couple of days. The words she would have gladly forgotten kept echoing in her ears. *Alone...alone...alone...*

And that day had come. Just when she was beginning to believe she and her lover were soul mates, she would be left on her own. It took great effort to choke back the tears—nay, the sobs—at the thought of breaking up. Burying her face in her pillow, she bit her lip. Crying would help nothing. She still wanted to cry. But not here. Somewhere where she could be alone, where she could bawl her heart out. Even the thought of breaking up with Seyit for good was terrifying. She felt sluggish. Drained. *I'll probably go out of my mind without him.*

Time seemed to be dragging on. Minutes and hours felt as long as days. No one had any appetite when Ismail Efendi's wife served a lunch of soup, pastry, and grapes. Seyit was all ears and eyes, waiting for news from Cemal.

At long last, Cemal turned up in the afternoon, and they had a hurried conversation at the doorway.

"Tatoğlu is ready, Kurt Seyit. He'll wait at midnight, out beyond the rocks to the right of the harbor. You know Cengiz, the fisherman? He'll be on hand too."

"That's great! I remember him, a stout fellow. Thanks, Cemal; thank you so much. Tell Tatoğlu one more thing, will you? The first match I light will signal I'm coming down the hill; I'll light a second when I'm on the shore. Tell him to watch out, all right?" A pause, then, in a voice that held hope and hurt at the same time, he asked, "Have you passed my message on to Father?" Surely his father could have made a bit of an effort to see him before he left.

"Of course I did," said the steward, wringing his hands. He fell silent.

"So what did he say?" prodded Seyit.

"'God give him speed; travel safe. If we don't see each other now, we'll meet again in the afterlife.'"

Seyit was crushed. With a bitter smile, he pondered how he had lost his father's love. So he wouldn't be able to see his family one last time. A sympathetic Cemal tried to explain, "Don't misunderstand, Kurt Seyit. They can't possibly see you now. They're under house arrest; they can't leave. And you can't go there."

A small mercy after all; he was sure his father would have summoned him for a farewell if the conditions weren't so perilous.

The farewell with the elderly steward was heartbreaking. Cemal was beginning to stoop, but he straightened to hug Seyit. Tears flowed freely between white eyelashes and got caught in the deep furrows of his face. "Oh, my little master, Master Kurt Seyit. When I taught you 'grab the handkerchief' riding on these hills! I remember it like yesterday. How time passes. Your father had such dreams for these lands and you..."

Cemal had been a second father. Giving him a fond hug, Seyit spoke, sounding as childish as the days he'd held on to the steward's hands when they had wandered between the vines. "Sadly, not all dreams come true, Cemal. We can't do anything about it."

"What can I do, Master Seyit—what? The land's gone, and you're going too; what can I do?" lamented the sobbing steward. He bowed his head and staggered out of the vineyard.

As darkness fell, Seyit and Celil returned to their earlier topic; it took nearly an hour of deliberation, but at long last they made their minds up. Unless Petro was eliminated, Seyit could never get away, nor could the other three vanish fully. The execution of the plan necessitated going back to the house Petro had commandeered. Hopefully he was still there, as Yasef had said. It was madness. The odds of getting there, doing what they needed to do, and returning within an hour—provided they found Petro on his own in the first place—were too small to even calculate. Except that letting him live was much riskier.

Seyit had kept Shura in the dark about his plans for the night. Truth be told, he had no idea how to say it. He was not yet reconciled to the idea of leaving her behind. What sort of incentive could he offer her to stay? He tried to imagine himself without her. His heart ached. It wasn't going to be easy—no, it wasn't going to be easy at all. This farewell would be different. There was no comeback. There was no way Shura could follow. He watched her, conscious that they had no more than a few more hours together. Earlier, she had briefly wandered in silence and gone back to sleep. Concerned that she was coming down with something, Seyit touched her forehead and cheeks. At the touch of her dried tears, he knelt and called out tenderly, "Shura, my darling Shurochka..."

She must have been sound asleep; she didn't stir. Kissing her on the forehead, Seyit stood up and cocked an eye to tell Celil he was ready. Tatiana was reading a book by the light of the gas lamp. Celil kissed her and whispered, "We'll be back soon, Tatya; don't go away. There's something we have to do."

Certain Shura and she were now being abandoned, Tatiana asked a silent question with her eyes.

Celil read her mind. "We'll be back, Tatya; trust me. I love you very much, darling."

She confirmed her trust in him with another kiss.

A few minutes later, pistols in their pockets, the two friends were climbing the hill they'd crept down only the previous night, and they were even more watchful this time. Their hearts were pounding by the time they reached the woods to the rear of the property. This was an enormous risk just so that they could buy a little bit more time. Gesturing for Celil to halt, Seyit crept past the bedroom and peeked in through the drawn net curtains. Petro was pacing irritably in the middle of the sitting room. He seemed to be on his own; there was no sign of anyone else. Seyit still waited to make sure. When Petro moved to the bedroom, as if to answer a call, Seyit drew back behind the trees. Thankfully his foe came nowhere near the window. Petro sat down on the bed, cigarette in hand. He flung his booted feet on the bed and placed a sheaf of papers on his lap. Taking long drags of his cigarette, he flicked through the pages. Then he chucked them away and went into the kitchen.

Signaling to Celil to take up a position at the window, Seyit slipped in through the open window. Repulsive traitor—daring to put his dirty boots on the bed Seyit had shared with Shura until last night! Grabbing a handful of the papers, he hid behind the heavy curtains separating the sitting room, his pistol at the ready. A quick glance at Petro's scribbles was enough to incense him—incense, terrify, and sicken. Petro had kept a record of the regions he had been responsible for all the way to Alushta. Place names headed lists of names of people, gentry or otherwise; their property; and executions. The number of people shot on grounds of suspected counterrevolutionary acts, treason, or theft of soviet property was appalling. Not a single one had been tried. Comrade Borinsky was prosecutor, judge, and executioner in one.

The footsteps returned. Seyit now stood hidden behind Petro in total silence. Glancing at the sheets he'd left on the bed, Petro halted. He took a look at the net curtains billowing in the cold wind as if he'd smelled danger. Just as he was about to put his hand on his pistol, Celil leaped up and trained his pistol on Petro.

"So it's you..." As the words hissed out between Petro's gnashing teeth, the ice-blue eyes seemed to move even closer together.

Celil said nothing.

"What's happened to your best mate then? Or has he sent you instead? You'd do anything for him, wouldn't you?"

Celil stayed silent, waiting for Seyit's move.

Given the others could turn up at any time, Seyit had no intention of dawdling. He took a single step and dug the muzzle into Petro's ribs. At the cold touch of the metal, Petro made a move to turn, but Seyit's low growl stopped him in his tracks. "Don't you dare move, Borinsky. You'll only hasten the end. Arms in the air."

He prodded him toward the window, where Celil gestured to Petro to climb out.

Their captive tried to sound brazen even as he complied. "You fools. They'll never let you get away with it if something happens to me. Where do you think you're going to run? You fools—it's over; don't you get it? No way out for you now."

Seyit pressed the pistol to this loathsome creature's neck. "One more word and your life's over—get it, you filthy pig?"

He grabbed a pick and a shovel without relaxing his hold on the prisoner.

They entered the woods. Petro's bluster was gone. He was beginning to panic. Every feigned stumble or attempt to ask a question had elicited a sharp prod from the muzzle.

"Where are you taking me? What're you gonna do?"

"Quiet! Keep walking."

Seyit called out in a while. "Halt! Halt and lower your arms."

Petro thought they would let him go now; they probably just wanted to give him a scare. They wouldn't dare do anything more. Regaining his former arrogance, he sniggered. "Don't know why you took such risks! Just for a little stroll?"

Seyit threw him the pick and shovel, keeping the pistol aimed all the time. He took a step back. Celil was standing on the other side.

"Dig."

"Are you crazy, Seyt? You having me on or something?"

"Or something, yes, like the tricks you've been playing."

Petro opened his mouth, but Seyit's restless finger stroked the trigger. "Not another word. Shut up and start. And hurry; we've got things to do. Hurry, I said!"

Petro now knew this was no joke, although he still had no idea what they wanted. Seyit told him to drop the shovel when the hole was roughly as long as a man's height.

"Now get inside and lie down."

Petro's cold, bland face paled visibly in the darkness. *Surely not...*His voice trembled. "No, Seyt, this is madness—"

"Shut up and get into the hole *now!*"

It finally dawned upon Petro that his fate was in his old friends' hands. He pleaded incessantly as he lowered himself. "Don't do it, Seyt; aren't we old mates?"

Seyit's eyes offered no quarter. Petro turned to Celil instead. "Celil, say something; Seyit must have flipped. For God's sake!"

"So now you remember God, Comrade Borinsky? Now you remember your old mates?"

Seyit's face flushed in fury; the man now pleading for his life had summarily dispatched dozens of innocents. He listed the names he'd read, keeping his voice steady and firm despite the tempest inside, despite the incandescent rage at the thought of Petro's victims. "Did those poor wretches beg to be spared too? Tell me, Petro: Did they beg for mercy? This is how you made them dig their own graves, isn't it? You filthy pig—I'd have torn you to pieces if I had the time. Just be grateful I don't."

Petro's hefty figure was racked with sobs. "Please don't do it; we'll come to an arrangement. I'll turn a blind eye; I'll let you get away—"

Seyit aimed at the heart of the man in the grave. "Comrade Borinsky, you have been found guilty of treason to Russia."

A crack...a truncated groan from the body in the pit...an echo waning on the hills...the flapping of wings...

Then the muffled sound of shoveled soil.

Restless birds were still fluttering when the two young men took the wooded road leading to the vineyard.

Farewell Alushta, Autumn 1918

A S SEYIT AND Celil hastened back, a shadow slipped through the darkness and tapped on the door of the little house in the vineyard. Fearful glances were exchanged between the household and the guests, who had been sitting in total silence for close to an hour. Ismail Efendi gestured for Shura and Tatiana to hide in the backroom just in case and concealed the door by unfurling a wall rug usually reserved for the coldest days. Then he walked to the front door and called, "Who's there?"

"It's me...Osman, Ismail Efendi."

The faithful servant opened the door. Osman burst in, flushed and panting, and shoved the poor man aside. "Where's Seyit? Where's my big brother? He's not gone yet, has he?"

Osman's distraught behavior unnerved Ismail Efendi. "Calm down, Master Osman; calm down. They'll be back soon. We're waiting for them too."

"How do you know they'll be back?"

"I know nothing, Master Osman, but that's what they said. Believe me—I know nothing."

Osman knew about the backroom; he lifted the rug and opened the door. Shura and Tatiana were sitting on the sofa, clasping each other's hands for comfort—too tense to sleep and unsettled by the raised voices in this strange tongue. When she saw it was Osman, a relieved Shura let go of Tatiana's hand and rushed over. "Oh! Osman! Thank God it's you! You frightened us so much!"

Ashamed that he had caused such distress, Osman hastened to bow gallantly as he tried to compose himself. "When did Seyit leave?"

Shura had to think about it before replying; keeping track of time had been difficult in the past couple of days. "Perhaps an hour, perhaps a little longer. What's wrong?"

Osman suddenly looked deflated. Gone was the brusque youth. Instead, he slapped his own head and sank at the edge of the sofa, dismayed, whining. "He's gone! Gone! Gone and left me here again!"

Shura was finally solving the puzzle that had been plaguing her for a while. Now she was totally alone. She had been left on her own. The man she loved had taken off without even bothering to speak to her. She tapped the shoulder of the youth sobbing into his hands, still hoping for a reply that would prove her fears wrong. Softly, she asked, "How do you know he's gone, Osman? What did he tell you?"

Osman moved his hands away and stared at her tearful eyes. Her heart breaking for the youth before her, Shura briefly forgot about her own predicament. His childish loneliness seemed much sadder than her broken heart. She stroked his hair. "You might be mistaken, you know."

"No, I heard; I heard it all."

She sat down next to him to listen.

"I heard Cemal talking to my father. Seyit's gonna escape to the other side tonight. But he was going at midnight. He'd asked for my father's blessings. I heard it all. I ran away to catch up. I ran away to catch up with my brother without anyone seeing. But..." His voice was barely audible now. "But he's already gone. I'll never see him again..."

The truth that had been staring her in the face slashed at her heart and mind like a blade of ice. She wasn't alone in her pain though; she glanced at Tatiana—who was equally shocked but then...Celil had given Tatiana his promise. Hadn't he said they'd be back? He couldn't have been lying. She stood up and came over.

"They can't have gone away yet. They'll be back, I know."

"They've gone, Tatya—gone and left us."

Shura's right hand wiped away the tears blurring her sight as she swore to herself she wouldn't cry again. If this was her fate, she would have to learn to cope. She had to cope for the sake of the love she'd enjoyed. But her heart and mind refused to listen.

An idea popped into her head. "Do you know how he's leaving?" she asked.

It might help to catch up with Seyit, thought Osman, and he blurted it all out in one breath. "'Course! I heard. He's going to escape in Tatoğlu's boat."

"Who's this...Tatoğlu?"

"Runs the salt boats in the harbor. Originally from Sinop but lives here now."

"Where's Sinop, Osman?"

"On the other shore of the Black Sea, in Turkey."

"Would you recognize this fellow if you saw him?"

"Of course I would."

Shrugging off the last vestiges of self-pity, Shura gathered her belongings. With a resolute look, she picked up a small travel bag, grabbed her coat and muff, and addressed the others. "Come on—let's go without delay. We might be able to catch up with him. You said midnight, right?"

Osman gaped. "Yes, I'd heard midnight mentioned. But it's been quite a while since Seyit left. He might have sailed already." He paused. "Anyway, isn't this really risky? It's really hard to reach the harbor. The Bolsheviks have blocked all the roads. Tatoğlu would keep his head down, and he might have sailed away already! It's very dangerous, very dangerous..."

"We both want to go with Seyit, don't we? In which case it's worth the risk, isn't it, Osman?"

Admiration for her courage and determination sparkling in his eyes, Osman stood up. "You're right; come on—let's go then!"

Wrapped up in their excitement, Osman and Shura failed to notice that Tatiana hadn't moved. Shura whipped around at the door. "What are you waiting for, Tatya? Come on—quick!"

Tatiana's resolve was different but no less firm for all that. She came over with open arms, speaking affectionately—and in total control of her emotions. "I'm staying, Shurochka; let's say our farewells."

Unable to believe her ears, Shura dropped her luggage and grabbed Tatiana's hands. "What are you saying, Tatya? They've gone; don't you get it? We'll only catch them if we move now. Or it will all be over—we'll never see them again! This is our last chance, Tatya!"

Shaking her friend by the shoulder was no use. This was no idle reverie for Tatiana, and time was running out. Shura had to make a choice between catching up with the man she loved and trying to persuade her friend to come along.

Of course Shura would hate to leave me behind! thought Tatiana. She kissed Shura on the cheek and reassured her in the same calm tone. "Please don't worry about me; I know Celil's going to come back. I can't vouch for Seyit, but I do know Celil is going to come back. He promised. Come hell or high water, he will come back. And I will wait here for him. He will find me here when he returns, whenever that might be."

They hugged like children, wept, and kissed each other. Tatiana braved a smile through her tears. "You know what? I used to think such farewells were a tad too theatrical. Seems I'd been rehearsing for real life all these years." Graceful dancer's fingers tucked a few stray strands back into the comb holding Shura's chignon. Another kiss. "Take care, lovely Shura; take good care of yourself. Write to me when you can." A sudden thought. "Not that I know what address to give you!"

"You too, dear Tatya—take good care of yourself. I'll never forget you."

"Nor I you. You know, in a way I'm glad you're going." Chuckling at the quizzical look, she continued, "My biggest rival in the beauty stakes is leaving Russia; I've got the field to myself now!"

Shura couldn't resist a chuckle in response; Tatiana's wicked sense of humor shone through even in their darkest hour. *It must be the drama training,* she thought, having no doubt her friend was crying silent tears too.

After a hasty farewell, Shura was given an enormous dark shawl, like the ones peasant women wore in the vineyard. It was hardly a total disguise for her big-city, aristocratic looks, but in the darkness, it would be perfectly adequate. Tatiana hugged her once more and gave her another kiss as Ismail Efendi's family prayed for safe travel at the door.

"I was teasing you just now, you know."

Had Tatiana changed her mind? No. She'd meant something else.

"Even if you go away, you'll always be remembered as the most beautiful girl in Russia."

Waving and blinking back the tears, Shura and Osman vanished into the darkness.

Ten minutes later, Seyit and Celil returned. Discarding all semblance of composure, Tatiana dashed over to hug Celil. "I knew it! I knew you'd be back. Thank God you're here."

His sweetheart had been terrified while he was away. Celil knew it was time to share his plans. He had to allay her fears at once, had to explain he would never leave her, that they would stay together. He turned at Seyit's question.

"Where's Shura?" He sounded desperately anxious.

Tatiana burst into tears again. "Oh, Seyt, why didn't you tell her?"

Seyit wanted answers, not questions. "Tatya, where is she? Where's she gone?"

"I don't know, Seyit; she and Osman left to find you."

Seyit couldn't believe his ears. "Osman? My little brother Osman? Oh, dear God; do they have a death wish? Where did they go?"

"They thought you'd gone and wanted to catch up."

Seyit started pacing in the tiny room, punching his palm. At one point he extracted his watch for a look. Looking at it, he recalled the day the tsar had presented the watch on a gold chain. He shut his eyes and shook his head to dispel the image. This was no time to indulge in nostalgia. Time was running out. He looked at Celil, who'd read his mind.

"No, Seyit; we can't go looking. The carts must be ready in a couple of hours."

Seyit was desperately restless. Nothing was going according to plan. Now his sweetheart and his brother were in danger. Chances were they would be caught as they tried to catch up with him.

"I'll never forgive myself if something happens to them. I can't leave them in danger!" But there was an even greater danger. "I don't know what to do, Celil. The stash in the storeroom has to be moved out tonight. Yasef can't look out for us beyond tonight. The arsenal will be found tomorrow, and that will be the end of it for my family and these poor people too."

Seyit cocked an eye at the household as he and Celil whispered.

"Look, Seyit—stop wasting time and get on with loading up. I'll try to find and stop them. They can't be far. At most they'd be waiting somewhere above the harbor, hiding from the guards. Don't worry; I'll shoot off now."

Seyit gave him a grateful look.

Celil wanted no answer. "I'm here anyway; I've got lots of time. Not like you; every moment counts. If you miss Yasef, all this preparation will have gone to waste." With a hug, he added, "Set off when you're ready. Don't wait for us. Don't worry; it'll all be fine."

They both doubted it; all the same, believing in their dreams promised a degree of relief. This was their last farewell; they would never meet again.

"There's so much to say and, sadly, so little time..."

"True. Then again, life's full of surprises. Who knows? We might get the chance one day. Please mind how you go, Seyit, please. I don't know how we could keep in contact now. I'll worry about you."

"And I you. Don't wait until the morning to leave; get away as soon as you can." Seyit took a deep breath and came clean. "Tell Shura everything when you find her. I was going to explain it all before I set off, but it wasn't to be." He pulled a pouch from his bag. "Give this to her. It should keep her going for a while. It would be great if she could come with you. I entrust my beloved to your care, brother. God keep you."

Tatiana had been waiting in the corner in tears.

Seyit hugged her, feeling awful that it wasn't his own darling he was taking leave of. He'd missed the chance of kissing Shura one last time. With a smile, he wiped Tatiana's tears. "Farewell, Tatya; look after Celil. You're a wonderful woman. May God never put you asunder."

"Oh, Seyt! Nothing will be the same without you!"

"Nothing is the same any longer, Tatya—not even us."

He caught Celil's eye. Murder was murder, even in self-defense, and it would weigh them down forever.

Celil charged out in search of Shura and Osman as Seyit made for the storeroom with Ismail Efendi, his son, and a couple of loyal vineyard workers. A horse cart emerged from the forest road and trundled to the storeroom. At whispered instructions from Ismail Efendi, the driver gave the horses a nosebag each to keep the noise down. A few minutes later, two more carts turned up.

First, the carts were laid with a bed of vine twigs. Then came the weapons removed from the crates. They added a layer of grape crates, more vine twigs and leaves over the lot, and ropes to secure the loads, and the arsenal was ready for transport once the wheels were oiled liberally.

Seyit hid something in the first cart, a small sack securely tied.

All this was done in pitch dark as Ismail Efendi's son kept a watch near the exit, lying at the bottom of the vines, his eyes and ears trained on the road.

Seyit changed into peasant clothes, knelt, and touched the ground. It was warm and soft. This was the last contact he would have with the soil of his homeland. He would miss it as much as the people he was leaving behind. He grabbed a handful, rubbed Alushta's fertile earth between his palms as though washing his hands, and watched it run between his fingers like the inexorable flow of life.

It was half an hour to midnight. Three carts were moving grape crates from the high vineyards of Alushta down to the harbor. The peasant driving the lead cart lowered his flat cap over his eyes a bit more. He looked no different from an ordinary vineyard worker with his shirt of coarse cloth, baggy trousers, scuffed shoes, and hands smelling of soil. Even the way he held the reins suggested an ordinary peasant who'd picked at the soil and carried crates around all day long in the sun. Stooping shoulders and a slouch completed the picture of someone who was as far from a first lieutenant in the tsar's Imperial Guards as possible.

However unsettling this false identity was, it still had to be better than the risk of being recognized.

The oiled wheels moved over the soft ground with a barely audible crushing of leaves and twigs. Seyit fancied—just for a moment—that Shura might emerge from between the trees. He was already regretting his decision to leave her behind. *I hope Celil's found her and Osman and brought them both back safe and sound*, he thought, when he was alerted back to the present by the approach of four horsemen. This would be the great test he'd been anticipating. The narrow road suddenly offered as precarious a support as the hair-thin bridge to the afterlife. Yasef didn't seem to be among the riders. He pulled the reins and stopped. One of the riders trotted over.

"Oi! Where d'ya think you're going? Don't you know there's a curfew on?"

Seyit looked around, thinking he might have missed Yasef the first time. No, he wasn't there. The reins would slip from his sweating hands if he wasn't careful. He held his breath and waited, lest his voice tremble and give him away. Things weren't going according to plan. The burly Bolshevik—almost too burly for his mount—prodded Seyit with his whip. "No ribbons yet then?"

Another horseman snorted.

"Maybe they want ribbons on their necks, eh? A red ribbon, bloodred."

He brayed at his own joke, drew his sword, and traced Seyit's collar. There was no doubt the threat would be carried out with relish.

"What's in the carts? Where are you going?"

Locking up his flawless Russian in an obscure corner of his mind, Seyit replied in the local vernacular. "Grapes. They're laden with grapes. We're going to the harbor."

"Who told you to go there?"

"Don't know. We just do what we're told. We was sent word at the vineyard."

The man mountain plunged his sword into the crates with an irate snarl.

"Who the fuck sent *word*, you bastard? Who—tell me! What the fuck d'ya think you're cooking up, you birdbrain? Where's this load going without our knowing, eh?"

The other two drivers waited, petrified, hoping they wouldn't be asked a question next. Seyit jumped down to deflect attention away from them. The first horseman's sword prodded his chest. "Oi! Hold your horses! Who said you could move? Just stop right there. Open these crates; I want to see them grapes."

Seyit climbed up and did as ordered. His tormentors fell upon the cart like vultures, smashing the grapes with swords and rifle butts. Once the top layer was ransacked, they made him open the second. The other two cart drivers watched the juicy grapes being crushed into pulp under the blanket of vine leaves, as if viewing their immediate future in the hands of these brutes.

One of the horsemen hawked, spat a huge gob of phlegm at the cart, and swore, wiping his frothing mouth.

"You fucking swine! You 'was sent word,' eh? Tell that to my hat! Whose property are you taking, you looters? We know how to deal with you lot."

It was all over. He might have escaped being identified as an imperial Russian officer or even mistaken for one who had joined the Whites, and now he was going to die as a peasant smuggling grapes. The end result was the same. There was nothing else to do. He glanced at the other two drivers, feeling terrible about risking their lives. "Them two, they don't know nothing. I picked the crop. Let 'em go."

The Bolshevik guffawed. "Let the drivers go? What the hell for? No cart drivers left in Russia or something? Two more, two less—who gives a damn?"

Seyit visualized being shot here, his body thrown over the cliff into the sea. So why not save them the trouble? He gauged the distance to the cliff to his right and had just started moving in the tiniest little steps when a fifth horseman suddenly galloped into view.

God hadn't forsaken him yet. It was Yasef. He drew to a halt alongside the others without a look at Seyit. "Greetings, comrades; what's the matter?"

The others drew themselves up and saluted; their demeanor suggested he outranked them all. "Smuggling his grapes, he was, and we caught him," said one.

Yasef snapped at Seyit, as if he'd never seen him before, "Which vineyard?"

Taken aback at the unexpected question, Seyit stammered, "The...the Eminofs'..."

Seemingly angered by the reply, Yasef tore him off a strip. "They're not the *Eminofs'* or *anyone else's* any longer. *No one* owns a vineyard any longer. Get it?" This was clearly part of the act. Yasef continued, "Number-two vineyard, I see." Turning to the others, he said, "It's all right, comrades. I was informed about this earlier. It's being shipped to Odessa first thing. Let them pass."

Seyit knew he wasn't out of danger just yet. Things happened in utterly unforeseen ways, and fortune seemed to be as fickle as it was purported to be. It was impossible to anticipate what might occur next.

After cantering around the carts, Yasef laid into the four horsemen. "Bloody hell! You've ruined the crop! You'll be asked to explain why, Comrade Tarvides; I'm sure you will. You've ruined soviet property!"

The others had slunk back. Now was the time to strike; Yasef had to make sure Seyit was gone before there were more questions. "All right now—away with you. And never leave without the proper papers again; is that understood?"

Seyit climbed back up to the driver's seat. Yasef trotted over to the right side, stared at the sea below the cliffs, drew a cigarette from his case, and asked, "Got a match, comrade? Time for a cigarette."

Seyit lit Yasef Zarkovich's cigarette. In the glow of the flame, his old friend saw the grateful look. He took a deep drag and mumbled, "Thanks, comrade."

"You too. Thanks...comrade," Seyit mumbled back and blew out the match.

The boat lying offshore started toward the rocks as Yasef called, "On your way!" Captain Tatoğlu Hasan had spotted the first match.

Seyit stayed on the road until he was certain they weren't followed. He turned off the harbor road into a narrow lane meandering down the cliff. It was too steep and too narrow for the carts to go all the way down to the shore. Soon he stopped and gestured to the others to follow suit. He leaped down and stood still, scanning the spot where the boat would moor. It was too dark to see. He pricked up his ears. Not a sound. The moon was obscured by a rush of thick cloud, offering only sporadic illumination—which was all Seyit had to memorize the location of the rocks below. He stood above the spot nearest the rocks to whisper and gesture to his men. "Unload the munitions and slide them down here one by one, all right?"

"All right, sir."

"I'm going down. I'll light a match. Start at once. If you see anyone, drop it all and pretend you were on your way. You don't know me at all, all right? And one more thing: unload the carts one by one, not all at the same time. Come on now. God bless you—thanks."

"God be with you, Kurt Seyit; safe sailing."

"And with you."

Seyit shook their hands and sped down the steep path. He didn't need to see his way; these were his childhood playgrounds. When he reached the end, he slid down on his heels and landed on the pebble beach. The narrow strip of land was lashed by noisy waves; the wind felt stiffer on the strand than on the hills.

Looking up at the cliff he'd just descended, he pulled out the matches. The first one fizzled out before it could be spotted from above. He knelt, hunched his shoulders, and tried again, this time with five matches shielded by a cupped hand. As soon as they caught, he withdrew his hand. The rifles started sliding down at once, skidding down one after another and piling up on the shore. Seyit turned toward the sea and signaled.

A figure emerged from the shadows at the bottom of the hill and called softly, "Kurt Seyit? It's me, Cengiz."

The two men grabbed each other's shoulder in a silent gesture of solidarity. Before long came the swoosh of a boat, and the fisherman and the fugitive flattened themselves on the pebbles until they were sure it was Tatoğlu.

The sound dropped; the prow appeared a few feet away. A match flared in the hands of the man standing astride the prow. The anchor dropped, and two figures jumped off, walking through the wash and onto the beach. Seyit recognized Tatoğlu Hasan and stood up. In total silence, the four men loaded the weapons in knee-deep water that occasionally swelled to their waists.

The weather was turning; dark, threatening rain clouds danced across the sky. Once the entire cargo had been loaded, Seyit strolled to the bottom of the cliff to make sure he'd left no trace behind. All three carts must have been unloaded now. Hooves clopped up the hill and faded away. His men had done a great job, far better than he'd allowed himself to hope for. It looked like his luck was finally turning. Casting one final look up, he sped over the pebbles to board without delay.

But he stopped in his tracks when someone shouted his name. He recognized the voice calling from the path he'd taken just now: it was Osman, his youngest brother.

Scrambling in the dark, he was yelling at the top of his voice. "Stop! Seyit *Abi!* Stop! I'm coming too!" He kept slipping, tumbling down, and getting back up to call again. "Abi! Wait for me! I'm coming! I'm coming too!"

The boat, the men waiting for him, and his precious cargo were all forgotten. Seyit called, "This way, Osman!"

He couldn't work out which came first: the moonlight shining through the clouds or the gunshots. Several men were aiming down from the cliff edge.

Seyit thought his back was on fire, hot like lava, and heard a roaring in his ears. He turned back to glance at the rocking boat. On board were three men who had risked their lives for him. It would hardly be fair to expect more; they would sail away soon. Behind him was his brother, trapped between the shore and the enemy, trying desperately to reach him.

Osman kept shouting for his big brother. "Save me, Abi; save me!"

The gunshots drowned the roar of the sea. Seyit scrambled up; his brother was only about fifty feet away. Osman had panicked; instead of running toward Seyit, he kept looking back at the gunmen.

Seyit urged him on. "Osman! Run downhill! Don't look back! I'm here—run!"

The wind drew the clouds apart. Everything was suddenly bathed in bright moonlight. Osman was approaching. But he wasn't the only one. As soon as they could see, the gunmen also started downhill.

Osman was one bend away. He yelled in joy when he saw his big brother, the bullets whizzing past suddenly forgotten. He opened his arms wide. "You're still here! You've not sailed away! Seyit Abi, you're—"

The yell of joy turned into a muffled moan. His knees buckled, and his arms came together as though he were picking stars from the sky and fell at his sides. Several more cracks. The soft soil under his feet gave way, and young Osman glided down to the shore, still staring at his big brother's open arms.

Seyit's scream echoed on the hills as he watched his eighteen-year-old brother smash onto the pebbles. "Osmaaannn!"

He tore off, half falling, half tumbling down, determined to lift Osman and take him away. The gunmen scrambling downhill were getting closer. He broke into a wild run and collapsed over his brother's body. Osman had rolled onto his back, eyes shut, waves frothing underneath his neck. Seyit couldn't bring himself to believe Osman was dead. He knelt, cradled his brother's head, and wept.

"Osman, my little brother—my brother—"

A bullet whizzed past his ear. Now the boat was returning fire. Much as he wanted to take Osman's body away, he knew he'd either be shot or captured if he delayed any further. With a silent glance at Cengiz—*Bury my brother; I beseech you!*—he waded into the swelling waves.

The moment he was hoisted over the gunwale, the boat moved out. The gunfire carried on relentlessly. Seyit grabbed a rifle and took up a position next to Tatoğlu's crewmen. Soon they'd moved out of the range of the rifles on the shore.

The heavy old boat, rendered even more sluggish by its cargo, fought hard to make its way against the growing waves. Seyit briefly wondered if they would actually manage to cross the Black Sea under these conditions.

The noises coming from the harbor wrenched him back to the present. Before long three vessels appeared, close enough to see clearly. As one moved to catch up from behind, the other two separated to pinch the Turkish boat between them.

Seyit looked at the armed crewmen and ordered, "One of you to port and the other to starboard—quick!"

They were only a couple of years younger than Seyit. What they lacked in size, they seemed to make up for in robust health and extraordinary agility. A life spent at sea had made them as sure of their footing as cats—and as dismissive of danger too. They obeyed his orders at once. Grabbing on to the gunwale to secure themselves, they crawled to their new positions. Seyit continued to load several more rifles as backup while a barrage of bullets opened up from behind.

Tatoğlu Hasan made a superhuman effort to protect his boat and passengers from the frenzied waves and the enemy. Wiping the sweat off his brow with a sleeve, he dodged the cross fire as he steered into the frothing, rolling waves. They would have been done for if a single one of the waves breaking over the prow had actually hit them.

"God damn you to hell, you *Moskof* swine! God damn you, and may the Black Sea swallow you up, God willing!" The old sea dog ground his teeth.

It was difficult to work out who had the upper hand in the infernal din of the roaring sea and the pounding gunfire. Perhaps there was no one left on deck by now. *The Moskof will soon surround us and finish me off,* thought Seyit—an unpleasant prospect that only served to make him sweat even more.

Turning his boat into the wave coming from the starboard side, the captain let loose another string of invectives in Turkish. "God damn you to hell, you abominable curs. I'd rather be buried in the Black Sea than give you the pleasure!" Slapping the wheel, he added in poor Russian, "Don't worry; God will look after us."

Seyit was trying work out the enemy's strength from the hail of bullets. Although there were three vessels in total, there couldn't have been more than a couple of men on board each, three on the outside. One of the three vessels could certainly catch up with them. He reached toward the trunk he'd placed at the bottom of the cabin door, momentarily ignoring the bullets whizzing overhead.

The boat lifted suddenly and seemed to hang in the air. Seyit slid back and banged his head against the hold hatch. It hurt badly enough to make him nearly pass out, but he fought the pain and snatched at a rope nearby. The boat slammed down into a trough. Water washed over the bow, grabbing the slithering rope out of Seyit's hand in the torrential downpour. Catching it with his foot at the last moment, he lashed himself securely before the next wave that was certain to come. The young deckhand on the starboard side was gone—either he'd been washed overboard or sucked toward the bow by the ebbing wave.

Seyit's first priority was to stop their pursuers. He seized a hand grenade from the trunk, held it gingerly, and scuttled aft, wondering how he could succeed without a visible target.

The pursuers were very close now. He had no other choice. This was their last chance. If his life was meant to end here after all he'd been through, then that was his fate. He could hardly do more. He couldn't fight fate, but there was one thing he *could* do—and that was to try for one last time.

"Help me, God."

Taking a deep breath, he sprang up, pulled the pin, hurled the hand grenade as far as he could, and threw himself back down to the deck. He had managed to dodge the bullets.

A bang—and the Russian vessel astern burst into flames. Wood and debris flew up into the air and fell down in a shower of sparks. The waters rose and opened, and the Black Sea swallowed the blazing vessel.

Tatoğlu Hasan whooped in joy at the sight of the flabbergasted enemy. "You're Tatoğlu's hero, man!"

Seyit took the opportunity to prime a second hand grenade.

The deckhand clutching the port gunwale was still bent double, still shooting. Seyit's next hand grenade found its mark but failed to sink the vessel in pursuit. All the same, the boat must have sustained significant damage, given the third boat immediately changed course, presumably to help.

The gunfire ceased. Seyit realized he'd been holding his breath for a long time. He sat down, leaned against the hold hatch, and took a deep breath. It had to be a miracle; he could hardly believe they had shaken off the pursuit. He cautiously scanned the surface of the sea; there was nothing other than Tatoğlu's boat and the waves. In the sudden stillness, Tatoğlu kissed his own palm noisily and stroked the wheel, looking much happier. "God bless you, my word! God bless you! Thank God!"

As the second deckhand materialized, rubbing his bruises, Seyit felt a huge weight lift off his chest. The young man had grabbed an open porthole at the last moment to avoid being washed overboard and had waited for that hellish racket to cease before rising to his feet.

It was calmer. Leaning on the aft gunwale, Seyit gazed mournfully back at the receding coast. Now that the immediate danger was over, his thoughts went back to the brother he'd left on the shore. His eyes moved up to the receding hills and vineyards of Alushta, where the trees seemed to wave back in the moonlight. He peered at the spot where little Osman had fallen. Seyit longed to return, embrace, and warm his brother's young body, which now lay cooling in the waves against the pebbles.

That familiar loneliness enveloped him again while the boat rocked and pitched as if made of paper. The sea lay beyond them, boundless and pitch black. Everything seemed pointless. Having lost so much, saving his own life did not seem to matter in quite the same way. His family, his home, his lands, his friends, his sweetheart: everything was left behind in the land now vanishing into a mist of dreams. And that wasn't the least of it. His soul, his heart...himself. All that was left behind. The man rocking in the boat in the middle of the sea was a forlorn wretch, lonely, robbed of his dreams and love.

A net curtain was drawing across the receding Alushta coastline. Seyit stared and stared, as if to etch into memory that last image of his homeland. An enormous wave slapped the stern; in the infinitesimal gap between its burst and fall, the coastline vanished altogether. It was over. His homeland had been visible one wave ago. All these years felt like a dream. Perhaps they were—a bad dream. He would awaken in the morning. And perhaps all he recalled would be a dream. Perhaps there never had been a town called Alushta. No one called Kurt Seyit had ever lived. What about the others? All his loved ones, everyone he'd lost; surely he hadn't dreamed them all? Wrapping his arms around himself, he tried to warm up. But he was frozen to the marrow. Nothing could warm up that chill. A souvenir of the steppes, one that would always make itself known like a shard of solid ice that never melted.

He had no idea how far they'd sailed. He'd spent so long in reminiscences that it could have been years. In actual fact, it had been only one hour. The ferocious wind had stilled, and the sea now swelled with broad and languorous waves.

Tatoğlu Hasan came over, bubbling with excitement. "Kurt Seyit, sir, God bless you. What a to-do! Hell, it was hell! Thanks to you, we're safe now."

The brave sailor had been ready to risk his boat, his crew, and his own life. Touched by the captain's expression, Seyit forced a smile. "You did a great job too, Tatoğlu. Anyone else at the helm, and we'd be at the bottom of the sea now."

Tatoğlu Hasan was delighted. Confident as he was of his own credentials as a great sailor, praise was always welcome. "You flatter me, sir; you flatter me," replied the captain, somewhat self-consciously. He carried on, unable to suppress his curiosity. "Sir, it's not my place, I know, but I was wondering if you knew anyone in Sinop or anything."

"An aunt married and moved there, but it was years ago. I have no idea where she is now. It's been a long time."

"Hm. Then it might be a little difficult. But don't worry, sir; Turkey's your homeland—not like you need kith and kin."

Homeland? How could a place be called one's homeland if you weren't born and raised there—if you didn't know it at all?

Tatoğlu pointed to the cargo. "If only you knew how much they'll be appreciated, sir! I know it's not easy, what you've just done, but once you see how happy people will be to see you, you'll forget your pain—even if only a little." Now that he was safe from the nightmare they'd left behind, his mind went to his own country's troubles. "The people are desperate in Turkey, sir. Homes are bereft of men. Anyone reaching eighteen goes to the front. The empire's in tatters. Where's all that Ottoman pomp and splendor that our grandfathers spoke of? Grab a pick and shovel to save a handful of land and go to war! It's pathetic... pathetic. That's why you'll see how they'll rejoice in Sinop when we dock." Then worried he'd been keeping Seyit up, he said, "Sir, try to sleep a little. We've got a long way to go and lots of sea to cross. When you're exhausted, this Black Sea looks interminable."

Seyit reached out to shake his hand. "Thanks, Tatoğlu. You've done a great job. I'll never forget it."

Tatoğlu's cheerful smile brushed it all off. "Don't mention it, sir! What's a few rounds, anyway? We're used to it, where we come from! I'm sorry we couldn't save your friend though."

"Not my friend," said Seyit. He gazed at the distant darkness over the sea and whispered, "It was my brother, Tatoğlu—my little brother..."

He choked. The captain felt terrible. He would have placed a hand on Seyit's shoulder in sympathy but refrained lest he offend a gentleman. "He'd be a martyr in God's eye, sir; God grant him peace. And God grant you patience. What else is there to say?"

There was nothing. Seyit was lost in thought again.

"Sir, it's best to be alone when you're grieving, I know. I'm at the helm; just ask the lads if you want anything at all. Would you like a blanket or something? It's getting chilly now."

Still lost in thought, Seyit replied, partly to humor the captain, "Good idea."

He didn't want to talk. He had nothing to talk about anymore. From now on he would be surrounded by strangers. They would listen as if they were hearing fairy tales. With no one to share or recall his memories, his sorrows and joys would be nothing more than tales. How could they possibly understand his experiences by merely listening? Where did he belong? He was nothing more than a fugitive escaping from an empire crushed by revolution, running into another empire torn apart by war.

A wave slapping against the gunwale brought him out of his reverie.

The wind at his back dropped all at once when a blanket was placed across his shoulders. That's when he realized just how cold he had been and swung around to thank the captain.

It couldn't be true. He must have lost his mind with all that nostalgic reverie. He couldn't swallow. He was gasping for breath. He wanted to touch this dream—to feel it. The face was in the shadow—the figure struggling to keep balance on the rolling deck. But Seyit would know this head, those shoulders, that posture anywhere. He reached out, and her name fell from his lips.

"Shura! Shurochka! My little darling..."

The shadow sinking down beside him was no longer a dream. For Seyit, it was like finding all that he had lost, everyone he had lost, all of his Russia. He hugged her close as she wept without a word. He inhaled her smell deeply, as if to inhale her into his lungs. No perfume—just a lingering of daffodils in the warm hollow of her neck. He opened the blanket, wrapped it around her shoulders, and drew her head against his chest. He buried his lips in her hair. Yes, here she was; Shura, his Shura, was beside him again.

Moonlight danced on their faces and hands. She had brought back all that was gone: the wheat fields in her thick blond hair, Alushta's sea in her blue eyes, Saint Petersburg's glory days in her scent, and all his loved ones in her gaze. She was the only person who knew his past, the only person who offered unquestioning trust. She was his past. She was the only person who knew about his childhood, adolescence, loves, affairs, family, and everyone he'd lost.

She was Seyit's Russia and Crimea that he'd thought he'd lost forever. He hugged her tighter. His self-control finally crumbled when he kissed her tears.

Men didn't cry. Soldiers didn't cry. But Kurt Seyit was crying.

Two Fugitives in
Sinop, 1918

THE SUN HAD yet to rise over the horizon on the second morning when the boat entered Sinop Harbor. As the nocturnal gloom lifted, the two passengers at the prow watched the approaching shore with bated breath, daring to indulge in a glimmer of hope on the threshold of a new life.

In an unexpected surge of optimism, Seyit felt the stirrings of anticipation, now impatient to set foot on land.

Shura, on the other hand, was happy to wait, drawing strength from the hand of the man she loved. She had no idea what to expect in a country she knew nothing about; so alien were its people, language, and customs that she resolved to follow Seyit and entrust herself to his decisions. She watched his sparkling eyes staring at the shore.

Their eyes met. Seyit squeezed her hand with a bright smile that belied the deep melancholy in his pupils. Shura smiled back. Her escape had been no less perilous than his. Osman had insisted they stick to the little-known paths to avoid detection; even then they had narrowly avoided being caught a couple of times. After entrusting her to Tatoğlu and insisting she hide until the boat was well underway, Osman had gone back to help his big brother. He must have kept to the same tracks, which would explain why he'd missed Seyit.

Fate played a fickle hand with human life.

Wending their way between fishing boats, Tatoğlu's boat docked—and was immediately greeted by a screaming pack of children that materialized out of nowhere.

"Come on now; stand back! Leave our guests alone," scolded Tatoğlu gently. The word *guest* had the effect of a magic wand. The children drew back one by one and stared in silence—except for one boy who ran, screaming, "Tatoğlu's back! Tatoğlu's back!"

Soon townsfolk turned up at the harbor along with the gendarme commander. An elder moved forward and greeted Seyit. "Welcome, sir. Welcome to our country."

On exchanging salutes with the commander, Seyit boarded the boat again to hand over his cache. The officer signaled a couple of his men, and the townsfolk helped unload this gift from nowhere. A chain formed at once to move the munitions from hand to hand. Hugging one another and screaming for joy like children, a grateful crowd surrounded Seyit, kissing his hands and cheeks in between prayers and tears. The children were no less impressed; one puny boy of about six or seven had thrown himself to the ground, taking aim with a long stick, writhing like a snake in his make-believe cover. His patched shirt had come loose from too-short trousers with a broken suspender that trailed in the dirt, his soles poked through the torn soles of his overshoes, and he kept readjusting his fez. "Bang! Bang! Bang! Shot the infidel—shot him!"

Seyit's eyes welled up. His unexpected miracle had given these people hope; this land that welcomed him with open arms was now his country.

Shura was so engrossed in this scene that at first she completely missed the gaping stares of young girls nearby. Fishermen's daughters in long floral frocks down to wrists and ankles, their hair mostly covered by scarves, stood transfixed by the revelation that the world held different women. This Russian looked nothing like them: she wore her blond hair in an uncovered chignon and a simple outfit they instinctively identified as expensive and chic.

A girl of about ten standing on a mound couldn't resist the lure of Shura's hair. She reached down to stroke it, blushed furiously at being caught, and rocked on the spot. Shura opened her arms in a universal gesture of warmth. She didn't speak the language, but a smile and terms of affection would have to serve. "*Davay, devochka; ne boysa.*"

The *devochka* understood instinctively that she was a *little girl*, took the rest to mean *come on* and *don't be scared*, and came over for a hug, sucking her finger. Shura gave her a kiss on the head and a cuddle. The girl was in seventh heaven: the Russian lady had picked her for a cuddle! She cast a look full of pride at her friends.

The cargo was off-loaded. The young couple took their luggage and followed the commander to the station, where they visited for tea and a chat for about an hour. A crowd accompanied them, waiting outside the gendarmerie and later forming a festive procession up to the house Shura and Seyit were given.

It was an adorable house of two rooms overlooking the harbor, surrounded by trees, and it had everything they might immediately need: sofas alongside the windows, a huge round copper tray in the middle, and an enormous hearth in the kitchen wall.

Alone at long last, they stood in silence for a while, as if to accustom themselves to a new world defined by a whitewashed ceiling and Sivas rugs on the walls and floor. There was a profusion of four o'clock flowers outside the window. Seyit caught his breath when he noticed the view. He moved toward the window. The harbor below the hill and the endless stretch of the Black Sea receding into the horizon...for a brief moment, he fancied that he was looking out from a hill in Alushta. It felt so real that he wondered if he had actually left his soul there.

No, he had no doubt. He now had a house in Sinop, but his soul was on the other shore.

That evening, every item they unpacked summoned a distinct memory. Seyit peered at the items he had placed on the small console between the two rooms. His uniform portrait, his decorations, the watch that had been a present from the tsar, and his diamond ring—they all looked alien, as if they belonged to someone else. *Remarkable!* he thought. *Memories never leave you, no matter how far you might be, yet objects you carry seem so far away.* His fingers wandered between the decorations, the watch, and the ring in an effort to return them to life, to regain a sense of ownership. The fob running through his palms conjured the humble, gentle, and warm gaze of Tsar Nicholas. Seyit recalled his first visit to the palace at the age of twelve and the kindly emperor stroking potted flowers. How long had it been? Fourteen years, no more. Time weighed his shoulders down as though it had been hundreds of years instead.

He returned the decorations to their boxes and placed them back in the sack filled with rubles and kopeks hidden inside two down pillows. He tied it securely and hoisted it up into the loft. That was all he had been able to bring from a lifetime.

Shura had only a few items of clothing that needed unpacking; after placing them in drawers, she sat down on the sofa. She felt dreadfully homesick in the dusk. She had never been so far away.

Seyit sat down beside her, drew back the net curtains, threw an arm over her shoulders, looked out, and murmured, "Come on, darling—sing me something sad."

Shura knew what he meant. Planting a kiss on his cheek, she began humming a song. She stared into the distance, as if she could see distant forested shores beyond the sea. Her mind went inland, into the steppes, and thence to the banks of the Neva. It snowed. Bells jingled as their troika sped over the crunchy snow.

By the time she had finished, her eyes were welling up. She flung herself into Seyit's arms. "Don't leave me, Seyt—never leave me. You're all I have in this world."

Seyit came out of his reverie, cupped her face, and gazed into her eyes. "And you're my everything, my darling—my everything..."

A long-forgotten heat emanating from his lap flooded in, down to the marrow of his bones. He grabbed her by the waist and drew her closer. His lips found hers. Stroking her curves, he realized he'd missed the yielding, yet firm flesh under his palms. His kisses went to the hollow of her neck. Shura indulged in the fancy that their lives were unchanged. Throwing her head back, she welcomed the tremors aroused by his lips. Hungry—yet unhurried—hands freed her from the shackles of shirt and lingerie, setting her breasts, belly, and legs on fire.

She couldn't hold back any longer; she was impatient to surrender and unite in flesh now that they were both ready. This was escape from the despair of contemplation. Breaths in unison, bodies rocking rhythmically, they relived happy times. Love was the only cure for homesickness—love expressed through their bodies. Bodies perfectly attuned to each other; when they took control, nothing mattered but the peak of that overwhelming pleasure—the contact of skin on skin. Breaths mingling, lips, arms, legs, and souls locked, they relished the most glorious expression of love as all that was far came close enough to touch. All longing came to an end, however briefly. Basking in each other's scent and warmth, they became whole.

Intrigued by the legendary tale of their daring escape, local dignitaries competed with one another to entertain the fugitives from Russia. Seyit and Shura's heroics merited a reward, and rewarded they would be, wartime shortages notwithstanding. Shura had little to do in the two-room house, thanks to a local woman who came in daily to help with the housekeeping, so she started writing her memoirs. Seyit frequented the coffeehouse where the men traditionally gathered, but *the men* were either younger than seventeen, too old to fight, or invalids lucky to have come back from the front; the *coffee* was made of ground chickpeas; the tea—kept boiling all day long—was stewed; there was no sugar; and the only topic was war.

The Great War raged on in its fourth year, but the tide had turned. The Allies now had the upper hand: Ottoman forces routed in the southeast lost Palestine and Syria. Having taken Baghdad, the British advanced all the way to Aleppo, where they came to a halt. The staunch defender was none other than Mustafa Kemal Pasha, the rising star of the Ottoman forces. No amount of military genius, however, could help him alter the course of events on his own.

As the Axis powers finally sued for peace, the once mighty Ottoman Empire had no choice but to follow suit. Its fate was placed in the hands of the Allies when the Treaty of Mudros was signed on October 30.

Profoundly distressed by the developments in his adopted country, Seyit lamented that all he had contributed was a boatload of munitions. He beat a path to the commander's door, hoping to put his military training and experience to better use, but he was sorely disappointed. His interlocutor welcomed him with open arms, listened, and apologized profusely. "Seyit *Bey*, thank you; thank you so much; you are so brave. You have offered us hope in our darkest hour...but, and I very much regret to say this, you are a Russian national, after all. Enlisting you under the circumstances is absolutely out of the question. Believe me; I am absolutely mortified to have to refuse you. Please don't take it as a personal affront; this is no reflection on your character. Quite the opposite—our trust in you is boundless. But the country is in such turmoil at the moment...I hope you'll understand."

"And if I were to take on Turkish nationality?"

"Then fine, absolutely, but again, it can't happen directly. These things take time, and doubly so if you've come from somewhere like Russia. Why not take this opportunity to enjoy yourself? I'm sure you deserve a bit of a rest after all you've been through."

Rising to his feet with a broken heart, Seyit accepted the gracious handshake.

"I suspect my ordeal's not over yet."

A healthy body, determination, military training, or skills: none of it would get him a commission in the Turkish army. Pitched into a coffeehouse in Sinop from the Imperial Guards of the Russian tsar, he felt useless, old, and tired.

As Seyit walked down the hallway, the commander called, "Seyit Bey, I'm really sorry..."

The young man waved without looking back and muttered, "Me too..."

He wanted to get away—to where, he had no idea, but one thing he did know was that life in Sinop was very difficult. He needed a new start, to find something to do. He was fed up with sitting in a coffeehouse all day, listening to boys, old men, and invalids talking of war. Shura was clearly in the same boat. She never complained, but she must feel stifled with no one to talk to. Even on the worst day in Russia, there had always been someone to share their troubles with—and in their own tongue. True, they had escaped certain death and fled to seek peace, but their present situation was also captivity of sorts, however willingly embraced. They lived among Turks in Turkey and were made to feel genuinely welcome. All the same, they were, and would remain, two fugitives of Russian nationality, which tied their hands. Their love remained as strong as ever, and they still needed each other as much as before. They had little cause for joy, but wasn't it sorrow that bound them together?

After days of deliberation, Seyit came to the conclusion that they ought to go to Istanbul. The empire might be crumbling, but the city that had been the seat of power for hundreds of years was likely to offer more opportunities, and there was a better chance of finding some friends there.

Shura was delighted at the prospect when she heard, not because she knew the city or anyone there but because the name *Tsargrad* evoked a fairy-tale image. *Istanbul*, she forced herself to think. *I must adopt its local name now.* Istanbul was the fabled city of splendor, color, empires, palaces, and vast fortunes. She allowed herself to fantasize as Seyit went to obtain travel permits.

One look at his face upon his return was enough to bring her back to reality. His answer to the silent question shattered yet another dream: "We can't go, darling; the British have occupied Istanbul."

It was November 18, 1918.

Amasya, June 1919

I N A MOVE calculated to stifle political opposition to Allied demands that he personally was willing to concede to, Sultan Mehmed VI, better known as Vahdettin, resolved the Ottoman Parliament. Emerging military and civilian networks outside Istanbul, however, remained out of his reach. Provincial resistance organizations springing from the earlier Young Turks movement were growing across the land.

The Allies asked Grand Vizier Damat Ferit Pasha, brother-in-law to the sultan, to quell the disturbances. Given the powerlessness of the Sublime *Porte* in the face of Anatolian insurgence, however, a military envoy to personally reestablish order was deemed essential. The name chosen for this assignment was Mustafa Kemal Pasha, now a brigadier, the legendary hero of Gallipoli. He was thus appointed as inspector of the Ninth Army that covered a vast portion of Anatolia. He would sway the people and the army, thought the *Porte*. More importantly, in contrast to Enver Pasha, he was no Germanophile, surely a point in his favor vis-à-vis the Allies.

On May 16, 1919, around the time the SS *Bandırma* cast off on her way to Samsun with Mustafa Kemal on board, the British military attaché Wyndham Deedes was waiting for an audience with the grand vizier. Justifiably suspecting Mustafa Kemal of being a less than willing collaborator (judging by his record of resistance to British forces), the attaché would have preferred someone else for this post. But the vessel had already sailed.

Well might he have worried. A formidable figure himself, Deedes was absolutely correct in his suspicions. This trip would alter the course of history for both Turkey and the world. By the time the SS *Bandırma* reached the Black Sea and steamed along the coastline, Mustafa Kemal's plans to assemble and lead an army beyond the reach of the occupation forces were advanced.

On landing in Samsun on May 19, he put those ideas into action. His first priority was to inspire nationalist feeling—where his legendary heroics would help. This was a leader who would stoke the latent fires of freedom. He summoned the fragmented resistance organizations to a congress in Sivas. It worked. Delegates, mostly traveling in secret, flocked in to meet their hero.

While Istanbul cowered in the pall cast by Allied warships, the seeds of the national struggle sown in Anatolia elicited hope, excitement, and joy. Allied politicians and occupation leaders who had underestimated Mustafa Kemal's ability to rouse a supposedly vanquished nation stood up and took notice. They were too late. He defied the order recalling him to Istanbul.

Seyit was in the Sinop delegation. He had been following developments for months, ruing the fate that forced him to sit on his hands. But a chance meeting with Kâzım Karabekir Pasha—the celebrated commander of the Fifteenth Army Corps—had indicated that Mustafa Kemal and his friends disagreed with the Istanbul administration. Seyit was desperate to join the growing resistance. The soldier inside was ready for duty. He longed for an opportunity to fight the enemies of his new country and conclude the battle he couldn't finish in Russia.

He couldn't wait to see the celebrated hero he'd been admiring from afar. When they did meet a few days later, Seyit was impressed beyond imagining by the constancy in that azure gaze. Mustafa Kemal seemed to glow with a magical inner fire that set him apart from the surrounding crowd. He wasn't particularly tall, yet his posture, gaze, attitude, and demeanor all spoke of an extraordinary personality. His greatest quality was an unshakeable conviction that he would deliver his nation, and he clearly knew what it would take.

Informed of Seyit's escape from Russia and delivery of munitions to the regional headquarters with no expectation of reward or remuneration, Mustafa Kemal offered him a warm handshake. Two pairs of blue eyes flashed. Seyit had never met any commander who had this effect on him. Mustafa Kemal's voice rang with cautious confidence as he shook Seyit's hand vigorously. "This nation will never forget your generosity. Rest assured it won't have been in vain."

The sheer power emanating from the man was unmistakable, even in that briefest of greetings. Seyit envied the delegation following Mustafa Kemal to Sivas. He, on the other hand, was denied the opportunity to accompany this great man in this great struggle. Despite several applications and even a personal petition to Kâzım Karabekir Pasha, he couldn't join the army. It was impossible before taking Turkish citizenship, and under the conditions, that was going to take years.

Seyit brooded on his return journey. He no longer had a reason to stay here. His gift of munitions was evidently all he could contribute at present. He was desperate to do more, but Turkey wanted no more. It was so hard to accept. He might as well go to Istanbul without further delay.

On arriving in Sinop, his request for travel permits elicited a caution.

"Seyit Bey, you are aware that Allies announced they would occupy Istanbul completely should the Sivas Congress go ahead? You might like to stay here until things calm down. At least in Anatolia, you're in resistance lands. I'm sure life is far harder in Istanbul than here."

"You know, Commander, it doesn't matter where you are when you're useless," replied Seyit with a wry smile.

"As you wish. I'll have your passes drawn up. Come and collect them tomorrow," came the sympathetic reply; insistence was futile.

The next day, handing Seyit a sealed envelope along with the passes he had requested, the commander explained, "My dear Seyit Bey, please don't lose it. One day, if we manage to deliver the nation, you may use it to receive what you're owed."

"You owe me nothing, sir. What I'm owed was left behind on the other shore," replied Seyit with a smile, casting a look at the sealed envelope. He shook the hand of the man who had been a close friend and great help all this time since his arrival in Sinop. They parted with a warm farewell.

Istanbul, Late 1919

T HE SPLENDID NEO-GOTHIC Haydarpaşa Station thronged with a customary crowd ranging between the extremes of wealth and poverty: women in veils and cloaks of every imaginable shape and style and men in smart *Istanbulin* frock coats and fezzes or shabby coats and turbans. One couple alighting from the train at Istanbul's Anatolian side instantly stood apart: a tall blond lady in an ankle-length sable coat and a matching hat and her companion in a European suit topped with an astrakhan kalpak. The foreigners were holding hands—a display of unimaginable intimacy for the time and place.

They each carried a bag and were followed by a porter carrying two suit-cases. What little they possessed would disappoint their envious audience, a far cry from what their outfits and demeanor implied. The sum total of their wealth consisted of Seyit's decorations, the watch, the ring presented by the dead tsar, and a sack of rubles. People born into wealth or the gentry, however, never lost a certain bearing that defied the vagaries of fortune.

Heads held high, hands still interlocked, the young couple who walked out of the station and silently greeted Istanbul were among the earliest Russian émigrés. They had no intention of going to the Russian consulate; despite continued resistance to the Reds across the sea, prudence was still the more advisable option for the time being.

It was nearly evening by the time they reached Sirkeci. They looked around, uncertain of where to go in this unfamiliar city under occupation, although they were probably more apprehensive about the future. Eventually Seyit led Shura to a phaeton.

"Do you know of a good hotel nearby?"

The coachman had never heard such well-dressed fare looking for hotels nearby; Pera was the more popular destination where a lady was concerned. Gathering his courage, he asked the young man with the foreign accent, "Pardon my curiosity, sir, but are you an outlander?"

Momentarily bristling at the label, Seyit relaxed into a chuckle. His Russian was much better than his Turkish, after all. "Yes, you could say I'm an outlander from afar!" The coachman was still staring quizzically. "We're from Russia."

Voyagers from Russia at a time of war, who clearly had arrived at Haydarpaşa and crossed to the European side! *It's all too puzzling*, thought the coachman, before he was struck by a flash of inspiration.

"Did you say Russia, sir? There are Crimeans staying at the Hotel Şeref in Tarlabaşı, near Taksim. I'll take you there if you like."

Crimeans! Great news! Seyit wondered who they could be. "Quick, take us there, wherever this hotel is!"

As he gave Shura an enthusiastic explanation, she mused she'd never seen him so animated before; she was pleased for him and a little sad for herself. When would she get such happy news? She berated herself silently at once. Wasn't she happy so long as he was? Had she not embarked upon this adventure, braved so much danger, just to be with him? Had she not left everything behind just to throw her lot in with his? Whether he offered her happiness or sorrow, she would share it with him. Gazing at his face, she recognized the sparkle in his eyes—the sparkle of anticipation and hope. She felt warmer, grasped his arm with both hands, and rested her head on his shoulder. She closed her eyes. Her mind flew back to their troika trip one snowy evening three years previously.

Snow fell in heavy flakes as the phaeton proceeded over Galata Bridge toward Pera. The road looked nothing like Moscow's Krasnaya Ploshchad or Kislovodsk's Narzan Gallery, but everything else looked the same. She was no longer troubled by her ignorance about their destination, the life that awaited them, or the people they would meet.

The Hotel Şeref looked nothing like the ones they were used to, but no friend could have offered a warmer welcome. The landlord personally greeted them and led them to a suite set aside for very important guests, wondering all the while what a woman in a sable coat and a man in a kalpak were doing in his establishment.

Seyit's question seemed to answer his unpronounced one. "I heard there were Crimeans staying here; are they still around? Would I be able to meet them?"

"Yes, sir, they are: Uncle Ali and young poet Hasan. They're recent arrivals too, but they left early this morning. I'll let you know when they're back."

The names didn't ring a bell, but Seyit was thrilled at the prospect of meeting someone from his homeland.

The old ceramic stove in the corner soon warmed the room. It was snowing heavily now. Shura drew the net curtains aside and rested her nose on the windowpane. Her warm breath instantly misted the glass. She wiped a clear patch to watch the scenery outside. Timber houses flanking a street of cobblestones, a sliver of a pavement, and a man in a fez alighting from a phaeton at the corner; how foreign it all looked! But the snow? The snow was the same everywhere. She looked up at the sky. Had the same clouds floated over Kislovodsk too? Snowed over her house too? Frozen the blue lake of Nalchik? If so, then those clouds carried the kisses of her dear mother and sisters, the smell of the River Don, the jingling of troika bells and the smell of the arctic chill blowing in from the steppes. She felt hot all over, opened the window and stuck her head out, closed her eyes, and took a deep breath. She felt the cold and the snowflakes on her face and hair, but it was no good. The sounds and smells were missing. She was about to wipe her eyes when a pair of arms embraced her waist and chest; she relaxed into that warm sense of security.

They watched the snow for a while. Soon the street, the pavements, and the roofs were covered. It piled on the windowsill, a white fluff already halfway up the pane. Seyit kissed Shura on the nape. "You know, darling? I've missed the snow."

"Me too..." said Shura.

He closed his eyes as he kissed her warm skin once again, drew her scent in as he always did, and held her narrow waist tighter. Shura hugged his arms and tilted her head back, abandoning herself to the lips wandering on her forehead and cheeks. The warmth of their breaths obscured most of the windowpane.

Blinking back the tears, Shura cast one more look at the sky before the last slice of clear glass also misted over.

Her enduring melancholy had not missed his attention. His lips wandered under her eyes and on her cheeks and descended to her lips. He desired her more than ever this evening, but he knew her too well to hurry. First he had to make her feel she was loved and wanted—that she wasn't alone. His tender kisses dried the salty tears on her lips. Freeing her hair from the pins, he let those fine threads of spun silk run through his palms. With no hint of haste, he unbuttoned her lace shirt and lowered his lips to her long neck and then to her breast, gingerly, loath to force her to make love on this emotional evening. Shura shut her eyes, abandoning herself to his kisses and caresses, but the sensation of falling in a void lingered. She didn't feel whole enough to make love, as though part of her soul was elsewhere. Then it occurred to her that this hesitancy might offend him.

"Does this ever happen to you too?" she asked bashfully.

"Does what ever happen, my love?" he asked between kisses.

Throwing her head back, Shura groped for the right words. "As if...hard to say...as if part of your body or soul is somewhere else..."

Seyit withdrew his lips from her shoulder, cupped her face in his hands, caressed her cheeks, and stared into her eyes as his blazing eyes bore through the darkness. When he spoke, it was in a tone that admitted his own melancholy was no less profound than hers. "But that's the reality, isn't it, my little Shura? That's the way it is, isn't it? We'll always feel this way. There's no remedy, my love..."

A remedy might have been precisely what she needed, but she knew they were in the same boat, that her man was burning with the same homesickness. She kissed his hand. "What...what do you do when that happens?"

Seyit wished he didn't love her this much; homesickness was incurable, and he knew it better than she ever would. The idea that her fragile soul and body suffered as he did was harrowing. He embraced her tenderly again, buried his face in her hair, and murmured, "Me? I complete my soul, my body, my everything with you, my darling..."

Am I doing him an injustice? she wondered. They weren't that different, after all, and his losses were far bigger than hers. She forgot her own grief. It was up to her to make him forget these sad moments and lift his spirits. Up to her to take him back to the good old days. *I complete my soul, my body, my everything with you, my darling*—that's what he had said. The union of their bodies and souls was the only way to put an end to the scorching homesickness inside.

Her velvet skirt and lacy petticoat rustled on their way down to the floor, and she presented her body to the man waiting patiently. Seyit was determined to rein in his customary haste. He picked her up in his arms and laid her on the cambric sheets; he needed as much love and tenderness as he wanted to offer her. He continued kissing her hair, face, lips, neck, and breasts as though they had just met. Shura trembled at every blazing contact.

The crackling logs in the ceramic stove, the tiny tongues of flame behind the iron grille, the broderie anglaise and net curtains: everything was like something out of a fairy tale—except for the heavy snowfall outside that had all but blanketed the window; it belonged to far distant lands. And the man she shared warmth, heartbeats, and the melancholy in the depths of their hearts with? He was a memento of the land of pure-white snow. She reached out to stroke his hair. When he grasped her body, she knew the time had come, the time when their souls and bodies would find peace.

***

During the next few days, as they tried to find their Istanbul legs, they eagerly sought the latest news from home. The other Crimean guests were a couple of men who'd been working in Baku: Uncle Ali and his nephew, poet Hasan. Ali was about forty-five and as avuncular as his moniker suggested. He had been the head butler in a wealthy landowner's mansion, and his only living relation was his sister's eighteen-year-old son, who had been an undergraduate in Moscow when his so-called best mate had shopped him to the Reds for refusing to participate in the demonstrations of March 1918. Uncle and nephew had run away together. Hotelier Şeref, Seyit, Ali, and Hasan frequently amused themselves with one another's accents and dialects, chattering away in Turkish and Crimean Tatar.

Christmas was approaching, and Shura wanted to go to church, but she didn't know where the Russian Orthodox churches were, or if there were any in the first place. Seyit asked around; yes, there were two: one in Galata and the other in Pangaltı.

On returning to the hotel that evening, however, she still looked agitated. Later that night, a restless Seyit opened his eyes to see Shura kneeling before her icon. She must have been there for quite a while. He watched without stirring, hoping to hear what his sweetheart was praying for. Was there room in her prayers for him? And even if there was, would they come to pass? How much longer would they stay together? All that he'd seen so far had shown that neither wealth, nor love, and not even relationships could last a lifetime.

She looked relatively more tranquil after crossing herself daintily; she stood up, approached the bed, and noticed Seyit's gaze. Embarrassed at having been caught despite their unspoken agreement to avoid overt demonstrations of piety and concerned that she might have offended him, she whispered bashfully as she came into his arms, "I hope I've not disturbed you."

He drew her into the bed, pressed her against his body, and kissed her forehead. "Why would you be disturbing me, my little Shura?" he asked, trying to catch her sad eyes. "Don't we ask the same God for the same things?"

"Are you sure our religions pray to the same God?"

"Of course, my love. Just as there is only one definition of love, there is only one God."

"What is the definition of love then?" she asked, evidently looking for answers to the very same questions in his mind. He hugged her tighter. Slowly hitching up the skirt of her full-length nightgown, he ran his hands up her warm, silky skin, murmuring, "Love, my darling, is the best thing God has given the world..."

As another night of melancholy turned into one of love in that hotel room, the wheels of history kept turning, altering the fortunes of two countries flanking the Black Sea—two countries that had once been great empires.

Bandırma

I STANBUL REMAINED UNDER occupation, war raged on across Anatolia, unemployment was rife, and destitution and hunger loomed for many—certainly for the thousands of Russian émigrés who had to start life from scratch. Neither the fortunes nor the titles they'd left behind meant much in a foreign land whose language and customs were totally alien, and living in the past was no help. They all needed work and money. Seyit's situation was no different. He had nothing other than the diamond ring on his finger, his decorations, his gold watch, and his stash of rubles, and he had absolutely no intention at all of parting with them even on his darkest day. No amount of ready money would last forever, at any rate. Accommodation and food had to be paid for, and Seyit knew it was high time for him to queue up for a job. Any job. Every morning, the hotel guests set out for whatever they could find around the city so that they could return in the evening with a few pennies in their pockets. They weren't proud either: porter in Sirkeci Station? Fine. Cleaning hotel toilets? Gladly.

One evening, as the guests were chatting in the lobby, the arrival of an elderly gentleman caused quite a commotion, an effusive display of respect that seemed to greet him whenever he came to stay. Basking in the hotelier's esteem, Hacı Bey stroked his white beard and moustache as he graciously condescended to join the new guests. A landowner seemingly happy with his lot despite the turbulent times, he frequently came to Istanbul to sell the produce of the vast İbrahim Bey Farm in Bandırma. His only problem, apparently, was a mysterious complaint that caused unbearable pain.

They chatted for quite a while. The guests were getting hungry. Bellies rumbled and mouths watered at the thought of a bowl of hot food and a couple of glasses of something. Uncle Ali took charge.

"Hacı Bey, place yourself in our hands, and you'll be cured by the morning. You'll be as good as new!"

Hacı sat up, his eyes gleaming hopefully; did these men from distant lands know of a remedy? "Cure me, and I'll give you whatever you want!"

"We don't ask much, Hacı Bey; don't worry! Give me some money, and I'll go get a few things. Get your room warmed up in the meantime, and keep a warm woolen vest to hand. I'll be back in no time at all."

And before long he was back, carrying bread, cheese, spicy sausage, rakı, a bottle of spirit, and some spices. Handing over the foods in the brown paper parcel, he crushed a generous quantity of camphor, blended it with mustard, and added it to the spirit. He made such an entertaining production of it all that by the time he'd shaken the bottle to blend it well and set off for his patient's room, Seyit and Shura were laughing their heads off.

Hacı Bey fell into a deep sleep after an energetic massage session that set his skin on fire. He'd been rubbed with this smelly concoction, pummeled vigorously, and enveloped in warm underwear. It was a cheerful Uncle Ali who washed his hands and returned to the lobby. "I guess I've earned that glass of rakı then!"

It was nearly noon when Hacı rose the next day, declaring he'd not slept this well in a long time and silently admitting that had been money well spent; he liked these men from Russia. A couple of days later, when he was about to leave, Hacı sought Seyit out—having identified him as the leader of the group of émigrés—to make him an offer.

"Seyit Bey, please don't take offense, but I see you're struggling here. I was wondering if you'd like to come to my farm. There's lots of work. I can't pay much: I'll give you somewhere to stay and food, and if things go well, perhaps I could offer a few pennies. Please don't misunderstand: I'm not trying to take advantage of you, but that's the only way I can make ends meet."

With no bargaining power, they knew room and board still presented a better prospect than nothing. They all packed and set off with Hacı Bey: Seyit, Shura, Uncle Ali, Young Poet Hasan, Handsome Yusuf, and Mehmet. They reached the farm several days later, had an early evening meal with their host, and retired immediately into their quarters. They knew they were receiving preferential treatment, since their rooms appeared to be far superior to the quarters of the other farmhands from nearby villages.

Seyit and Shura's room raised a smile when they first stepped in: the walls, floor, and sofas were all covered with a profusion of kilims in a range of clashing patterns. Fortune moved in mysterious ways, but at least they were together.

Shura stood shivering. The only source of heating was a brazier in the middle; Seyit cuddled her. His mind went back to a time when he'd listened to the crackling of the logs in the fireplace, watching the flames with a tumbler of vodka in his hand after a fascinating show at the Mariinsky. It wasn't hard to guess that Shura was recalling a similar memory even as she gazed at the deer in the landscape on the wall kilim.

"You know, my love? I miss Tchaikovsky."

She turned toward him with a chuckle. "Whatever made you think of this now?" Her eyes were sparkling; she didn't look unhappy with her lot.

Seyit cheered up, opened his mouth—and was startled by gunshots outside. Pushing her aside for safety, he bolted to the window. About twenty horsemen thronging outside the farmhouse were firing into the air. Hacı scuttled out, still in nightclothes and nightcap, put down his lamp, and shook the hand of one of the burly horsemen who had dismounted. Seyit watched Hacı bow repeatedly and talk in an unbroken stream, although the words were impossible to make out.

"What's happening, Seyt, for God's sake?" asked Shura.

"We'll soon find out; don't leave the room, and lock the door behind me."

The rest of the Hotel Şeref contingent were milling in the hallway by the staircase when a breathless Hacı dashed upstairs. "Don't say a word now; best they don't know who you are."

That deferential welcome was not sincere then, thought Seyit. *Something stinks here.*

"Who the hell are they, Hacı Bey? What do they want from you?"

"Please, Seyit Bey, don't say a word. Just smile. This is Black Ali's gang; they're here to eat. They'll stay awhile, eat, drink, and then leave. We have to treat them like guests. Otherwise, God forbid, these bandits will show no mercy. Come on, come on; help us lay the tables. I've put a lamb on the spit. They're hungry."

He hastened down the stairs, waving at his new recruits to follow—and they had no choice but to comply. Storming about without a single word to betray their accents, they all pretended to be local farm staff. Tables were set outside the farmhouse despite the chilly night. A lamb was already roasting, and the bandits fell upon the bottles of rakı like a gang of jail breakers. Young poet Hasan was so scared that he invented tasks in the kitchen to stay out of their sight. The other four men kept refilling frequently emptied plates and glasses all night long, their hearts in their mouths.

It was nearly time for morning prayers when the Black Ali gang loaded up provisions and galloped away, firing into the air as they did so. Too tense to go to sleep, the new arrivals set about their duties instead.

By the evening, they were barely able to lift their spoons to their mouths. After a sleepless night and a long and exhausting day on the farm, they were desperate to catch up on missed sleep.

It wasn't to be. Another bout of gunshots and whinnying horses jolted them all out of bed.

Seyit hastened to get dressed again, grumbling, "Every night? It's getting to be a little too much. At this rate, there'll be no food left to feed staff either!"

This time, it was Çerkes "Circassian" Ethem's bandits, who wanted a bit of rest after having trounced the Black Ali gang. Hacı Bey and the farmhands laid the tables as before, slaughtered a lamb, and flung it into the oven. As the glasses were filled with rakı, the brigands fell upon the feast, tearing meat off the carcass on the table, smacking their lips, wiping the dripping fat with the backs of their hands, and regaling one another with the crudest japes—just like the previous night's uninvited foul mouths. Seyit felt sick at their lack of table manners, which were in such contrast to the exquisite courtesy of renowned leader Çerkes Ethem.

In a repetition of the previous morning, Çerkes Ethem's gang also left before daybreak—not, however, before they'd commandeered several horses and additional provisions.

At dawn, Seyit and Uncle Ali set to work in the stables. As a head butler in a nobleman's mansion, Ali's sense of pride was hurt at having to muck out, whereas Seyit regarded it as the best job they'd found. He loved horses, loved grooming them, and certainly didn't see mucking out as beneath him. In his imagination, he was back in the cavalry regiment stables, looking after his wonderful Socks. Fantasy helped.

Then he heard a rattling gasp from Ali. The poor fellow's eyes were bulging out at something in the hay, pitchfork frozen in his hand. At first, spotting the blood on the prongs, Seyit wondered if Ali had inadvertently injured someone. Grasping the man's hand, he glanced at the hay. He gasped too. Cold sweat poured down his back.

A severed head was looking out, covered in blood, eyes half open and ears sliced off. Seyit looked around for the poor victim's body, but it was nowhere to be seen. It wasn't a familiar face, not one they'd seen on the farm in the past couple of days, although the murder must have been recent. He dragged Ali out of there.

"Maybe they brought him along. Maybe it's one of their men. Let's pretend we've seen nothing, Ali. Come on; let's get the hell out of here."

"What are we gonna do now, Seyit Bey? What an ominous place! What are we gonna do now?" Ali wailed in a barely audible voice.

"Ali, we've not seen it, all right?" asked Seyit, trying to calm the older man down. "We've seen nothing and know nothing. And we'll tell no one. Not even our own people. Or we might get into trouble even if we could get away. Now pull yourself up and get to work next door. We've not been here at all today. We've seen nothing today—don't forget. I'll think of something."

Seyit pondered all day long how to escape from the farm. He had no wish to discuss anything with Hacı Bey and no reason to trust the scalawag who would easily shop them in order to save his own skin. There was nothing to suggest that Hacı Bey didn't belong to one or more of these bandit gangs. If Seyit were to suggest they wanted to go back to Istanbul, Hacı would pry, demanding to know what had suddenly prompted this change of heart. It was best to get away without telling anyone anything.

Seyit was watering the horses when he saw Hasan loading a cart.

"Hullo, young man, what are you up to?" he asked, rushing over.

"Off to the dock, Seyit Abi; I was told to load the garlic and the potatoes."

Glancing around, Seyit moved closer, pretending to be helping with the loading. He whispered, "I'm going to ask you for a favor, my young poet friend. But it's going to be our secret."

The younger man was thrilled at the prospect of sharing a secret with his hero. "Of course, Seyit Abi—anything you ask!"

"Don't load them all." Hasan gave a perplexed stare, and Seyit prodded him back to work. "Open a few sacks, sell the produce, and bring me the money. All right? Not a word to anyone else now." Hasan looked bewildered by this apparent suggestion of theft. "No, it's all right; trust me. You'll be doing us all a favor. I couldn't leave the farm now on a credible pretext; that's why I'm asking you. But careful now—don't get caught, all right?"

"Won't we get caught afterward though?"

"God is great, Hasan; he'll look after us. Have a good day. Safe travel!" said Seyit, cuffing the younger man affectionately on the back of the neck, raising his voice at the approach of a few farmhands. He went back to work.

Later that night, Seyit hid the cash Hasan had surreptitiously slipped into his hands and explained as a silent Shura watched inquisitively, "We're going away, my love, and at once, now we have a little money. Once I retrieve our passports, that is."

She was afraid, but what they'd seen the last two nights was far more terrifying.

Seyit continued, "I know where Hacı's hidden our passports. I'll get them in the dead of the night, and we can leave at once provided we're all ready."

"What if something goes wrong?"

"It's not like we haven't always assumed the worst so far, is it?" He chuckled, stroking her cheek.

Seyit then alerted his companions; they would meet at the stables at midnight.

When his gold watch chimed eleven, he snuck out on tiptoe. Silence reigned in the farmhouse, but Seyit knew his companions waited, alert, behind their doors. Hacı must have been in a deep sleep after two sleepless nights; he had retired immediately after nighttime prayers. Seyit put his ear against their employer's door; all he could hear was snoring.

The wooden staircase was going to creak horribly in the stillness of the night though. He decided to slide down the banister instead, grinning at this childish pleasure.

He slipped into the office where the account books and other documents were kept. Three days ago, when they'd arrived, he'd watched Hacı stash away their passports and identity papers in the locked cupboard covering an entire wall. It would have been preferable to open the lock without breaking it, but since they were going to be away by the morning, it wasn't going to make much difference. He extracted a knife from his pocket, slipped the blade between the two wings of the door, and wiggled it until the lock sprang. He found what he was looking for.

He stepped out and spotted Shura at the bottom of the stairs in the dark. She had packed and followed him downstairs. Holding hands, they walked out of the kitchen door at the rear. The others soon joined them. Seyit gave them a brief explanation, and they set off. They walked all night long.

It took ten days of trekking, catching rides on horse carts, and spending nights in small villages to return to the Hotel Şeref in Tepebaşı.

A New Life, 1920

A FEW DAYS later, Shura and Seyit started working for Mr. Konstantinides in a laundry on Kalyoncu Kulluğu Street, a stone's throw away from the bustling thoroughfare that was the Grand Rue de Pera—a street that, like countless others in Istanbul, had been named once for some purpose that had lost its relevance in the annals of history. (In this case, it referred to a police force entrusted with the security of the shipyards down the hill.)

Istanbul, or Constantinople, as their new employer insisted on calling it, was never without a surprise. Thousands of years of history distilled into a melting as well as nonmelting pot of races and languages and religious affiliations. Mr. Konstantinides spoke Greek and would have been called Greek by any European, but as a *Rum*—Anatolian Roman—he knew his ancestors had been on these lands for a very long time indeed, certainly well before the present rush of occupiers.

As Shura ironed all day long, Seyit collected dirty laundry and delivered clean items to local restaurants, clubs, private residences, and hotels. These weren't their dream jobs, but they were the best they could get under the circumstances. Seyit knew he cut quite a figure in a three-piece suit, tie, and kalpak; several ladies now looked forward to their pressed laundry deliveries from this handsome young man with flashing blue eyes. Thanks to his flawless French and German, he got along famously with the Europeans and Levantines. The one thing he couldn't stomach, however, was tips. True, they needed every penny; true, beggars couldn't be choosers…but he was too proud to accept a few coins tucked into his pocket—an ignominy thankfully forestalled by his dignified conduct and sartorial elegance.

The only willowy fair blonde in the ironing room, Shura stood apart from the gaggle of olive-skinned girls in cambric shirts displaying plump arms and ample bosoms under rolled-up sleeves and undone top buttons. She couldn't have looked more out of place if she had been a rare garden daisy in a meadow of wild herbs. She wore her golden hair plaited into a chignon at the nape. Every once in a while, as her iron danced over an enormous broderie anglaise tablecloth, she recalled her mother's supper tables in Kislovodsk, her sister Valentine's piano and songs, and guests leaving on their colorful troikas. Memory after memory flashed past her eyes, each a lovely scene framed by the steam on the white cloth. Less talkative than the others, she preferred to evade politely prying questions posed in appallingly accented French—and the perpetual chatter around her fell back into Greek soon enough. She worked silently at the ironing board all day long, lost in her dreams and feeling utterly alone until Seyit's return.

Their living quarters consisted of a room upstairs allocated by a munificent Mr. Konstantinides, who had made it clear that this was a special privilege. Not many laundry owners got to employ White Russian gentry, after all.

It was only after closing down for the evening that the lovers regained their own little world. The moment they were alone, their heartbeats quickened, and their souls and minds resumed living for real.

Since accommodation was now free, they could afford to dine out. Even on their poorest days, a good evening meal with drinks and singing was a necessity. On occasion Seyit brought over Russian dishes from Volkov Restaurant and complemented this feast at home with a bottle of vodka. As the evening progressed, they snuggled up and invariably chatted about the good old days. Seyit dragged out many tales from his childhood he'd never told her before. She never tired of listening with a smile on her lips, gazing fondly and stroking his hair. They never argued. Neither attempted to dominate. They loved each other utterly and completely.

No amount of hardship was going to stop Shura from taking it all in her stride. Her gentle and cheerful disposition never wavered. She was happy to listen to him for hours and rest her head on his chest when he wanted silence. They had come to know each other better than they knew themselves.

Her unquestioning love extended into listening to his past tales of woman-izing; she had absolutely no doubt that they were all left behind, short stories that provided life with the spice of variety. Encouraged by that total trust, he lay his past bare before her. It always took them a little while to return to their new world after having revisited yet another memory, but return they did, happy to have shared it.

Recounting memories was only a part of the joy of Seyit's life. Making love was as vital as eating, drinking, and talking. If anything, it was even more impor-tant. It was only during those hours of passion that privations, nostalgia, or sor-row of any description were laid aside. Only then were they certain that all they needed was each other.

One thing Seyit was adamant about was that they avoid dipping into the sack of rubles. That money was for something big: they might go back to Russia one day or immigrate to America. But Seyit needed a second job to save for a rainy day, or even just to save.

He hit upon the ingenious idea of supplying several restaurants in Tepebaşı with lemon vodka: every evening, he distilled white spirit, filtered it through coal, and flavored it with glycerin and cloves. It was then bottled with neatly sliced lemon peel and left to age. Before long, he was working practically all night to supply growing demand. Secrecy was another issue; he had to keep Mr. Konstantinides in the dark about the moonshine still that sat above the laundry.

A little money was now put aside every day. Whenever he counted it, he couldn't repress a chuckle, thinking about the dashing young officer who'd have blown more than this paltry amount in the course of one single night of revelry without blinking an eye back in the old, wild days in Saint Petersburg. The hope of spending his savings in Saint Petersburg once again won over the desire to go to America. One thing that kept his hopes alive was the constant trickle of news from Crimea; the Whites seemed to be on the ascendancy.

When Denikin resigned, General Baron Pyotr Nikolayevich Wrangel, who had been in Istanbul until April, was recalled to Crimea. He took over, reformed the voluntary White Army that had been in disarray after several defeats, imple-mented a series of successful policies, held off the Reds, and even forced them to retreat at several locations.

The émigrés all devoured foreign newspapers and conversed endlessly as they waited for news of the White Army's ultimate triumph. They now allowed themselves the luxury of talking about the future. Seyit and Shura were one of thousands thrilled about the prospect of resuming the life they had left behind, shattered as it was.

"I'll kiss my father's hand the moment I land," mused Seyit. "There wasn't the opportunity when I left." He then smiled wistfully. "We might make it to harvesttime. I'll then take you to Kislovodsk, and we'll look for your mother and your sisters and brothers."

"That would be lovely! I miss them all so much!" chirped Shura, taking his arm.

The possibility that their homes and nearest and dearest might be gone was banished from their minds; no one wanted to consider that awful news might be waiting around the corner.

What they needed now was good dreams. What they needed now was hope.

Those hopes were dashed to the ground. The Bolshevik regime made peace with the Poles and thus freed up troops to fight the Whites in the south. Wrangel's last stand failed. Sevastopol fell on November 15, 1920, the day after over two dozen vessels evacuated Crimea. Wrangel's fleet, as it came to be known, was crammed with the last vestiges of his White Army and any civilians fortunate enough to have made it on board. Many more had already fled to Istanbul, the unknown being a better alternative to the certainty of the gruesome fate that awaited them at the hands of the Reds.

By late November, the Bosphorus was thick with vessels sailing in one after the other, bringing exhausted soldiers, generals, coachmen, counts, baronesses, dancers, doctors, and prostitutes: Russians from every class and every walk of life. Before long hundreds of thousands descended into Istanbul, and the majority of this hodgepodge of humanity dispersed into Pera. All in all, approximately two hundred thousand White Russians landed in Istanbul; many others were settled in Gelibolu, on the Isle of Lemnos, and in the Balkans. When the last ship from Crimea docked, Seyit and Shura knew they would never return now. This was a new chapter in their lives.

Not a day passed without them meeting yet another fellow White Russian. All social and cultural barriers were down now; fate had brought them all together. Everyone asked everyone else about their nearest and dearest, trying to glean some information from somewhere. Families had been left behind in that frantic rush to escape. Spouses and children had been separated as people scrambled to board. Everyone asked for names and addresses. Chaos reigned.

The Russian pharmacy where Shura had been working as cashier for several months was one of the most popular spots for such inquiries; every White Russian who made it into Pera dropped into Zezemsky's in Taksim.

Shura and Seyit considered themselves much more fortunate than these thousands knocking on doors and looking for work. The new arrivals weren't proud; they would take anything, no matter how poorly it paid. Who cared about titles when destitution loomed?

At Seyit's request, the laundry had taken on two young Russians. They claimed to be the daughters of a general and said they had been studying in Moscow. One look and Seyit knew their education had involved no academic knowledge; rather, it would have been of the practical kind, in a field more commonly known as the oldest profession. He didn't let on; Mr. Konstantinides liked them anyway.

Before long, familiar faces began to turn up among fellow émigrés. Manol was one of Seyit's brothers-in-arms from the Carpathian front. He had left his young wife and baby in Kiev years ago when he went to war and neither saw nor heard from them ever again. He had later served in General Wrangel's volunteer army and had made it to the last vessel by the skin of his teeth, which is where he'd met an Azeri by the name of İskender Beyzade. A tall, well-built, and extremely handsome son of a rich landowner family from Baku, İskender had managed to sneak through the Reds that had surrounded their home one night. He'd taken his younger brother along, but they had been separated on the way.

Seyit invited them both for dinner that night. Only Seyit and Manol had known each other before the revolution, yet all four got along like long-lost friends. Shura had done justice to the food from the Volkov. Vodka tumblers filled, Seyit stood up and lifted his drink to toast his friends. "*Na zdorovie!*"

Manol and İskender stood up and repeated the toast as Shura raised her glass, her eyes glistening. "*Na zdorovie!*"

The drinks were downed in one and refilled at once. At the sight of this feast—the likes of which the guests had quite forgotten about—of pirozhkis, Russian salad, smoked fish, and duck, the guests raised their glasses in a toast to their hosts this time. Then to the tsar, next to Istanbul, and then to the guests, and again to the hosts...the first bottle must have had a hole at the bottom. The second was cracked open.

As Manol and İskender launched into an account of the events of the past two years in Russia, however, the sounds of cutlery ceased. No fiery sip of vodka could still the pain of reopened wounds. Seyit asked about Crimea, knowing full well he ought to have anticipated the reply, yet it came as a blow all the same

"It was ablaze as we retreated, Seyit. The Reds wreaked their wrath on Crimea. God spare anyone left behind!"

Seyit and İskender said, "Amen!" as Shura crossed herself and then glanced at Seyit. He moved his chair closer, placed his arm over her shoulder, and kissed her head. They might pray in different religions, but the prayers and hopes were the same. She placed her hand on his knee, as if by snuggling closer they could protect the families they had left behind. Seyit asked another question, this time on Shura's behalf—the question she had been unable to voice: "What about Kislovodsk? How are things over there?"

"Same. Attacked before Crimea. Mansions were sequestered, and any gentry they captured were either killed or taken away no one knows where. They've not been heard from since. Families were scattered to the winds, Seyit. So few have managed to get away with their kith or kin."

Shura was weeping silently, one hand over her eyes, wishing she'd never learned the answers to the questions that had been plaguing her for so long. She'd been deceiving herself up to now, hoping for the best, but now that she knew the truth...that was that. She took a sip from the tumbler Seyit held to her lips and rested her head on his shoulder. She was so fortunate to have him there.

Manol fell silent. It was İskender's turn to speak; he sounded incongruously sensitive for someone of his size. "They gathered babies and little children. God knows where they took them. And they did the same in Crimea, I hear."

"They must've taken them to children's camps. They'd be no good to the Bolsheviks, would they, if they knew how their parents were murdered and their property looted and torched? Who knows how they will be inculcated in the virtues of Bolshevism now!"

Manol wiped his eyes, downed his glass in one, and mumbled as he refilled it, "My baby...must be around four now. Who knows?"

Silence reigned over the table. Silence and tears. Seyit hugged his sweetheart tighter and started humming a song. The others lifted their glasses; exchanged glances; and, one by one, all joined in. The song of the snowy steppes and of the Don Cossacks rose from the first-floor window of a laundry in Pera as four young people cried for their lost country.

It was twilight when Seyit and Shura saw their guests off. They shut the door and hugged instinctively. They stood in total silence, rooted to the spot. All they could do now was to console each other after what had been discussed. They understood each other so well. There was no need for words; no word or glance could offer more consolation than this embrace. Shura was still crying. He wiped her tears. She took hold of his hand and kissed the palm.

"I'm very sorry, darling. I can't stop myself."

He ran his fingers through her hair and drew her closer. "Cry, my lovely Shura; cry. You'll feel better. I wish I could cry like you." He wasn't sobbing, but his face buried in her hair was drenched in tears.

Locked in an embrace, they moved to the bed illuminated by the street lamp. They had lost so much that was irreplaceable. Their only link to the past was their love. Seyit kissed her cheeks wet with tears; kissed her neck; and nuzzling the silky cascade of her hair, inhaled her scent. He'd fled Russia with his young sweetheart; now he wanted to protect her and spend his life with her. He needed the same tenderness, love, and understanding, and it was this young woman embracing him who understood him better than anyone else. She ran her hands through his hair, held his head with one hand, and held his shoulder with the other, just like a mother cradling her child on her lap. Lying in that maternal hold and alert to her sensual abandon, Seyit's blood surged in his veins. His heart and mind were in turmoil, assailed by a multitude of contrasting emotions and sensations: his quickening pulse as he unbuttoned her shirt, the melancholy at kissing her tears, the comforting touch of the long fingers in his hair. She was the culmination of every emotion he could ever desire or yearn for. She was his one true love, everything about his childhood, adulthood, excitements, passions, and longings. His lips wandered over her body as her moans were punctuated by the occasional sob.

"Seyt, Seyt, my love. Don't leave me. Don't ever leave me—"

Silencing her with a kiss, he wrapped his arms around her and held her tight.

She recognized the passion building up in the body she knew so well. He would soon scoop her up from the edge of the cliff, soar with her in the skies, and fly her to the clouds and higher. She closed her eyes and yielded to the pleasures to come. Seyit untangled himself and stood up. She slipped her shirt over her shoulders and head. He took a generous sip from his glass and bent down to her lips. She swallowed the vodka that set her on fire. A thirsty kiss to douse the fire within.

"My love, my beautiful darling..." whispered Seyit.

She didn't want to hear the rest. Her head was spinning, her heart was pounding, and her blood was on fire. Cupping his head in her hands, she drew it to her lips. "Don't speak. Just make love to me..."

One more night of love worth hundreds of words.

By the time they stretched out in each other's arms, worn out with weeping and lovemaking, the first rays of the new day were ready to pierce the net curtains.

The First Heartbreak

D ETERMINED AS THEY were to avoid taking sides in the Russian civil war, the Allies occupying Istanbul unanimously tolerated the flood of White Russian émigrés, although every vessel was kept offshore for extended checks to identify any Red spies. The faces of émigrés fortunate enough to obtain landing permits were like an open book of the horrors, brutality, and terror they had suffered. Agonizing over their loved ones left behind in the bloodbath that was their homeland, most could hardly believe they had gotten out alive.

New hardships awaited the White Russians welcomed with open arms in occupied Istanbul. Hardships they had to brave and overcome, for their own sake as much as that of their families, so long as they had a dream to cling to: the dream of returning to Russia one day. One day. The dream they all clung to, the dream that kept them all going.

Just like Seyit and Shura. *One day* was the wish that safeguarded the rubles in the pillow.

This new rush was a welcome change for the lovers; no longer did they feel quite so alone. Russian rang through Pera; Russian was heard far more frequently than any other language, even Turkish! It was well-nigh impossible not to come across a former bon vivant White Russian at every step of the way on a stroll between Tepebaşı and Taksim. Elegant partygoers, exquisitely dressed and beautifully educated, these new guests were like a breath of fresh air in the Ottoman capital, which had never before hosted so many aristocrats at one time. White Russians were distinctly different from the Levantines and members of foreign missions that had provided the European flavor up to then.

This sudden influx would soon have an impact on the lovers' lives.

It was a cold evening in late November. Shura was tidying up the shelves in the pharmacy. The doorbell tinkled.

She caught her breath when she saw who it was. Eyes open wide in joyful surprise, she didn't even notice the bottle that fell from her hand and shattered into smithereens. Flinging the duster aside, she ran to the door. "Yevgeny! Yevgeny!"

The handsome young man was none other than her cousin Yevgeny Bogayevsky, her aunt Nadia's son. They hugged. She couldn't believe her eyes: her cousin was here, in Istanbul! Grabbing his hand, she led him to the Thonet sofa at the rear.

"Come, Yevgeny, come; sit down and tell me everything!"

She sat down next to him, firing off a barrage of questions that gave him no chance to open his mouth. Eventually he patted her hands for silence.

"Hold on, Shura; hold on for a moment. I'll tell you everything, if you'll only let me!"

But she wouldn't settle down. "Tell me, Yevgeny: Who else came with you? Is my mother here? What about my auntie Nadia?"

"I'm very sorry, Shura; your mother's sadly not here. No amount of insistence on Father's part helped. She wouldn't leave Kislovodsk."

"What about Valentine?"

Worried about her sister and uncle ever since they had left the train in Novorossiysk, she gave him a searching look, hoping for some good news. He shook his head with a smile. "Dear Shura! Honestly! We were hoping to surprise you. Well, if you're going to get this excited, I might as well tell you everything from the beginning." Glancing at his watch, he asked, "What time do you leave?"

"I can lock up in about ten minutes."

"Then keep calm, and don't ask too many questions. I'll wait for you. We'll leave together."

"Where are we going?"

"Shura, please keep calm and enjoy the surprise."

Wondering which of her relations she would soon see, she tidied up in a rush, leaving a couple of small accounting tasks until the morning; she was too excited and tense at any rate.

At seven o'clock, she locked up and linked her arm through Yevgeny's, hurrying him along, impatient to reach their destination as soon as possible, afraid to lose her family before she'd even found them. The snow weighing down the clouds burst free in a light sprinkle. Shura took a deep breath, threw her head back, and sent a silent prayer of thanks up into the heavens.

The two cousins walked toward Tarlabaşı arm in arm.

***

Seyit had good news for his sweetheart. Mr. Konstantinides must be planning to move to Greece; he wanted to sell the laundry and would be happy to come to an arrangement—"If," he'd said, "Kyrios Eminof had a modest amount in the way of savings?"

Those savings were nowhere near the amount Mr. Konstantinides named as *a modest amount,* a far from an inconsiderable sum, as it happened. Seyit had been contemplating it since their talk in the morning; he had no idea how to put the money together, but he did have a week to decide. He could exchange his rubles, of course. They needed to make a living in Istanbul, and the laundry was lucrative; they would soon recoup the investment. Becoming the boss instead of knocking on doors to deliver starched laundry was very tempting—too tempting to refuse. Fine. He would find the money one way or the other.

Thrilled now that his mind was made up, he couldn't wait for Shura to return; he would tell her at once. He put the ledger away and locked the desk drawers. A chill wind whipped his face when he walked out of the laundry, harbinger of snow. Seyit smiled. He loved the cold. Sniffing the approaching snowfall, he walked uphill from Tepebaşı, turned toward Taksim, paused to check his watch, and slowed his steps: there was no need to hurry. Shura couldn't leave before seven. He still had another quarter of an hour. Eschewing the horse tram passing by, he carried on, on foot. He loved walking in the cold.

He recognized two attractive—and equally poised—ladies walking in the opposite direction, Russians who worked at Park Hotel, one in room service and the other in the restaurant. Recognizing him, they returned his gallant salute with a smile and a faint bow. Seyit mused with astonishment that he'd been faithful to one single woman for quite a while.

Crossing Taksim Square, he spotted the lights in the Russian pharmacy going out one by one. He picked up speed and then broke into a run. His sweetheart walked out. Seyit waited for the car blocking his way to pass. It started snowing. He straightened his kalpak and raised his collar. He stepped down from the pavement and froze on the spot.

A man walked out of the pharmacy after Shura and stood, waiting for her to lock up. She took his arm; they both looked happy—looked cozy. Seyit couldn't believe his eyes. He watched, tormented by jealousy, as Shura chuckled and rested her head against the young man's shoulder. They were about to cross the road to where Seyit stood. He had no idea what to do. Stay put and confront them? What would that solve other than insulting his sweetheart and offending his pride? He snuck into a darkened doorway. Shura passed by with her companion. He followed them for a while. By the time they started downhill from Pera to Tarlabaşı, he had no doubt. She had another man in her life.

His whole world crumbled. She was cuckolding him. This was far worse than being deserted. His good news now meant nothing. The woman who was his *raison d'être*, the woman who kept his memories alive, was now with someone else. He was raging inwardly on his way back. Raging against himself, Shura, his fate… against everything. Someone had to be culpable. Someone he could punish. Ruminating as he walked in the snow, he blamed his fate. He wondered where he might go next and decided to return to his room. He was in no mood to meet anyone else. He wanted to be alone.

The ironing room girls were leaving; as they simpered good-byes, Seyit stepped in and shut the door. He hung his coat on the rack, placed his kalpak on the stand, and moved toward the staircase when he noticed a light at the rear. He turned to check; he wasn't alone. Holding her coat, Marushka looked about to leave. When she saw Seyit, she came to an abrupt stop and pressed her right hand on her chest. "Oh, good God! Seyt Eminof, you scared me!" Then she noticed the confusion on his face. Tilting her head with genuine concern, she asked, "You don't look too well, Eminof; what's wrong?"

Seyit had no time to waste on this little trollop; he walked back to the stairs, impatient to be alone with his thoughts. "You may leave now, Marushka; thank you."

She followed, evidently having no intention of leaving him alone. "Is there anything I can do?"

It was a solicitation rather than an offer of help. Seyit knew the tone well and knew the standard question favored by Petrograd's top courtesans and the passionate, black-eyed gypsy dancers alike.

He turned his head to size her up from head to toe. She was pretty in a common sort of way. Too much of a strumpet for a stroll down the road, but one who was probably a great lay.

Why not? he thought. Hadn't Shura gone off with someone else? Wasn't he all on his own tonight? This was probably what he needed to deal with the rage inside. He stared into her eyes to make sure. No, he wasn't mistaken. All she waited for was a sign. The moment he held out his hand, she dropped her coat and bag at once, her eyes sparkling with a smile that said, *You won't regret it.*

He was baffled by his own actions. Why was he taking this woman to bed? He'd seen her every day for nearly a year without being in the least bit interested! He felt so little for her that were she to drop his hand now and tell him she'd changed her mind, he wouldn't feel at all offended. That, however, was clearly the last thing on Marushka's mind. She couldn't wait to hop in bed with him and started tugging at her clothes, prattling on in a husky voice. "You know, Seyt Eminof, whenever you went up with Alexandra Verjenskaya, I dreamed it was me with you. That day has finally come! You'll see; you'll love it!"

Seyit wasn't at all convinced. Her uncalled-for familiarity grated on his ears, her inappropriate reference to his one true love doubly so. He opened the bottle of vodka on the console listlessly and downed a tumbler as quickly as he'd filled it. Resting his arms on the console, he watched her in the mirror as she undressed at the other end of the room. Her haste suggested a professional anxious to serve a customer without delay. How blasé she looked! Her skirt was already on the floor, as was her petticoat. Her shirt buttons were undone. Did such women always undress in reverse order? Did they think this was somehow more titillating?

Marushka lit the lamp by the bed and waited for a move. He stayed put. She sashayed toward him, the only garment on her naked body the unbuttoned shirt, from which her ample bosom spilled out. Seyit stood motionless, watching her in the mirror without the slightest tinge of desire. Evidently unbothered, however, she wrapped her arms around him and started to unbutton his shirt, whispering in his ear and kissing his neck all the while. Shaking his head irritably, Seyit pushed her off. But Marushka wasn't in love; all she wanted was to have sex with a man she fancied. She wasn't going to let anything stop her now. She grabbed his waist from behind and pressed her breasts against his back. A plump leg captured his. Her hands slowly slipped under his shirt.

He was horrified to acknowledge utter indifference to the woman whose hungry hands and legs were stroking his body. Instead, his eyes sought the one he shared this room and this bed with, on their darkest, loneliest, and poorest days. His lovely little Shura. The woman who should have been here with him now. The one who should have been making love to him now. Why had she done it? Why? It was Shura he wanted, Shura he needed—who was somewhere else, with another man.

Didn't that give him the right to be with someone else too? Not necessarily Marushka, but she was here, and she was available. Since Shura was cheating on him, he had every right to lay another woman in this bed. He swung around and took Marushka in his arms. Her initial smile changed from triumph into one of bewilderment when she lay on her back; she'd thought she'd aroused him, but his face spoke of something else. He was thinking of the woman he loved. He was possessing the woman he loved. By the time it had dawned on Marushka that she was simply a vessel, it was too late.

Still frustrated, and unresponsive to Marushka's unfamiliar flesh, it was only when Seyit imagined he was holding Shura that arousal finally came.

He'd lost everything he loved. Everything. His homeland, his family, his brothers-in-arms, and his last remaining support: his one true love. *Why? Why?*

At the climax of this loveless coupling, his head fell down on Marushka's neck and he muttered, "Shura, my little darling…"

He pulled away testily, sat up, lit a cigarette, lay back, and rested his head on his left arm, furious with himself for having slaked gratuitous thirst on a woman who wasn't responsible for his foul mood, furious for this pointless coupling.

Dawn had yet to break when Marushka awoke and accepted that she meant nothing to the man beside her. She got up, got partly dressed, and tidied up her hair before the mirror. Evidently having changed her mind about not saying anything, she turned at the door, fingers fumbling with her buttons. "You've got it bad, Seyt Eminof; you're head over heels in love."

Seyit hadn't slept a wink. He lay in bed in a fugue of cigarette smoke, his mind elsewhere, watching the snowflakes flutter outside the window.

She shrugged as she shut the door behind her. "Whatever. It doesn't matter."

Her heels clacked down the stairs. He waited for the front door to shut; he couldn't wait for her to go away. Perhaps then he could pretend this had never happened.

Jolted by the sound of women's voices coming from the entrance hall, he leaped up; it was too early for the staff.

When Shura unlocked the door silently and snuck in to avoid waking Seyit, the entrance was in darkness. She moved, feeling her way: the wall, the office door. As her hands sought the banister, she nearly tripped over something. She stopped and bent down; her eyes were getting used to the darkness. What she'd just picked up was a handbag. She looked at the door at the top of the stairs. Her eyes still on the door, she bent down and picked up a coat. She had no doubt there was a woman with Seyit. One shameless enough to discard her things at the bottom of the stairs before going up for sex.

Tears sprang to her eyes. There was a lump in her throat. She didn't know what to do. Go upstairs and throw this stuff at the woman in bed with her lover? What would that achieve? Could she even stoop that low? And in any case, if Seyit was so eager to bring in another woman the moment she was away, clearly she had no place in his life. How could he do it? How? After all they had suffered—after all they'd gone through?

She was still rooted to the spot, battling with herself when the door upstairs opened at precisely the same time as the high landing window admitted a pale gray light. It fell on the woman buttoning up her shirt as she skipped downstairs. Shura let out an inadvertent moan as recognition dawned.

No less shocked, Marushka froze on the step, her hands crossed over her chest. She tried to speak, mumbled something unintelligible, grabbed her coat and bag from Shura's hands, and bolted out.

Shura felt no anger toward her. That woman had looked too pathetic and too common for anger. She wanted to go upstairs, see Seyit, and ask what was going on. Perhaps this was a regular occurrence whenever they were apart. Which could only mean she wasn't the only woman in his life.

She felt abandoned, betrayed, utterly alone. Her world had come crashing down upon her head. She dashed out the front door in tears.

At the sound of the slamming door, Seyit dashed to the window. *Marushka's never coming back then, if that's how she chose to leave!*

But the woman running away in the snow now wasn't the tart who'd just left his bed. It was Shura.

Seyit had the shock of his life. He flung open the window and hung half out. "Shura! Shura! Shura!"

She paused and turned for a look, but nothing could keep her there any longer. She carried on running in tears.

Drowning in guilt and remorse, Seyit pulled on his trousers and ran down the stairs, putting his arms into the sleeves of his shirt. He had to stop her. He needed her. It had been a big mistake; he had to take her in his arms and explain it all. He charged out, leaving the door open, and ran all the way to the corner. Her silhouette was not far; he'd catch up with her in no time at all.

By the time he'd reached the crossroads, however, Shura had already boarded the first Taksim tram of the day. Seyit's clenched fists dropped to his sides. She was gone. Gone for good. Their love must have been too fragile to survive even the slightest hurt. On this snowy November morning, they were both wounded.

Shura turned her face to the road and wept in silence. What was going to happen now? There was an enormous void in her life. How strange: she had found so many of her closest relations in Istanbul and lost Seyit in the meantime. A loss that tarnished everything else. It was far too early yet, but she went to the pharmacy all the same. She unlocked the door, entered the shop, locked the door behind her, and sat down in the armchair behind the shop window. She needed to be alone.

At seven thirty, it was still quite dark. It still snowed. Taksim Square was white, as were the roofs of the buildings around it. Everything looked empty and cold. The pharmacy was dark. Shura cried as she watched the snowfall through the net curtain behind the shop window. Suddenly her pulse quickened. He'd followed her; there he was. Seyit stood across the road. He was crossing the road. He was coming. Now they would meet again, embrace, tell each other everything, and start anew. She jumped to her feet and stood behind the door. She would open the door before he rang the bell, and she would throw herself into his arms.

Seyit stood at the curb, staring at the pharmacy windows. He was sure she was there. She must have seen him. She could have emerged if she'd wanted to. Perhaps she'd only popped into the laundry to say she was leaving him! She had heard him call her name and seen him run after her. And wasn't it she who had left with another man only the previous evening?

He regretted coming all that way. He turned back and crossed the road again.

Shura unlocked the door when the sound she'd been anticipating failed to materialize. Seyit was striding away. Reaching out as if she could see and stop, she sobbed.

"Seyt..."

Fate Tests the Lovers

I T PROVED TO be a day of heartbreak and pining for them both. Seyit still wished to see her that evening, meet her after work, and talk to her. If Shura was in love with someone else, he wanted to hear it from her own mouth. He was so tetchy all day long that no one dared to ask him anything. A small mercy—one that was highly welcome all the same—was that Marushka hadn't turned up. He had spoiled everything, and he had no wish to see his accomplice ever again.

A drained Shura with bloodshot eyes kept making mistakes on her calculator and dropped a few bottles in the laboratory. On this day, which ought to have been her happiest day for the past two years! Yevgeny's surprise had been waiting at 143 Tarlabaşı, the house where several members of her family now lived: her sister Valentine; half brother Vladimir Dmitriyevich Lissenko; maternal aunt Nadia; Nadia's husband, General Bogayevsky; and her younger cousin Boris. All this time she'd thought she'd lost them for good, and here they were! That reunion punctuated by laughter and tears led to a supper that lasted for hours. This was a miracle.

And a truly great miracle it was too. Wasn't any succor that followed disaster defined as a miracle, anyhow? Their families torn apart, homes torched, and loved ones unable to flee brutally murdered, the homeless and destitute survivors had resigned themselves to their fate. Reunions were rare, and all the more rapturous for it.

That Shura had found her nearest and dearest in Istanbul in that maelstrom was a miracle indeed. Strictly speaking, it was they who had found her, not that it mattered who found whom. Fate clearly had other plans for her though; instead of rejoicing in the reunion, she had now lost Seyit.

Loath to offend her family's sense of propriety, she had been understandably circumspect about her domestic arrangements, which in turn precluded any excuse not to stay with them that night. She had set off first thing to inform Seyit. Had she known about the nasty surprise awaiting her, she would never have gone in the first place. *There still has to be an explanation*, she thought, wiping the tears rolling down. If Seyit was tired of her, he had to say it to her face. After agonizing for hours, she resolved to confront him that evening.

Life seldom offers the helm, and we usually miss our chance when it does. Our powerlessness only registers when fate has trumped us once again, by which time it's too late.

Seyit and Shura both made plans with the best of intentions. But fate would test them again. Around six thirty, her cousins entered the pharmacy. Now she couldn't go to the laundry unless she sent them away first.

"Dearest Yevgeny, dearest Boris! How lovely to see you here!"

"We're here to fetch you, Shura; we're on our way to get a Christmas tree and thought you might like to come along," said the brothers, kissing her on the cheek. With a deliberate look at the wall clock, ostensibly an employee who would have loved to leave early, she whispered, "I've got another half hour to do here. Why don't you go? We'll meet at home later."

Mr. Zezemsky overheard. Shura's state hadn't escaped his notice, and he'd felt sorry for her all day long. It would be good to let her off early for once.

"It's all right, Alexandra Julianovna; you may leave with your company. I can manage for another half an hour. Off you go—what are you waiting for?" He added with a naughty wink, "Ah! Youth!"

Horrified that he'd got the wrong end of the stick, Shura knew the only way to spare her employer's blushes was by introducing everyone present.

"Leonid Arkadyevich, allow me to introduce my cousins: this young man is Boris Afrikanovich Bogayevsky, and this is his elder brother, Yevgeny Afrikanovich Bogayevsky; Leonid Arkadyevich Zezemsky."

The pharmacist broke into a wide smile as his eyebrows lifted in delight. "No! Incredible! How wonderful; then you really do have an excuse to leave early."

Meeting Seyit would have to wait until the following day; donning her coat, she left between her cousins.

Twenty minutes later, Seyit entered the pharmacy and waited for a couple of Levantines to be served first. Once they had left, the assistant in a white coat started scribbling in the ledger, wrinkled his nose to lift his slipping spectacles, and gave Seyit a blank look. "Yes, may I help you?"

"I was looking for Mademoiselle Alexandra Verjenskaya. Has she not come today?"

"She has, sir; she's just left."

"Do you know where she went?"

The assistant's right hand scratched his neck under the collar as his lips curled, and he shrugged his shoulders. It was quite a production for a simple no. Seyit thanked him all the same and was walking out when additional information was volunteered out of the blue.

"She left with a young man and a boy. Don't know where though—I don't speak Russian."

As he walked out with another thanks, Seyit cursed himself for having come here, berating himself for having run after Shura in the morning, and beside himself for not having enjoyed Marushka more.

It was time to accept that Shura was now out of his life.

This was easier said than done. Striking her out of his life would mean striking out all his life so far. He recalled the moment he'd found her on the boat after sailing away from Alushta. God! How great was their love! How all embracing; how soothing! She had been barely eighteen when she had dived headfirst into that terrifying adventure with the man she loved. And now? What had gone wrong?

His mind in turmoil, Seyit spent many a sleepless night.

As did Shura. She put a brave face on all day at her newfound family home and cried under the covers all night long. She wanted to live her life again—but with a few changes. She wanted to relive the night she'd met Seyit in Moscow, the night she had placed her hand in his at the Bolshoi. Then she recalled the first time they'd made love in Tatiana's forest home. That's when her lips dried and her body felt like it was on fire. Wasn't the meeting at the Novorossiysk Inn one of the highlights of her life? As a matter of fact, she wanted to relive every moment with Seyit again—every moment except for the other night. Which had happened. There was no turning the clock back.

His love life in tatters, Seyit pondered Mr. Konstantinides's proposal, and eventually made his mind up. He could put some of his rubles into the business—an idea that made sense only if he were determined to stay in Istanbul. If, on the other hand, he had any intention of emigrating to Paris or America, there was no point in tying money up in a business here.

It was early afternoon on Christmas Eve. Having given the girls the afternoon and the next day off, Seyit sat in the office, his head buried in the accounts. There was a knock at the door. He looked out the window, threw his pen away, and hastened to the door. It was Shura. He did his best to keep his composure when he opened the door. He wasn't the only guilty party here, after all, was he?

Shura looked drained. Her hands in a muff and a sable hat on her head, she looked like a postcard from Petrograd. The hurt in her enormous blue eyes was unmistakable. They stared at each other stiffly; they both had sufficient reason to hold back.

Seyit drew aside to invite her in. "Come on in; why didn't you use your key?"

Shura bit her lips. She'd sworn not to cry. Lifting her proud head, she replied, "I regretted it last time I did. And I don't think I shall ever use it again." She extracted the key from her bag and laid it on the table. She stood at the bottom of the stairs and spoke in the same cool tone. "Now, I would like to collect my things, if I might. I'm sure your guest will appreciate the drawer space."

Without waiting for a reply, she mounted the stairs. Seyit followed, shut the door behind them, and leaned against it. He was astonished at her intractability. What had happened to his tender, warm sweetheart? She must want the other fellow so much that she wouldn't even give him a chance. Brushing the bangs away from his forehead, he crossed his arms and waited for her to speak. They could still sort something out if they at least spoke and vented their anger.

Shura took her lingerie out of the drawers and clothes off the hangers and folded it all, acting as though she were alone in the room. One word from Seyit and she would relent, which was the last thing she wanted. But she couldn't hold back the tears when she picked up her valise from the wardrobe. She lifted the lid and started packing, averting her gaze from him. How many memories were carried in this little valise! How many moments from Kislovodsk to Novorossiysk, thence to Feodosia, Alushta, Sinop, and now Istanbul! Was this the end of the road then?

Her eyes fell on the bed. She recalled the nights when they'd hugged in tears and made passionate love in it, the bed where the other woman had lain, in the arms of her lover, making passionate love, listening to terms of endearment.

She let the tears flow freely.

Seyit, who had been wondering how to approach her, now knew he couldn't wait any longer. His sweetheart was suffering as much as he was. It was time to put an end to it. He moved toward her slowly and waited by her side, waited as he always did for a sign from her that she wanted him.

She was crying, scrunching the scarf she'd been given on her way out of Alushta. She buried her face in her hands and tried to stifle her sobs in the fabric.

When Seyit opened his arms and wrapped them around her, the vibrations spreading into his entire body from his palms and arms shouted that he had found the other half of his soul. Burying his head in the hair of the sweetheart he'd been pining for, he closed his eyes and mumbled, "My God! What have we done to each other? What?"

Lifting her head from his chest, where she'd rested it willingly a moment earlier, she spoke through her tears. "I've done you no wrong, Seyt—no wrong."

He preferred to close the topic. "It's all right, my Shura; whatever happened, happened. It's all over now. You don't have to tell me."

Anger flashed in her eyes as she threw her head back. "You don't understand; nothing's happened. I did not cheat on you. If anyone's been cheated on, it was me."

With a flash of recognition at Seyit's quizzical look, she exclaimed, "Oh, for God's sake, Seyt! I couldn't get back here that night because my cousin turned up at the pharmacy: Yevgeny Bogayevsky! They'd all made it to Istanbul safe and sound."

She raised her arms as if to indicate a miracle and let them drop wearily. She perched on the edge of the bed and placed her hands on her lap. After telling him about the arrival of the Bogayevskys, along with her sister and brother; the house in Tarlabaşı; and the whole story of the happy reunion, she looked into his eyes. He had no such rational explanation, however. He sat down next to her and took her hands in his.

"My little Shura, I don't know what to say. I must have gone berserk when I saw you. I can't tell you how awful it was to watch you disappear into the night with another man." He gave her a kiss on the forehead. "But I swear to you: there was only one woman here with me all that time you were away."

Shura wiped her tears and stared at him, waiting for the rest.

"And that was you, my darling—believe me."

They couldn't bear to torment each other any longer; the yearning in their eyes said, *Embrace*. They fell back onto the bed. The suitcase tumbled down with a thud, the snow caressed the window, and the only other sound was their quickened breathing. Seyit gave her a kiss and got up to feed a couple more logs into the stove. He left the door open so that the flames could illuminate the room; it was only around four o'clock, but the sky was rapidly darkening in the height of the winter. He removed his shirt and lay down next to Shura, whispering, "I've missed you so much, my darling, so much! Never leave me again."

Saddened at the thought that they'd come so close to losing their love, Shura wrapped her arms around his neck and drew him closer. "I've missed you too, my love. Very much."

They'd never made love with such wild abandon before. Now they knew what they lived for, that they were two halves of a whole, their desire multiplied. Seyit knew his sweetheart was no longer the inexperienced, timid girl she once had been, but every time they made love, he felt the same thrill as the first time. It was Shura's serenity that aroused his reaction, her sensitive patience that offered love before sex, and her childish innocence under the exterior of a mature woman. It all suited his own disposition perfectly—his excitable, demanding love and admiration that demanded the same in return. Tender, silent kisses through to frenzied hours of passion—he loved it all, loved to make love to her until they fell back exhausted. Then, and only then, did they know they had found the other halves they'd been missing.

Several hours later, Shura stirred awkwardly. Seyit turned to look at her.

"What is it? Your arm gone to sleep?"

"No, darling…" she said, patting his cleft chin. It was obvious she had something to say.

"So what is it then?" he insisted.

Shura sat up on her heels and tugged at the sheet to cover her breasts. Pulling back the corner of the sheet, he asked, "Are you cold?"

"No, oh no."

"Then leave them be. You're so beautiful; let me watch while we talk." He chuckled. "You know, I used to find women much more attractive after a few drinks. You, on the other hand, are the only woman I love watching even when I'm stone-cold sober!"

"Is this meant to be a compliment?"

Seyit sat up, placed a kiss on her perfectly rounded shoulder, and lay back down, an arm under his head. "Yes, my little sweetheart; what do you want to tell me?"

"Seyt…I have to go." She pushed him back gently when he shot up. "No, no, don't misunderstand. It's just that I can't stay here with you any longer. All my family is together. My uncle has rented a house in Tarlabaşı; they're all there, including Uncle Bogayevsky's aide-de-camp and secretary. They're all there. There's…there's no way I could explain that I'm living with you. You must understand. I can't tell them."

"What did you tell them about your escape then?" asked Seyit, crestfallen.

"Pretty much everything. Except for the fact that I'd been living with you, naturally." She saw he was hurt. "Believe me, Seyt; this has nothing to do with you. But my family would never accept it—me living in sin. Please try to understand me."

Seyit took her extended hand and brought it to his lips. "I do understand; of course I do."

"I'll come here whenever I can. Nothing's going to change."

There was no point in insisting. He had no right to wrench her away from her family. His mind went back to his own father's attitude toward Shura; at the time, Seyit had chosen his love over his own family and possibly broken their hearts forever. So why wasn't she doing the same now?

It was best to chase away such uncharitable thoughts. He spoke instead about his plans to buy the laundry.

Meanwhile, Shura had risen, gotten dressed, and resumed packing. She listened cheerfully. "That's great news, Seyt—wonderful!" She grew more serious and added, "I could probably find a little too...if you wanted?"

Seyit stroked her cheek. "You're so considerate, my love. But it won't be necessary. I might be able to delve into my rubles."

"Are you sure?"

Embracing her shoulders, Seyit kissed her and murmured, "Yes, I'm sure." He was elated; not even the fact that she was going away could spoil his cheer. He kissed her again, as if they'd just met. "Merry Christmas, my love."

Shura ran her hand through his hair with a smile. "Thank you, my darling."

***

The Orthodox Christmas Eve falls on January 6 in the Gregorian calendar. In early 1921, Istanbul was home to an extraordinary celebration. Hagia Pantoleimon, Hagia Andrea, and Hagia Elia thronged with White Russian émigrés who lit thousands of candles and sang hymns. This was totally different from Christmases past, when they would have dressed in their newest outfits, swooshing over powdery snow in their troikas to alight outside churches bedecked in marvelous icons, and chanted joyous tunes celebrating the birth of the Messiah. No one prayed for wishes now. Instead, they pleaded for the return of a stolen reality—for their distant homeland, a place they could never go back to. For their nearest and dearest left behind. The ones lying in pools of their own blood in their own gardens. The ones who'd fallen back to the quay in Yalta as the rope slipped from their hands.

Isn't it strange that when things are going well, we think of little to ask of God? At most we ask for frivolous things, things of no consequence. But prayer comes easy when people have lost everything. Only then do they know what they miss, what they're bereft of, and what to pray for.

And so it came to pass that in January 1921, the most woebegone supplications rising to God from Istanbul's churches came from the hearts of the White Russians.

Selling Memories

I N THE FIRST week of 1921, as they celebrated Christmas, Shura, Valentine, and their half brother Vladimir moved out of the crowded three-story Bogayevsky house in Tarlabaşı into a rented flat in nearby Altın Bakkal Street—another colorful Pera street name, this time referring to a "Golden Grocer." A curtain separated the girls' bedroom area from the combined dining and sitting room; it was a far cry from their glory days, but since this was their new life, they had to make the best of it. Too many of their fellow émigrés suffering from a miscalculated sense of divinely granted entitlement to aristocratic privileges had refused to dirty their hands with work and ended up destitute. Pride comes before a fall. The three siblings had no intention of falling into the same trap. They would, with God's help, cope one way or another.

Shura kept her frequent meetings with Seyit a secret from Valentine and Vladimir. After that incident, the lovers gave each other the benefit of the doubt, a little more space, and no grief about their times apart.

One day, quite out of the blue, Mr. Konstantinides turned up, having been missing for months. No one knew where he'd been or what he'd done since he'd given Seyit one week to decide. Seyit confirmed he would buy the laundry and pay in rubles. His boss stroked his beard cheerfully, and the banknotes were counted and placed in the latter's palm. The cash went into a bag, the two men shook hands, and Mr. Konstantinides set off for the bank.

That evening after work, Seyit could hardly contain himself, pacing up and down as he waited for Shura. He finally had a place—nay, a business—of his own. He sat down at the desk, settled into the chair, and leaned back. He was beaming when Shura arrived; in answer to her questioning look, he stood up and opened his arms to welcome his sweetheart.

"Celebrations are in order, my love!"

"Congratulations, Seyt!"

Hand in hand, they were moving toward the stairs when there came a knock at the door. It was Mr. Konstantinides, looking none too happy. He burst into the office without waiting for an invitation, plunked the black bag on the desk, and stood, arms akimbo. He pursed his lips and shook his head.

"No good, Kyrios Seyit." He snapped open the bag, pulled out the wad of rubles, and spread it out on the desk as they gaped. "Sorry, Kyrios Seyit. The bank no longer accepts these tsar notes."

"Why not?"

"Romanov rubles are no longer legal tender. Can't be converted either. Forbidden."

"What on earth are you talking about, Mr. Konstantinides? Since when is the imperial ruble no good?"

"Since yesterday morning when the bank received instructions. I'm sorry, Kyrios Seyit, but what can I do? It's the Bolsheviks who banned it. What good is worthless money to me?"

Seyit slumped into the chair and huffed with a wry smile. Shura was furious but kept it to herself; instead, she placed a tender hand on his shoulder in silent sympathy for this devastating setback.

Stroking his beard, the Greek snapped his bag shut as he carped on. "I don't know what's gonna happen now. If you've got money, fine. Otherwise I'll have to find another buyer."

Seyit gestured for patience as he stood up. "Hold on! There's no need for haste. Let me think a bit."

We might still have a deal then, thought the older man, grinning to himself; after all, how many other cash buyers could he whip up in the turmoil of war and occupation? He climbed down at once.

"Far be it for me, Kyrios Seyit, to ever lean on you! All this time we've worked together! I'd happily vouch for you. Please, by all means, do take the time to consider it further. I'll stop by again tomorrow."

"Thank you."

Mr. Konstantinides left saluting and bowing nonstop.

The lovers were lost in thought when there came another knock at the door. This time it was Manol and İskender, who'd dropped by on their way to Pera Palace for supper, and they were intent on taking Seyit along. On hearing what had happened, they changed their plans; they would all dine in together. After all, their rubles were also worthless.

By the time a bottle of vodka was gone, laughter had replaced sorrow in the room above the laundry. Seyit was roaring with laughter now. "Can you imagine: hide all that money for three years in a pillow, put up with hunger and poverty, pull it out when you need it, and what happens? All you've been saving is a sack of newsprint!"

"What else is in the pillows, Seyit?"

"Best take it out before it's too late!"

They were laughing with tears in their eyes, joyless tears of frustration fueled by alcohol. Seyit got to his feet, spread the banknotes on the table, and picked them up one by one.

"Come on—up: we're going out."

"Where?" A unanimous question.

Seyit was no longer laughing. "Given they are now history, we ought to give them a decent send-off, don't you agree?"

It was nearly midnight when incredulous passersby on Galata Bridge watched four well-dressed foreigners laugh their heads off as they scattered thousands of Romanov rubles over the Golden Horn.

Early the next morning, Seyit went to the Grand Bazaar and entered the first jewelry shop in a row of hundreds in the ancient covered market. The jeweler laid the necklace he'd been polishing back on the counter and peered at the arrival. Judging by his clothes, he was a well-heeled foreigner, and the kalpak said White Russian. Another émigré resorting to selling valuables. An unctuous grin split the jeweler's face as he stood up, rubbing his hands.

"Welcome, sir, welcome. Please be seated, sir." He pointed to the only chair by the counter. Chatty was the last thing Seyit felt. If anything, he looked distinctly uneasy about having come here in the first place. He seemed to hesitate. But the jeweler hadn't been a Grand Bazaar merchant for all these years without having learned something about human nature. "How may I be of assistance, sir?

Please, do sit down, I beseech you; have a cup of coffee. You don't have to buy anything."

"No, thank you. I don't want coffee." Seyit shook his head.

The jeweler insisted. "I won't hear of it, sir. You've come all this way and honored our shop with your presence; it would be rude not to offer you a cup of coffee!" Sticking his head out the door, he called out to a young boy standing outside the shop opposite. "Two coffees here!" He then returned to his seat, rubbing his hands all the while; he couldn't wait to see what the foreigner had to sell.

Seyit reluctantly pulled out two velvet boxes. "What would you offer for these?"

The jeweler put his spectacles on as the boxes were opened and their contents placed on the counter. He had got to know the tsar's coat of arms and insignia well in the past few months. The calculator that was his brain operated at lightning speed as he stared at the enameled silver medals and decorations. He knew exactly what they were worth. Not that he was prepared to disclose it.

"Magnificent...they're magnificent...but..." He curled his lips. "I don't know what to say, dear sir! They are precious, except times are hard. Surely you're aware we've seen nothing but war and occupation for years and years now? No one's got money to invest in such items. Everyone's counting pennies."

Seyit had no time to waste. He inquired in a formal tone, "Please tell me how much you could offer."

The jeweler turned and twisted the medals in his hands, as if that would have an impact on their value, obviously considering the lowest figure he could get away with. Not surprisingly, his paltry offer prompted Seyit to place the medals back into the boxes and shut the lids at once. The jeweler grabbed his arm.

"But sir, please, do hold on; you're a valuable customer. Let us see if we could improve the offer."

The affected royal *we* grated on Seyit's nerves. "I've got no time for haggling. There's no way I'm parting with them for twenty-five liras," retorted Seyit, secretly pleased at the unattractive offer.

He grabbed the boxes, placed them in his pocket, tugged at the chain at his waist, and opened the lid of his watch. Just then the watch chimed ten o'clock.

The jeweler pursed his lips and emitted something between a whistle and a gasp of awe. A greedy hand reached out and then drew back. "May I take a look? What a lovely watch! I've not seen the like—ever! It must be a very special make."

Seyit mumbled as he snapped the gold lid back, "Yes...yes, that it is."

"Magnificent workmanship, absolutely magnificent!" exclaimed the jeweler, scanning the diamond-encrusted coat of arms and the ruby monogram. Realizing Seyit was on his way out, he clapped his hands as though struck by a great idea. "Tell you what, dear sir! I can't do much for the medals, but if you would consider selling the watch too, I'd be delighted to offer you two hundred and fifty liras for the lot. And that only because I value your custom, sir."

It wasn't an ungenerous sum under the circumstances, but it was nowhere near what Seyit needed. He shook his head, offered his thanks, and left even as the jeweler exclaimed, "Go around the whole bazaar, dear sir, but believe me: I gave you the best price."

Seyit turned into the Bedesten, the oldest part of the Bazaar—effectively an interior arcade—and entered another shop. This was one of nearly a dozen jewelers or gold dealers, all of whom could have been in cahoots. A couple even referred him to the first shop he'd been to. He felt trapped and eventually struck a deal with an Albanian jeweler who paid two hundred and seventy liras for the medals and the watch. That was clearly the best offer he was going to get.

His heart broke as he gazed at his memories rather than the physical mementos he placed on the counter. They seemed to hold a strange power to keep the past alive, and now he was about to break the last connection with his old life in Russia. A life that flashed past his eyes. The thrill when Tsar Nicholas II pinned the medals on his chest.

He stroked the watch lid one last time and left the Grand Bazaar in an indescribable state of anguish. He felt like a traitor, one who had betrayed his memories, who had sold the last vestiges of his past. His medals and pocket watch would henceforth pass into new hands that had no connection or memories with them whatsoever.

Mr. Konstantinides gleefully accepted the two hundred and seventy liras and instructed the balance should be paid in monthly installments to his nephew Hristo in Pangaltı.

"He'll know where I am and where to send it," he added as he took his leave.

This was to be the start of a year of very hard work for Seyit. He was paying off the balance on the one hand and trying to grow the business on the other and hoping to rent a decent flat in a Pera street soon, if all went well.

Shura's family commitments meant they couldn't spend as much time together as he would have liked. Occasionally their paths crossed at Park Hotel or Taksim Gardens, and each time they were forced to conceal their relationship—whose sporadic nature naturally steered them toward new groups of friends.

In the meantime, Seyit had discovered some Crimean relations in Istanbul: Yahya, Mustafa, and Selim had managed to flee on Wrangel's fleet. The first two were Seyit's elder maternal uncle's sons, and Selim had married his paternal aunt's daughter a couple of years ago.

Yahya now intended to marry the wealthy German lady he'd met and fallen in love with during their crossing. Senta said little, but she had obviously left a family behind in Russia.

Selim and his wife had a young son too—but he'd lost them both during that hellish scramble to board the ship. He had called their names up and down the decks throughout the crossing and the entire ten days of waiting on the Bosphorus. Painful as it was, reason dictated that he had lost them forever.

The ties that bound these people were singular, far beyond those of blood relations, fellow citizens, or speakers of the same language. Hearts bled longest, even around long tables where the alcohol flowed as liberally as the singing and the laughter. Unshed tears glistened in every eye even through the laughter. Melancholy was their relentless companion even at their merriest. Homesickness ravaged their bodies like a fever, and only those in the same boat could sympathize. In a silent pact, no one mentioned a single personal tragedy, yet they all knew one another's pain.

Late in the summer of 1922, as White Russians were now settling in Istanbul, and the city was getting accustomed to this latest influx, the country stood poised on the brink of a new dawn. At the conclusion of decades of war, Turkish faces shone with hope. From the ashes of the Ottoman Empire rose a new nation under Commander-in-Chief Mustafa Kemal Pasha. Decades of armed conflict were finally coming to an end: the Balkan Wars, the Great War, and finally the War of Independence. Empowered by a new parliament on the steppes of Anatolia, the Nationalist Army triumphed on the battlefield on August 30, 1922. The Greek occupation of western Anatolia ended ten days later.

On September 11, Istanbul, the straits of Bosphorus and Dardanelles, Edirne, and Eastern Thrace reverted to Turkey according to the Armistice of Mudanya signed between the Nationalists and the Allies.

As Turks set about building a modern country on the lands they had managed to salvage from the tatters of the once mighty Ottoman Empire, the White Russians of the once mighty Russian Empire came to terms with their own prospects. Some decided to settle permanently in Istanbul, and others flocked to the consulates of Bulgaria, Yugoslavia, France, the United States, or Canada in the hundreds of thousands. The fortunate souls rewarded with the necessary permits then had yet another interminable journey into the unknown to look forward to, a journey crammed into trains or ships.

Those who chose to stay in Istanbul faced other challenges. New conditions, hardships, new acquaintances, living from day to day, the struggle to survive one more day—in short, their lives were dictated by fate. Wasn't that the description of fate, after all? The force that steers life outside human wish or control. If perchance the outcome answered prayers, it was called luck—otherwise simply fate.

One night in 1923, White Russians had gathered as usual to sing of the old country in the popular night spot of Tepebaşı Garden. The pianist was none other than Valentine. In another life, she had been a child prodigy who had played for her upper-class family in Kislovodsk and later blossomed into a sought-after performer at society parties. Blushing under the stares of handsome young aristocrats, she would acknowledge the applause with a curtsy and consider herself the happiest girl in the world.

When still an adolescent, Valentine had been asked to perform at a reception in honor of Princess Maria Pavlovna. After the recital, her music teacher, Maria Ivanovna Vassilievna Maharina, had led her to the princess. Valentine would always remember how everyone who had kissed the royal hand before retreating walked backward.

The most unforgettable occasion was playing for her young husband, Baron Constantine Clodt von Jürgensburg, however. Only twenty-two at the time, the nobleman had listened without moving a muscle, one arm resting on the piano, adoring eyes never leaving her.

Memories flashed by as fast as her fingers danced on the keys. What had happened to her mother? Did Kislovodsk still stand there? The last time she'd seen her darling husband, he'd been cheerfully waving astride a tank on an open freight car as the armored brigade departed for the front. Had he survived the battles with the Bolsheviks? What about everyone else, all her acquaintances and loved ones?

She wasn't the only one plagued by questions. There wasn't a single musician or patron present whose mind wasn't similarly tormented as they accompanied the song to a pair of dark eyes:

Ochi chyornye,
Ochi strastnye,
Ochi zhguchiye...

By the time Seyit, Manol, Yahya, Sergei, and Selim arrived, the entertainment was in full flow. Seyit's heart leaped: Shura was sitting with her back to him near the stage. He excused himself and got up. At her table were two other women and a man. Seyit recognized one of the ladies as a dancer from Kiev; bowing to them, he leaned down to whisper in Shura's ear, "Good evening."

She turned her head, looking pleased, surprised—and a little guarded.

"Good evening, Seyt," she replied, her eyes darting right and left.

Perplexed by her jumpy state, Seyit lowered his voice even more. "You're very beautiful, and I miss you very much."

It couldn't have been the others at the table; they seemed to be oblivious to the exchange between Shura and Seyit. But she looked ill at ease, and there was something different in her gaze. Seyit thought he must be mistaken. What could there be, anyhow?

"May I invite you to our table? We'd all have a good time together."

"Best not, Seyt. We're about to leave soon. I have to be at work very early tomorrow."

"All right, my love; I hereby take my leave. Consider yourself kissed."

"Good night, darling."

By the time Seyit resumed his seat, a young man in a merchant navy uniform had settled into the chair next to Shura. It hit him like a bucket of cold water. He'd been right. Now he knew what was in her voice and behavior.

"Seyt Eminof, are you well?" asked Manol, a hand on his shoulder.

"I'm fine; I'm fine."

Yahya had followed Seyit's gaze and pretty much figured out what was wrong. He and Manol knew Shura as the love of Seyit's life, after all; they'd all dined together and even spent a weekend on Prinkipo on one occasion. Why Seyit was upset was no secret.

"We could leave now if you like, Seyit."

Seyit started filling their glasses, a woeful smile curling on his lips. "We can't escape everything that life throws at us. Come on—*Na zdorovie!*"

Shura's party stood up. Their eyes met, and Seyit raised his glass once again, looking her in the eye. Shura responded with her usual warm, gentle, and affectionate gaze. Seyit cheered up at once. *My God! She's so beautiful!* he thought.

He did feel much better now. He even thought of dashing over to her, but the French captain held her arm. She averted her gaze and left Tepebaşı Garden.

Their relationship was cracking. Their spiritual world was no longer the same. Their new lives were driving a wedge between them. It was inevitable. Then why was her gaze still full of love? He could kick himself for not having gone over and taken her arm, which would have only put her on the spot. If she wanted another man in her life, Seyit had no call over her. Perhaps it was time to forget the Russian fairy tale against that long-gone backdrop of snow, glittering lights, the muffled clip-clop of troika horses' hooves, church bells, polkas, and Tchaikovsky's tunes. Perhaps it was time to forget his flaxen-haired, huge blue-eyed sweetheart who smelled of flowers. Perhaps their love had never been real.

All night long he mulled over what the coming day might bring. He felt sick. But he heard nothing from Shura on that day or on several others that followed. Surely she could at the very least offer him some explanation? He could think of nothing else, reliving everything since they had first met. He missed her; he wanted her beside him. Night after sleepless night, he agonized over whether to go to the pharmacy to see her. No. Damned if he would! She was the one who had walked past on the arm of a stranger, so she was the one who had to make the first move. He waited in anguish.

The next evening, Manol threw a party for some friends who were moving to America. Still out of sorts, Seyit still agreed to go. But he cheered up as soon as Manol answered the door: the first person he spotted was Shura, conversing with a couple of Russian ladies. A piano, a balalaika, and a guitar played in a corner. Seyit accepted a glass of wine and made his way toward her, greeting ladies on the way; some got a handshake, others a kiss on the cheek, and a few dreamy-eyed lovelies received a rakish smile. No matter how much he loved the most important woman in his life, he wasn't totally oblivious to the charms of others. Someone tugged at his arm, and he turned to look.

"Sergei, old chap! Delighted to see you here!"

He had to suppress a smirk when Sergei introduced his "fiancée," a lady considerably his senior. Why Sergei had resorted to his well-known ruse to ensure devotion from his latest conquest was baffling, given the lady in question was nearly old enough to be his mother.

Shura was still chatting to her friends when she heard a familiar laugh nearby. Startled, she turned her head for a look. It felt like déjà vu. They locked eyes. Seyit stood in a group of four or five people. It felt as though she were back in the winter of 1916, at the Borinsky mansion in Moscow.

My God! she thought. She trembled as the blood in her veins heated up. She felt dizzy at the sight of his deep-blue eyes ablaze with love. They exchanged a long look as if they were meeting for the first time and had fallen in love at first sight. There was urgency in Seyit's gaze and attraction in Shura's bashful eyes.

At Manol's invitation into the dining room, the guests began to file in.

Seyit and Shura were facing each other. Neither knew what to say. Shura groped for the right words, and Seyit had no wish to sound accusing. They were both astonished by this staggering inability to find something to say after all these years.

"Good evening, Alexandra Julianovna Verjenskaya."

It was the first time he had addressed her so formally, partly in retaliation for her sustained distance.

"Good evening, Seyt...You're not cross with me, are you?"

"Cross? Cross, did you say? What did you expect, Shura? What would you like me to do? How else should I feel when the woman who is half my life withdraws from me?"

"So we finally understand each other then."

"What do you mean?"

"You remember the night when I left the pharmacy with Yevgeny and the following morning? Can you now appreciate what I felt when I came back and saw what I saw?"

"But Shura! I thought we were over it. If only I'd known where you were and with whom..."

"And that's what the matter is, Seyt. That's precisely why I had a fling. I couldn't bear sharing you, so I wanted to make you suffer like you'd made me. Believe me; it wasn't planned. It just happened, and I only realized afterward why I'd allowed it to."

Seyit knew what she meant. People deceived themselves when they tried to deal with the hurt of betrayal by doing the same. It never worked. All it did was to make everything worse. Oddly enough, they had grown so close that they were now repeating each other's mistakes.

"So what happens now?" asked Seyit, expecting a reply.

She turned toward the window and twisted the glass in her hand. After a brief period of silence, she broke into soft sobs. Seyit placed his glass down and moved closer. He placed his hands on her shoulders and leaned down to give her a kiss on the cheek.

"Please don't cry, Shura. All I ask is that you tell me what your intentions are from this point onward. You know I would never pressure you into a decision."

Shura placed her hand in the palm of the man she'd been missing. "I know, Seyt; I know."

"Do you recall what you told me once?"

With a curious look, no longer sobbing, she asked, "What was it?"

"You said, 'Never did regret a single thing I did with you, Seyt, not a single thing,'" he said. He squeezed her hand and asked, "Do you still think the same?"

With a smile, Shura pressed her fingers down in reply. Their expression altered at the contact. They both knew what it meant. Neither food nor dance was on their minds now. All they wanted was to be alone together. Propriety demanded a couple more hours at Manol's party, but leave together they eventually did. She stared at his firm, handsome face as they descended hand in hand. She loved him very much indeed.

They alighted from the carriage in Kalyoncu Kulluğu Street, filled with anticipation. Seyit took her in his arms the moment they stepped inside. Shura leaned against the front door, flung aside her bag and gloves, and wrapped her arms around his neck. Her lips wandered on the sharp lines of his face and on the cleft of his chin. His kisses wandered on her hair, neck, and throat, rediscovering the smell and her firm flesh he'd been missing. He took her in his arms and mounted the stairs, his eyes locked on hers.

The question of who had been in here since she'd been gone was shooed away at once. The last thing she wanted to do was to ruin her night. Oddly enough Seyit's thoughts ran along the same lines. He was no longer her first and only lover. A stranger had come between them, a strange man who had touched his special woman. Alarmed at how tense that thought made him, he waved it away. Now he knew how he'd tormented the woman he loved when he'd slept with Marushka—and Shura had found out in the morning.

What was done was done. They were together now, and they loved each other. That's what mattered.

All these thoughts flashed past in the blink of an eye. Seyit grasped her and whispered into her ear as he ran a hand through her silky hair, "Let's not hurt each other ever again, Shurochka. I love you so very much."

"Oh! Me too, Seyt; I love you too. So much."

Elated at having won her back, Seyit covered her face, hands, and fingertips with leisurely kisses and caresses. Shura responded in kind, calming the urgency she knew so well. They had all night. They would enjoy every second. Like drinking the last drop of a sweet sherbet or an ice-cold tumbler of vodka, they would savor every contact of the lips and relish the indescribable pleasure of every touch on the skin.

He lay back, drew her to his chest, and tenderly held her waist-length hair.

"You're so beautiful. You know, you're even more beautiful now than when we first met."

Shura smiled at the compliment. "Could be the alcohol speaking!"

"You're right," teased Seyit. "Women look prettier when I'm drunk. You, on the other hand, are the only woman I find beautiful even when I'm sober. You know that; I've told you before."

He cupped her face in his hands, stared into her eyes, and whispered as he sought her lips, "And always desire..."

Young Fiancée

T HAT NIGHT MARKED the start of a new period of ups and downs for Seyit and
Shura. No other couple could have been more passionate—whenever they
met, that is. Every time they did, they reaffirmed their love, convinced more than
ever that they were made for each other. Yet whenever they were apart, Seyit
threw himself into an ardent pursuit of daring, thrill-seeking beauties. He had no
doubt that Shura also had the occasional fling.

Jealousy and unrest plagued them both, since neither wanted to share the
other. That being said, something was clearly amiss: the happiness they felt when
they were together drifted farther away whenever they were apart.

They no longer met as frequently either. While Shura waited for a sign of
commitment, Seyit painstakingly avoided making a claim over the woman he
had loved for years. They were much more than lovers after all the terrifying
ordeals, sorrows, and homesickness. Perhaps she wanted something new in her
life. Agitated and downcast, he reasoned that she had to make her own choices.

In the meantime, it was time to set a definite course for his life. The only
thing that went well was his finances, and he was looking forward to renting a
fine flat in Aynalı Çeşme.

It was the end of the workweek; he had just paid the wages and locked away
a satisfactory surplus and was about to pour a drink. There was a knock at the
door. It was Selim, not Shura as he'd hoped.

"Come on, Seyit; get ready. I'm taking you away."

"Where, pray tell?"

"To a wedding."

"Who's getting married?"

"You don't know them."

"Why on earth would I go to a stranger's wedding?"

"No strangers, Seyit; my wife's milk sister's getting married at their home in Aksaray. Come along; it'll do you good. You've driven yourself into a rut, doing the same thing day in, day out, with the same people all the time, thinking you're still in Russia. Come on; get away—get some fresh air. You can leave whenever you want if you find it too tedious. Stop dawdling."

Seyit didn't want to upset him, especially as the wedding party involved an unusual tradition: a wet nurse's children and her charges would be considered siblings for the rest of their lives.

"Fine, let me have a bath and shave first. Actually, why don't you go on ahead? Don't waste time waiting for me. Give me the address, and I'll come later."

"Now don't you dare let me down, all right?"

"I promise I'll come. I may be a little late, but I'll definitely come."

He took a bath, got ready, and swung by Pera Palace first for a swift drink with Sergei and Manol at the bar. He hailed a cab, although he was in no particular rush to get to the wedding and certainly had no intention of spending the whole night there. He was going to keep his promise to Selim—that was all.

Before long, the glittering, music, and laughter-filled nightlife, the come-hither merrymaking, had given way to the quiet, peaceful, unassuming evening of the residential areas. By the time Seyit got there, the marriage ceremony had been concluded, the feast was consumed, and the men had withdrawn to a corner with their drinks. Women's voices came from the adjacent rooms. Seyit had never attended a party where the men and women sat apart. It wasn't a strictly segregated house, since ladies regularly came in with fruit and drinks, yet they seemed to prefer having fun in separate quarters.

After a whispered exchange with his wife, Selim spoke to Seyit. "Seyit, up you get; I'm taking you upstairs."

"Oh no, you're not!" Seyit chuckled. "I'm not staying the night! I'm off soon, anyway."

"No one's inviting you to stay. There's someone I want you to see." He stood up to lead the way. "Wonder if you'll like her?"

Seyit carried on laughing as he followed. "I ought to have known you'd have something up your sleeve!"

The daughters of overnight guests, mostly relations from afar, were getting ready to settle down for the night in a big room. Stretched out on mattresses on the floor in their nightgowns, platters of fresh and dried fruit at the ready, they were having a little party of their own. They couldn't wait for the real highlight of the night: a fairy tale from Mürvet. She'd always been their favorite storyteller, one who would embellish every tale with new details each time and always had a surprise ending. She was in a new, white, ankle-length cambric nightgown; her mother had accented it with scalloping on the cuffs and collar when she made it. Mürvet let her hair down, brushed it, and took another look in the mirror. A very pretty girl smiled back, one who would have looked equally charming even without the help of candlelight: dark hair contrasted with the white nightgown; large, expressive eyes were lined with kohl; and she bore a small upturned nose and full lips. She decided not to wash the makeup off yet, at least not until she was ready for bed; instead, she dabbed a few drops of rosewater on her cheeks and neck from a tiny vial she'd extracted from her bag. As soon as she settled on her sofa, the other girls surrounded her with shrieks of joy. The gas lamp on the copper tray in the center and the smell of roses made the atmosphere perfect for a gripping tale.

As the younger girls all waited with bated breath, Mürvet threw her hair back, took a moment to collect her thoughts, and opened a window into another world. Her soft voice floated her audience away into a land of fantasy, enchanting words animated by elegant gestures and her dancing eyes, opening wide at times and narrowing into a languid squint at others. The light played on her lips and prominent cheekbones. So transported were she and her audience that no one noticed the two men watching from the shadows of the hallway. At one point Mürvet turned her gaze to the door, as if she'd sensed someone else's presence, but there was no one to see. Just a faint draught of air.

The two young men slipped back to the staircase.

"So Kurt Seyt, how do you like my cousin? She's lovely, isn't she?"

Seyit was still laughing. "She is, no question about it, but isn't she too young? How old is she? Fifteen? Sixteen?"

"Mürvet must be seventeen now. If you like her though, best ask for her hand without delay. Such a pretty girl won't be left alone for long. I hear families with suitable sons are already queuing up."

"That's all very well, but she's just a child! Look, she's still telling fairy tales." He shook his head and added, "And she might even be in love with someone else anyway. Has anyone asked her?"

"Seyit, no one asks the girls anything much around here. So long as her parents agree, that's all there is to it."

They grabbed a drink each on their return downstairs and moved into a small room that happened to be unoccupied just then.

"She's a great housekeeper—the hardest-working girl in the family, you know," said Selim, still waxing lyrical.

"Yes, fine. That's fine, but that doesn't necessarily mean she's ready for marriage. I think she's too young."

"No, she's not. Trust me: if you don't grab your chance now, she'll be married off to someone else before you know it. Don't let her get away; that's what I say."

"Selim, my brother, thank you. Nothing could be farther from my mind than getting married though." Seyit popped a few roasted chickpeas into his mouth, allowed a sip of rakı to soften them in his mouth, and carried on pensively. "I've not yet decided what to do with my life. Not even sure I'll stay here. I might sell the business and go to America or France."

"Don't be a fool! Business is good. You've finally started making some money after all you've been through. With a lovely young wife beside you, you'd be set for life. And if you still want to leave, take her along. What's the big deal?"

"I'm not ready for marriage, Selim."

"Are you still carrying on with Shura?"

Downing his thimbleful in one, Seyit leaned back. He brushed his bangs away from his forehead, threw his head back, closed his eyes, and gave an audible sigh. Selim realized he'd touched a sore point.

"You can't carry on like this, Seyit. Get married, have a home, family, settle down."

"Home? I've had so many homes, Selim: the one I was born and raised in, the ones I shared with lovers, the house I hid from the Reds in...my last memory of every single one of them is heartbreak. I had to leave them all. I had to leave them all behind."

"Fine, but no one's pursuing you now, right? No more Bolsheviks on your tail. Stop bemoaning the past. You say peace has always eluded you—fine! Now's your chance to grab it! Why not give yourself a break?"

Seyit filled his tumbler and upended the bottle; resting an elbow on the table and his head in his hand, he watched the last few drops trickle down.

"Selim? Would you rather be sand in an hourglass or rakı in a bottle of rakı?"

Selim shook his head with a sigh. He had long since learned to leave Seyit alone whenever this mood hit. Neither man spoke for the next five minutes or so. Selim waited patiently for his troubled companion to shake off the nostalgia. When Seyit spoke, he looked like someone who'd just awakened from a dream.

"What were you saying, Selim? I'm sorry."

"Don't worry. I was saying we should ask for Mürvet's hand for you."

"Seems you're determined to become my in-law again!"

They exchanged a bitter smile. Selim's first wife had been Seyit's cousin; the eighteen-year-old bride and her one-year-old infant son had vanished on the Crimean shore, and neither man would ever forget the pain. Accepting that he had to make the best of things, Selim had later remarried.

"If you won't let go of the past, you'll never live in the present, Seyit. Build a new life; enjoy yourself. You won't regret it."

"Is it so easy to let go of the past, Selim? Do memories ever leave you alone?"

"Just accept it; time will see to the rest." He hesitated before forcing himself to continue. "And Seyit...how about breaking up with that girl? You'll never be able to let go—so long as she is in your life."

Seyit's expression changed at once, and he snapped, "Don't speak of her, Selim. Never speak of her again. She is very special to me. I'm not about to make any promises to anyone about my relationship with Shura. Am I making myself clear?"

Selim had to backtrack. "All right, Seyit, fine; calm down. I was just trying to be helpful—that's all."

Seyit's temper stilled as quickly as it had flared; he reached out with a friendly pat on the arm. "I'm sorry, Selim; I know you'll humor me." He raised his glass and leaned over the table. "How are we going to ask for this little girl's hand then?"

Selim jumped for joy and grabbed Seyit by the shoulders. "Great, Kurt Seyit, wonderful! Consider it done. You'll see; you won't regret it..." His voice trailed off. "Do you think I've ever forgotten about my young wife and baby? No...absolutely not. Every night when I go to bed, I'm plagued by thoughts eating into my mind, images that haunt me and squeeze my heart. But I manage to go on; I have to go on living. There's no other way." Pulling himself up, he continued, "Mürvet is very young. If you marry her, you'll be able to mold her the way you want, and she'll become a good companion. She's pretty, she's capable, and she'll learn fast. Her mother's a formidable lady, actually. She may be a little short tempered and reticent, but she has good reason. They suffered so much: Emine Hanım is the niece of Hacı Yahya Pasha; she was very young herself when they fled Silistre in 1892, leaving everything behind in what is now Bulgaria. As you can imagine, as refugees themselves, for years and years they suffered in poverty here. She was the one who looked after the entire family throughout the war. Looked after a sick husband and raised the children on her own when he died in 1919. Mother *and* father. Mürvet's her greatest help, so she might drag her feet a little at first."

The next day, Selim got his wife, Şükriye, to intermediate; they raised the subject with Mürvet's mother and elder brother and sang Seyit's praises for hours. Dumbfounded at the news that his proposal had been accepted, Seyit purchased a solitaire and a diamond-and-ruby cluster ring. Life was so strange: marriage had been the last thing on his mind, and he had, not that long ago, sold a watch and medals that had meant so much. If only he could buy them back now!

The rings and a photo of Seyit in his Guards uniform taken in Saint Petersburg went to the new fiancée's home. Seyit was incredulous: all he had to was to send a ring, and he was engaged to a girl from Aksaray's Tatlıkuyu district! To a girl he'd yet to see close up, a girl who'd not even caught a glimpse of him. How could a young girl marry someone she'd never seen, someone she didn't know at all... with no idea whether she would like him? Selim was quick to reassure that this was the custom here.

Still filled with nostalgia for the first thirty-one years of his life, Seyit wondered if he was ever going to get used to these strangers and their alien customs. How was he going to live among them, with one of them? Was he making a dreadful mistake?

As well he might have worried. The rings and the photograph were returned three weeks after they had been delivered to the fiancée. A cringing Selim turned up at Seyit's new flat, placed the gifts on the table, and started hesitatingly, "I'm very sorry Seyit...but all hell's broken loose."

"What happened?" asked Seyit, with no relief—much to his surprise. He must have taken a shine to Mürvet after all.

"You know the hotel you stayed at when you arrived in Istanbul?"

"Yes, the Hotel Şeref. What about it?"

"Seems the hotelier's daughter is a friend of Mürvet's and a close one at that. She recognized your photo and blabbed about your Russian mistress, how you'd been living together and everything...threw the cat among the pigeons, in other words. Emine fetched up at our door in the blink of an eye. Mürvet was in floods of tears; her mother was crying bloody murder; and as for her brother...well, you can guess what *he* said."

"What did they say?"

"That no daughter of theirs is marrying a man who has a mistress. And they won't budge an inch."

"Why didn't you tell them it's all off between Shura and me?"

"Are you sure? Can I really say that?" Selim gaped.

Seyit reflected briefly. "Yes, yes, of course you can. What about Mürvet, though?"

"Devastated—what do you expect? Your photo's been tucked under her pillow ever since she first saw it. Poor girl's off her food and everything."

The gaslit picture of the pretty girl with the slanting black eyes and neat little upturned nose flashed before Seyit's eyes. She was so young, so innocent! It must be awful to have her dreams shattered by such betrayal. He felt terrible. Perhaps he really was about to let slip a union that would have made him very happy.

"Selim, take it all back and inform them I don't have a mistress or anything; nor do I live with anyone. I've got a good mind to go to America if this falls through, anyhow."

It turned out to be quite a job to persuade Mürvet's mother, but relent she eventually did at the sight of her daughter crying night and day. Head over heels in love with the handsome young man in uniform, Mürvet had been bursting into tears at the sight of her finger bereft of those precious rings.

They were placed back on her finger a fortnight later, and Seyit dispatched Emine forty liras for the wedding preparations, equivalent to five months' salary for a senior civil servant. The wedding was scheduled for the end of September.

Seyit carried on living it up in Pera, but his fiancée frequently popped into his mind now. He was growing fond of this stranger who would one day become his wife. This was nothing like his love with Shura, not that he was prepared to go through the same thing again.

The key was the word *stranger*, however. An engaged couple ought to get to know each other. Except he had been cautioned in no uncertain terms that they would be allowed to meet only after the wedding.

Seyit wasn't prepared to wait that long.

He spent a whole afternoon in Pera's elegant boutiques, purchasing silk lingerie, scarves and shirts, perfume, and ivory hairpins, all wrapped in delicate European tissue and adorned with silk ribbons. He couldn't have been more thrilled if he were on his way to delight a little child. So she'd been crying for him and after only seeing a photograph too! Men can rarely resist a woman in love. Her devotion, before they'd even been introduced properly, was melting his heart. Convinced that she'd be overjoyed by this surprise visit, and laden with parcels, he hailed a cab at Tünel.

It was dusk on July 15, a time for the megapolis to radiate the heat it had absorbed all day. Crickets sang in gardens illuminated by a bewitching moon emblazoned upon that summer evening sky.

Strange Customs

MÜRVET COULDN'T WAIT to wear her wedding dress.

It was after supper. Her mother, Emine; brother, Hakkı; and sister-in-law, Meliha were drinking coffee in the back garden. Mürvet sat upstairs in the room overlooking the street in her white nightgown with the scalloped edges, cheerfully preparing her trousseau with the help of her neighborhood friends. Various items lay on the sofas as the girls sewed, embroidered, and sang merrily.

The singing ceased on hearing a knock at the door.

"Behire's back." One of the girls had just nipped out to fetch a thimble and a spare pair of scissors from home. Mürvet flipped her long hair over her shoulder, leaped to her feet, skipped downstairs, and opened the door. Dazzled by the moonlight falling on her face, she exclaimed, "Selim! Welcome—come in, do."

His face obscured behind a pile of parcels, all that was visible of the man on the doorstep was hair rising above the top parcel with a huge bow. He said nothing. Mürvet repeated, "Come on in, Selim; they're all round the back: Mother and the whole family."

The man leaned out from behind the parcels. Mürvet's hand flew to her mouth. This wasn't her brother-in-law, Selim; this was the man whose photo lay under her pillow. Her fiancé. Freezing on the spot, a white dot illuminated by an accommodating moon, she crossed her arms to cover her flimsy nightgown. With a raffish wink, he placed a kiss on her hair.

She gave an inadvertent yelp and flew upstairs, stunned and elated, trembling like a leaf when she reached the sofa. Her heart was pounding out of her chest. A curious gaggle of girls surrounded her at once. She couldn't stop blushing at the memory of the kiss on her hair.

Hakkı had darted indoors at hearing the scream. With a glacial welcome, he bade Seyit enter, showed him into a room by the door, went out into the garden, and prevented Emine from coming in. "Don't go in; it's Seyit."

"Fine, son; shouldn't I be greeting my son-in-law?"

"No, absolutely not! What cheek! Turning up out of the blue, on his own, at this hour! And whatever he did to Mürvet at the door just now, the poor girl yelled and ran upstairs. Molested her, if you ask me! If you appear, he'll take that as an invitation to stay for hours. Then he'll fetch up whenever the fancy takes him. Better give him the cold shoulder; I'll send him away."

"You're right," she replied, curbing her curiosity. But her stepson was right; this foreigner with strange customs had to be kept at arm's length. She returned to her seat in the garden.

Hakkı mumbled something about how they would welcome his visit some other time, provided there was sufficient notice. Taken aback by this cool reception, a vexed Seyit placed his presents on the table and moved to the door.

"Fine, please give my fiancée her presents. See you some other time..."

Back home an hour later, he vented his displeasure. "Never seen the like, Selim! I can't see my fiancée. She doesn't know me at all. I go there laden with presents, and no one has the courtesy to greet me. It was worse than being sent off with a flea in my ear! I'm not prepared to put up with it any longer. If they don't intend to let their daughter marry me, then they should stop messing around. I don't play such games. They put the ring on, they take it off—they won't even bother talking to us...I'm through with this nonsense."

"Don't fly off the handle, Kurt Seyit. You're right: their customs are different, but you have to understand them too. You've seen the girl and liked what you saw. She liked your photograph. The rest comes after the wedding. You can't just knock on the door unannounced and enter a girl's house whenever the fancy takes you, with no rhyme or reason! You'll embarrass them before the neighbors."

But this time, Seyit was determined to stand his ground. "Fine; then we go announced tomorrow evening. Please go over in the morning and announce our intention to visit that evening—that's the rhyme—and tell them we have a reason. There's your rhyme and reason. Then they can't complain. All right?"

"You won't drop it, will you? So what's this reason then?" laughed Selim.

"Well, you're their relative, anyway. And I want to give my fiancée some presents."

"Again? Didn't you just do that tonight?"

"Even so, they were little trinkets. I'd like to give something better than just the rings. All right?"

"All right, Seyit; I'll do my best."

They parted with a hug, Selim still chuckling at Seyit's bloody mindedness. This new son-in-law was going to be no pushover.

Mürvet had unwrapped the parcels to exclamations of admiration from her friends as one chic surprise after another blossomed into tissue papers revealing imported fineries.

Behire sighed. "You're so lucky, Mürvet! No one around here ever had it so good!"

Certain of their friendship as she was, Mürvet sensed envy. It was flattering, but she was afraid of the evil eye. "Kismet, Behire! I'd never have believed it myself. Destiny."

She carried on gingerly, reluctant to rip or tear any of the delicate wrapping, rolling up the ribbons and folding the tissues neatly.

"Just look at these stockings, Mürvet: real silk! Oh my God! And in so many colors too!"

"Wonder what's in that tiny box. Hey, girls! It's perfume, and it's European. Mürvet, why don't you open it? Let's have a sniff. It must smell divine."

"This scarf is silk too. Oh! It's fabulous!"

"Will you look at this lovely lace collar!"

Mürvet was sitting on her heels on the sofa, mesmerized—and practically inebriated—by these luxuries she had seen only in pictures and on the ladies visiting Nazire Hanım's mansion.

Later that night, she tried on the turquoise silk dress with the cream French lace trimmings and gazed at her reflection in the mirror. It clung to her bosom and waist and cascaded down the hips in frills, a world away from the baggy flannel or cotton dresses gathered at the waist that she normally wore. Cautiously, scared of laddering it, she slipped one silk stocking on. She had no shoes to wear with such a dress, so she rose on tiptoe, went to the console, and picked up the vial of kohl. She lined her eyes carefully, stepped back, opened her arms out, and twirled on her toes. She watched the silk fabric stroke her body, swing out, swish, and drape itself back. It was like a dream. An evanescent dream of the rings on her fingers, the silk, everything but everything. She couldn't take her eyes off the mirror. She had never felt this close to womanhood, so...on the verge of maturity.

The door swung open; it was her mother. Mürvet stood nailed to the spot, mortified at having been caught. She started wringing her hands before her mother's stern gaze. As she feared, Emine lashed out.

"What do you think you're doing, Mürvet? What do you think you're doing in that dress? Might as well be naked! You can see everything. No decent girl or woman would ever be caught dead in anything like that! Take it off at once. Take it off, and don't let me ever see it again."

Recalling the day her mother had tugged her rings off, Mürvet clenched her fist. She wasn't going to let it happen a second time. Neither did she have any intention of giving her dress away.

"But Mother...it was Se..."

"I know, I know. I know who sent it. Flaming Moskof! Wish I'd never agreed in the first place—I'd never give you away. Can't go back on my word now. Turns up out of the blue, molests you at the door, and then gives you such shamelessly naked dresses. And you're only too happy to wear them. Good God! What's the world coming to? He's gonna disgrace us all before the neighbors!"

"Mother, he did nothing untoward. He didn't even touch me. I swear to God."

"Shut up! I know what happened. Take it off now. And wipe that filth off your face. Come back to your senses. Good heavens! Whatever next!"

Protest was futile. Afraid of annoying her mother any further, Mürvet removed the dress, hung it up, washed her face, and went to bed. She blew out the gas lamp and fell asleep, praying for happiness, a silk scarf in one hand and Seyit's photograph in the other.

The next morning Selim came over to announce their intention to call. Flustered as she was, Emine knew further refusal would have been churlish and set about preparations for the evening.

Hakkı worked as a typesetter at the İkdam Press and always came home for lunch. That day, he flew into a rage at hearing about the plans for the evening.

"Who the hell does he think he is? So he was an officer for the Russian tsar? Big deal! We are the grandchildren of an Ottoman Pasha! Mr. Grand wants to turn up whenever he wants, with or without prior notice. Outrageous! Keep indulging him this way, and he'll never marry the girl. He'll keep coming over and split one day. Bloke's used to living with a mistress; he doesn't believe in marriage vows."

"I can't do anything about it now, Hakkı. My sisters-in-law, Selim—they're all coming! What more should you do? How can you say no to a guest? Bite your tongue this evening. He won't repeat it. Come on; help me a little here."

"All right, all right. Tell them I don't want to see that man here again until the wedding though."

Just then Mürvet's paternal aunts dropped in with their daughters.

"Seyit and Selim will visit in the evening," said Şükriye. Somewhat cheered up by their arrival, Emine chattered as the women laid a table in the garden. Dusk was settling when Selim and Seyit knocked at the door.

Taking Mürvet aside, Emine hissed. "Off you go into Meliha's room, and stay there. Understood?" She added irritably, almost under her breath, "If only this evening were over. I swear I can hardly breathe!"

It was like a bucket of cold water. Mürvet stared at the closed door, crestfallen; she had no place at the table! And all this time she'd been dying to meet her fiancé and chat with him. Her eyes welled up. Cross with anything and everything that was conspiring to keep her apart from the man she loved, she stole over to the window to watch the garden from behind the net curtain. At least she might catch a glimpse of him from here.

But Seyit was given a seat with his back to the window, and Mürvet was sure it was Hakkı's doing. No matter which side of the window she stood, she just couldn't see Seyit's face.

Hours went by. She felt like a prisoner when her sister-in-law brought up a tray with her dinner.

Her fiancé was regaling everyone with his jokes and unaffected charm—everyone except for Emine and Hakkı, that is. Mürvet couldn't hear the conversation, but she was envious of everyone sharing a table, a chat, or a joke with him.

There was a lull in the laughter. The only voice she could hear was his. Silently unlatching and lifting the sash, Mürvet pricked up her ears. Seyit spoke confidently yet firmly in a beautifully modulated voice despite his distinctive accent: "I appreciate that was the earlier agreement, but I suggest we don't wait that long. I propose we wed at the end of August."

Hakkı and Emine protested at once. "What's the hurry? Won't everyone wonder why?"

Mürvet couldn't see the look Seyit gave Hakkı, but she had no doubt it was a withering glance. Refilling his glass, a patently unruffled Seyit replied, "I've just named the date. It's up to you to accept or refuse. If you accept, that's fine; we'll wed on August 30. If you don't, that's also fine, and we'll call the whole thing off. I've got friends moving to America; I might as well join them if there's nothing to hold me here."

Hakkı shot up in a fury with Emine on his heels. *That must be what "You could cut the air with a knife!" means*, thought Mürvet. *Now it all falls apart again!* She couldn't bear it any more. Her head was throbbing. Her nose ached with the trickle of warm blood. She pulled out a handkerchief, tilted her head back, tamponed her nostrils, and crept toward the door to overhear what her brother and mother were discussing in the hall. Hakkı was ranting and raving.

"Haven't I told you? Eh? He's so full of himself! Has to have everything his way! Who the hell does he think he is? Is he taking a girl from an orphanage? Thinks he can lord it over us just because he's brought a couple of scraps of silk?"

Emine was trying to pacify him. "Hush, son, hush! Everyone can hear you! We'll never live it down! All the windows are open; everyone's out in the gardens! What difference does it make, a month later or a month earlier? Anyway, weren't you scared he wasn't going to marry her? See, he does want to marry her."

"Can't you see though, he's making things difficult? He'll just shove off if we say no to the end of August. And Mürvet's gonna be left on the shelf. Who'll marry a girl who's broken off an engagement?"

"Hush! Bite your tongue! Now listen. Let's not dig our heels in. The sooner it's done and dusted, the better it will be all around. Anyway, he's been to the house several times now. Who could vouch for her virtue now? How are we gonna convince everyone we've kept them apart? And if it all falls through, how do we explain to the neighbors why? Come on; let's sort it out once and for all."

"You're right. Let's not drag it out. Fine, let's go back out."

Mürvet's legs gave out under her. Her nose wouldn't stop bleeding. Feeling quite sick, she collapsed on the bed.

She was just beginning to pull herself together when footsteps pounded up-stairs, the door was flung open, and the girls rushed in with the good news. In the meantime, Emine was organizing the overnight guests, fumbling in the linen cupboard.

"Come on, Mürvet—come and help me make the beds."

Şükriye and her younger sister Adalet would sleep in Mürvet's room, and the aunts would stay in another. It was taken for granted that Selim and Seyit would leave. The girls gathered in Mürvet's room after wishing their mother good night. Mürvet offered Şükriye her own bed and took one of the mattresses on the floor. Hugging her knees closer to her chest and her back to a pillow and blushing in anticipation, she waited for an account of the conversations in the garden. This was no joke. She was getting married in a month. Just then, after a knock, the door opened to reveal Selim.

"What are you all doing here? A girls' convention?" he asked his wife.

Şükriye folded the cover and moved toward her husband. "What does it look like? We're about to turn in. Aren't you two leaving?"

Selim was taken aback. "Where? I'm sure you can find beds for us too. We're family, aren't we?"

Şükriye had no idea what to say. Of course Selim could stay. But neither Emine nor Hakkı would allow Seyit to stay the night. The fur would fly again. She was about to explain it to her husband when she spotted Seyit, peering over Selim's shoulder. Mürvet froze in the bed where she was sitting. This was the second time she'd locked eyes with her fiancé, and she was in a nightgown again. She saw his smile and wished the ground would open up and swallow her. At the thought of Hakkı's fury, she dived into the bed and drew the sheet over her head, still blushing like a beetroot when Şükriye stepped outside to move the men away and shut the door.

The men must have left, judging by Hakkı's yells ringing in the hallways. "One more, just one more imposition, and I'll kick out these Moskofs, I swear! Family or not, I'll kick 'em out; I swear!"

Knowing Hakkı tarred her husband with the same brush, Şükriye patted Mürvet's cheek, and they exchanged an uneasy smile.

Thus was the wedding date set.

The Wedding,
August 30, 1923

A UGUST 30 DAWNED upon a nation still buoyant with the Treaty of Lausanne signed five weeks previously, a nation looking forward to the day's double celebrations. This, the first anniversary of the decisive Nationalist victory at Dumlupınar, happened to coincide with the Feast of Sacrifice, the day when wealthy Muslims sacrifice a sheep and distribute a third of the meat to those less fortunate; feed neighbors, relations, and visitors with another third; and save the remainder for the family.

There was a third occasion this year, however: one that meant far more to Mürvet. This was to be her wedding day. Hard as it was, she did her best to contain herself. It was unseemly for a maiden to appear so eager to wed.

As per tradition—and Atatürk's secularist reforms still being some way off—the religious ceremony was held in separate rooms. Seyit and Mürvet had yet to see each other face to face. After the wedding, the women left the house; the men would stay at the bride's home to eat and drink and have fun, while the women would proceed to the henna party elsewhere.

The venue was Nazire Hanım's mansion next door. Upon her retirement from royal service, she had been showered with a considerable pension, an enormous mansion, and servants of her own by her longtime employer, Princess Naciye Sultan. The neighborhood's very own courtly lady's gracious offer to host Mürvet's henna party had been gratefully accepted by Emine. Her modest house would have been too cramped to host separate men's and women's parties on such an occasion.

Matrons and maidens alike gathered in the mansion. Nazire Hanım had lent Mürvet her own palace robe, a silk velvet *bindallı*: a fabulous long cream kaftan adorned with silver, coral, ruby, and sage embroidery; a matching cap with silver coins; and a broad belt. Mürvet's feet went into velvet slippers with pointed, curving toes ending in red pom-poms. Her long hair was dressed in the customary forty braids; a silk veil pinned to the cap skimmed over her shoulders and cascaded down to her waist.

Everyone else was in the traditional henna party dress of satin top and baggy trousers, mostly hired from the Grand Bazaar, although no one could outshine Mürvet or Nazire Hanım today.

The henna party would take place in the big reception room, where a long table was bedecked with sherbets, lemonade, desserts, and helvas. Two ladies playing the oud and the kanun on the seat in the oriel soon found vocal accompaniment among the more confident singers in the party. Before long, classical songs gave way to folk tunes, and zils were procured—seemingly out of nowhere—as dancers kept rhythm with their finger cymbals, and those less energetic clapped in time from their seats. Mürvet was dragged to the center of the dancers pivoting and spinning merrily.

The music stilled when the henna was brought out. The party settled in a large circle on the massive carpet. Mürvet sat at the center, flanked by a girl holding the henna bowl and Nazire Hanım, who scooped up a handful of the green mixture and placed it in Mürvet's palm, intoning prayers throughout. She then wrapped Mürvet's fist in a handkerchief, planted a kiss on her forehead, and got up. It was time for the henna bowl to pass from hand to hand.

On returning home in the early hours after more songs and poems, the ladies were faced by the mess the men's party had left. Not a single plate or glass was left untouched, the tables in the garden were covered in the detritus of food and drink, and the kitchen was piled high with dirty pots and pans.

Neither Emine nor Mürvet got much sleep that night. First, they made the beds for the aunts and cousins. Next they washed and scrubbed and wiped and polished and put away until the dawn call to prayer. The only thing that punctuated the silence throughout their toil had been Emine's grumbles.

First thing in the morning, two sheep were slaughtered. After the share for the poor was distributed, the remainder would be sautéed for the evening's feast.

Emine was taken aback at the sight of her sisters-in-law and nieces getting ready to go out; she had been hoping they might give her a hand, and here they were, leaving for the fairground! It fell upon the bride and her mother to cook the feast before the afternoon's bridal bath ceremony.

"Don't know how we're gonna get it all done! God help us. Here I am, rushed off my feet, and no one to help. Never mind—at least they're out of the way. Thank God for small mercies..."

Mürvet beavered away without complaint. As if it wasn't the same house that had been spring-cleaned the day before, the rugs were wiped, and the windows and patio were polished. Next, fresh coffee was ground and confectionery bowls refilled. Mürvet's bed was made with the new broderie anglaise linen and finished with bridal pillowcases and bedspread in gold satin.

Emine and Hakkı had objected to Mürvet moving out to Seyit's flat in Pera. That was a den of iniquity, a land of infidels. Seyit seemed to concede the point for the time being. Mürvet straightened up the bedspread once more, drew back, and stared. This had been her bed, her bed as a young girl, and tonight she would be sharing it with her husband—a prospect that made her blush. She wasn't at all prepared. It all had been fine up to now: getting engaged, receiving expensive presents, a handsome fiancé to love from afar...but what next? She was utterly ignorant of what conjugal relations might involve. None of her elders had illuminated her on what to do once left alone in a room with a strange man, let alone share a bed! How would she cover herself? Many years earlier, a totally innocent question had been rewarded by a slap from her mother. Mürvet had never again dared to ask another, and the pain was still fresh in the mind. She wasn't about to open her mouth to ask anything now.

Then again—surely she wasn't the only girl getting married! So perhaps you learned certain things after the wedding.

Her mother's voice jolted her out of her contemplation. "Mürvet! Mürvet! Where are you, girl? These tablecloths need pressing. Come on. Any time now they'll descend on us. No time to waste."

Mürvet set the tables in the garden once again. The white linen tablecloths with a floral appliqué border were her own handiwork. After placing roses and four o'clock flowers from the garden in vases, she stood back to admire the effect; yes, the blossoms looked lovely against the snow-white tablecloths.

The mezes, vegetable dishes, and desserts were transferred into serving dishes to cool when a knock at the door announced the return of the merry gaggle of aunts and cousins. Before long, neighborhood women started flocking in, bath bundles in their hands. It was time for the next ceremony. A convoy of carriages took the bridal party to the Cağaloğlu Hamamı.

The two-hundred-year-old Turkish bath uphill from Hagia Sophia had always been popular not only for ordinary weekly bath day treats but also as a venue for bridal baths for Jews and Muslims alike. A traditional twin bathhouse open all year, it served both sexes in separate quarters with mirrored floor plans set at right angles. Bathrooms were standard in larger residences as in Crimea; the more modest amenities in smaller houses, on the other hand, made regular trips to the city's myriad bathhouses not only a necessity but also a cheery outing to look forward to. A bridal party was an even more joyous occasion.

Mürvet and her guests entered the women's section, got undressed in the changing booths, and moved into the hot chamber. Decorously covered in bath wraps, naked women tottered on high sandals toward the marble washbowls set into the walls to pour bowls of hot water over themselves as they watched others in their party already stretching out on the central stone. The enormous octagonal marble plinth where more than a dozen patrons could lie at once was the heart of the Turkish bathhouse. The skin, softened after several minutes of sweating, would then be subjected to a vigorous massage with a raw silk mitt. More scrub than massage—given the fervor of the bath attendants.

That afternoon everyone was dancing attendance on Mürvet. The first step was the sugaring; no bride—nor any other woman—would even dream of meeting life's challenges with a single stray hair on her body. Then came bowlfuls of hot water in preparation for the scrub.

Unaccustomed as she was to being the focus of attention, Mürvet was both embarrassed and not a little flattered. She lay on the central stone and submitted to the expert hands of a bath attendant. Before long her body was bright red with the heat and the scrubbing. Her friends led her to a washbowl, where they washed and rinsed her hair twice, singing all the while. They then pinned her hair up and washed her body.

No amount of scrubbing would remove the henna on her palms and fingers though. By the time the bathbowls, wraps, and sandals were packed and the party returned home, Mürvet could hardly contain herself. It was time to put her wedding dress on. Her sister-in-law came into her room to help her dress. Taking the opportunity, Emine led her sisters-in-law to the kitchen so that they could finish the preparations. Mürvet put on the white chemise with the scalloped trim she had made herself and a pair of long drawers with elasticated cuffs at the calf. They looked incongruous next to the lacy silk garters and ivory silk stockings Seyit had given her; but there was nothing she could do about that.

The wedding dress was laid out on the bed. It looked so lovely that Mürvet was afraid to touch it lest she mark the fabric. Seyit had sent her the white silk fabric and the lace adorning the collar and sleeves, and Emine had made the dress modeled on a picture Nazire Hanım had found. Seyit had also sent her the white satin heels with an ankle strap and a bow. As Mürvet stood before the mirror, Meliha powdered her face to tone down the blushing cheeks, lined her eyes with kohl, used heated tongs to curl her bangs into two cascades framing her face, and put up the rest of her hair in a chignon.

The floor-length veil was a solid length of lace matching the trim of her gown. Mürvet could have cried with joy at the reflection in the mirror. Repeating *Maşallah* over and over again between feigned spits to fend off the evil eye, Meliha straightened Mürvet's hair and skirts and picked up the tiara that had caused Emine such grief. Affluent folk might purchase such items outright, but the less well-off tended to hire one for the big day. Emine had been disheartened with the selection within her budget; none of them went with the lovely silk dress. Thankfully her younger sister-in-law's husband stood surety with a Grand Bazaar jeweler friend, and an elegant tiara was duly procured. Mürvet was ecstatic at the result when the tiara went over the veil. She looked just like the pictures in the magazines she'd been admiring for years...no, she looked more beautiful and richer. Clapping her hands, Meliha flung open the door.

"Everyone! Come and see how a bride should look!" She walked around Mürvet, who was still mesmerized by her own reflection. "Off with the evil eye! Maşallah! Maşallah, my girl! What a fortunate fellow this Seyit is!"

"I'm fortunate too, Meliha," hazarded Mürvet with a bashful smile.

"Of course you are! None of us had such a lovely wedding gown or rings! You could be going to a pasha's mansion. Maşallah."

Was there a trace of envy there? wondered Mürvet, just as the other women and girls rushed in, clapped and screamed, and led her out of the door, holding her veil and skirts. In the blink of an eye, Mürvet was placed on the sofa in the sitting room. Her companions lined up to admire the bride as though they were staring at a shop mannequin. Fethiye and Necmiye were speechless at the sight of this fairy princess instead of their big sister usually found scrubbing the floors on her knees in a flannel skirt or doing the washing. The proud mother suddenly realized just how young Mürvet was. Emine's eldest daughter, now barely seventeen, had been her mother's help like an adult for so many years. The girl had been given little opportunity to enjoy her childhood and was now on the threshold of womanhood; she'd missed out on the stage between.

Emine shook her head. There was nothing she could do now, other than pray for her daughter to have an easy life from this point forward.

Tying Mürvet's sash fell upon Hakkı as the man of the house. As per tradition, he wound a broad red satin sash around her waist, tied it twice, and undid the knot twice before tying it for the third time and drawing back to let Meliha undo the knot. Emine tipped her daughter-in-law, who brought over the ribbon, which symbolized chastity and strength.

The front door barely had time to shut between arrivals. Sherbets, lemonade, and sweets greeted kith and kin and neighbors and friends coming to congratulate the bride.

It was late afternoon when the stream of visitors finally dwindled to a trickle until only close family were left, and the male relatives turned up one by one. The food was spread out on the tables. The sound of laughter and cheerful chatter rose up, tantalizing the bride, who had been forced to sit and wait instead.

How she wished she could join the party in the garden, to chat and laugh! More importantly, to see the man who was her husband before they retired into the nuptial chamber. But since tradition outweighed her desires, she had no choice but to bide her time.

As evening descended, lamps were lit. Judging by the volume of laughter wafting up into the room upstairs, drinks were replenished repeatedly. Mürvet gathered her veil and skirts and went over to the window to watch the party from behind the net curtain. Her eyes picked up the three strangers in the crowd; one of them had to be Seyit, but since all she could see of them were their hands raising their glasses and their backs, she couldn't be sure.

There was a gaggle of giggling young girls at the other end of the table. Mürvet thought it was so unfair. This was her wedding, and everyone was having fun except her. She sighed and looked out again. It was hot. Not a leaf stirred; nor did the net curtain. Lifting her veil, she fanned her throat with a lace handkerchief. Why couldn't she be sitting at the table in her lovely gown?

The diners rose. The men left the garden, and the ladies hastened to clear the table. Mürvet withdrew from the window, heart beating in anticipation. She didn't want to be caught there. She settled back on the sofa to wait, and before long the door opened. It was Meliha.

"How are you, love? Come along; time to go to the nuptial chamber."

Mürvet held her veil with one hand and Meliha's hand with the other and followed her sister-in-law. It was hard to believe she was in her own house; she felt lost, unable to think what to do or how to act. On reaching the bedroom, Meliha led her to the sofa, lowered the veil over her face, and left.

Mürvet could see little beyond the lace veil and the net canopy over the bed. When the door opened a couple of minutes later, she thought her heart would jump out of her chest; her heartbeat was pounding in her ears. Realizing it was Meliha carrying a couple of prayer rugs, Mürvet calmed down somewhat. Meliha spread the rugs on the other side of the bed, and two men entered as she left. They looked alike, too similar for Mürvet to tell which was her husband. Other than his photograph and one meeting when she'd been dazzled by the moonlight, she had never really seen Seyit.

The men performed the bridegroom prayers, stood up after a bow, and placed some money on the rugs. One slapped the other affectionately and left. That had to be the best man, which meant the one in the room now was her husband.

Mürvet feared she would pass out now that they were alone. The idea of marriage that she'd been looking forward to was suddenly a metal band constricting her heart. Sitting tensely, she crushed the handkerchief in her hands as Meliha entered and in total silence collected the tip, rolled up the rugs, handed it all to someone outside the door, and came over to Mürvet to lead her to Seyit's side. Meliha put their hands together and left.

Blushing furiously at the touch of a strange man, Mürvet kept her eyes on the hem of her skirt, unable to control the trembling of her legs and hands. Seyit waited without a sound but without letting go of her hand, as if to allow her to get used to his touch. Footsteps retreated outside. Still holding her hand, he reached out with his other hand and lifted her veil. He held her wrist to slide on her *first sight* gift, a fabulous gold bangle surrounded by diamonds. Mürvet caught her breath as she looked from between half-open lids. Her wrist and arm were so slender, however, that he had to push it almost all the way up to her elbow. He was smiling at his young wife's shy, innocent diffidence. Lifting her face gently by the chin, he forced her to look at him. When their eyes met, Mürvet thought her heart would stop. The pupils of his deep-blue eyes blazed like embers. The smiling lips under the neat, thin moustache murmured words she couldn't hear. Trembling like a leaf now, she felt the hand grasping hers squeeze a little tighter. Her legs were about to give way. Her strength was gone.

Seyit was pleasantly surprised by how pretty his young wife was, much prettier than he'd anticipated. Her prominent cheekbones, dark, slanted eyes, and slender figure were enchanting. Her bashful gaze was reminiscent of a schoolchild terrified of an exam. He was certain that she was utterly ignorant of men and what a wedding night involved. Carefully, lest he frighten her, he removed the tiara and the veil and placed them by the mirror before carrying her trembling body to the bed. Petrified she might pass out or, at the very least, have a nosebleed, Mürvet couldn't lift her gaze from her dress to meet his eyes. She felt his warm breath on her hair and forehead. The touch of his lips on her cheeks, around her eyes, and on her chin set her face on fire.

The first time he addressed her directly was in a whisper: "Murka...my little Murka."

The Newlyweds

MÜRVET FELL HEAD over heels in love with her husband straightaway. Besotted Seyit might have been with his young wife, but the course of love never did run smooth, as they found out within a week of the wedding. So different were their backgrounds that goodwill alone was never going to suffice to prevent friction.

The first dispute arose over lingerie. Seyit rejected outright the cotton underclothing Mürvet had spent weeks making for them both. The morning after their wedding, she laid it all out on the bed, and he promptly put it all away. Neither would he wear a nightshirt or pajamas. Mürvet's anxiety—*What if someone walks in?*—only raised a chuckling retort: "Anyone who enters my bedroom ought to be ready to see me as I am. Better make sure they know!"

Needless to say, Mürvet steered clear of the subject altogether.

The following day, Seyit arrived home with his hands full, grabbed his wife's waist, and planted a noisy kiss on the edge of her mouth. Emine and Hakkı pursed their lips and exchanged a sour look. Poor Mürvet was between a rock and a hard place, living in a permanent state of trepidation, seeking approval for everything Seyit and she did. Instead of kissing him back, therefore, she recoiled. Thankfully he didn't seem to mind.

"Here, Murka—for you. Let's go upstairs," he said, handing her the parcels.

"Erm...I was just about to lay the table."

"There's still time. Let's go upstairs. You can chat to me while I get changed."

At Mürvet's pleading glance, Emine grudgingly conceded. "Up you go then; go with your husband. Fethiye can lay the table this once."

Seyit dragged his wife upstairs with another passionate kiss. "Don't you want to see what I got you?"

"Of course I do." She smiled back.

"Unwrap them then!"

Seyit removed his shirt, draped a towel across his shoulders, and started to shave as he watched Mürvet stare spellbound at the silk lingerie pouring out of the parcels. The bed was covered in a froth of slips, briefs, and brassieres in white, black, ivory, and blue.

"Oh, Seyit! They're lovely!" she exclaimed.

"You like them?"

"I love them!"

"Good. From now on this is what you wear, all right? I never want to see you in those dreadful long flannels with elasticated cuffs."

Mürvet blushed furiously even through her delight; she had been married for only a day, and it would take a long time before she was comfortable discussing such matters.

Soon they descended to the dining room. Seeing Emine, Hakkı, Meliha, and the children were already seated, Seyit was less than impressed.

His reproach was courteous, yet unmistakable. "I apologize; I had no idea you were in such a hurry. I would never consider dining unshaven..."

Mürvet could almost hear Hakkı grind his teeth.

After supper, Seyit and Mürvet retired to their room, but before they'd finished undressing, a commotion broke out downstairs: Hakkı and Meliha were having a right old dingdong. His upper body bare, Seyit pulled his trousers on and stormed out. Mürvet followed. Her brother and sister-in-law were fighting outside their room, and Emine was trying to pacify them.

Meliha was bawling, one hand on her bleeding lip, the other grabbing her husband by the shirt, who in turn was yelling as he rattled her by the shoulders.

"Let her go!" yelled Seyit. "Who'd rough up a woman? Leave her alone!"

Emine was felled by an almighty slap Hakkı had intended for his wife. Meliha took this opportunity to run into her room and slam the door.

"You ought to be ashamed of yourself!" shouted Seyit. "Call yourself a man? Look what you've done!" He tried to give his groaning mother-in-law a hand up, but her legs wouldn't carry her. Cradling the frail woman, Seyit carried her upstairs to her room as Mürvet brought a drink of water and rubbed her temples with some cologne. They waited at Emine's bedside until she came around.

The following morning Seyit left for work before anyone else was up. Hugging and kissing his wife on his way out, he said, "Murka, let's have some rakı and meze tonight." He traced her cheek with a finger. "That's what I'm used to. I'm not dining on a one-pot dish and water every night."

Later that morning, Mürvet gathered her courage to raise the subject with her mother when they were cooking. Emine seemed to have forgotten about the son-in-law who had rescued her the previous night.

"Meze and rakı, huh? As if we'd not just feasted for two days running! Who can afford to buy mezes and rakı every day God sends? He can buy it himself if that's his liking. I'm too old to be looking after a son-in-law!"

Mürvet bit her tongue to hide her vexation. Now a married woman, she did not welcome her mother's rebuke.

Seyit had earlier consulted Selim on how to manage household expenses as a son-in-law living with his wife's family. "Under no circumstances should you offer to chip in," Selim had cautioned. "Best to buy provisions and presents in lieu." Anxious to avoid offense at any cost and still out of his depth in his wife's family, Seyit did as he was advised. Lavish gifts for his wife had to be acceptable, he'd thought, but there was always something he couldn't quite put his finger on. Hoping for a jovial dinner table, he came back laden with rakı, spicy sausage, cheese, and pickled bonito. Mürvet breathed a sigh of relief as she unwrapped the delicacies, since no one else had any intention of buying what he had asked for. With a glance at the food Mürvet was setting out, Emine grumbled, stirring the pan of beans with mince constantly, her words clearly intended to be heard.

"Call this a contribution to the kitchen? Just brings what *he* wants to accompany his alcohol."

Their customary dinners that started with prayers and carried on with food bolted down were unlikely to ever appeal. Seyit missed what he was used to: taking a sip of his drink, relishing every morsel, and enjoying good conversation with everyone around the table. But no one here wanted to keep him company. Annoyed at eyes watching his every mouthful, he cut his meal short and rose from the table with the rest.

Nearing the end of that first week, Mürvet gathered their dirty clothes and went down to the laundry. As the whites were boiling, she set about washing her delicate new lingerie. Checking up on Mürvet on her way out to the shops, Emine's eyes widened at the sight of the fineries in her daughter's hands.

"What's that lot then?"

"Erm...my underwear, Mother."

Emine fished a flimsy piece of silk from the washbowl, held it at arm's length, and shook her head.

"Tsk...tsk...tsk...call this underwear? What happened to the garments we made; why aren't you wearing them?"

"My husband bought them, Mother."

"Like I couldn't guess! Who wears such filth—do you have any idea? No decent woman in her right mind would wear any of this. No one's got any shame nowadays. Look at this...and that..." her hands kept churning the washbowl. "Wash them all and put them away. He'll turn you into a slut at this rate, if you wear everything he brings you."

Mürvet was fuming by the time her mother stormed off. She wasn't allowed to enjoy anything her husband brought! Then again, that was her mother. Surely she wanted what was best for her? Of course she wouldn't want to look like a tart. On finishing her chores, she took a bath and put on the voluminous flannels.

When they retired that night, Seyit slipped into bed naked as usual...and sprang up, bemused by the scene at the foot of the bed: his wife was attempting to wriggle into her nightie without removing her clothes first.

"What on earth are you doing? You look like you're wrestling with your clothes. Come here; shall I give you a hand?" He chuckled.

"No, Seyit, no; it's all right. I'm nearly done," she replied, flustered.

She donned her nightie, hung up her dress, and came to bed. Sensing an unusual timidity in that childish behavior, Seyit stroked her hair, turned her face to him, and asked, "What is it, Murka? What's the matter?"

"Nothing; nothing's the matter. Come on; let's go to sleep."

Seyit bent down to kiss her, and his eye fell upon the chemise visible between the buttons of her nightgown. He drew back.

"Why are you wearing this...dowdy stuff again? Murka, I've told you: I don't like this type of underwear. Why don't you wear what I've bought?"

Mürvet began crying. "I'm not wearing them again."

"Why's that? What have they done to you?" teased Seyit.

"I'm not wearing them," declared a tearful Mürvet.

"But why?"

"Because that's what sluts wear. I'm not a slut."

Seyit threw his head back and laughed out loud. "So that's what the matter is. So only sluts wear silk lingerie, eh? Says who?"

"Mother does."

Seyit sat up, resting on an elbow. "And how does she know what sluts wear?"

Mürvet knew there was no way she was going win the argument, but she had to repeat what her mother had said. "Mother says that's what Pera women wear..."

Seyit was still laughing. "I see. The sluts of Pera, eh? And has your mother ever been there?"

"We never go there."

"Why?"

"Because Muslims don't live there."

Seyit nodded as if learning something of enormous import. "I see. So silk lingerie is worn by non-Muslim sluts."

"Yes, that's right."

Seyit put an arm under her body, drew her close, kissed her hair, and spoke. There was no laughter in his tone. "Look, Murka, my little wife. That's all nonsense. Pera is the finest district of Istanbul, if you ask me. Of course there are good people there, and wicked ones too, as you would get anywhere. There are Muslims and non-Muslims. No one forces anyone else to convert. There are pashas' sons, duchesses, countesses, and princes too. Every diplomatic mission is in Pera. Think they're all evil? Think all their wives are sluts?"

Mürvet's tears dried up at this description of a world totally beyond her experience. Basking in his warmth dispelled all her problems with the family.

"Everything I bought you is what elegant and wealthy ladies wear. Wearing them doesn't make you a slut; it makes you chic, which is what I want my wife to be. I never want to see this stuff again, all right? Deal?"

She nodded. She loved her husband.

The next evening, now in her stylish lingerie, Mürvet laid the table, paying special attention to Seyit's mezes, looking forward to his return. She had resolved to wash and dry her laundry when her mother wasn't looking. Just as she greeted him at the door, they heard shouts outside and opened the door again. An old man was yelling his head off, one hand grabbing Fethiye's ear and the other waving his walking stick in the air. "Whose brat is this?"

Seyit went over to rescue Fethiye. "I'm her brother-in-law; what's the matter? Why are you hurting the child?"

"I'd have broken her legs if I had the strength! She should thank God I don't! Climbed my fig tree and broke all the branches, horrible little tyke! God punish her! Now you, you chastise her. I'll whip her next time I see her in my garden."

Oh, God! Mürvet sighed inwardly. They'd not enjoyed a single quiet night since Seyit had moved in. There was something every day. Later that evening, just when things were calming down, Hakkı and Meliha went at it hammer and tongs again and ruined their dinner. No one spoke a word at the table. And later still, no one slept a wink as Meliha's baby cried all night. Mürvet knew her husband tossed and turned and eventually got up before sunrise. She knew he was getting dressed in the dark but didn't dare open her mouth to ask. He must be going to work early; he'd had no sleep anyway. Seyit shut the door quietly as he left, and Mürvet stared at the first rays of sunlight with bloodshot eyes.

He didn't return that night or the next. The family was at one another's throats. Hakkı was blaming Emine for letting such a man marry into the family, and Emine retaliated by pointing out it was Hakkı and Meliha's domestic problems that had driven the new son-in-law away. They ended up closing ranks against the newcomer all the same: he was the outsider; he was the one with the strange customs and behavior who failed to fit in. Mürvet took to her room in tears. Gossip ran rife in the neighborhood by the end of the first day. The next afternoon the neighboring women flocked over. Everyone wanted to know why the new son-in-law wasn't back and how the bride was faring. No amount of evasiveness on Emine's part helped; she heard the whispers as the women left.

"See, that's what happens when you give your daughter away to a Moskof."

"Bet he's an infidel and all!"

Emine sulked at Mürvet as if it was all her fault.

The rest of the family had already retired when Seyit turned up after supper on the third day. Mürvet gave him a subdued greeting; they went upstairs straightaway, and she broke into tears.

"You must regret getting married, Seyit."

"Whatever makes you say that?"

"You've been gone for days! This isn't normal around here. Tongues are wagging up and down the street. And do you have any idea how worried I was?"

Seyit embraced his wife. The proximity of their bodies couldn't reach over the chasm. He explained slowly and deliberately, "Look, Murka, I told your mother right at the start. This is too far for me. I don't work in an office; it's not like I can work regular hours. It's too far to commute day in, day out. Either we move to Pera or carry on this way."

He released her, sat down on the sofa by the window, leaned back, and stared at her quizzically. She was in a quandary.

"How can I tell my mother, Seyit? And Hakkı Abi? He'll never let me go there!"

"I'm telling you, Murka. I understand your customs, but you might like to come halfway too. I can't enjoy a pleasant meal with conversation and a drink or two. That's what we're used to; even on our darkest day, the table is a place of joy. Even on our worst day, we sing, albeit a sad song at times. I come home to hear Hakkı and Meliha scrapping and then their brat screeches all night next door. As for your sisters, I love them both, but I'm already sick of the sound of children's voices before I've had a child of my own. There's not a single moment's peace in this house. If I wanted to bring a couple of friends home, where would I entertain them? Do you understand me?"

He was right, but Mürvet's problem was raising the topic with her mother. Raise it she did the next morning though. And Emine told Hakkı, who went ballistic as usual, ranting and raving as Mürvet trembled in her room.

"Just what I was afraid of! No way is anyone going to Pera from this house. If he can't cope with the distance, he can divorce the girl and marry someone more up his own street from Pera!"

That night, in the privacy of their bedroom, Mürvet recounted the reaction. Seyit dropped his customary good humor for the first time. "Look, Mürvet, I am wedded to neither your mother nor your brother. I took you as my wife; you are my wedded wife. So long as I am your husband, where I go, there you follow. You've lived as they dictated for all these years; from now on, you will live with me. It's my life you will be sharing; I'm not interested in what anyone else thinks."

A pensive Mürvet curled her lower lip. There was one more thing she had to say. She hesitated and then blurted it out. "But the neighbors are saying really nasty things."

"Oh yeah? Like what?" scoffed Seyit, cocking his head.

She was already regretting it, mortified at having to repeat it for her husband's ears. "Erm...they're saying..."

"Go on, go on! Tell me. Seeing as the whole neighborhood knows it anyway!"

"They're saying, 'That Moskof! Bet he's not even circumcised!'"

Seyit roared with laughter and sat back. "And who was it who said that?"

She was puzzled at his reaction; anyone else would have been outraged! Yet here he was, laughing his head off. With a sigh of relief, she carried on. "Makbule Hanım's husband, Şevki Bey—seems he told her."

Seyit couldn't believe his ears or the mentality of the people around him; it all sounded like a joke. Still chuckling, he teased his wife, "I see...so Şevki Bey told his wife, Makbule Hanım; Makbule Hanım came over and told your mother, your mother told you, and you're telling me. Amazing the number of people interested in my circumcision." He patted the seat next to him. "Come, Murka; sit here. Sit down so that we can sort this out. We have to quash such rumors, after all."

He looked and sounded so solemn that she thought he did want to find a solution. She sat down next to him and waited. It wasn't long before his eyes regained their teasing glint and his lips the usual playful smile. Taking her hand in his, he spoke slowly. "Now, sweetheart, go tell your mother to pass a message to the neighbors. Seeing as Şevki Bey wishes to learn whether I'm circumcised or not, the solution is easy. Tell him to send me his wife one night; I'll show her.

That will sort it out once and for all." He burst out laughing and stroked Mürvet's cheek, hoping to lift her out of her bemusement. "Murka, I couldn't care less what the neighbors think. That's what I was afraid of anyway. It's impossible for us to enjoy any privacy or peace here. We have to have our own life. Do you understand me?"

His adamant tone suggested there was no point in protesting; in that first week, Mürvet had come to acknowledge that her husband did what he said.

So she couldn't wait for morning to come. As soon as Seyit and Hakkı had left for work, she sought her mother and explained the situation—albeit with a good deal of stammering and hesitating.

"You want him that much, eh? Gagging for it, are you?" snapped Emine.

I love my husband, she wanted to reply, *and I don't want to break up*—but that unjust accusation had put her on the spot. All Mürvet wanted was to be with her husband. She spoke in what she hoped was a persuasive tone. "Mother, I'm already married. Wouldn't it be a disgrace to get a divorce? Would you rather I did that?"

"Do you know where he's going to take you? What sort of a life he's offering you? If you leave this house, that will be that. Might as well know you won't be welcome if you come back with your tail between your legs."

With that, Emine walked out, leaving Mürvet gasping for breath. Her mother had said neither yes nor no. Mürvet had to choose between her mother and her husband, a dreadful dilemma that constricted her chest. Thank God Seyit had refrained from pressuring her in the morning. Was it possible he had changed his mind? That would have solved things.

One morning two months after the wedding, Mürvet was sick. The nausea recurred the next morning and the next, alerting her to the fact that she was pregnant. It was not something she was ready for; they had yet to set up their own home; they had yet to enjoy each other's company on their own. And she'd never had time to herself, in actual fact, looking after her sisters all her life and recently her baby nephew too. The neighborhood midwife quashed all her hopes that she might have been mistaken. She was due mid-June.

Seyit didn't appear to be over the moon at hearing the news, although he embraced her with a tender kiss at once. He sounded sad on her behalf. "My little Murka! You're still a child yourself. I wish you'd had a little time to grow up first."

He didn't need to say it. She was painfully aware of her own shortcomings, of the gaping abyss between their education, experience, and sophistication. She was desperate to learn, to catch up with her husband, but was held back by the taboos, bans, and sins that had accompanied her upbringing, not to mention her family's disapprobation. She was caught between two worlds.

Unwilling to spook her, Seyit was in no hurry to introduce Mürvet to his friends or the life he had been living up to now. Instead, he spoke of life in Russia so that she may begin to appreciate what his expectations were.

These tales of his family and home, his childhood, family home, growing up in Saint Petersburg, the Tsarskoye Selo house, troikas sliding over the snow, their bells jingling, the Nevsky Prospekt ablaze with lights, operas, and ballet shows all transported Mürvet to a world she couldn't even begin to imagine. She cried like a baby listening to accounts of the Carpathian front, the revolution, the massacre of the tsar's family, her husband's escape, and the youngest brother left on the shore. His suffering broke her heart, but she had neither the words nor the wisdom to dress his wounds.

Seyit freely spoke of his relations with the fair sex too, starting with the baroness in Tsarskoye Selo, and moving on to the alluring gypsy dancers and the lovely Larissa in the forest of Yalta. He left nothing out, and Mürvet wept tears of jealousy in Seyit's arms; covering her with kisses, he would swear all that was left in the past. Far from bringing them closer, however, his intention to hide nothing from her only backfired. She ate her heart out at the thought of those lovely foreigners, each and every one better educated, more beautiful, sophisticated, and alluring than she was, tormenting herself that they had all embraced and kissed and even shared a bed and delighted him with their bodies. By the time Seyit realized how much these tales hurt her, the damage was done. She grew distant, consumed by jealousy, in a permanent tearful sulk.

The worst blow came with the change in his voice when he spoke of Shura; every time she heard it, Mürvet regretted having married him in the first place. Jealous as she was of all the others, her jealousy of Shura was beyond compare. Seyit described a breathtaking beauty with long blond hair and blue eyes. Shura had been nearly sixteen when they had first met, which would make her younger than Mürvet now, and which meant this particular rival had to be at the height of her glory now. To add insult to injury, Shura plainly held a special place in his heart. It was an extraordinarily disturbing thought.

Mürvet had another, much more valid reason. Seyit's other flings had all stayed behind in Russia; they were no more than a memory now. Shura, on the other hand, was here in Istanbul, just a stone's throw away.

Mürvet sought in vain for some affirmation in his voice that the affair was over, and in the absence of any such reassurance, she felt awful.

There was something else. She couldn't stop herself from secretly admiring this particular rival. Shura had gamely shared all his suffering all this time; left her home, family, and country behind; and put up with years of hardship and poverty, all for the love of Seyit. At times Mürvet wished they could swap places. Except she'd never be brave enough—she could never leave her mother or even step out without her brother's permission. As for embarking upon an adventure of any kind? Forget about it. Every time she tormented herself with these thoughts, her jealousy intensified. Her husband had survived the most unforgettable and irreversible upheaval in his life with that woman. Shura's image would probably never leave them alone.

Worst of all, Mürvet couldn't be sure that her husband had forsaken Shura, given how he spent all day in Pera and frequently stayed the nights too.

They had been married for nearly three months when, one late November morning, Seyit grabbed his wife by the waist and kissed her as she was drawing back the curtains. "Get dressed; we're going out this morning."

"Where?"

"Out."

"Out?" repeated Mürvet, thrilled and not a little apprehensive. "But where?"

"Don't worry—not somewhere wicked. We're going to visit Selim and his wife. Come on; let's not tarry."

She opened the wardrobe eagerly and stared. Seyit spoke beside her. "Wear the blue dress I sent you for our engagement, the one with the lace collar."

"Isn't it a bit too chic for the morning?" she asked, picking up the dress she'd not dared to wear since her mother's rebuke.

Seyit kissed her lips. "My dear Murka, a chic lady is chic day or night. Mornings included."

"I never wore anything this fancy to visit them before!" she protested with a bashful smile.

"Things have changed: now that you're my wife, you'll look the way I want."

And before long she did. Her belly was beginning to swell a little, but the dress was still a good fit. They set off in a hired carriage. She soon realized this was an unfamiliar route and ventured to ask, "Seyit, where are we going exactly?"

"Got something to do first."

His silence suggested a surprise. Mürvet's knowledge of Istanbul ended at Karaköy; she was fascinated by the difference in the fabric of the city. The timber houses of varying sizes flanking the road gave way to splendid edifices in stone liberally adorned with marble columns, carved portals, and statues. Shop windows displayed hats, scarves, and fabrics of unimaginable loveliness. Mürvet's eyes were like saucers as she stared, enchanted by the colors and elegance of this new world. Smiling, Seyit took her hand, thrilled at her awestruck interest. His wife was like a pupil learning a new word every day.

The carriage eventually drew to a halt outside a building in Kalyoncu Kulluğu Street. He held out his hand to help her alight.

"Here," said Seyit. "This is where I work."

So this was the place she'd been dying to see. So this was Pera, the place her mother decried as a despicable den of iniquity.

So this was where Seyit had lived with Shura in the flat upstairs!

Seized by an indescribable fit of jealousy, Mürvet silently gritted her teeth. No, she wasn't going to torment herself with images of her husband and his great love living here, drinking and making love.

Seyit guided her inside. What it lacked in width, it made up for in depth as several interconnecting rooms led to a large garden at the rear. Four young women were working in the first room and two more in the next. *Probably Russians*, thought Mürvet, given Seyit spoke to them in a foreign tongue before leading her into what had to be his office.

"Remove your coat, Murka, and wait here for a while. They'll bring you coffee. I've got something to attend to; I'll be back soon."

As he kissed her on the cheek and left, Mürvet cast a sneaky glance at the other women watching her husband. Two looked quite young, possibly only a year or two older than she was, but they all moved with a natural grace...and they were all lovely. So her husband was working with these lovely women day in and day out and sometimes even stayed the night. Her stomach was cramping. She saw her black ankle-length cloak for what it was: out of place, inviting ridicule. She slipped it off. That was better. She had to look even more attractive than the rest in her lacy silk dress and diamond brooch and bracelet. She crossed her legs in a pose she assumed suited her outfit.

A window in the wall opened to the room next door, where a man was working at a desk behind a mountain of ledgers and other papers. Amused by the sight of the somber-looking clerk in thick-rimmed glasses and sleeve protectors, Mürvet smiled to herself.

A carriage halted outside. She looked up, thinking it was Seyit, and got up for a closer look. Two ladies alighted, made for the entrance, and opened the door of the office. One was in her early twenties, and the other had to be a couple of years older. They could have walked out of a magazine in their tailored suits, tilted berets, and capes over their arms. They were both beautiful, although the younger was by far the more stunning. Her golden-blond hair waved onto her shoulders. She moved with confident grace into the middle of the room, caught Mürvet's eye, smiled at the bookkeeper who had come out to greet her, and asked in accented Turkish, "Where's Seyt Eminof?"

Mürvet wasn't at all happy that this foreign woman sought *her* husband by name. Yet she couldn't keep her eyes off this beauty. Suddenly her chic outfit felt overdressed next to this blonde.

The foreigner started chatting to the Russian madams in the other room in a relaxed manner that suggested they all knew one another well.

It was the first time Mürvet had been in her husband's office, and she was flustered by the overwhelming presence of this sophisticated foreigner who seemed to know everyone, wandering around as though she belonged here. Mürvet felt like a sad, insignificant little child in her chair. Seyit's accounts of Shura raced through her mind. Just then one of the ironers entered the office, and Mürvet asked her, "Who are these ladies?"

"Ironed here. Must want a job again." The woman shrugged, assuming an air of knowledge she didn't possess; her Turkish wasn't brilliant either.

Mürvet kept watching the blonde surreptitiously.

Then her prey bolted to the door, opened it, and breathlessly yelled a string of words, the only one that Mürvet could make out being *Seyt!*

The owner of the name looked astonished at seeing who it was. The woman he'd been longing for throughout his lonely days and nights was finally here.

"Good morning, Seyt."

"Shura!"

Seyt hastened to Mürvet's side at once. Shura halted and resisted the temptation to move closer; the girl she'd ignored just now had to mean something to Seyt.

"Is it true, Seyt—what I heard?" Shura asked, her voice calm.

"What did you hear?" countered Seyt unemotionally.

"That you got married?" Shura's gaze wandered over Mürvet, who was at a loss for what to do and how to act. They had to be talking about her. The blonde's eyes were filling up. So she wasn't the only one whose heart was breaking.

As if to punish the lover who'd tormented him for a long time, Seyt leaned down to plant a kiss on Mürvet's cheek and laid his hand on her shoulder—a clear indication of his choice. "Yes—this is my wife."

"Seyt..."

She didn't finish. Her eyes had filled, but she wasn't crying. Holding her head up, she walked to the door, exchanged a couple of words with Seyt, and left.

In total silence, a despondent Seyt gazed at the door for a while and gave an abstracted sigh.

"Did you see Shura?"

Mürvet feigned a nonchalance she hadn't felt, certainly not for the past quarter of an hour. "Didn't notice." After a pause, she couldn't contain herself. "Why was she even here?"

"We had an account to settle," answered Seyt in a tired voice, riffling through the documents on his desk.

It was a far from satisfactory answer. What Mürvet needed from her husband just now was a reassurance that he loved her and had no regrets about marrying her. More importantly, she needed to know he had nothing to do with other women any longer.

He said nothing.

She also knew she couldn't hold back anymore. She flew out, ran to the bathroom at the end, locked the door, and started bawling. She had no idea how long she stayed there. At long last she calmed down; splashed cold water over her face, streaked with kohl and reddened from crying; reapplied her makeup; and had to concede that her swollen eyes and nose told a different story.

Meanwhile, Seyit stood immobile. How long had it been since Shura had left? Two minutes? Perhaps twenty? Perhaps even longer. All thirty-one years of his life flashed by. His memories had receded another step or two with her. He could smell her cologne and recalled the touch of her hand when she had opened the door. All his past had been in his hands a moment ago and had gone away now. He felt unbelievably lonely. Disappointingly, marriage had solved nothing. He wished his wife were here right now, running her fingers through his hair, lifting his spirits, comforting him about the loss of a life he would never have again, cuddling him, kissing him, making him forget his yearning. But he was alone. Utterly alone. His young wife was incapable of understanding him.

Mürvet returned on tiptoe, averting her gaze to hide the signs of her crying. She slipped her cloak over her dress.

"Come on; let's take you home," said Seyit wearily as he stood up to help.

They returned in total silence.

"Please let's not mention what happened today. I don't want Mother to hear," begged Mürvet as they alighted outside the door.

Later that night, when they were in bed, she sensed she would never possess her husband in full, that there would always remain some elusive spot in his mind and soul. She wished she'd never married. And now she was going to have a baby. How would she cope, with all these women around him? At her age, and with her devastating inexperience in all matters? She burst into sobs.

Seyit couldn't sleep either. He wanted to talk to his wife, tell her everything about his past life, and then make love. Perhaps then he would be free of the weight of the memories threatening to crush him. But broaching the topic with Mürvet now would only cause her grief; she would yell and cry and alert the whole household. They had no chance of privacy in this house. No chance at all of getting to know his wife or building a warm relationship.

Shura would have shared his silence whenever he was troubled. Gentle and warm, she would have waited until he spoke and dispelled the worries besetting him with her love. He missed her so. She would have consoled him if she were here now.

Mürvet's sobs brought him out of his thoughts. He gathered her hair spread upon the pillow, put his arm under her neck, and drew her to him. Smelling her fresh skin cleansed with rosewater, he kissed her wet cheeks.

My God! he thought. *I love her too!*

Caressing her swelling belly, he nuzzled her neck and cheeks. He appreciated the jealousy that was eating his little wife but sought in vain for the words to soothe her. Instead he rocked her in his arms until she stilled. When she finally felt safe enough to fall asleep in his arms, Seyit stared at the ceiling, pondering what course their life would take.

In the morning, Mürvet awakened to the sight of her husband dressed and ready to leave. He was staring out of the window, hands in his pockets. He came over and gave her a kiss when he saw her open her eyes. "Come on, Murka; get dressed. We're going."

"Where, Seyit, so early in the morning?"

"To our new home."

"To our new home?"

"We ought to have gone yesterday, but it wasn't to be. Get ready."

"How am I going to tell Mother?"

"Tell her what? Mürvet, I'm your husband, your lawfully wedded husband, and I am taking you away. To home, to our home. Our own place. Somewhere we can be on our own, do what we want. Why worry about your mother?"

Mürvet recalled the events of the previous day. She didn't trust him, and her mother's warnings rang in her ears. She had no idea where this home was yet instinctively knew too many questions would only annoy him. She loved him madly, but her handsome husband was a proven womanizer. At least here Mürvet would have her mother's and brother's support if things got too sticky. But once she'd left, she would never be able to turn to them. She stared at the floor, brooding, until Seyit perched at the edge of the bed.

"Look, Murka—this is our chance. Our chance to get to know each other and love each other more. We'll dine tête-à-tête; you'll be the mistress of your own home. We won't have to answer to anyone else. Do you understand me? We'll be happier." Chuckling, he traced her cheek with his finger. "Come on; don't be scared: we'll live among Muslims."

At a loss for what to do, Mürvet dressed listlessly. She didn't want to lose her husband, but she couldn't decide how to break it to her mother either.

Morning prayers over, Emine was having her coffee. Mürvet stood at the door to gather her wits, a little tongue tied at her mother's deliberately slow turn of head with a quizzical stare. She composed herself, swallowed, and heard the words tumble out. "Mother, we're leaving."

"Where?" Emine's chilly question indicated she knew this didn't refer to an outing.

"I don't know. Wherever he takes me."

Emine turned her head to look out of the window, sitting unperturbed to all intents and purposes, but when she spoke again, it was in a peeved voice. "Fine. I'm not sending you on your own though. Take Necmiye. She may be only ten, but she's your sister."

"I'd be delighted to, Mother," said Mürvet, scrambling for a response.

Emine turned her brimming eyes to the dregs in her cup. "Well, go with God then."

Mürvet hesitated. Her mother wasn't even looking her in the eye. She wanted to go over and kiss her hand, but Emine sat in such stony silence that she didn't dare. She asked almost too softly to be heard, "Have you nothing to give me, Mother?"

"What? You want furniture? Take your bed and your trunk." She stood up, went to her room, and returned carrying something wrapped in newsprint. She held it out.

"What is it, Mother?"

"From my own trousseau. A coffee set. Don't say your mother never gave you anything."

Seyit turned up at the door with a phaeton and a cart, which took all their goods with room to spare. Mürvet silently wondered if every bride felt so lost on leaving the family home. Everything seemed to be a problem in their marriage.

Thankfully Seyit was happy that Necmiye was coming with them; she was his favorite among his wife's family, and she reminded him of his sister Havva.

Mürvet kissed her mother's hand before mounting the phaeton. "Mother, you'll come to visit, won't you?"

"If you deign to give us the address, why not?"

Seyit shook his mother-in-law's hand and mounted. Necmiye sitting between the newlyweds, they set off toward their new home.

Loneliness, Unshared

THE TWO HORSE-DRAWN vehicles drew to a halt outside number 7 in Hacı Hüsrev Hill. A delightful two-story house in a garden awaited its new owners descending from the phaeton.

Still bemused at having left the family home, Mürvet wandered inside. The house consisted of a kitchen, a bathroom, and a room on the ground floor and a large bedroom and a second one only fit to be called a boxroom upstairs.

Seyit had arranged for a thorough cleaning a few days previously, which didn't stop Mürvet from going over it once again. The cart was unloaded, the marital bed was placed in the larger of the rooms upstairs, and a temporary floor mattress made Necmiye's bed in the smaller one. As Mürvet made the beds, placing the pillows in lacy cases, she kept telling herself she was now the mistress of her own home. Out of her trunk came her crocheted nets and thicker curtains for the windows.

Refusing to succumb to the gloom of the descending evening, Mürvet kept a sunny front for her sister's benefit. Seyit lit the gas lamp, went out, and returned before long, laden with Russian food from Volkov Restaurant for their first evening meal in their new home. No makeshift table of newspapers laid on the floor could dampen his cheerful spirits; opening a bottle of vodka, he pinched Mürvet's cheek with a wink.

"Oh, Seyit! Not in front of Necmiye!" she whispered, embarrassed by this display of affection in front of her sister.

"In my own home, Murka, I can fondle my wife whenever I want, all right?"

"Hush, Seyit, please!"

"Have a glass with me?"

"I don't drink, Seyit."

"Never mind. I'll drink on my own then. *Na zdorovie!*" he said, but he looked crestfallen.

Mürvet stayed silent, not knowing how to cheer him up. Since Necmiye wasn't much more talkative, Seyit felt as though he were babysitting a couple of children. He poured himself another drink as his wife and sister-in-law cleared up.

"Go on; go to bed. You must be tired, you two."

Mürvet washed up and went upstairs with her sister, wondering why their relationship was so up and down all the time. *God*, she prayed when she went to bed, *please don't make me miss Mother's house.*

Seyit sat with his back against the wall, alone in the empty room downstairs until the bottle of vodka was gone. He pulled his knees up, rested his arms and head, and pondered. Happiness seemed to elude him, and he didn't know what to do. This was their first night in their new home, a night when he'd been looking forward to a good meal and a few drinks with his wife and then embracing in bed and dreaming of a better future.

All he had for company instead was this tumbler in his hand. He could feel the alcohol dilate his veins. He felt hot. He got up to open the window, took a few deep breaths, and filled his lungs with the bitter cold of December. He lit a cigarette, watching the flame of the match until it nearly burned his fingers. He was restless. There was something missing in his life, an enormous void that he couldn't fill. He started humming a song in Russian. The lyrics, the sips of vodka, and the cold rushing in from the window joined forces to transport him back to Saint Petersburg.

The next morning, Mürvet awakened alone. Seyit was nowhere to be seen, and even his pillow looked untouched. She cried in secret so that Necmiye wouldn't see. There, her mother was right after all! Her husband had got up and left her, all alone in this strange place.

Only an hour later, tears of joy replaced those of despair when she answered the door to find a cartful of furniture Seyit had sent home. Mürvet watched, happy as a child as the dining table, chairs, mirror, console, china, spirit cooker, and foodstuffs were unloaded. Together with Necmiye, she pushed and pulled and changed the arrangement this way and that. There was no one to interfere or tell her what to do. This was her home. These were her things, and she could place them wherever she wanted. So she did, singing to cheer Necmiye up.

Much later, still musing on how much she loved and missed her husband, Mürvet noticed the time. It was nearly evening. She cooked the evening meal and even prepared some mezes.

On returning home, Seyit breathed a sigh of relief at the enthusiastic welcome. Mürvet looked radiant enough to make him forget the despondency of the previous night. He smiled when he saw the beautifully arranged table by the window. Things seemed to be on the up. Giving his wife a kiss, he went to wash.

It was a wonderful dinner. For the first time since their wedding, they were enjoying a good meal free from the bile of domestic discord, talking of things that interested them. Mürvet even indulged her husband and drank a glass of wine to keep him company. Halfway through the glass, she felt warmer, a pleasant dizziness. Her eyes were blazing now. Seyit had just finished his meze. Gazing fondly at her sparkling eyes and reddened cheeks as she got up to get the meat, he grabbed her slender hand as she reached out to collect his plate and pulled her to him. Startled as she was by this uninhibited—and thoroughly unaccustomed—show of intimacy, she bit her tongue. Thankfully Necmiye had already retired for the night. Seyit turned sideways in his chair, wrapped his arms around Mürvet's expanding waist, and rested his head on the pronounced swelling of her belly. Placing a kiss over the navel, he nuzzled against her warmth. Unwilling to protest yet still too timid to respond in kind, she drew back even as she wanted to hold his head and shoulders.

"The meat's on the grill, Seyit; it'll burn."

"All right, go on—let's not burn the meat," he teased, caressing her hips.

He broke into the wide grin of a contented man watching his wife's back.

Things did seem to be on the up indeed. Seyit sent home a few pieces of furniture every day and brought food home in the evenings. Whenever he was late home, he ordered their meal from the Volkov.

His parcels often contained a gift or two for Mürvet and Necmiye. But there was a thorn in Mürvet's side; Necmiye had niggled and whined a little at first, but recently she'd been crying all day long. It broke Mürvet's heart; she had raised her little sister, but clearly Necmiye missed their mother.

Mürvet broached the subject with Seyit, who was happy for them to visit their mother. The two joyous sisters got ready and set off, and Emine was delighted to see her daughters. Mürvet explained Necmiye was terribly home-sick. "She doesn't want to come back with me, Mother; she cries all day long."

"Fine," replied Emine, smugly petting her youngest at her feet. "Necmiye stays; take Fethiye along. She's fourteen. She can cope better."

Uncertain of Seyit's reaction, Mürvet was still too timid to protest—which might offend Fethiye, at any rate.

In the afternoon, Mürvet and Fethiye arrived at the Kasımpaşa house. Seyit did chafe at his mother-in-law's interference, as Mürvet had suspected. Would his wife's family ever leave them alone? He felt trapped. From time to time, espe-cially when he'd had a little to drink, he was overcome with the need to talk of his old life in Russia; whenever he did, Mürvet's eyes filled at once, and she burst into tears. She couldn't cope with his old life, with all he'd lost. More importantly, she was beside herself with jealousy whenever he spoke of things they had not shared.

As a result, much as he would have loved to, Seyit didn't dare invite his Russian friends home, nor could they meet out: any suggestions to go out were met with vehement objections as if he'd made an indecent proposal. Happy as he was to wait until she got used to his ways, Seyit longed for the dinner tables where drinks and music flowed and where sorrow was shared.

Their first guests were Gül and İbrahim.

Like hundreds of thousands of others, they had managed to flee in 1920. Born and raised in the mansion of the Lord of Baku, Gül Hanım was an exquisite young beauty with delicate features. İbrahim Bey, an unassuming man who paled in comparison, came from a Crimean village called Korbuk. When the lord was killed by a shot that came through the window, Gül had fled the Bolsheviks be-sieging the mansion and somehow made it to Wrangel's fleet. İbrahim was one of the thousands on board. Like thousands of penniless female émigrés, Gül had married the first man who offered her protection, regardless of the disparity in their backgrounds. They now had two sons called Sermet and Rüstem.

Mürvet was spellbound by Gül Hanım's grace and gentle good manners. They lived close enough for the two women to visit frequently.

Mürvet may have been grateful for Gül's friendship, but it was different for Seyit. Even in his poorest days, he'd managed to enjoy something of the good life so far. The tranquil—nay, prim—atmosphere of home could never rival the temptations of Pera. Loving his wife wasn't enough to solve everything. Since she could not yet fit in with the lifestyle he preferred, he decided not to rush her.

It was January. The bitter winds of the past week had finally given way to a heavy snowfall that covered the stairs, the windows, everywhere. The snow gave Seyit a new lease of life; he was cheerfully chopping wood in the garden in trousers and an undershirt. Mürvet watched his broad back and muscular arms swinging the ax, desperately jealous of women she would never know.

"You'll catch cold, Seyit. Who'd go out in this weather half naked, for God's sake?" she chided as he came in carrying a basket of logs and shook the snow off.

"You don't catch cold in the snow," replied Seyit.

"You don't?"

"I've told you, haven't I? Sled dogs in Russia dig a hole in the snow to sleep in. They're toasty warm when they wake." Chuckling, he set about cleaning the stove with a song on his lips.

Winter or summer, his hot baths always ended with a bucketful of ice-cold water from the well. Her querying gaze often elicited an explanation such as, "Whenever it snowed, we swam in the lake in the Yalta forests. You have to acclimatize the body to the cold at all times so that you're prepared for the day when you can't get warm."

Oblivious to her growing irritation with these frequent reminiscences of a time *before, before her,* in Russia or here, he never stopped mentioning them.

One day Seyit left quite late; it was nearly noon. He kissed his wife and walked out, intending to proceed on foot. He loved hearing the snow crunch under his shoes, loved this pure-white world. He burst into his favorite tune.

Mürvet waited in vain at his usual time of arrival. And waited. And waited. She reheated dinner, fed Fethiye, and put her to bed.

She sat at the window to wait. It was still snowing. Snowdrifts had risen halfway up the garden gate. By midnight, she was clutching her handkerchief, unable to peel her tearful eyes away from the road, tormenting herself in a fit of jealousy. The ticktock of the carriage clock counted the minutes.

It was past two o'clock when a knock came at the door. She leaped up eagerly and let him in. Seyit grabbed her tipsily, but being in no mood to humor him after hours of crying, she recoiled. Seyit doffed his hat, shook the snow off his hair, and broke into a merry chatter. Mürvet averted her bloodshot eyes, unable to understand what he was saying. He was speaking in Russian. With no response from her, he eventually paused, slapped his forehead, and chuckled at his own mistake. He cuddled and kissed her.

"Really! What am I...for a moment...forgot." He slurred his words. Caressing her cheeks, he went on, "Come on, my Murka; you must be sleepy. Go to bed if you like. I'd really appreciate it though if you could warm up some water. I want to take a bath."

With a hug and a kiss on her cheek, he strode off to the bathroom. Mürvet went into the kitchen wordlessly to put the big kettle on the cooker.

Thoroughly sobered, Seyit mounted the stairs in his bathrobe, singing and whistling merrily. By the time Mürvet arrived in the bedroom, he was lying in bed, watching his cigarette smoke. He smiled at his wife—who was in no mood to reciprocate. She didn't know what to say or do. All she wanted to do was to bawl her eyes out. Choking on her sobs, she turned her back to him, leaned against the door, and burst into tears. Seyit put his cigarette down, leaped up, hugged her, turned her to face him, and stared. His heart broke at the sight of the little mouth pinched in disgust at his betrayal, the eyes brimming with tears, and the nostrils quivering in rage. He had hurt her again. He wanted to make it up to her, to make her feel better, but it was so hard to explain. Would she understand if he said he'd met Shura, they'd chatted a bit, had a few drinks, and somehow ended up making love, but it really didn't mean much? All it would achieve was to fill Mürvet's innocent, jealous heart with suffering. He cupped her head and rested it against his chest. Exhausted with crying and waiting for hours, she didn't resist. A dizzying smell of soap and lotion rose from his warm skin under the bathrobe. Seyit carried on caressing her hair and cheeks. He wanted to say something... but it didn't come. "Oh, Murka! My childish little Murka!"

Mürvet was still crying. Seyit's mind went to the other woman, the tearful parting not so long ago. He missed her already. But he also loved the woman hungry for his love, her head on his chest, his baby in her belly. Stroking and kissing her cheeks, he tried to soothe her.

This was a hell made for three people. He was miserable, and so were the two women he loved. He knew he didn't have much choice to rectify the situation.

His mind was reeling even after Mürvet fell into a deep sleep.

Despite their earlier pact to stay apart, he still met Shura—despite her un-equivocal stance once she'd heard of the baby on the way. She had put her foot down; they could never get together again. The occasional fling was one thing; marriage was another. She felt betrayed. In fact, she had announced she had no reason to stay in Turkey any longer. And yet, they had still fallen into each other's arms and made passionate love. Afterward, however, they had parted with no promises or hope. Perhaps it was time to make a choice once and for all and renounce Shura for good. Then he closed his eyes and shook that notion off. No, he could never renounce her. Only she could make that decision.

He glanced at his young wife in sighing slumber and stroked her hair, his heart full of compassion. He could have been angrier; he'd said time and again he didn't want children. That he didn't feel ready to become a father. Now they'd have to deal with a baby too in the midst of all this turmoil. He felt trapped again. If only Mürvet weren't pregnant! Then he could have made a better deci-sion, with a clear mind. In all this time, Shura had never burdened him in this way. Why hadn't Mürvet managed it then? In his heart he knew he was being unfair, that precautions could have been taken—which he had done all his life as advised by his father. Mürvet had been totally ignorant of even the most basic tenets of conjugal relations, never mind avoiding pregnancy.

He sat up in bed, elbows on his knees, face in his hands, as if to compress the impotence he felt into that small area between his palms.

At the end of January, they moved across the road to a slightly larger place. It belonged to the same landlord and also had a garden but benefited from two extra bedrooms, which Seyit thought would come in handy for a growing family.

It was around the same time that Mürvet's family house in Tatlıkuyu was sold. She insisted on contributing to the family budget with the thirty gold liras that was her share, but Seyit was adamant. He wouldn't take it; instead, he said she should save it for a rainy day.

They lacked for nothing. Having grown up watching every penny, Mürvet now basked in the luxury of ready meals and constant flow of good food supplies.

Her wardrobe was full of new dresses and shoes, and Seyit eventually forbade her from wearing the cloak. On this particular matter, like thousands of progressive Turks, he referred to Latife Hanım: Atatürk's elegant wife had shown the way by discarding the old hijab-style coverings in favor of stylish modern outfits.

"Are you going to set tongues wagging about the ghoul I'd married? Garbing yourself like a cockroach! I never want to see you in this stuff again."

Rather predictably, the first time Mürvet visited her mother in a dainty fur-trimmed hat and coat, she was torn off a strip. "What do you think you're wearing? How dare you turn up, hair and face uncovered for all to see? What will the neighbors say, when you left in hijab? Never come to my house in this getup again, Mürvet."

On returning home in tears, she was doubly hurt to note her husband was out. Instead of seeking consolation in Seyit's arms, she spent all night crying at her mother's words and her husband's absence. At such times no amount of elegant dresses, shoes, or expensive jewelry meant anything. All she wanted was to be happy, to have her husband by her side, and to not fall out with her mother. No one understood her. She sat on the lookout for a silhouette to appear in the snow. Moving closer to Pera hadn't helped. Seyit still came and went as he pleased. He might spend a very happy evening home and not turn up at all the next night, or only come back in the wee hours. He seemed to live a double life.

It was one of those nights.

The room upstairs from the laundry in Kalyoncu Kulluğu Street was in darkness except for the beam of light that caressed the falling snow on its way to the windowpane, passed between the open curtains, and fell upon the face of the fully dressed man lying on the bed. The smoke rising from his cigarette glowed in the deceptive warmth of the gas burning in the light outside.

He had wanted to be alone after yet another night of partying at the Pera Palace. Mürvet would be waiting in tears again, and he was in no mood to put up with weeping, immaturity, or jealousy. All he wanted to do was to think on his own in the dark. He needed to talk to and listen to himself. Did he actually love his wife? he wondered. Yes, he did. That didn't mean he was prepared to fully commit. He missed his friends, life, homes, and land he would never see again. What he needed was love that would offer him all the affection and warmth of everything he was missing, and that could only be Shura. He knew no other woman could offer him the same peace that she did. Sadly, they both had other people in their lives now. Could they possibly join as one in the same love if they got together? Did she miss him in the same way right now? He needed to feel her in his arms and embrace her. He stubbed out his cigarette, laced his hands behind his head, and closed his eyes. Memories soothed him somewhat. Sooner or later he would have to return home to his wife. Tomorrow if not today, or the day after. And he had to come up with a lie to explain why he had stayed away. He preferred saying nothing instead of lying, except that didn't stop Mürvet's insufferable silent tears.

It had been hours, and he still couldn't sleep. He was exhausted. He wanted to forget everything and lose himself. He got up and walked toward the balcony at the rear. He opened the door, and snow piling up on the doorstep fell inside. He picked up a bottle from a basket covered in snow. He came back to bed, carrying the ice-cold vodka, and stretched out. The crystal tumbler was filled and refilled over and over again. It solved nothing. He loved and pitied Mürvet but longed for Shura. An irresistible yearning.

He made his mind up. He would see Shura the next day.

***

Five minutes before the black clouds looming overhead unleashed a torrential downpour, the *Closed* sign was hung on the door of the Zezemsky Pharmacy. The young woman at the till was totting up the day's takings as the sales assistant locked drawers and cupboards one by one.

A rap on the window made her look up. She would know that silhouette anywhere; she caught her breath as her right hand pressed down on her chest in an attempt to still the pounding of her heart.

The assistant called out from behind the locked door, "Closed—we're closed now."

Shura dashed out from behind the till. "It's all right; it's for me."

With a shrug, the assistant resumed his task. Shura opened the door to her drenched lover and invited him in with a wounded look. "Come in, Seyt."

Once he was settled in the wooden chair opposite, she went back to the methodical scrutiny of the figures on the sheet in front of her. Seyit's heart ached at the glints on her golden hair and the hurt on her gentle face. He was overwhelmed by a desire to take her in his arms and nuzzle her hair, face, and neck. Uneasy at the thought of someone else in her life, he waited patiently; they would soon be alone together.

Time seemed to drag its feet. The rain beating at the shop window sounded unnaturally loud in the silence inside, occasionally broken by the jangle of the bunch of keys in the assistant's hand.

Seyit knew he'd missed Shura more than he could have imagined—missed her and everything about her. He longed to draw in her voice, gaze, smile, smell, and warmth, like a long-awaited breath.

At long last the two employees started turning out the lights in the pharmacy. Seyit stood up. He had no idea what would happen next or what to say. Perhaps they'd walk out the door and simply go their separate ways. He held her umbrella as Shura locked the door. They set off side by side, at first in total silence, as if neither knew what to say. Seyit moved the umbrella to his other hand and grabbed hers; she flinched but didn't pull her hand away.

"Seyt. This isn't right."

"Holding your hand?"

"Not just that; you know what I mean. This...thing—it's all wrong."

"What would you rather we did?"

"I don't know. Maybe it's best we stop seeing each other."

"Are you sure that's what you want?"

Seyit clasped her hand tighter. At first there was no reply. He halted, planted himself before her, and stared at her welling eyes.

"Seyt, you're the one who married another woman. You're the one who's going to become a father. There is no room in your life for me any longer."

There was nothing to say. It was all true—except for the bit about no room in his life. They walked on, still hand in hand. Now that it was raining even harder, Seyit moved to hail a cab at the corner, but Shura stopped him. "I want to walk."

"Then I'll walk you there," he said, taking her silence as consent.

They walked side by side without a word until they arrived at 32 Altın Bakkal Street. He opened the door with the key she'd pulled out of her bag, stood aside to let her in, and only spoke as he laid the keys in her palm. "Funny how we can't find anything to say to each other."

"So it is...very funny." Shura halted with a foot on the bottom step.

Seyit pushed through the door to join her. "Shura, darling, I had things to discuss with you. But I guess this is not a good time." He held out his hand. "I guess you want to be alone. Good-bye."

Their hands met. A cold touch. It was time to part.

At that featherlight touch, their hands grew warmer. Seyit leaned down to give her a kiss on one cheek. Then on the other...and took her in his arms when her lips found his cheek. Their self-control vanished. They fell into each other's arms, breathless kisses making up for the time wasted in silence. As they unlocked the door to the flat and stepped in, Seyit hesitated; he knew Shura shared the flat with her sister and brother. Shura read his mind.

"Tinochka's going to be late; she's playing in two restaurants tonight, and Vladimir's out."

Seyit enveloped her in his arms. "What's happened to us, Shurochka? What's happened to us?"

"You know, Seyt, I miss those days. When we lived in Sinop, when we'd first arrived in Istanbul."

"Like a fairy tale, all in the past now." Seyit smiled and gave her a kiss.

"When we only belonged to each other."

Staring into her eyes, aware that they shared the same loneliness, he said, "We always belong to each other, Shura, and always shall, no matter what. We are in each other's blood, in each other's memories. That will never change no matter what the conditions."

He wiped the tears rolling down her cheeks and kissed her cheeks. When their lips met, they both knew what would happen. Hours of love that would solve nothing. Nothing would change. Other than taking refuge in their own world, their love, and reliving the past once again—albeit fleetingly.

Farewell,
Spring 1924

N O AMOUNT OF alcohol would help him sleep. He had nightmares whenever he dozed off. He felt he was losing control of his own life, drifting between night and day. At the time he fled Russia, he'd thought he was embarking upon an adventure on his own, that he'd only be responsible for his own safety. How could he have been so wrong! Everything he did now, every decision he made, affected two women. Two women...so uniquely beautiful and so important to his happiness—each in her own way. There were the flings he rarely saw a second time, none of whom allayed the dreadful sense of loneliness that plagued him. He had secretly hoped Mürvet would help him assimilate in his new country. But she was so young, such a child still, that Seyit had to teach her everything day in and day out. She had yet to shake off the oppressive customs inculcated in her. Seyit was fed up with the jealousy, anxieties, and crying fits.

Shura was his only link to his home country, past, childhood, and daredevil youth, his only connection to a long-lost life he would never stop missing. She was the only witness to, and his only partner in, an indescribable romance, a thrilling adventure pierced by wounds and heartbreak. But now everything was rapidly changing. Neither Shura's presence helped with the homesickness nor Mürvet's love made him feel at home.

Except for one thing. He had married an innocent child and invited her to share in his destiny. The young girl who had accompanied him on his way out of the Alushta coast, on the other hand, had abandoned her own family and country out of love. She had come to a totally alien land to be with him, had uncomplainingly put up with all their trials and tribulations. She was also decent enough to share at least some of the responsibility for the way they had drifted apart, regardless of the hurt his marriage to another must have caused. Sweet, beautiful, devoted Shura: she would always be special, one who long since deserved to be happy. That happiness would clearly elude her in Istanbul under these conditions. It was beholden upon him to persuade her to leave, to go to Paris as she'd always wanted to. It was going to be tough, but he had to do it for her sake.

He was confident this was the right decision. Carefully, so as not to awaken Mürvet from her deep slumber, he rose from bed, got dressed, and left. On his way toward Pera, he repeatedly came close to changing his mind.

But no. No more would he repeat that mistake. Shura deserved her own life. He walked on.

***

Suffused with the first rays of the new day, everything in the bedroom gradually took shape and color: the satin curtains, the console, the mirror above it, a perfume bottle, a strand of pearls. The sheer mosquito net over the brass bed was drawn back, and the bedspread had slid to the floor.

The blond man shifted to his side to gaze at the young woman, rose on his elbow, and placed a kiss on her hair. His fingers trailed softly on her shoulders and back, careful not to wake her. How long had it been since he'd met this exquisite creature? Six months, eight at the most. This foreign woman in another foreign land was much more than an infatuation; she was an obsession now. He admired the dignified stoicism behind the sunny charm that concealed past suffering, the loving gaze that never allowed him a peek beyond the curtain of melancholy.

It was nearly time for him to leave. Whether he would ever return to Istanbul, he didn't know. The thought of never seeing Shura again drove him up the wall. He hugged her tight and waited for her to open her eyes. Awakening with a low purr in her throat, she spoke in a sleepy, muffled voice. "Bonjour, Alain."

She held his hands encircling her waist and waited for him to say what he evidently had to.

"Shura..." he started hesitantly, placing a kiss in her palm.

"Yes?"

"Will you come with me to France?"

"To France? Why?"

"I don't want to leave you all alone here."

"I'm not alone: I've got Valentine and some very old friends."

"Shura, Valentine's married. So is that old friend too, right?"

She lifted his hand off her back. Her slender finger twisted his wedding ring, her face dropping like a child whose wound's hurting again.

"And I won't be alone in France? Tell me, what's the difference?" Her right arm stretched up over the pillow. Her gaze wandered among the white folds of the net, as though she sought something or someone. She carried on, still as softly. "I'm destined for a lifetime of loneliness. Doesn't matter in the least where. I made this decision a long time ago, and I'll abide by the consequences. Don't you worry about me."

"But I don't want to leave you, Shura. You know I love you more than this ring on my finger."

"Don't, Alain—please stop pitying me. You owe me nothing. You have a wife and children to go back to. If by some chance your travels bring you here again, who knows, we might meet again. Kısmet, as the Turks say."

"You still love him, don't you?"

"Love? I don't know...I've long since forgotten where it ends. He represents everyone and everything I've ever loved. When I look at Seyit, I see Kislovodsk and snowy pines and hear the hooves of troika horses and the toll of church bells. This is far beyond love. This is like needing to breathe, Alain; I don't expect you to understand. He is the living image of my homeland I can never go back to. Even if I never see him, just knowing that he wanders and breathes in the same city, in the same places as me, is enough. He is my Russia in Istanbul."

Alain drew her close to peer into the eyes brimming with melancholy. Yes, she was telling the truth.

"Look, darling, I'm not asking you to leave permanently. Come with me. Treat it like a trip. I understand what he means to you, but you must give me a chance." She was still holding his ring. "Look, it means nothing. We've not even seen each other for six years. You'll see; I'll sort it out as soon as I'm back. She was the one who asked for a divorce anyway; I'd been dragging my feet all this time lest wagging tongues harmed my prospects for promotion."

"And now? What's different now?"

"So much is different: you're in my life now, and I want to keep you there. And to hell with this thing!" But the ring wouldn't budge. "*Putain!*"

Shura kissed his hand. "Alain, it's all right. Throwing the ring away solves nothing. Once something's permeated our body and soul, they can't be dislodged quite that easily. Drop it now; let's enjoy what little time we have left."

Besotted, Alain didn't know what else to say to persuade her. "I'm running out of time, and I've not had enough of you." He covered her mournful face with kisses.

Ten minutes later, he was dressed in his uniform with his valise by the door. He embraced Shura one last time. "My darling, I will wait for you—don't forget."

"I love you too. But this...this is something else altogether."

"I understand. I will wait for you."

"Bye, Alain."

He slipped out and descended the stairs quietly, looking back several times at Shura, who waited at the doorstep. On reaching the floor below, he quickened his steps. One more flight down, and he narrowly avoided colliding with a young man running upstairs.

The two men paused to look each other up and down. Alain recognized Seyit from the photos in Shura's room, but the man who still ruled her heart was much more imposing in real life. He had a far more stirring gaze and commanding presence.

What flashed through Seyit's mind was a question: Who was this blond man in uniform leaving Shura's floor, and what business did he have there? Valentine had married, Vladimir and the Bogayevskys had immigrated to France, and Shura lived on her own. It hit him between the eyes: a man leaving a single woman's home early in the morning could only mean one thing.

The stranger had gone out by then.

Seyit ran up the stairs in twos. The woman he'd been agonizing over all night was openly living with someone else. He was panting for breath by the time he reached her door.

Shura's mind kept churning as she looked out the window to watch Alain's departure. She could love him. Perhaps she already did. And she had always dreamed of going to Paris. Except it would be so far away from Seyit.

The doorbell rang. Alain must have left something behind. She hastened to the door...and froze on the spot. Her heart beat out of her chest. The man she would have followed anywhere, done anything for, was standing before her.

"Seyt!"

Then she noticed his blazing eyes. Glowering. He strode in without a word. His state spoke volumes.

Seyit pushed the door shut, grabbed her shoulders, and shook her.

"What's this farce? Who the hell was that?"

"Stop, Seyt—you're hurting me."

"Tell me: Who was it? How long have you been together? No, wait, let me guess. That first night you left me and vanished—that was him, right? I wasn't married then, remember? Tell me! I was waiting for you, and you were screwing this bastard, right?" He was wild with rage. "And now what? Now that your lover's gone, are you with me again? Or is there someone else in line? Tell me!"

She couldn't believe her ears. The man she loved was accusing her of the most unspeakable treachery, the man she had devoted her life to! It was unfair. Trying to free herself, to make him understand, she pleaded. "Seyt, please listen to me."

All at once she felt the weight of his hand first on one cheek and then the other. Her skin and eyes were on fire, her face started swelling, and a howling ran through her mind. The grip holding her was released, but she couldn't stand upright any longer. Trembling, she slumped to the floor.

Seyit was horrified at what he had done. He fell down on his knees and pulled her close. He had to make sure she was all right. Stroking her hair away from her forehead, he cupped her face. Her lip was bleeding, and handprints glared an angry red on both cheeks. She was crying silently. Mortified, Seyit hugged her tight with tears in his eyes.

"Forgive me; forgive me, Shura! I don't know what came over me. I couldn't control myself. I must have been insane. I should never have done it. My God! I must have been insane."

Shura felt her heart break into a thousand pieces. "You don't need to apologize, Seyit. You're right. I did spend the night with him. And other nights too."

She stood up lightly as ever and walked to the bathroom. Seyit spotted the mussed-up bed and the towels in the bathroom as he followed. The masculine scent in the air caught in his throat. Why had he picked this day, this hour, to come here? This had to be the latest trick of fate to break them up.

Using a soaked towel as a compress on her cheeks, Shura entered the bedroom and perched on the edge of the bed. Seyit had no wish to stay there though.

"Can't we go to the sitting room?"

She replied without moving, her voice muffled behind the towel. "You may sit wherever you wish."

He realized she wasn't following, turned back, picked up a chair, and perched on it opposite her. "Listen to me, Shura; we have to talk."

She removed the towel reluctantly, eyes still averted. "What's there to talk about, Seyit?"

"Shura, my Shura, please, I beg of you, please forgive me for what happened just now. I know it's really difficult, but please try. The reason I'm here..."

She froze him with a blank look.

"At any rate...I met him on the stairs. Who was it? How long have you known him?" he mumbled.

"Alain...the captain of a French liner. I met him seven or eight months ago."

"Does he love you?"

"Are you sure you want to know?" she asked, staring in amazement.

In the gentlest tone he could muster, Seyit tried to reassure her. "Yes, please tell me: Does he love you?"

"He says he does."

"What about you?"

Shura burst into tears. "Seyt, it's you I love."

He picked her hands up and put them up to his lips. He looked devastated.

"Shura, my dearest Shura, I'm no good to you. How much does this bloke love you?"

"He wants to take me away."

Seyit left the chair to sit next to her. "When's he leaving?"

"The ship sails this afternoon."

Seyit stood up and pulled her up by the hand. "Pack; you're leaving too."

"I'm leaving, am I? Where, pray tell?"

He sat back down, gazed into her eyes, and spoke authoritatively. "Shura, you're to go with the man who loves you."

"No! You're not sending me away!" she screeched.

"It's what's best for you, darling."

"No! I'd have gone long ago if I'd wanted to! I said I don't want to!"

Irritated by that shrill yell, Seyit slapped the bed. "Is this how you intend to live the rest of your life? Waiting for a man who'll swan up whenever it pops into his sweet head? Trying to forget your loneliness with others when it doesn't? How much longer do you think you can live like this? Another ten years? What about twenty?"

Shura collapsed on the bed in floods of tears. Punching the pillow and shaking her head as if to banish what he was saying.

Seyit lay over her, hugged her shoulders, and stroked her hair. She'd had it bobbed since he'd last seen her. That lush golden cascade now curled up at the shoulders. His fingers ran through the silky strands. Their happiness had run through their fingers in the same way. He started in a gentle voice. "Shura, you're very important to me. But so much water's gone under the bridge; nothing's the same. We've shared so much, you and I. You were mine, and mine alone, for such a long time. What happened to us? Why did we hurt each other so much? Why are we so far apart now? I don't know. All I know is that I want you to be happy. You should have a life of your own. Have a family. We both need to move away from the past and live our new lives. Believe me, my darling: wherever you are, you will always be my other half."

Shura fell silent. She rolled over gingerly. Her face looked dreadful. She lay back and cast Seyit a resigned, desperate look—the despair of impossible love.

Her eyes sparkled with unspent tears. She tugged him by the hands toward her. Hugged the man she loved with all her heart.

Full of regret, weary of their trials, Seyit wrapped his arms around her delicate body. They wept silent tears on each other's shoulders and stayed locked in that embrace without moving or saying anything. They wanted to inhale each other's warmth forever. How time passed! How quickly all these years had flown by! Only a year ago they couldn't even begin to imagine living apart, and now it was time to say farewell.

Seyit eventually broke the silence with a whisper. "Forgive me, my darling."

Shura sobbed. "And you too...forgive me, my love. Shall we ever meet again?"

His words of comfort were meant for them both. "Why not? Did we have any idea we would meet seven years ago in Moscow? Fate might have another surprise for us."

"I wish we could be back in Moscow now."

Seyit contemplated her imminent departure. How would he cope with losing her? Yearning had already colored their gazes. They embraced even tighter and kissed with wild abandon, as if to mark each other's skin with an indelible memory. Eyes and bodies locked; between sobs and silent tears, they made love for one last time.

Softly, he released her. Shura slipped out of bed and went to the bathroom. She dressed in total silence, chose a blue two-piece suit and matching shoes to travel in, powdered her face, and applied a muted lipstick.

Seyit watched enchanted as her every move brought her closer to their parting. She was composed as she placed a valise on the bed and packed her clothes out of the wardrobe and drawers, so unruffled, as though she had always been planning to leave. Then again, that was her way. He had witnessed how level-headed she had been when she'd found him in Novorossiysk and how serenely she had hidden in Tatoğlu's boat. Wasn't her dignified temerity one reason they had enjoyed such a wonderful relationship?

She pinned her hat woven of silk ribbons in place.

"Blue is your color," said Seyit, caressing her cheek. "Now you look just like that little girl in the winter of 1916."

Shura braved a smile, her right index finger tracing his face. "Do you recall, Seyt? Recall what you said while pointing at the cupids in the fountain?"

"I do, my love."

"Can you say it again now?"

"Absolutely."

"Then say it. I know it changes nothing, but I want to hear it anyway."

Seyit embraced her, captured her lips with a long kiss, and murmured, "You know, I'd like to swap places with them. I'd like to freeze with you in my arms, as I'm kissing you. Then you'd be in my arms, kissing me for all eternity."

She swallowed back the threatening tears, wiped her welling eyes, and freed herself to pick up her bag and gloves. Casting one last look at the flat, she reached the front door.

It was a different person who walked out half a heartbeat later. There was no sign of the woman who had been breaking her heart for the past couple of hours. She might have been sad, but her steps were firm.

She asked the taxi to wait outside Valentine's home, went upstairs to say her good-byes, and returned ten minutes later.

Seyit and Shura arrived at the quay with two hours to spare. Handing her luggage to a porter, Seyit told him to follow. They hastened through ticket control, and he explained when challenged that he was seeing off the captain's wife; a young sailor was told to escort them to the captain's cabin.

Alain was working on his maps when there was a knock at his door.

"*Entrez!*"

The sailor put his head through the door and saluted. "Captain, your wife's here."

Alain swung around, surprised. "My wife?" He stared at the man he'd crossed on the stairs a couple of hours earlier. Seyit led Shura in by the hand, addressing him in impeccable French. "Yes, that is my only condition. You may only take her away if you promise to marry her."

Alain gazed at his lover, ecstatic that this chap called Seyt had succeeded where he had failed. It was a bitter triumph, but she was with him now. He held out a hand in gratitude. "I promise, *Monsieur Éminof.*"

Bemused by the careful pronunciation of his name, Seyit gave Shura a curious look, but she was staring out of the window with her back to them both.

"I need to trust your word; she deserves to be happy and forget all the suffering. She is special."

Alain sensed that this love far transcended a long-lasting passionate affair. Seyt and Shura were connected by something beyond the merely physical—a recognition he was gallant enough to concede.

"Monsieur Éminof, I love her very much indeed. What I cannot stake my life on, however, is whether she will accept the happiness I offer."

"What do you mean, exactly?"

"I don't know how you managed to bring her here. No amount of pleading on my part worked." Answering Seyit's querying gaze with a wry smile, he carried on. "She had chosen to stay with you."

Seyit choked up. He had done her such wrong! What could he possibly say to her now to make it up? He gazed at her. But she was no longer there with them. Upright and dignified, she kept staring at the port. Her eyes though...they were fixed somewhere far beyond.

Without letting go of the captain's hand, still gazing at Shura, Seyit continued.

"An even greater reason to make her happy." He moved toward the window and held her by the shoulders. "Farewell, Shurochka."

She replied without turning. "Farewell, Seyt."

Her eyes were misting far too much to see out. She wanted to be left alone to cry. To cry herself to death.

As he walked away, Seyit looked back up to the ship, but the face he longed to see wasn't there. He reached the road in a void. Despite a flicker of inner peace, something was crushing his heart. Was that it? Was that his last connection to the past? He had left one-half of his own life, his memories, his great love. He was now half a man. The tears springing to his eyes flowed back into his heart. A ship would sail to France, taking away the warmth of his body and the vigor of his soul. His little Shura was going away, and he was already missing her. He had no doubt that her absence would only amplify his longing. He felt as lonely as he had all those years ago as a twelve-year-old in Saint Petersburg—a grown man suffering fits of loneliness like a little child.

The ship blew its horn in the distance.

"Bye-bye, my love," he murmured.

Once Seyit had left, Alain went over to Shura, tenderly held her, and leaned down to her ear. "Everything will be fine, my darling. I will make you very happy." He summoned a cabin boy, handed him the luggage, held Shura's hand, and gave her a kiss on the cheek. "Go on, my darling; you must be exhausted. Unpack, settle into the cabin, and rest a little. I'll come over once we're underway."

Wiping her cheeks, Shura forced a smile, pecked him on the cheek, and followed the cabin boy out.

The horn blew repeatedly as she stepped into the cabin; they must be getting ready to raise anchor. With a rumble, the engines burst into life. There was no point in crying any longer. Like an exile resigned to her fate, she placed her luggage on the bed, opened the cases, looked out of the porthole, went out, and made her way to the top deck.

Most of the passengers were there. Despite the warmth of spring in the air, Shura shivered. Moving away from the crowd, she leaned on the rail to watch the ship pull away from the quay. White froth trailed back from the stern before regaining the inimitable blue-green of the Bosphorus. A brief temptation to dive into that boiling blue cauldron was swept away equally swiftly. What would that serve, other than being a monumental act of idiocy? Instead of fleeing from her own sorrow, she would leave behind a mourning lover. Perhaps even two. Would Seyt hear? And even if he did, what difference would it make?

She peeled her eyes away from the waves to watch the shore. It had been similarly warm when they had left Crimea. Was this to be her lot, sailing away with a man, and then another, leaving one land for another, leaving one life for another?

The liner was passing Sirkeci. Images of poverty—theirs and that of other White Russians—flashed past her eyes, as refugees arrived in the capital of a dying empire under Allied occupation. No amount of despair or anxiety about their future had made her as unhappy as she was now.

She fancied she'd spotted Seyit waving from Seraglio Point.

All at once, snow covered everything. Pines and firs and larches...century-old evergreens wore their pristine whites. The man she loved was galloping toward her. She saw herself standing on a snowy mound, waiting with open arms. Seyit rode over, leaned, grabbed her waist, and placed her in front of him. Shura reached back to hug him tight. They were flying over the snowdrifts now. She heard the bells of the Kislovodsk church. Troika bells in the distance. Valentine was playing Tchaikovsky on the piano. Tatiana was pirouetting under the pines in a tutu whiter than snow. All that she had been missing—then Seyt lowered her to the powdery snow and vanished into the woods.

She shook herself. Even daydreams seemed to condemn her to loneliness. Topkapı Palace, Hagia Sophia, and the Blue Mosque in the background played tricks with her eyes, morphing into Saint Basil's Cathedral lit by the street-corner fires in Moscow.

She looked at the Bosphorus receding behind her now. How close Istanbul was to Russia! A wave of her sea or a breeze of her wind still reached these shores, even if nothing else did. But now, as land grew ever more distant, she knew she had never felt such a powerful longing as she did today. It was as if she were leaving her homeland and her fellow Russians for the first time. She shivered. An icy loneliness seeped into her bones as the tears started rolling down. Her words drowned in the whoosh of the waves.

"Farewell, my Russia; farewell, my Seyt—my only love, farewell."

Epilogue

I T WAS WITH great reluctance, in 1992, that I ended the novel at the point where the lovers parted. Kurt Seyit's great love, Shura, initially nothing more than a name, had gradually assumed a body and soul in my imagination. I grew to admire her rare beauty, courage, and single-minded devotion to her lover in the face of great adversity, which she took in her stride.

That she did make it to Paris was all I knew at the time I had finished writing *Kurt Seyt & Shura*. My grandmother Murka mentioned a letter Shura had sent in 1928, four years after her departure: it seems she was seriously ill and wanted to see Seyit one last time. To his credit, Seyit refused Murka's selfless suggestion that he could go. A reunion would result only in added misery for his wife and two daughters, whom he point-blank refused to abandon.

Even though the trail ended there, I was secretly hoping she was still alive and might one day read the novel and look me up. An overwhelming sense of anticipation said I would find Shura, as though she kept calling out, "Find me… I'm so close!"

Thankfully, destiny would lend a helping hand.

The late Jak Deleon was working on his *Beyoğlu'nda Beyaz Ruslar* when I consulted him—a breathtaking quirk of fate that led me to an old lady called Valentine Taskina, who was none other than Shura's sister Tinochka. Baroness Valentine Clodt von Jürgensburg, née Valentine Julianovna Verjenskaya, or simply Tina—as she insisted we call her—preserved a nobility of spirit fiercely defiant of reduced circumstances. Every Tuesday afternoon for six months, I paid my respects with homemade blinis and Russian vodka. We chatted, ate, and drank until late in the evening as Tina spoke of life in Kislovodsk, Moscow, and Saint Petersburg; of the death of her first husband; of fleeing the Bolsheviks in

Wrangel's fleet; and of settling down in Istanbul when so many other White Russian émigrés ultimately left for France or America. As I hung on her every word, she thrived with each new thread; the joy of remembrance is a powerful remedy for nostalgia. She looked forward to our Tuesdays as eagerly as her amanuensis did, rising from her sick bed with beautifully styled hair, a powdered face, rouged cheeks, pink lips, jewelry, and a shawl over her shoulders worn more glamorously than a fur stole.

In the spring of 1992, she handed me documents, family albums, and other boxes pertaining to a time going back one hundred years. We both burst into tears that afternoon. I was torn between the thrill of holding traces of a past I was pursuing and sympathy for their sufferings. That turned out to be our last Tuesday. Soon after playing the piano for us, she departed this world, her work done. Perhaps it was a sense of closure that had moved her to tears.

My one regret is that she never got to read the novel. I will miss my dear baroness very much indeed.

By this time, locating the woman whose spirit had guided me was looking increasingly difficult. Oddly enough, the character fleshed out in my imagination was precisely the sister Tina told me about.

Shura had a daughter. One address or telephone number led to another and another beyond it. Convinced of some higher purpose that had inspired me to write this novel, I never lost hope—even when the trail appeared to come to a dead end. I was duty bound to gather the pieces of a shattered whole and present the entire story. I had progressed this far and was not about to give up.

One thing I deliberately avoided during the writing period was visiting Russia, dreading the stifling effect of a land in the death throes of a failed system. All I knew about the other members of the family was that Mirza Mehmet Eminof had been imprisoned in the vineyard house soon after his eldest son's escape, and the entire family had been tortured and kept under house arrest for many years. It was time to learn the rest. In August 1992, my late husband and I visited Crimea in the mistaken belief that it might cure the relentless sorrows in my heart. Instead, that trip carved fresh wounds.

Osman had been shot as he tried to join Seyit in 1919. Mirza Mehmet Eminof's youngest daughter, Havva, was taken away for questioning one day and never came back. Mahmut and Mümine had been dragged out of their home, tortured, and killed late one night in 1928.

Sixteen years later, in May 1944, Stalin condemned over two hundred thousand Crimean Tatars to exile—those who weren't killed outright, that is. Ostensibly to rout out "non-Soviet elements in the region," this mass deportation and massacre took a mere two days. No evidence of the purported treason was ever provided, nor did a single trial take place. Today this is recognized as genocide. A return to ancestral lands several decades later has failed to dress the wounds, and Russia has since employed a highly controversial referendum in March 2014 to annex Crimea once again.

Mirza Mehmet Eminof was appointed gravedigger to bury his own people slaughtered by one of the most savage regimes in history. He was eighty when he fell into a mass grave where the dead and the quick were thrown together. Whether his heart gave out or he was kicked by a jackboot, we may never know.

After days of pounding the streets of Alushta, looking for *Gort Alushta, Sadovi Ulitsa* in search of a trace of my family, or perhaps the sound of a single breath, I finally located one single building: a dilapidated house, its garden appropriated by a road, and the little stream that used to run between those vanished trees carved into a street. All that remained of its past glory were the lace net curtains. Threadbare, they billowed out of rotten window frames in a silent lament to their tormented owners. A dozen families had been crammed into what must once have been a lovely house.

What I believed to have been the home of Mahmut Eminof's turned out to be Osman's, as confirmed on a telephone call in late August 2017.

In order to eliminate potential confusion for my readers, I changed the names of some secondary characters who had the same name as a previously introduced hero. For example, Selim, Seyit's cousin who appears in the story in Istanbul, was actually named Osman, too, just like Seyit's youngest brother.

Another character whose name was changed for the book is Rüstem, whom we encounter during the Carpathian front. His real name was also Osman.

I will always be grateful to Tatiana Shekhsheyova, the director of the Alushta Museum and Library; her colleagues; and the leader of the Crimean Tatar Parliament, Mustafa Cemilev, for their support in publicizing my request to find any surviving members of the Eminof family. Quite unexpectedly, cousins in Saint Petersburg, Moscow, and Alushta got in touch and together filled in the blanks in our family tree.

The only other find was a monumental, two-hundred-year-old mulberry tree that stood alone long after the Eminof Mansion in Sadovi Road had been razed to the ground. It rose in the middle of a plaza, a silent witness to all that bloodshed, a venerable sage reaching up to the heavens with a canopy that hovered over the ground. Dinnara Yamalaeva, my kindly correspondent and devoted reader who sent the photograph of the tree, had enclosed a few dried leaves so that the brown and green veins of the Eminof mulberry could speak to me.

There was more to discover.

The Ottoman major captured at the Carpathian front turned out to be none other than my paternal grandfather, Ali Nihat Bey: an indomitable soul who survived a hellish trek to Siberia that took months and whose escape back to Turkey from a godforsaken village two years later deserves a novel in its own right. In yet another mysterious twist of fate, Ali Nihat's son Vedat married my mother, Leman, in 1953, by which time Seyit had been dead for eight years. Sadly, Seyit and Ali Nihat never met after that one time in the Carpathians.

I continued looking for Shura. On the eve of a trip to the United States, a call came from a Sandra Wells in Pasadena, California—Sandrochka, as her mother used to call her—Shura's daughter.

The next day I was at her doorstep, trembling with excitement. I cannot even begin to express my sense of anticipation. It was a highly emotional meeting. Seventy years after the lovers parted, one's daughter met the other's granddaughter. Like family members reunited after a long time, we shed healing tears together as we dressed old wounds. Sandrochka is a warm, lively, gracious, and charming human being blessed with, as might be expected, impeccable manners.

On visiting Shura's final resting place in the Glendale Forest Lawn Memorial Park, I pictured her as she had posed for Photo Kazbek in Istanbul in 1922, an exquisite beauty who brooked no sorrow to cloud her clear brow. As I laid a bunch of irises—her favorites, as it turned out—I felt a tremendous sense of peace, of having carried out this self-assigned duty. Introduced to her on a snowy night

Nermin Bezmen

in 1916 in Moscow, I had followed her every move once she had entered Seyit's life...until, that is, the day she boarded that ship bound for France.

After she left, Seyit resolved to look after his wife—my grandmother—and two daughters, occasionally being admitted into Atatürk's company in Florya. He did, on the other hand, seek oblivion in Pera's glittering nightlife of wine, women, and song, attempting to drown the incurable yearning for his homeland, family, and Shura. Disappointments and crushing poverty chipped away at his passionate nature but never made a dint in his dignity. Too proud to call in his debt, he never once used the IOU related to the boatload of munitions he had donated to the Nationalist cause in 1919. *Kurt Seyt & Murka* relates the years between 1924 and 1944, including much more on the ordeal of Crimean Tatars.

As for Shura, as I paid my respects in Forest Lawn in September 1994, I began to appreciate why she had captivated my imagination. I am convinced that Kurt Seyt and Shura met again in my own person—or in my lines. And I sincerely hope that their spirits are now at peace, free of the sorrows, yearning, and heartbreaks they suffered in their lives.

Shura kept reminding me of my promise to tell her story beyond 1924. I owed it to her to keep her alive, to keep her beside me, but I had no idea she had so much more to say! She filled the air beneath the wings of my mind, speaking softly into my spirit and heart, and I am delighted to announce that *Shura* was published in November 2016.

Kurt Seyt & Shura has, to date, been printed forty-six times in Turkish and published in twelve countries across the world. History is a bounty that seduces with a glimpse into hitherto undiscovered gems; the deeper I rummage in that treasure chest, the more I learn about the people and events that ultimately shaped us today. Every new edition, therefore, is enriched with new detail or a minor tweak that smooths the narrative flow.

One such astonishing piece of news came out of the blue in late August 2017; two distant cousins rang from Simferopol to say that Osman Eminof had not died on the Alushta shore! He was nursed back to health by the fisherman who had helped Seyit escape; later he got married, lived quietly on Sadovi Road until he was conscripted into the Red Army in 1941, fell prisoner, was exiled to

Siberia afterward—which is how the USSR rewarded combatants returning from captivity—and survived a ten-year sentence.

In a strange twist of fate, his son Hüseyin died the day after informing me about Osman. The past beckons with many more stories yet.

Two loyal and beloved friends to Seyit and Shura, Celil and Tatya remained in Alushta in order to allow Seyit and Shura a safe escape. We have no knowledge of their fate after that night. We have no letters or news from them. Whether they were killed or escaped elsewhere remains a mystery hidden in history. There is always hope that someone who knew them or an offspring may come forth with the rest of their story after that night.

In 2014, *Kurt Seyt & Shura* aired on Turkish TV for the first time. Largely based on my novel and beautifully cast, this spectacular production became an instant hit, first in its homeland and soon across the world. Within weeks of *Kurt Seyt & Shura*'s debut on Netflix, I was inundated with fan mail.

It was time to update the text with facts that had emerged since 1992 in a new English edition. I am thrilled with this beautifully seamless translation and hope readers in Australia, Canada, New Zealand, South Africa, the United Kingdom, and the United States—English-speaking readers everywhere, in fact—will share my passion for Kurt Seyt and Shura's real story.

The outburst of fan enthusiasm on social media has inspired me to dedicate a couple of hours daily answering their questions. More detail will have been revealed in the pages you have just read, and *Kurt Seyt & Murka* and *Shura* offer further information into the lives and events of the past century. The characters depicted in these novels were real people; they made the decisions they did for reasons that might appear unfathomable through the lens of time. Certain moral and social codes today are different from those of the early twentieth century. I would beg the reader's indulgence: I chose not to judge but to narrate.

We never die so long as our stories live on. Long may we continue to learn about past generations, as we hope our grandchildren will remember us equally affectionately.

September 2017, New Jersey

A Family Album

KURT SEYT
&
SHURA

The author's grandfather, Kurt Seyt. First Lieutenant Seyt Eminof, cavalry in the Imperial Guards. Upon his return from the Carpathian front—Saint Petersburg, 1917.

The beautiful Alexandra "Shura" Julianovna Verjenskaya.
Istanbul, 1922. (Photo: M. Kazbek, Beyoğlu)

Shura and Tina with their nanny—Kislovodsk, 1905.

Tina, Julian Verjensky, and Shura—Kislovodsk, 1910.
Verjensky troikas on their way to the Narzan Springs—Caucasus, 1910.

Shura in the garden with her dog—Kislovodsk, 1913.

Dinner in the Verjensky Mansion—Kislovodsk, 1915.

The Verjensky Mansion—Kislovodsk, 1914.

The church where Valentine Julianovna Verjenskaya married Baron Constantine
Clodt von Jürgensburg as the Great War and the revolution raged on—
Novorossiysk, 1917.

Baron Constantine Clodt von Jürgensburg

Nermin Bezmen

Constantine with his brothers and brother-in-law at the front, 1917.

Standing L to R: unnamed nurse, Sergei Clodt von Jürgensburg, Constantine, Shura, and Tina's elder brother, Vladimir Dmitriyevich Lissenko.

Sitting: Boris Clodt von Jürgensburg

Tsar Nicholas Alexandrovich Romanov.

Nermin Bezmen

A scene from the Bolshevik Revolution—Kislovodsk, 1917.

Turkish, Hungarian, and German prisoners of war at the field hospital, prior to setting off for Siberia. Major Ali Nihat in light uniform in the middle, standing on the second step behind the nurse, the Carpathian front, 1917.

Major Ali Nihat in exile in Siberia, 1918.

Shura's mother, Yekaterina; eldest sister, Nina; niece Katya; and
family and friends. After the revolution—Russia (undated).

Osman Eminof, his wife, an unidentified guest, and Mirza
Mehmet Eminof—Alushta, after 1919.

The Summer Residence of the Russian Embassy—Büyükdere, Istanbul, 1920s.
Le Foyer Russe, Winter Garden, Sakız Ağacı Road—Pera, Istanbul, early 1920s.

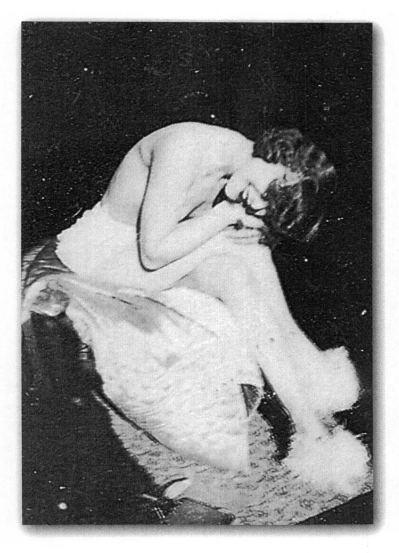

Shura—Istanbul, 1922. (Photo: Kurt Seyt)

Baroness Valentine "Tinochka" Clodt von Jürgensburg—Pera, Istanbul, 1920.

The Russian Balalaika Orchestra—Pera, Istanbul, 1920. (Photo: M. Kazbek)

Tinochka, now Valentine Taskina, pianist with the Milowitz
Orchestra, the French Theater—Pera, Istanbul, 1920s.

What remains of the invalid Romanov or tsar rubles strewn off
Galata Bridge by Seyit, Manol, and İskender, 1922.

Shura by the River Seine shortly after leaving Istanbul—Paris, 1924.

Shura by the River Seine shortly after leaving Istanbul—Paris, 1924.

Kurt Seyt's cousin Arif at the Eminof Mansion entrance—Alushta, 1928.

Mürvet "Murka" Eminof—Pera, Istanbul, 1928.

Seyit Eminof with his cousin Hulki; daughter Şükran; wife,
Murka; and daughter Lemanuchka—Istanbul, 1928.

Baroness Valentine (Tina); the author; and Theodor "Todori" Negroponti, Tinochka's partner of forty-seven years—Istanbul, 1992.

Tina tells Pamir Bezmen he made her feel thirty-five, with Todori—
Istanbul, 1992.

The author outside Osman Eminof's dilapidated house, now shared by a dozen families—Bağlıkova (the former Sadovi Road), Alushta, August 1992.

Exploring Alushta, guided by Tatiana Shekhsheyova, director of the Alushta Library.
*"The hundred-year-old lady said she had seen much, but all she
could recall was death."*—Author's note—Alushta, 1992.

The author at the Tsar Nicholas II Fountain—Livadia Palace, Yalta, 1992.

Pamir and Nermin Bezmen on the balcony where the Romanovs
enjoyed the Black Sea breeze—Livadia Palace, Yalta, 1992.

Nermin and Pamir Bezmen at Karagöl, nearly eighty years after Seyit
and his friends enjoyed a midnight dip—Yalta Forest, 1992.

Pamira and Nermin Bezmen, Sandra Wells, and Pamir
Bezmen—Pasadena, California, 1994.

Sandra—Pasadena, California, 1994.

Nermin, Sandra Wells, and Pamira—Pasadena, California, 1994.

Kurt Seyt's granddaughter Nermin Bezmen with Shura's daughter,
Sandra Wells, placing blue irises on Shura's grave—Forest Lawn Memorial
Park, Glendale, United States, 1994. (Photo: Pamir Bezmen)

KURTSEYT & SHURA

~ Join the family ~

THE STORY OF Kurt Seyt & Shura has touched many lives beyond ours. Our readers have taken our story into their hearts, and given our ancestors new life.

Almost 100 years after their first kiss, Kurt Seyt & Shura continue to enchant us today.

Through their story, we have connected with millions of new friends, who have joined us in feeling their love, passion, sorrow, joy and heart ache.

Join our growing family at
www.kurtseytandshura.com

and on our Facebook group Kurt Seyt & Shura English
www.facebook.com/KurtSeytandShuraEnglish/

If this story has touched your heart, we would be delighted it if you shared it with your loved ones.

Made in the USA
Lexington, KY
05 February 2018